OVERTIME
positions

A.M. MCCOY

This book is what happens when a wholesome Hallmark movie gets drunk at the bar and ends up bent over against a brick wall in a back alley by a Lifetime Network thriller...
...and a filthy smut book films it all from the shadows, taking notes.
Here's to bad decisions, beer league boys, and the kind of small-town chaos that deserves an NC-17 rating.

Welcome to **Cedar Bluff**,
where hearts collide, rules break,
and love always goes into **Overtime Positions**

1 - FRANKIE
Safe in the dark

MY EYELIDS CLOSED as I took a deep breath in the quiet, cold air, letting it fill my lungs as I imagined it moving through my veins, pushing away the fatigue. The heavy black weight of exhaustion kept my eyes closed as I leaned against the freezing cold shelf, resting my forehead on it.

I just needed a moment to collect myself, and then I'd go back out to face the day. Just one quiet second.

"Yo, Boss," a voice interrupted my solitude, and I jumped, whacking my head on the top of the shelf and cursing as I rubbed the spot. "Wait, were you sleeping?"

"No, I was doing a fucking jazz number," I barked in frustration, staring at the man who irritated me like it was his full-time job. "What do you want, Rick?"

The old man stood up taller as if my tone offended him, but I knew better. He ball-busted twenty-four seven.

"A beer. It's ten after eight. If I don't drink two brewskies before hitting the ice—"

"You'll break your hip," I droned on, brushing my bangs off my face. "I'm on it."

I went to step around the jolly green giant, who kept the entire rink afloat most days, but he stopped me with a hand on my arm. "Hey, are you alright?"

"Perfect," I said and then sighed when his face tightened annoyingly. "How do you do *that?*"

Pleased with himself, he crossed his arms with a smirk. "I spent years studying misfits who were silent verbally but said everything they could with their actions."

"You were a teacher at a *prep school*," I glared. "And don't call me a misfit."

"Spill it, kid."

"I'm not a kid either."

"Spill it, *lady?*" he joked, leaning on the heavy metal door, still blocking my way.

"I'm just tired," I sighed. "Toby was up at three."

"Ugh," he grimaced, "Stomach ache, or insomnia this time?" he asked, moving aside and following me out of the walk-in cooler to the rink-side bar. Some days he made it hard to ignore that he knew my kids better than their—nope, never mind. Not a spiral I was about to go down.

"Worse." I went behind the bar as he took his usual seat, glancing at the scores above my head on the television. "He wanted to know how caterpillars grow wings inside their cocoons."

He snorted and shook his head. "That kid is too fucking smart."

"Agreed." I cracked the top of his beer and grabbed his

mug from its honorary hook behind the bar, pouring it in. It was a gag gift from years ago when he took on the imaginary position of coach and captain of the team, and it stuck. Watching him drink his brew from a coffee mug that said *World's Okayest Coach* always made me smile.

It didn't hurt that the man who gave him that mug made me smile for no reason at all, he was just that great.

"You'd think a simple Google answer would have sufficed, but no." I rolled my eyes. "We had to watch three Nat Geo shows to quench his thirst for knowledge."

"Thank God you get to sleep in tomorrow, huh?" He picked up his beer for an air cheers, and I nodded, moving down the bar to set a round of cans up on the end.

"Small miracles."

I bartended the night shift at the ice rink on Wednesdays and Saturdays, which meant I usually crawled into bed after my kids were deep into their REM cycles. Thankfully, my mom kept them over for sleepovers on those nights so I could actually get some sleep.

Lucky for me, she lived right next door—and Emmie and Toby loved her more than me most days.

I would be lost without my mom.

Even at thirty years old, she was my best friend, the only thing that kept me afloat when the single-mom chaos got to be too much. I moved back home four years ago, with a one-week-old strapped to my chest and a two-year-old on my hip. Alone, scared, furious, and ashamed.

And my angel of a mother opened her arms, gave me one of those warm hugs that reminded me of sunshine, and patted my head, telling me I'd be fine, and everything would work out in time.

Four years later, I was still waiting to feel fine.

As soon as I set the last beer on the bar, the doors opened

and the team started filtering in, joking, roughhousing, totally amped up to do their favorite thing in the world—drink beer and beat the shit out of other smelly, sweaty men in an old man's hockey league.

Beer League, as we called it.

"Ay Boss," Billy *The Bull*, called as he shouldered his bag and snagged his beer. "Always looking out for your favorite team."

"Eh, I'd hardly call the Net Crashers my favorite." I grimaced with a smirk, drying a glass from the sanitizer tray.

"Yeah, sure," Slick Sam walked up behind him, picking up his can, "But we all know Sam's your man."

"Oh, fuck all the way off," Mitch, *The Brick*, slapped the back of his head with his beefy hand. "We know Boss is sweet on *Sunshine*."

My cheeks reddened as I hid behind the counter, just as the overly charismatic firefighter in question—Elliot *Sunshine Torres*—showed up.

Was I sweet for Elliot? No. That'd be weird. We couldn't be more different. I was a black cat, for fuck's sake. Sarcasm was my love language, sass and dry humor were my fallbacks, and I couldn't remember a time in my life when I felt as bright and optimistic as Elliot was daily. He was the coffee mug guru, for Pete's sake. He was perfect.

The man oozed freakishly happy vibes.

I oozed day-old coffee and fatigue.

Opposites.

Did that stop my stupid stomach from getting butterflies every time he winked at me? Also no.

"Hey Boss," Elliot said with his pretty-boy smile, "Cheer loud for me tonight."

Rick, their honorary captain and the father of the entire rink, chuckled from his seat, giving me a knowing eye as he cut in. "She might, though I'm not sure you have what it takes to handle all of Frankie, Sunshine. She might have better luck annoying *Saw* into smiling with her sass."

Insert blush number two for the night. Damn it, it was only eight p.m.

Travis *The Saw* Hayes followed his best friend Elliot to the bar for his drink. And once again, I peeked out from behind my wayward bangs to watch the two men—polar opposites—existing in the same space in their weird yin-and-yang way.

Travis stood six and a half feet tall, and nearly as wide, covered in dark-tanned skin from working outside at construction sites every day, with tattoos running up and down his hands and arms. He never smiled unless he was slamming some poor son of a bitch into the boards or celebrating another victory with his buddies. And that stare—the one that held mine like a silent movie, captivating me with no words until I was lost on the other side of it.

Damn.

Elliot, on the other hand, was—well, Mr. Sunshine.

Tall, lean, with ripped and defined muscles under his tight shirts that hugged his biceps like another layer of skin, full of smiles, charisma, and witty one-liners to entertain even the surliest of beasts that he skated circles around for fun.

Yet, they were two peas in a very odd pod.

Teammates on the Net Crashers, the best beer league team on this side of—well, I wasn't sure. There weren't many stats for their league, but they were pretty good around these parts in sleepy little Cedar Bluff, Wisconsin.

I didn't dare make eye contact with Travis as he picked up his beer, but I could feel his stare. That was the thing about him, he was just so damn intense.

Everything he did felt monumental.

Which was why I kept my eyes down as the rest of the team grabbed their superstitious beers and disappeared into the locker room before their practice.

I had no business getting wrapped up in a headfirst tailspin over the big, surly attack dog, or his golden retriever bestie.

Life was complicated enough as a single mom, living next door to my mom in our sleepy hometown, slinging beers at the skating rink while simultaneously finishing a degree in business management.

Twelve years ago, when I left my small hometown, I had stars in my eyes, watching the world pass by from the back seat of a motorcycle, ready to take it on.

And all I got in return was heartache and bruised dreams.

"Hey Boss." Rick's voice pulled me from the stack of glasses I'd been zoning out over, lost in the what-ifs and has-beens and everything in between.

"Yeah?" I looked up at him and found that thoughtful, knowing look in his eyes.

"It's good to have you home." He sent a wink my way as he finished his first beer of the night.

"I've been back for four years, Ricky." I rolled my eyes at him. "Is the dementia hitting already?"

He chuckled and stood up, taking the last can off the pile on his way to the locker room and pouring it into his mug. "Either way, this is where you belong. Even if you don't think so."

A snort escaped my lips as I shook my head. "Maybe, maybe not. I guess only time will tell."

THE HUM of the cooling system was the only noise in the massive arena; the lights were off in every rink besides the one I stood in, and the whole place was empty. Which was the only reason I even dared to step off the rubber mats in the bench box and place one skate onto the fresh ice.

If Rick knew I stayed late after closing and messed up his freshly smoothed ice on Wednesday nights, he'd have a coronary. But it was the only time the place was ever truly empty.

And my embarrassment didn't require an audience.

Wobbling onto the ice, I held onto the wall and then forced myself to take a few deep breaths before pushing off.

I had to get the hang of it. There was no other choice.

I couldn't let my girl down any longer, she only had me.

One foot push, one foot glide.

It was easy. Or it should be. I watched people skating every single day, yet the second my own feet stepped onto the ice, I felt like a newborn giraffe.

All leg. No coordination.

I struggled my way around the rink, staying close enough to the boards that I could get to them to pull myself back up if I fell, but not too close that I'd hit my head on them and knock myself out.

Intrusive thoughts were a real bitch as a mother, and I refused to become a bloody popsicle during a secret skating session after hours for the maintenance crew to find in the morning.

That was a headline I was not interested in being part of.

After two laps, I forced myself to try bending my legs, folding at the waist to get some momentum up as I skated. It felt awkward and worse than dancing with two left feet, but I pushed on.

"You're going to pull something in your back skating like that." A deep voice called out from behind me, and I screamed in surprise, whipping my head around to see who had snuck in.

Of course, the momentum of turning around competed with my momentum forward, and my two left feet went in opposite directions, and my tailbone was the next thing to hit the ice.

"Fuck." I groaned, rolling onto my stomach and holding my ass as I pushed my forehead into the ice, begging the surface to melt and swallow me whole. "Ow, ow, ow."

"I'm sorry." The gruff voice called, getting closer, and I looked up as Travis ran across the ice effortlessly, wearing his tan work boots instead of skates and still made it look like it was the easiest thing ever. "Shit, stay still."

"Ow." I hissed for dramatic effect before trying to get up onto my knees to get off the wet surface. My clothes stuck to me from the short time star-fishing across the ice, and my palms burned where I braced them.

"Hey," Travis came to a sliding stop, getting on his knees in front of me. "Hang on."

"I'm fine." I bit out, gritting my teeth as my cheeks turned red, making everything else far worse. "It's okay."

I tried to stand up, stupidly I might add, since I wasn't holding onto the wall, and my feet flailed out from under me, almost like I was—on ice.

My embarrassment bloomed so bright my stomach cramped from it before Travis reached out and put both of his massive hands on my upper arms, stabilizing and then lifting me by them like it was once again, fucking effortless.

Men with natural-born muscles and abilities pissed me off.

Especially when I was sexually attracted to them and it made me even more uncomfortable and awkward.

"You got it?" He asked, keeping his hands next to my arms but not actually touching me as I got my bearings.

"Yeah, I'm fine. I already said that." I blew my bangs out of my face and breathed through the pain radiating up my ass crack to my teeth.

"What are you doing out here?" Travis asked, dropping his hands and crossing them over his wide chest. "Because I know you're not planning to try out for the Net Crashers."

"God, no," I grunted and shook off the idea like it was repulsive. "And it's also none of your business."

His eyes widened slightly with the raise of his dark, brutal eyebrows and then relaxed. The stupidly attractive ball cap he always wore just made the darkness of his stare, shrouded in shadows, that much hotter. "Fine. Keep it to yourself, just like everything else."

Travis turned away from me and walked back towards the boards, and my shoulders sank for being so mean to him. He didn't deserve that, not really.

I didn't remember Travis from when I was growing up; he was a few years older than me and didn't hang around with younger kids. But when I moved back, he was always around somehow. Living his mostly silent, and to himself life, yet at the same time he was part of everything in town.

His construction company was one of the best-known names in town, his men were on site at every project going on. And the homes he built, God. Talk about dreamy.

His parents still owned the truck dealership on the edge of town, and everyone local bought their vehicles there. Some even traveled back to Cedar Bluff for them, bypassing anyone else for the honest Hayes Family Dealership. And then there was the rink I worked at.

He worked on the Zamboni and other miscellaneous machines, keeping the place afloat, he played for the Net

Crashers, and he coached various hockey clinics in his free time.

Travis Hayes was like a steady and strong fixture in the community. And one of the most loyal people I'd ever met, even if I avoided him because of my stupid little crush.

"I'm trying to learn how to skate." I called out, surprising myself and grimacing when he turned to look at me over his shoulder. "For Emmie."

Turning to face me again, he slowly started walking back. "For her hockey team?"

For some reason, the fact that he knew my daughter was on a hockey team made my stomach flutter.

With my cheeks ablaze, I nodded and tucked my hands in my flannel sleeves. I really needed to remember gloves the next time. "Parents are supposed to go out on the ice with them at practice, to help, but I can't. And I'm failing her because I can't help her. None of the coaches will help her. They just ignore her the whole time."

His jaw tightened slightly as he came to a stop. "What about her dad?"

I barely refrained from rolling my eyes because the truth was, I didn't want to talk about Danny with Travis. He wouldn't understand.

"Not around." I shrug, "It's just me."

He took a deep breath and looked out around the empty ice. "How long have you been doing this?" He glared at me again, "Using the ice alone at night, when no one else is around to help you if you get hurt?"

Rolling my eyes, I turned away from him as I tried to skate confidently. "A few weeks."

"And that's the best you've got?"

I glared at him as I circled him, and his face twitched a

little, almost as if he wanted to smile, but stopped himself. "Not helpful."

"Get off the ice." He said curtly, walking away from me without another glance, and I stopped pushing, gliding to a stop.

"Excuse me?"

"Get off the ice." He repeated, "It's too damn late, I'm too tired to stick around and babysit you and I'm not willing to leave you alone here, bound to crack your head open and become a bloody popsicle."

I brushed off the common thought we both had about my abilities and bristled at his tone instead. "No, thanks."

Damn, that felt bratty.

And *good*.

"Frankie." He snapped, glaring at me. "Get off the ice."

"No." I pushed off away from him, annoyed.

"Damnit."

"Go home, Travis." I argued, "I'm fine!"

"You're not fine!" He said gruffly, closer to me than I expected him to be, and I shrieked when I sensed him right behind me a second before his body was in my path and then I was falling over his dropped shoulder.

"Damnit, Travis." I screeched as he stood up, carrying me over his shoulder off the ice. "You're a Neanderthal."

"And you're terrible at accepting help."

"Help?" I cried, slamming my hand against his back and cursing as he adjusted me on his shoulder again, putting his hand on my upper thigh, precariously close to my no-no zone. "You're not helping me! You're bossing me around."

"So I can help you!" He argued, tightening his hold on my thigh and making my body go haywire. Why did I have to wear my skinny jeans? I could feel the heat of his hand right below my ass, and my mouth watered at the dominance in it. "I can't stay and help you tonight, but I can help you next week." He flipped me over his shoulder, and I landed on my feet with a huff.

"You—?" I stammer in confusion.

"Next week, after practice. I'll help you." Travis put his hands on his hips and stared at me. Even with my skates on, I barely came up to his chest.

"Why?" I squinted my eyes at him, waiting to figure out what his motive was. "Why would you do that?"

With a shrug, he backed up a step. "Because your daughter deserves to have someone out there on the ice with her." He said, my shoulders deflated. Whether he meant it or not, that one sentence made me feel even guiltier.

"Gee, thanks." I whispered as he walked away as if nothing had happened at all.

2 - TRAVIS
Teamwork

I WALKED along the upper observatory deck of the rink, watching the chaos going on below. It was Friday night, and the Tiny Tot Hockey team was in full swing practicing — and I meant that term loosely.

Very fucking loosely.

Six-year-olds rolled around on the ice, throwing them-selves into dog piles and playing tag willy-nilly, ignoring everything the coaches said.

Well, not coaches. *Parents.*

They were the worst coaches ever. Kids never respected their own parents at that age, and then you gave them skates, sticks, pucks, and friends, and it got even worse.

I leaned my elbows on the metal railing, watching with a

grimace. Most of the kids on the ice wouldn't be back next year. Either they weren't interested in the sport at all, or their parents would be unwilling to pay hundreds of dollars in fees and gear for them to fuck off.

And of the ones who came back, only half of them would ever actually be any good at the sport.

I clocked a few of those kids skating laps around everyone else at breakneck speed, some held a stick, some managed to pass the puck around as they went. Those were probably the only ones who had a chance to do something on the team.

As I scanned the ice again, I caught a player on one end of the ice and my eyes ended up stuck on the teeny-tiny little kid, dwarfed in a jersey three sizes too big, hanging to the top of their skates as they did circles around the net.

I wasn't sure why, but there was something about the way they skated that kept me entranced. It was almost as if their feet didn't touch the ice at all; they just walked above it.

It wasn't textbook skating at all, but it was—fast.

And clean.

The kid stopped and turned to go in the other direction, aimlessly circling the net with zero direction from the coaches or other parents, in their own world.

But then I caught the name on the back of the jersey, and I cursed myself for not figuring it out on my own at first.

Blake.

As in Frankie Blake.

"Emmie!" A loud, sharp voice called from below me, and I leaned over the rail, looking down at the glass where a fierce woman beat on it, yelling to the tiny kid on the ice being ignored by the grownups. "Go ask for help! Emmie!"

Frankie put her hands on her hips and bowed her head, frustrated as her daughter wasted time on the ice, invisible to the coaches who were too busy either chasing after the good kids or trying to wrangle the hooligans treating practice as playtime.

And Emmie just slipped through the cracks.

Full of potential and natural skill.

Before I could believe what I was doing; I headed down to the locker room, laced up my skates, and made my way out onto the ice. None of the coaches or parents said anything to me, but I felt *her* eyes as I skated past the glass.

Frankie's eyes.

I couldn't pay attention to that though, as I neared her mini-me daughter skating herself dizzily around the net.

"Hey."

The girl stopped skating with a fast turn and stood tall and still, like she hadn't been doing circles for the last half hour. "Sup, Saw?"

The little girl calling me by my hockey name took me back, but I guessed it shouldn't. She was her mother's daughter, after all. Getting closer, her bright green eyes — identical to her mom's — burned into mine through the dark lens of her helmet.

"What are you doing?" I asked.

With an unimpressed shrug, she looked around. "Same thing I do every practice at this wasteland."

I looked out over the chaos, trying to see it through her point of view, and almost shuddered at the pointlessness of it.

"What exactly is skating in circles going to do for you?"

With another shrug, she resumed her same path around the net. "What are speed drills going to do for me?" she countered, "I'm a goalie, and we don't have a goalie coach."

"You don't have a single coach at all," I muttered, and she clapped back with a grunt.

"No shit."

I could feel her mother's stare burning holes through my

skin, and I glanced back at her over my shoulder. Frankie held her hands up in a *what's going on motion*, and I looked back down at her daughter.

"Grab your stick," I told her, picking up an extra stick off the top of the net and collecting lost pucks from the boards, long ago forgotten by the other players now wrestling on the other side of the ice.

"What for?" Emmie questioned, even as she picked up her stick.

"Goalie drills." I skated out of the crease and stood waiting for her to get ready. "Defend."

She dropped into a stance and blocked the first shot, caught the second in her regular hockey glove, and then missed the third. I hadn't expected her to block any of them, given that she didn't have any actual goalie gear on.

Standing up out of her crouch, she stared at me, blinking, waiting for me to say something.

"Carter!" I bellowed over the chaos, catching the attention of the head coach for the Tiny Tots league. The ice went silent, and for the first time since the first kid put skates down, everything was still. "Where is her gear?"

The man glanced over at Emmie and then at me, looking dumb as shit. "She's wearing it."

"Her goalie gear!" I snapped in frustration. "She's a goalie!"

The man shrugged half-heartedly. "We don't need another goalie, we have one," he said, nodding to a kid on the bottom of a dog pile, screaming for his mommy, before turning away, giving his attention to the kids he deemed worthy. The boys.

I could almost feel Frankie's mind boiling as I locked eyes with her through the scuffed glass.

This was what she meant when she said her daughter needed her.

She was risking physical pain to protect her daughter from the bullshit she knew Emmie would face.

Not on my watch. No fucking way.

Turning back to the small girl standing in the crease, I put my hands on my hips. "Do you want to play with these kids?"

Emmie looked up at me and blinked. "They're the only team for my age."

"That's not what I asked you."

Again, she blinked and looked out over the group of boys, actively ignoring her like she didn't matter to them. "No." She looked back up at me and stood an inch taller. "But I want to beat them."

Five minutes ago, I couldn't have told you what Emmie Blake looked like, let alone what she was capable of doing on the ice. And here I was, ready to commit myself to helping her prove that the people who were supposed to be nurturing her natural-born interest and talent were the ones unworthy — not her.

"Then we practice," I nodded to her. "Hard. Every Friday."

Emmie's face lit up slightly, but she reined it in to give me a hard glare. "You're going to help me? Why?"

I gnashed my molars to keep from calling her out for being as stubborn as her mother when someone offered help. "Because you deserve to have someone that will," I said as the coach blew the whistle, signaling the end of practice. "And when you're far better than everyone else, they'll have no choice but to put you in."

"Thanks," she said almost wistfully before skating off to the locker room.

She wasn't one to fuss over stuff, apparently, and I kind of liked that. I recognized that.

Instead of heading back into the locker room to take my skates off, I headed to the bench where Frankie paced, waiting for me.

"What happened? What did she say?" She rapid-fired the second my skate touched the rubber mat. "Why do they think it's okay to treat her that way?"

I leaned back against the boards, eyeing her up. She looked frazzled and tired, but in the same breath, she was still strikingly beautiful. She had always been, even when she was younger.

Age didn't dampen that at all, even if life tried to wear it out of her.

"I'm going to talk to Rick. Carter doesn't have what it takes to run that team, and if I can't get him to realize that, then I'll coach Emmie myself," I said, and Frankie stopped pacing suddenly, staring at me like I had four heads.

"Why—"

"I swear to God, woman," I groaned, holding my hand up and cutting her off. "Just say thank you and feed that kid something with protein for dinner. I'm going to blow her over with my bad attitude if you don't."

I wasn't sure why, but that seemed to catch her off guard and irritate her. Instead of snapping at me like she always did with the guys when she was at the bar, she simply nodded her head curtly. "Thank you."

"Don't mention it."

"Frankie!" Stew, the crotchety old man who ran the snack bar across the rink, yelled over the PA system for the whole place to hear. "Toby's treating the nacho cheese machine like a drinking fountain again! Get your damn kid before I sell him to the circus!"

Frankie audibly sighed and picked up her bag. "I have to go."

Before I could say anything, she walked away toward the snack bar, slinging her arm over Emmie's shoulders on her way by the locker room, and I stood there, watching.

Why? I couldn't tell you.

But my feet didn't move again until I watched her pick up a squirming, cackling little boy with a cheese-wiz smile off the counter and carry him off under her arm like a football toward the exit.

Only then did I tear myself away from the sight of her and her family, and head toward the office I already knew Rick would still be in, pretending to work while he watched hockey on TV.

The Tiny Tots coaching crew was in desperate need of restructuring.

And he was the man to get it done.

"I NEED your help next Friday night." I said as I finished sanding a cabinet door.

My best friend looked up from his spot across from me, working on his own door. "What's her name?" Eli winked and took a drink of beer before going back to sanding. "I mean, it's been a hot minute since we tag-teamed—"

"Shut up." I cursed, second-guessing even involving him in the whole thing, but I was up a shit creek and needed help. "I'm coaching the Tots on Fridays from now on, and I need someone out there with actual fucking skills if I have a hope or a prayer of making something useful out of the time committed."

Eli stopped mid-sanding stroke and stared at me. "You're what?" He laid the wood down, leaned on the bench, blinking at me. "The Tots? Are you fucking nuts?"

"Yes." I replied instantly, and his mouth snapped shut in shock. "But I have a damn good reason."

"Oh, I can't wait to hear this." He grabbed his beer and waited expectantly.

"Frankie Blake." I said, as if that was explanation enough, and his shoulders deflated a bit, so I went on. "Her daughter plays for the Tots."

"Emmie." He said the words, and I was surprised that he knew her name. "I know. What does that have to do with you? And now, me?"

"Did you know Frankie stays late at the rink after everyone else leaves to practice skating so she can go out with Emmie during practice?" I asked, and Eli's brows furrowed over his eyes. "Or that she can't skate worth a damn, even after weeks of trying." I sighed and felt the same bite of frustration returning after finally letting it go the night before. "Or that not a single coach on that team will even notice that Emmie is a fucking natural in the crease. They ignore her. They leave her to kill time doing nothing all practice long, and Frankie is trapped on the bleachers because she can't skate. And Emmie suffers for it."

"Jesus, Saw." Eli sat down in the chair behind him and took another drink off his beer. "You've got it bad, huh?"

"Oh, fuck off." I snapped in frustration that he'd even think anything had to do with Frankie after what I just told him. I hated the fact that I had ever opened my stupid mouth months ago and told him I was into Frankie. It was pointless because she was too closed off to even notice anyone giving her any authentic attention, and his constant razzing of it had been insufferable since. "Never mind." I huffed, "I'll ask

Trace." Maybe the goalie from the Net Crashers would be a better help to coach Emmie than Eli, anyway. Eli was a center after all, so what the hell did he know about goalies other than how to score on them.

"The fuck you fucking will." He snapped, standing up and pointing his finger at me. "That was rude. Take it back." His eyes rounded as he glared at me, waiting for me to actually take it back in an over-dramatic way, and I flipped him off.

"Well then, stop being a dick about it."

"I'm obviously going to help you." He huffed, lowering his drama queen flag and sitting back down in his chair. "I just wanted to pull your leg about Frankie for a second."

"Well, don't." I looked back down at the cabinet door in my hand. "Nothing is going to happen there, but she needs help. So we're going to help her."

"Nothing's going to happen, huh?" He asked, and I could feel his eyes on me. "Then you don't mind if I shoot my shot with her then?"

My blood heated to a boil, but I kept my head down. "Since when are you interested in Frankie Blake?"

"Since she kicked Tyler Sharpe's ass in tenth grade for taking up-skirt pictures on the bleachers during the football game." He replied as if it were a no-brainer. "But I graduated, and she was so wrapped up with that kid from Hillgrove High, she never even knew I existed."

He was talking about her tenth-grade year, meaning I had already graduated and was in the Marines.

And there was that Hillgrove kid.

Danny Masters.

Emmie and Toby's dad.

Deadbeat asshole prick who didn't deserve to breathe the same fucking air as any of them.

"So, you'll help then?" I asked, but his face was buried in his phone, as usual, and I shook my head. "Right, got it. Thanks."

A second later my phone pinged in my pocket with our team group chat tone, and Eli pocketed his phone, looking smug.

"What did you do?" I asked, fishing my phone out and opening the message up.

SUNSHINE

> Saw's the new coach of the Tots league—practice is at six every Friday. Be there or don't show up for our games on Saturdays.

> Oh, and Frankie's the team mom, so... brownie points with her for helping.

"You're a royal pain in my ass." I snapped, glaring at Eli.

He gave me one of his signature playboy grins, and then the responses came in.

RONNIE THE ROCKET

> Does she give snacks or blowies in thanks?

NATE THE NOODLE

> If it's blowies, I'm in. If it's snacks, I'll have to check my calendar.

MITCH THE BRICK

> I'm in. I can't wait to see Saw trying to wrangle toddlers.

SLICK SAM

> I'll drink on the bench.

TRACE THE TRAMP

> That's all you do at our games too.

BILLY THE BULL

But back to the blowies? Anyone have info on this because I'm interested.

MITCH THE BRICK

You're not her type. Fuck off.

SLICK SAM

Sam's her man, back off.

COACH RICK

I'm in. Oh, and did you forget I added Frankie to this chat last year?

BILLY THE BULL

Gulps

SLICK SAM

Hey Frankie, you got plans this weekend?

"Jesus fuck." I groaned, trying to remember if Rick was pulling our leg or not. Our team chat was—rabid. Absolutely not at all appropriate for Frankie to be part of. I was also worried that someone might have said something about me being into her in the chat without us even remembering that she was in it.

Eli snorted and laughed, reading the messages. "I totally forgot about that. Well, that makes things more interesting."

RONNIE THE ROCKET

buys shovel now so you can bury me alive Frankie

RONNIE THE ROCKET

The first-round tonight at our practice is on me. See y'all there.

BOSS FRANKIE

.... *Eyeballs*

BOSS FRANKIE

> See you there. No blowies included. But I'll bring brownies to Tots.

"I hate you." I cursed, pocketing my phone as Eli chuckled.

"Yeah, I know." He picked up his sandpaper again. "But you're stuck with me, so deal with it. Besides, maybe if she knows we're into her, she'll bite when we toss out our pick-up lines."

Grunting, "She'll bite alright," I got back to work, sanding down the cabinets to my new kitchen. "She's fierce, that one."

"Just how we like 'em." Eli said, and I looked up at him, catching his wink. "May the best man win."

3 - ELI
Babysitter

FOR SOME REASON, I was on edge walking into the rink before our Saturday night practice.

Anxious?

Nervous?

Worried?

Earlier, I'd sent out a mass text to the team to help Trav and me out with coaching the Tots league, but I had no clue Frankie was in that group chat.

After the blunder, I searched the chat, and she had never once responded to any of our bullshit. She simply existed in silence, reading or maybe ignoring us completely.

However, when searching for her name to see if she had ever texted back, I found one hundred and four mentions of her name in the conversations. Forty-eight of them were from me.

Kill me.

Frankie Blake couldn't have been more different from me. When I smiled, she glared. When I laughed, she said something sarcastic. When I was easygoing and made friends everywhere, she acted as though she sat upon a deserted island, watching everyone float on by without even trying to wave hello.

She existed in her own little black cat bubble, with her sharp eyeliner, ripped jeans, and scuffed Converse.

But she hadn't always been like that. When we were in high school, she was two years younger than I was, but I knew who she was. Everyone did.

Franchesca Blake was the wild child of our little hometown. She smiled and flirted with everyone, in a nutshell, she was the girl everyone wanted either to be or to date. It was no surprise when she got wrapped up with an asshole bad boy, but we were all surprised when he talked her into leaving it all behind for him.

Broke her mama's heart to watch her ride away on the back seat of his motorcycle with nothing more than a quick goodbye.

A couple of years ago, she pulled back into town, this time in an SUV with a couple of car seats in tow, and no smiles for anyone. Now she was right back where she never wanted to be, to begin with.

I couldn't find it in me to be sad about that though, because it meant she was around people who cared about her. People who watched over her.

Men who would take care of her.

Something happened to her in her time away from Cedar Bluff, and it darkened her soul. It changed who she was.

When her mama had mentioned that Frankie was coming back, and looking for a job, I mentioned the rink was looking for a couple of different positions.

A few weeks later, Frankie was the newest bartender, working five shifts a week.

And for the last four years, she slowly unwound herself from the mental turmoil she hid behind, and started integrating with locals, building new relationships as the woman she was today.

I had almost convinced myself to do more than shamelessly flirt from my side of the bar top when Trav made a comment about being interested in her. God, that was a shitty night.

It was the first time in our nearly two decades long friendship that I had considered competing with him for a girl. We had completely different types in women, so it hadn't happened before. To be honest, Frankie was the perfect woman for Trav. Their darkness matched energies, and their dry humor, or better yet, their incredible lack of any humor at all, was identical.

All that being said, I couldn't figure out why I was interested in her at all, outside of physical attraction. That was easy to figure out because, fuck—she was sexy. Then there was the way she was with her kids. She was an incredible mom. Emmie and Toby were terrorists in their own ways, and ran Frankie ragged, but she never complained.

She just showed up every day for them, without fail.

Then there was also the way my body reacted every time she was near, *that* was hard to ignore. There was something in her smile. It happened so infrequently that when I could get one out of her; it felt like the sunshine had broken through the clouds in a storm, for just a second before it disappeared again.

Worth every second of corny one-liners, and over-whelming moments of annoying her for them.

My attraction to her made little sense, so that was why I never acted on it. I thought maybe it'd fade and blow over after the appeal of the shiny new toy vibe she brought to town ended.

Four years later, I was still fucking waiting.

Scratch that, I wasn't waiting anymore. I was tired of ignoring it. Even if it meant stepping on Trav's toes. If it was meant to be between her and me, he'd get over it. And if it wasn't, then it wouldn't matter, anyway.

But I had to try.

Leading me to nervous jitters as I walked through the rink's public space, toward the locker rooms, directly past the bar.

Directly past Frankie.

She was behind the bar, washing glasses, with her signature knot of long dark brown hair tied up on top of her head, dark makeup and a black-and-white checkered flannel.

I was early, and our team beers weren't sitting on the bar top yet, which had been my plan. So, as I neared the busy bar, she hardly glanced up at me before continuing what she was doing. "I'll be right with you." She spoke.

"No hurry. I've got time." I replied, taking a seat, and her head snapped up in my direction.

"Elliot." She looked at me confused and then up at the large Budweiser clock over her cash register. "I thought I was running late for a minute."

"You're all good, I'm early." I smiled, hoping she'd relax if she saw I was. Instead, she tucked a wayward piece of hair behind her ear and dried her hands off.

"Can I get you a beer?" she asked.

"That would be great." I pulled my wallet out and laid a

ten on the counter as she exchanged it for a Coors Lite, my drink of choice. Even if Coach Rick ordered us all Labatt each night. I drank it because it was free, and I was a dude who didn't look at a cold beer in the face without drinking it. But having my favorite was better. And knowing Frankie remembered it was even better. "So Tiny Tots, huh?" I asked and smirked when she let out a huff, blowing her bangs back.

"If you ask for a blowie, I'm going to steal the keys to the Zamboni and run you over with it." She deadpanned, pointing her bottle opener at me before cracking the lid off a bottle for another customer.

"Asking for them takes all the fun out of it, so you're safe. Unless you're offering?" I joked with a wink, and I couldn't be sure, but as she turned away, it seemed like her cheeks started blushing.

And then she avoided me altogether at the other end of the bar.

"Harassing my favorite ball buster?" Coach Rick asked, sliding onto the stool next to me with a nudge. "I wouldn't recommend it. You don't have thick enough skin."

Frankie smirked and made her way back to my end, as if with Coach Rick at my side, I was safer.

Interesting.

"Don't you boys have pucks to chase?" She asked, sliding a beer across the counter to him and leaning on her elbows. "Or puck bunnies to chase?"

"Ooh," I grimaced, grabbing my heart. "You wound me, Black Cat. When was the last time you saw me flirting back with one of those?"

"True." Rick clanked his beer to mine, "But they chase *you* a whole lot."

"It's incredible actually," Frankie sassed, "Who knew beer

league hockey was so popular. You'd think you were famous with how many groupies you have."

"Hmm." I leaned forward and tilted my head to the side, "You sound jealous. Want to join my fan club?"

"As if." She cut back without missing a beat, "Pretty boy jocks aren't my thing."

"What is your thing then?" I asked, rejoicing in how she didn't back off or deflect me like she usually did. Her standing still long enough to bicker with was refreshing. And exciting. "I've never seen you pay any man, jock or not, attention."

Rick snorted, standing up off his stool as Frankie instantly handed him another can to take with him. "And that's my cue to leave."

We both paid him hardly any attention, as Frankie raised one perfect dark eyebrow at me. "Maybe it's men that aren't my type."

"A lesbian?" I pretended to be shocked, "Now that's a date I want to be a third wheel on."

She rolled her eyes, barely cracking a smile. "You wish, Sunshine."

I opened my mouth to tell her just how much I did, when a shrieking whistle broke our stare off, drawing our attention to the entrance.

Frankie's son Toby and his sister Emmie ran in through the front doors like two wild tornadoes full of energy and chaos. Toby had a whistle between his lips, blowing his freaking mind off as Emmie passed a puck back and forth between her stick, wearing a Yosemite Jersey that hung to her knees.

"What the hell?" Frankie leaned back, shaking her head. "What are you guys doing here?"

"Grandma got the shits." Emmie deadpanned, laying her

stick across the bar top as she crawled up on the stool next to me.

"Emelia Elizabeth!" Frankie snapped, pointing her finger at her as Toby blew his whistle loudly again.

"Swear jar!" He yelled like an official on the ice, complete with hand motions. "Two dollars for a four-letter word not starting with an F!"

He tried climbing up onto the stool on my other side, and slipped, but I caught him just in the nick of time and put him on the seat. He grinned like a playboy and winked at me.

Emmie didn't miss a beat and shrugged her shoulders. "It can cross out mom's *fuckballs* from this morning. Which is five dollars times two because it was before eight am."

I choked on my beer and coughed right before it came out my nose.

Emmie blinked at me without a lick of embarrassment, and I decided she was my favorite. The girl was just like her mom. "That's very generous of you."

"I'm cool like that." She fired back.

"What in the ever-loving world is going on right now?" Frankie interrupted, hands on her hips as we all looked across the bar at her.

"I told you." Emmie looked over her mom's head at the Yosemite game playing. "Grandma's sick. She can't watch us tonight."

"She just dropped you off?" Frankie asked, pulling her phone from her back pocket. "I didn't even get a call from her."

Her daughter sighed as if the whole thing was tiresome, "She was shi—I mean, pooping her brains out, Mom. She said she was going to have to stand in the shower and let it come out both ends like you did that time you ate oysters at that cookout on a date with that weirdo from the seafood truck that delivers frozen shrimp here."

"Enough!" Frankie rubbed her forehead, chancing a glance at me before groaning in frustration. "I can't do this right now, Emmie. I have to work."

"And Toby and I are going to be perfect angels while we wait for you to be done." Emmie said in a robot voice, like she was repeating strict instructions from their grandma herself.

"Are there nachos tonight, Mama?" Toby asked, leaning up on his knees to look at the snack bar across the wide-open space, and Frankie snapped her fingers in his face, drawing his eyes back to her.

"If I catch you anywhere near that snack bar tonight, I'm going to sell you to Stew. And he's going to sell you to the circus. Do you hear me, sir?" She sighed, looking out over the space. "What the hell am I going to do?"

She wasn't talking to me, and in reality, I had no business answering her. But I did anyway.

"You're going to sell them to me." I said, glancing at Toby, whose eyes rounded slightly. "We have all kinds of things that they can help with tonight."

"Really?" Emmie cut in, pulling on my sleeve. "On the ice things?"

"Hockey!" Toby let out a shrill scream, throwing his hands up into the air and blowing his whistle. "Hockey! Hockey! Hockey!" He chanted like he was calling for a fight on the ice.

I snorted and looked at Frankie. "We can keep them busy for you."

"No." Frankie shook her head and then looked over my shoulder, stiffening slightly. "No, I'll figure something else out."

"For what?" Trav asked, coming up behind me as Emmie jumped onto her knees to face him.

"My grandma's sick, Mom's stressed, and Sunshine said he's going to buy us."

Trav gave me a side-eye as I chuckled before explaining. "Frankie is in a jam, we're not doing anything crazy tonight at practice, and we're going to entertain the kids while we do it so Frankie can relax."

She snorted behind me with an exasperated look on her face. "I haven't done that in years, fellas. Besides, you have no idea what you're getting yourselves into."

"We got it." Travis said without missing a beat, which surprised me. Not that he didn't like kids, he coached youth clinics regularly, but he also wasn't the type of guy to invite chaos into his life. Respectfully, Frankie's kids were chaos wrapped in a feral raccoon layer of sticky energy. Maybe with all twenty of us guys on deck, we might be able to keep them out of trouble until the end of her shift. Maybe. "Don't worry about it."

I looked at her and hated the way she didn't bite back at him or argue like she did with me. Instead, she chewed on her bottom lip, looking like she wanted to, but ended up sighing and deflating a bit. "I'll see if I can get someone to come in and cover me."

"Don't worry about it." I said as I stood up and caught Toby mid-superman jump off his stool, before lowering him to his feet. "We've got this."

Frankie snorted as Travis and Emmie turned off toward the rink with doubtful eyes. "Good luck. And thanks."

"Don't mention it." I winked, "But if you're offering payback—"

"Zamboni." She warned, cutting me off with a lethal stare that cracked a little at the end with a soft smile. "But good try."

4 - FRANKIE
Toby's Hustle

THE BAR CALMED down after the last game got over at the other rink, and I could walk away for a minute to check on the guys. I didn't need to check on the kids; I knew they were undoubtedly being minions, but I needed to check that the guys were still alright.

I half expected them to be tied up in the corner while Emmie and Toby terrorized them.

Instead, I found Emmie in the goal at the far end of the ice, working on stick work with Crasher's goalie, Trace. Travis skated around the crease, sending pucks at my daughter, who wasn't wearing her hockey gear, but avoided any impact thanks to his strategic aim.

He was in his hockey gear, and dammit—my mouth

watered. Like usual. His black hockey pants sat on his hips, and then the tight athletic shirt he wore was cut off at the sleeves, baring his massive biceps and tattoos to my stupidly depraved eyes. Travis was just so dang big, he defied logic, and my body couldn't help but wonder if all of him was large.

I hoped to the shiny sun goddess above that he was, because a man like that deserved to have a big dick.

Not that I'd ever see it, but that didn't stop a girl from fantasizing.

In another life, Travis was exactly the kind of man I could see myself with. Strong. Reliant. Protective. Dominant. All the things that made the girly parts inside of me go sweet. But those parts of me never saw the light of day anymore, life had dulled them out and hardened around them.

Now, I didn't go for men at all, thanks to self-celibacy and a downright refusal to trust again, they kept me on the outside looking in. Which was fine, since I was too busy to want anything for myself anyway.

But in moments like that, watching him care for my daughter and help her, I could almost stop moving long enough to wonder.

"Mom!" Toby rushed over to me, climbing up the bleachers in his uncoordinated fury. "Can I have an empty jar?"

"A what?" I asked, pushing his dark brown hair back off his forehead. "What is all over your face?" I rubbed my thumb over the brown smear up the side of his cheek. "Is this poop or chocolate?"

"Chocolate." He replied instantly. "Coach Sunshine got me a hockey puck made of chocolate out of the vending machine!"

Because of course Elliot gave my kid sugar.

"Jesus." I muttered, "Where's the rest of it?"

He blinked up at me for half a beat and then pointed at his stomach. "Right here."

"You ate it all?" I hissed, counting the minutes until he no doubt puked it all back up. His stomach was weaker than my sense of humor after eight pm.

"So, the jar?" he asked again, hopping from foot to foot. "Can I go get one?"

"What do you—" I stopped myself and stared at the ceiling for a moment. "You know what, I don't even want to know what for. There's a plastic one behind the bar, have at it."

"Sweet!" He jumped up and then took off toward the jar he no doubt planned to put something incredibly gross into.

Elliot skated over to the open boards, and I had to focus on getting down the stairs in one piece without falling on my face, because he was shirtless and covered in a delicious layer of sweat that made me wonder what his abs would feel like pressed against my bare breasts with him on top of me. "Hey Boss." He winked. "Come to steal the gremlins from us already?"

Get a grip, girl.

Elliot was insanely ripped; his washboard abs and defined pecs made my mouth water like a dying man in the Sahara staring at an oasis mirage. He looked so good, but I knew he wasn't real—remember I had a depraved mind, after all.

Snorting as I got to the bottom step. "I would have thought you'd be begging for reprieve by now."

He scoffed and grinned, "Not me, no way. I'm having a fucking blast."

My heart pitter-pattered a little at the genuine joy on his lit-up face. "Seriously?"

"Seriously," His smile dropped a bit. "Why?"

I shrugged, hating the guilt I felt at expecting everyone to hate being around my kids like that. "Never mind."

"Hey," He dropped his smile completely and pulled me to the boards by my wrist. Even being a step above him, he still towered over me in his skates. Tipping my head back to look up at him, I was instantly reminded how good it felt to feel small next to a strong man. In a feminine way. "What's wrong?"

Sighing, I tried to deflect like usual, "Nothing. I appreciate you watching them for me."

"Frankie." He urged, pressing me with the steady firmness of his kind voice. "You can talk to me." His hand lingered on my wrist, and I didn't ache to step away like I normally did around men. Part of me even *wanted* to be close to him. It was the same way I felt the other night with Travis, watching him help Emmie out on the ice. What the hell was wrong with me, getting my head all twisted around two different men suddenly, after years of indifference. "Please." Eli added, and I groaned.

"Don't be kind to me." I whispered, closing my eyes to all the other noises and sights in the rink. "I can't do kind."

"Is that why you fall in line for Trav so easily?" He asked, and my eyes popped open in surprise. One, what the hell was he talking about, and two, why the hell was he talking about it? We were running straight past acquaintance conversation and falling into something that felt way too personal. "Because he isn't kind?"

"Excuse you?" I asked firmer than I probably needed to, and his answering smirk made my scowl deepen.

"Yep." He let go of my wrist and sighed, "There it is."

"There what is?" I asked, putting my hands on my hips, slightly offended, even though I had no idea what he was talking about. The man talked in circles, distracting me with his pretty-boy good looks and charisma. I hated that.

I hated that it worked, even more.

"That wall." He shook his head, "That impenetrable wall you keep up, forcing everyone to stay just far enough away so you can shoulder everything on your own."

"Got it!" Toby called out, flying down the stairs at breakneck speed and forcing us to pay attention to him. "Hey! Coach Grumpy!" Toby waved around the jar. "You owe me ten bucks for double no-no words!"

Travis looked over at us, and his eyes went from Elliot to me, standing on each side of the low wall, and darkened, before he turned his attention to my little boy waving the plastic jar around. "I'll even up after practice." He called, and his dark eyes traveled back to me before he turned away completely.

"Ha!" Toby chuckled, "Swear jar for the win!"

"No." I replied, "You're not charging them for the swear jar."

"Why not?" Toby whined, "*You* have to pay into it."

"Because I'm your mom, and I'm desperately trying to be a better person so I can be a good example for you two. Random guys at the rink who are trying to help us out are not going to pay your fee!"

"Aw, c'mon." Toby whined, walking away down the bleachers in defeat, and then I was forced to acknowledge the six-foot Greek god standing in front of me again, toeing the line of wants and can't haves with me.

"I think maybe you should take a look around, Frankie." Elliot said softly, skating backward away from me. "We're not all just a bunch of random guys at the rink." His normally kind and cheerful face pinched together like he was disappointed in me. "If you'd stop pushing us all away, you might find that one or two of us could be exactly the kind of example that your kiddos could use."

"What's that supposed to mean?" I pushed, crossing my arms.

Elliot shook his head in frustration. "It means you don't have to do everything on your own, woman." He raised his brows pointedly, and I hated how his tone excited me more than it offended me. I'd never seen him be serious before. "You could let a man in and let him take care of things." He held his hands out, showcasing the way the entire team was rallying, pitching in and helping with my kids in a pinch.

Sure, he was right. Any of the men on the team would be a good example for my kids to have in their lives as my partner, I wasn't dumb enough to ignore that.

But I *was* too broken to allow it.

"Sure thing." I replied, backing up a step and putting my hands in my jean pockets. "I'll ask Coach Rick out sometime. Thanks for the idea."

He rolled his eyes but cracked a smile. I could tell he was frustrated with me, men always were, but he was too sweet to hold it against me. Even if I wanted to box his ears for thinking he could be.

"Sure thing, Black Cat." He replied, using that new nickname for the second time tonight. I didn't even hate it. "While you're at it, ask your mom if she's free next weekend. I've always had a thing for sweet ol' Mrs. Blake."

I turned away, flipping him off over my shoulder as Toby's annoying whistle blew. "Bird flying!" He screamed for everyone to hear. "Five bucks!"

I waved him off and hollered back, "Coach Sunshine can pay my bill."

Elliot's chuckle from the ice was enough to bring a smile

to my lips as I walked away. But only because no one could see it. Couldn't have anyone thinking I was nice or something.

I EYED THE CLOCK AGAIN, knowing that if I stayed any longer, the kids were going to be bears in the morning when they had to get up. But I also had a bar full of people and no one to take over for me.

Mom fail number eight thousand.

And that was just this week's tally.

I took a deep breath to keep from crumbling under the weight of it all and stopped short when my mom walked in through the front door on a breeze like she was walking some runway in Milan.

"Mom?" I shook my head, walking around the bar. "What are you doing?"

"Picking the kids up." She said effortlessly. "I told them I would be back at nine."

"What?" I rubbed my forehead as I tried to understand what was happening. "They said you have a stomach bug or something."

"Hey, Lucy." Coach Rick greeted my mom with a quick peck on her cheek. "You look beautiful tonight."

My mom swatted his arm playfully, "I look beautiful every night." She sang in her fairytale-sweet voice. She was right, she always did, in an effortless Elizabeth Taylor way I always envied. In everything she did, she was soft and nurturing, unlike me, I was sharp and snarky. I had questioned how we were related too many times to count.

"Mom." I interrupted as Crashers started filing out of the

team hallway, suspiciously without my kids. "Where were you?"

"On a date." She replied, "I told you three times I was meeting Charles for dinner tonight. That's why I dropped the kids off; I was on my way across town." She pursed her lips. "You forgot, didn't you?"

"I—" I stammered like an idiot as Travis eyed me suspiciously as he took a seat at the bar next to Rick. "So, you're not sick?"

"Heaven's girl," my mom rolled her eyes, "Do I look sick?"

"Well—no." I huffed, replaying the way both kids effortlessly made up the story earlier and planned my revenge.

"Where are the kids? I want to get them home and in bed before they fall asleep standing up. I'm sure they're exhausted from playing here for the last few hours."

"Mom." Emmie showed up out of nowhere and pulled on my sleeve. "We have a problem."

Glaring at her, "You mean besides the fact that you lied about Grandma being sick?"

"Bigger than that." Emmie swallowed, glancing around the group and hiding behind my side when she clocked Travis watching her. "*Much* bigger than that."

"What?" I asked, suddenly on edge and suspiciously aware of Toby's absence. "Where's your brother?"

"Uh—" She shrunk more and whispered. "In the vending machine."

"I told him not to take any money from anyone for that damn swear jar." I snapped and glared at my daughter before she could dare to point out my curse. Turning to Travis, "Did you give him money? The last thing he needs is junk food right now."

Trav raised one brow at me, and I felt like a scolded child

before he calmly answered, "I didn't settle my tab with him yet."

"No, Mom!" Emmie pulled on my sleeve roughly, "He's not *at* the vending machine." She widened her eyes as she hissed. "He's *in* the vending machine."

"In—" Fuck, I tore off at a sprint towards the team vending machines by the ice. "Jesus Christ!"

Travis was hot on my heels as I ran down the stairs, and he cleared them in half the time, getting to the machine right before me.

And in the candy one, there sat my boy, pressed up against the glass with a chocolate-covered grin as he ate a candy bar, waving the best he could in his tight confinement. "Hi Mama!"

"Get out right now!" I hissed, fighting the panic building in my gut as I uselessly tried to pry the door open.

"Can't." Toby shrugged, "I'm stuck."

"Boy, I swear to God!" I smacked the side of the machine, and Travis pulled me away from it as more guys came out of the locker room.

One of them being Elliot.

"Get the keys from Rick!" Travis barked at his friend, who paled when he came around the corner and saw Toby stuck in the machine.

"Damn, kid. Five minutes alone." Elliot warned, "That was it."

"I'm fast!" Toby cheered, and I cursed under my breath.

Rick was already on his way down the stairs, slower than Travis, and I ran down them, followed by my mom and Emmie.

"Take a deep breath, he's fine." Travis said quietly behind me, pulling me further away from the machine. I wanted to fight him and tell him where he could shove his advice, but when his hand slid over the front of my stomach, pulling me into his chest so Rick could get to the panel on it, I froze. And heated into an inferno of confusion and physical reactions as I felt the intensity of his body heat against me. "Frankie, take a deep breath." He said against my ear.

I gritted my teeth and felt Elliot's eyes on me from the other side of my mom as I did what Travis said.

Fuck them all.

But he was right, I needed to calm down now that I knew my son wasn't in any danger. Though he was in a whole big can of trouble the second he was free.

"Toby," Rick stood at the front of the machine, putting his hands on his hips to stare at my son. "We talked about this. I thought we agreed you weren't going to do anything to scare your Mama again. The joyride on the Zamboni last month nearly put her in the hospital with a heart attack."

Toby's shoulders sagged a little as he negotiated through the glass. "Well, she said I couldn't go to the Snack Bar. And she told me I couldn't collect swear jar money! I was hungry."

I rolled my eyes but kept my mouth shut as Rick shook his head.

"No, this was not an acceptable alternative. And you know that." Rick warned, and Toby wilted further. I softened as my anger and worry melted into sadness as someone other than me disciplined my son. Even though there were days I wanted to send my kids to Mars on a one-way ticket, I would rather be boiled in a pot of tar than watch someone else discipline them. But Rick wasn't just anyone, and he was never unfair or over the top with my kids or anyone else for that matter. "Okay, so you're never going to do this again, right?" Rick asked, putting the key into the machine but didn't turn it until Toby replied.

"Yes, Sir." He nodded his head eagerly, ready to get broken out of his candy-filled jail.

"Good." Rick popped the door open, and Elliot picked Toby up out of it, setting him on his feet.

My boy hung his head and ran to my side, burying his face in my stomach as Travis backed up. "I'm sorry, Mama." Toby said thoughtfully, blinking up at me with his innocent and remorseful eyes.

"I know." I leaned down and kissed his forehead, unable to say anything else as my own emotions bubbled up. "I know, baby."

"C'mon." My mom held her hand out, and Toby ran to her side as Emmie held her other hand. "Let's go home and get to bed." She gave me a pointed look as she backed up with my kids in tow. "They're just kids, doing kid stuff, Frankie. Don't worry, I've got it now."

I nodded, unable to respond because I knew if I unclenched my teeth, tears would fall before the words did.

Silently, I watched my kids walk away, safe in my mom's arms, out through the front door, and the moment they could no longer see me, I turned and walked away.

As I started cracking, desperate to escape, I felt the guys' eyes on me. I didn't pay attention to where I went, I just needed somewhere private to lose my hold on the tight control I always hid behind, and when I was in the abandoned equipment room behind the rink, the tears fell.

Covering my mouth to stifle the sobs, I doubled over as so much grief crashed over me.

"Shh." Elliot's gentle voice found me in the darkness, I hadn't even realized he was following me in my panic. Struggling, I bucked against his hold as he pulled me into his big chest, before all the fight dissolved in my tired muscles, leaving me no choice but to give in to it and lean into his strength. "Get it out."

Shame, guilt and embarrassment dragged me under as he held me, but for the first time in years, I couldn't muster up the strength to push away from it.

So, I let it out.

I cried.

And I cried.

And I *fucking* cried.

All while a man I had no business darkening with my bullshit held me up.

"You're okay." Elliot whispered against my temple, running his hands over my back and arms, soothing me the whole time as I clung to him. "They're okay. Everything is going to be okay."

"I'm failing." I whispered into the darkness around us, finally speaking the truth out loud. It had been suffocating me for years, but I couldn't pretend everything was okay. Not anymore. "I'm failing them."

"You're not." He replied firmly, shaking his head. "Not in any way are you failing those kids, Frankie." More sobs shook my shoulders as his words broke through the walls that held my spine up under the weight of the world most days. "Those kids are incredible; they are free-spirited and ornery because they know they are safe and loved. They are kids, because you shoulder everything in the world, so they can be."

"I can't—" I hiccupped, digging my fingers into his shirt. "I don't think I can do it all anymore."

"And you're not going to." He stated, sliding one hand against the side of my cheek and pulling my head back to look up at him, while simultaneously keeping me pinned to his body. "You don't have to. You're surrounded by people who want to help you. You just have to let us."

I groaned, dropping my forehead against his chest again. "It's not your responsibility."

"You're right, it's not." He stated. "It's their father's responsibility to be in their lives and help you. But he's not. And if I know a single thing about you at all, I know there's a damn good reason he's not. So, you can either do it all on your own and continue feeling like you're harming them somehow, or you can let us help. We want to help."

"We?" I snorted, shaking my head. "You and what army, Elliot? Because that's what it's going to take."

"Travis." He said instantly, and I scoffed as he went on. "Rick and the guys. We all care."

"Travis hates me." I snap. "He thinks I'm failing them too, and he's right."

"He doesn't." The sound of Elliot's scoff echoed in the confined space as he pushed me against the wall, and my head snapped back. The rough texture of the wall scraped against my body as he loomed over me. "Travis is a hard-ass and even harder to read than you are. But he's my best friend, and I know him like the back of my hand. And there are a lot of things he thinks about you, Frankie." He said pointedly, and my stomach flipped slightly even as he pushed on. "But I assure you none of them are in a negative way."

"I don't understand—"

"Good." He smirked, barely visible in the dim light. "Because I'm messing this up by trying to convince you that he's into you. Even if he is my best friend, I'm not trying to ruin my own chances with you."

"God." I sagged into the wall, and he grinned bigger. "You're crazy."

"Crazy enough to make a move on a girl in a stinky equipment room who just wiped snot all over my shirt."

A laugh broke through my lips before I could even recognize it, and I shook my head, giving in to the universe, which was obviously trying to humiliate me in every way tonight.

"You're an incredible mom, Frankie." He stated, more serious now. "It was one of the first things I noticed about you when you moved back. But you want to know what else I noticed, probably long before I saw you with the kids?"

"Do I dare ask?" I deadpanned, being snarky like my normal hard-ass self.

"I mean besides that dump truck—" He joked, and I pinched his side, making him chuckle. "It was how drawn to you, I am." I bit my lip to keep from pushing him away like I usually would as he went on. "It doesn't make sense, and I know that, but it doesn't mean there isn't something there that I'm interested in exploring when you're ready."

"And what if I'm never ready?" I whispered the fear I had every night, falling asleep alone for the last four years. "Because I don't think I know how to be that girl anymore."

"Do you want to be?" He asked, running his thumb over my cheek. "Because I remember the girl you were in high school. I remember how full of life and love you were. You were like a flame, and all of us were the moths, daring to fight the heat to be close to you."

"Elliot." I sighed as if his words were arrows aimed directly at my armor.

"Experiment with me for a moment." He said, as his voice took on a huskiness I'd never heard before. "Ask me to kiss you." My chest deflated as my breath left my lungs, faced with something I had thought about more times than I could count in the darkness of my own fantasies, but never expected to happen in real life. "Don't give me one of the millions of excuses I'm sure you are already thinking of. Just tell me to kiss you. Just once."

I gave in, falling headfirst into the dreamland he was

dangling in front of me like it was something I could actually have. "Kiss me, Elliot."

Tomorrow, I'd regret it and have to come to terms with that loss.

Tonight, I was going to give in.

"With fucking pleasure." He growled, and then his lips were on mine, and my moans were in his ears as he pressed me into the wall.

I wasn't sure what I expected a kiss with Elliot Torres to feel like, but I knew I didn't expect the intensity that I was getting from him, that was for sure. His teeth nipped at my lip, and I opened, teasing his tongue with mine as my body burned everywhere he touched me. He kissed with such dominance and confidence that it made me weak in the knees.

Damn it, he kissed like I would assume Travis would, all full of power and control.

Fuck—was I really thinking about Travis as Elliot's hips pinned me to the wall? Was I moaning for Elliot while I suddenly wondered if Travis would be as assertive as his best friend was?

"Sorry to interrupt." A gruff voice said from behind Elliot, and I shrieked, finding Travis standing there, staring at us locked in—whatever the hell we were just doing, and I instantly felt guilty.

Damnit!

"You have impeccable timing, man." Elliot laughed without turning, wiping his lip with the pad of his thumb as he braced one arm over my head against the wall. "What's up?"

"Mrs. Blake wants you to drive Frankie home. Rick is closing down the bar and said to send her home."

"What?" I snapped, ready to argue with being told what to do, even by my own mother and Rick.

"Burdens." Elliot murmured, stopping me. "You agreed to let us shoulder some of it, remember?"

"I don't remember agreeing to your plan." I deadpanned, and he leaned up off my body as he turned to face his friend.

It was then that I noticed Travis had my bag and jacket in one hand, the other one shoved in his jeans pocket in a fist. His face was shadowed, and I couldn't quite see the intensity of his eyes, but I could feel it.

"Here." Travis handed my stuff to me and then turned away.

"Thanks." I whispered, falling on deaf ears as he was already walking away.

"Wait." Elliot called, looking down at me. "I'm going to regret this." He whispered to me before cracking his neck and talking to his friend. "I have to get to the station. I forgot I picked up an extra shift."

"It's fine," I ran my hand through my messed-up hair. Elliot must have pushed his hands into it when we were— well, anyway. "I'm fine to drive."

"Meh," Elliot whistled, "I'm not willing to risk the wrath of Mrs. Blake by disobeying her direct orders." He winked at me, "You know she's my end goal, anyway."

"What are you doing?" I asked, confused as Travis hovered in the doorway.

"Trav will drive you home."

"He what—?" I shook my head, "No, I can drive."

"I'll drive you home." Travis stated authoritatively before pushing open the door. "Let's go."

Without another glance back from him, he walked out, letting the door swing shut behind him, leaving a confused me and a smirking Elliot back in the darkness.

"What the fuck?" I whispered to myself.

"Do me a favor." Elliot said, walking deeper into the

equipment room towards the secondary entrance to the locker room. "Think of me when you kiss him goodnight."

I scoffed at the absolutely ridiculous alternate universe I fell into when I walked into the dark room in the middle of a mental breakdown moments ago. "Sure. Whatever you say, lunatic. Where are you even going?"

He hooked his thumb over his shoulder with that signature pretty-boy smirk. "To go jack off in the shower before I lock myself away in a bunk room with a bunch of other dudes for the night."

"Ew." I grimaced dramatically as a joke and then decided to play dirty and try to remember who the girl was from so many years ago that he talked about. "Think of me when you do it."

"Oh, baby." He purred, "You're the star in all of my one-handed daydreams lately." Elliot smirked and disappeared through the door, leaving me alone.

And suddenly, I was trying to decide which door I wanted to walk through more at that moment.

The one to a steamy shower with a naked Elliot, who kissed like a God. Or the one to a cold, tense ride home with an unmovable brick wall that excited me just as much as his flirty friend.

Decisions, decisions.

5 - TRAVIS
Kisses in the Dark

SHE KEPT her head down as she jumped up into my truck, closing the door next to her with zero strength behind it. Which meant it didn't latch.

My classic square-body pickup truck was a collector's item, but that didn't mean it worked perfectly all the time.

"What's the trick?" She asked, pulling on the useless handle that didn't work right all the time either.

"Here." I leaned across the bench seat and yanked it just right and then slammed it shut. "Like that."

I could smell her shampoo when I leaned across her, and I hated that I liked it. I shouldn't fucking like it.

Liking it felt wrong now. Since seeing her with Eli a few minutes ago. Kissing him. Damn, she was really fucking kissing him. When I first walked into the dark room, I thought maybe he had been pushing her into it, using her emotional distress to get her to finally fold to his charm. But that had only lasted a moment, because in the next she moaned, and pulled him closer, gripping his shirt and leaning up on her toes to kiss him back.

Deeper.

Harder.

And it all became so painfully obvious to me in the darkness.

I couldn't give her that.

Sure, the physical connection I could compete with, I knew without a doubt that if I somehow convinced Frankie to kiss me, there would be an explosion of chemistry. I wasn't talking about that.

I was talking about what happened before and after their kiss.

The emotions.

Eli told her she was incredible. He validated her fears and struggles. He comforted her.

I couldn't do that. I didn't know how. There wasn't a tender bone in my body, and she obviously wanted that—wanted him.

Which made the tension in my truck cab, built in the silence around the hum of the heater and the soft breaths from her in the passenger seat, even worse for me. That's all it would ever be—tension.

On my part, not hers.

I was hanging on by a thread, every annoying tick of my turn signal threatened to push me over the edge as I drove her across town.

Part of me wished she'd yell at me for spying on them, or even give me some crass, snarky jab about making her ride home with me. Yet she just wouldn't fucking budge, and with each second of silence, I cracked, getting dangerously closer to telling her the truth.

Eli's hushed words echoed through my brain as I left the room, I knew I wasn't supposed to hear them, but that didn't change anything now.

"Think of me when you kiss him goodnight."

What the hell was that? He handed her off to me to drive home like it was some—team effort. Like I was there to pick up where he left off and help out with the cause.

Fuck, that made me angry enough to clench the steering wheel so tight my knuckles ached, groaning in sync with the stitched leather.

I wasn't angry at Frankie, not really. Even though I wanted to be after watching her kiss Eli so passionately. That part didn't even really bother me, aside from making me green with envy. I wasn't even angry with Eli for making a move on her.

I was angry at how badly I wanted to be *that* guy—the one who always knew the right thing to say. The one who made people feel safe and secure just by smiling. The one who made even Frankie Blake melt and soften for him.

Instead, I was the rough-edged man who sat there, feeling like a third wheel in my own goddamn truck.

When I pulled into her driveway, my headlights sliced across the front lawn as I parked by the small front porch. Still, she didn't speak.

Still, I didn't move.

Say something, Trav.

Do something!

Nothing would come to mind though, or better yet, millions of things came to mind, I just didn't know how to do them. I was no good at that stuff.

"You're mad." She breathed, and my hands instinctively tightened around the wheel again as I stared off into the darkness.

"I'm not mad."

"Bullshit."

The quick snap of her strong voice was enough to draw my face around in her direction and make me look at her.

Really look at her.

Her cheeks were still pink, but not from the harsh cold air outside. Her eyes were glassy but sharp. She cried not long ago, and she looked like she might do it again.

Though she looked more like she might rip my head off instead.

Instead of fighting her on it, I shook my head, staring at her glowing green eyes, and asked "What do you want me to say, Frankie?"

"Whatever it is that's making you act like you're trying not to feel anything at all." She demanded.

I let out a humorless laugh and shoved the gearshift into park. "Fine. I saw you and Eli. I watched him kiss you and say all the right shit and make you feel seen. Good for him." I turned on the bench seat and faced her, putting my arm against the back of the seat, "And I'm trying to sit here and act like it doesn't gut me."

Her lips parted, "Travis," her breath hitched.

"You don't owe me anything," I added quickly, tasting the bitterness of it. "He's your type, right? Smooth, charming, outgoing. Everyone loves Eli."

But even as I said the words, I knew there was more to it. I forced myself to trust my gut. And my gut told me that there was something in her eyes all those times she would look at me over the last few years. All those times her lips wouldn't say all the things her mind wanted her to.

"Are you seriously jealous of your best friend right now?" she asked, stunned.

I scoffed, sitting back against the door. "Are you seriously trying to pretend that you aren't torn between the two of us?"

That shut her up.

The words hung between us, thick and dangerous. Her chest heaved, and my blood roared as we stared through the darkness. Somehow, it felt like we were burning bridges we'd never be able to walk back over once the sun came up.

"I didn't ask for any of this." She whispered, "I'm *not* asking for it. I don't even want it."

"Sure." I scoffed, angry with myself for admitting that I was hung up over her and jealous of Eli, now that she was admitting my biggest fear. She didn't want me.

"Why the hell are you making me feel like the villain for being caught in the middle?" She snapped, shoving me with her fist against my chest.

I didn't rise to the bait though, because she was right. Frankie was stuck in the middle between two guys who wanted her. Yet she wanted only one back. That wasn't her fault.

"You kissed him back." I said quietly, more for myself than for her.

I'd been biting my tongue for years. Watching her. Wanting her. Yet I never stood a chance.

"Yeah," She whispered, and her shoulders fell as I finally looked back at her, "But I haven't stopped thinking about what it would feel like to kiss *you* since."

My blood ran cold and heated to lava in the same second as her white teeth bit into her bottom lip.

Her face didn't show anger or frustration, from my outburst or pitting her as the bad guy.

No, that would have been easy to deal with. That would have been familiar to me.

When I stared at her in the dark, silent cab of my truck, I saw something new on her face.

Need.

It wasn't casual. It wasn't flirtatious.

It was raw.

Honest.

Wrecked.

And suddenly, I didn't think. I moved. Before I even knew it, I was out of the truck and around to her side, yanking the door open and catching her as she jumped out. Her breath puffed into the air in quick pants; her eyes were wide.

Then her hands were grabbing the front of my shirt, and mine were on her face, pulling her into me as I kissed her.

Fuck.

I was kissing Frankie Blake.

Dammit if she didn't kiss me back with the same enthusiasm I had envied seeing with Eli earlier. I could feel her desperation with every move she made.

Teeth. Tongue. Hands. Fingernails.

Frankie gasped into my mouth as her fists curled into my shirt, pinning herself between me and the seat of my truck. I growled when my hard-on pressed against her stomach, and she pushed back against it.

"Is this what you were wondering about, Frankie?" I said against her lips, baiting her and toying with the fire she always tried to burn everyone with.

"You kiss like you fight on the ice." She whispered breathlessly. "I knew you would."

"And you kiss like you need saving." I murmured back. "But don't make me your safe place unless you mean it."

She scoffed, and I could see the moment she went to make

a smart-ass comment back, but stopped herself. Instead, she paused and then replied, "What if I want both?" She asked gently. "What if you both make me feel safe in different ways?"

And then it was my turn to stay silent. I didn't reply because I didn't have an answer for her.

Instead, I kissed her again.

And she kissed me back.

Even though her kids were next door at her mom's for the night, and I wanted nothing more than to take her inside and spend the night in her bed, I didn't. But only because as I walked her to her front door and waited for her to walk inside, and turn off her porch light, the same question ran through my head on repeat.

What scared me more?

The fact that I finally had something I wanted to win—or that I might be willing to share her just to keep from losing her?

Double Team

THE ICY STILLNESS of the morning usually soothed my errant mind, while pausing my tired body after a long eventful shift. But not this morning. I sat on the back bumper of Engine Twenty-Two and tried to find that familiar peace that could only be found after a bad call in the middle of the night and before the world woke up for their normal, mundane day. That space when people were none the wiser about the terror that we faced while they slept peacefully in their homes.

I longed for the comfort I normally found in that space. My mind had been wreaking havoc on me all shift, a shift I wasn't even supposed to be working and regretted volunteering for since last night.

Right about the time I walked away from Frankie and her

sweet, sinful lips so I could push her and her desires into my best friend's eager and capable hands.

Damn, Trav was going to owe me big time.

My body tightened again, remembering the way Frankie had asked me to kiss her. The way she tasted, the way she sounded when I eagerly obliged. She had felt perfect, pinned to the wall, kissing me back with such vigor and need.

I knew for sure that no one had touched her body with only her pleasure in mind for a long time. She might have dated or hooked up with men since returning to Cedar Bluff, but I could just tell that no one had taken care of her needs the way she deserved.

Or maybe now, after she went home with Trav, someone had.

Last night I'd pushed her toward my best friend with a joke on my lips, and something like a blade twisting in my chest.

Think of me when you kiss him goodnight.

I'd said it like it was funny. Like it didn't matter. But it did.

And I thought about it all night long. I thought about her.

Her mouth. Her eyes. The way her fingers curled into my shirt like she didn't want to let go.

And then—the look that Travis had in his eyes when I turned around and found him watching us. Watching her.

Like she was something he'd been trying not to need and just couldn't anymore. Part of me felt good for giving my friend the push he needed to make a move on the woman he had lusted after for years.

And the other part of me felt gutted that Frankie was that woman in the end. Something happened between them after I went to work, I could feel it in my bones. But it didn't hurt me to think about.

That was the part that messed with my head the most. I didn't feel like I lost something as Travis gained it. It felt like we were sharing something we weren't supposed to be allowed to have in the first place.

So even though we were splitting the prize, it was still a win for both of us.

Fuck, that sounded sick and twisted.

"Morning," A gruff voice called out behind me.

Travis.

I had heard the familiar rumble of his classic truck when he pulled in but couldn't muster up the courage to walk out and greet him.

Looking over my shoulder, I found him holding a drink carrier with two coffee cups in it and a look on his face like he didn't know whether to flinch or grin.

"Is that a peace offering?" I asked, arching an eyebrow at him.

"Figured you were probably all up in your own head." He handed me a cup. "Thought maybe I'd try to caffeinate the overthinking away."

I snorted and took the coffee, shaking my head. "So, rip the band-aid off, tell me what happened."

He took a seat on the bumper next to me and sighed before letting the silence stretch around us for a while. Finally, he put me out of my misery.

"We kissed."

I nodded, letting his words sink into my mind as the caffeine started to hit my bloodstream. "Was it a good one?"

He groaned and widened his eyes.

Damnit.

"Well, shit." I grunted.

"Don't act like it wasn't a grand slam when you had her in

the equipment room all to yourself," He deadpanned, "I saw enough to know better."

"I'm not." I whistled, taking another sip.

"You're not mad?" He asked after a while, like he had been waiting to ask.

"No," I replied instantly, and that made him blink like he wasn't expecting it. "I'm—" I trailed off, trying to find the right words. They didn't come easily, nothing about the whole situation did, but I leaned on the decades of friendship between us to lead the way. "Relieved? I'm relieved."

His brow furrowed, "Relieved I kissed the woman you like? And that she enjoyed it?"

I laughed softly and shook my head again, "Relieved I wasn't wrong. That she wants both of us."

Silence again hung between us, but it wasn't the bad kind.

"And you're okay with that?" he asked cautiously, like he didn't want to tip something over an invisible edge and ruin everything.

I looked down at the cup in my hands, fingers drumming lightly on the lid. "It's weird as hell in a way," I admitted, "But I don't feel—threatened. I feel like—" I took a deep breath and looked over at him, finding his penetrating gaze locked right onto me. "Like we're better at this if we're not pretending it's a race."

Travis stared at me for a long moment before letting out a long breath, and I realized that was what he'd been waiting to hear.

"You're saying you want to date her together?" He asked, looking for clarification.

My jaw flexed, I hadn't said it out loud yet. Not even to myself. But the second the question left his mouth, the answer was there, solid and settled in my chest.

"If it's what she wants," I said quietly, "Yeah, I do."

He didn't say anything back, but after a long time, he held his coffee cup out to me, and I chuckled, bumping mine against his with a grunt.

That was enough.

A truce.

No, that wasn't the right word.

Permission?

Permission to make what we wanted out of the situation without worrying about anything else.

There was a shift in the air between us, thankfully. A new kind of game had been started, without either of us realizing it until now.

And I couldn't stop smiling. Because as messed up as it all sounded, I fucking loved the idea of a little playful competition for the woman that had been driving us both mad with need for years.

The challenge.

The chaos.

The shared obsession.

Frankie Blake was right in the middle of it all, loud, stubborn, sexy as hell and somehow on the receiving end of all the overdue care and devotion she had been missing her whole life.

Hope she was ready for us.

"OKAY, LINE DRILLS!" Travis yelled, blowing his whistle, and the tiny tots scrambled to the blue line. "Set." He warned, and they all dropped their shoulders, getting into position. "Go!"

The kids shot off, skating to the next blue line and resetting, ready to race back to prove who was fastest. Parents lined up against the glass, watching their kids excel at practice for the first time, probably ever. Even the kids who lacked skills but had heart competed and proved they had a right to be there.

And Emmie—damn. The girl took shot after shot, and every kid on the ice cycled through drills, ending with shots on each goal at opposite ends of the ice. The goalie the old coach kept in the crease missed more than he stopped, but he was getting the hang of it.

Emmie didn't need any guidance; she just *got* it.

She got the game. She got the mechanics. She got the puck.

Every. Single. Time.

She was natural. Travis had been right, and if she worked hard, she could go big with her skills. It felt incredible to be a part of it all. Helping the girl and her teammates finally craft their skills and dive into something worth spending time on.

Never mind the fact that it felt really damn good to feel Frankie's proud gaze from the sidelines too. That made something in my chest all gooey.

God, she looked fucking good too. Perhaps I was just imagining things, but she appeared to have put a bit more effort into her look as she came down the bleachers before practice.

Her black jeans looked painted on, and her white sweater embraced her curves like a caress I wanted to be a part of. Instead of her signature topknot of dark hair, she wore it down, letting the long locks dance around her shoulders and down the long line of her spine to the top of her ass.

An ass worth worshiping too, if I did say so myself. I wasn't even an ass man by choice, but I'd still fall to my knees behind Frankie any day of the week because hers was that damn sexy.

"Sunshine!" Emmie screeched from goal. "Take a shot. I bet I can stop it!"

I chuckled as Trace cheered her on from next to the net, "Yeah, give it your best shot!" He called.

I grabbed a puck and started toward her, skating fast, keeping the puck moving like I would in an actual game, and she hunkered down in net, locked in. I passed it back and forth, trying to trick her and even did a quick spin, faking to the left before shooting it at the top right of the net.

As it soared toward her, it was like the whole rink quieted, watching to see if she managed to stop a full speed puck.

She started to the left, where I led her before shooting, but she quickly corrected and got her glove up into the right corner, plucking the puck out of thin air and dropping it onto the ice to show her prize.

"Boo-yah!" She cheered and broke out into a fancy little moonwalk dance as she pumped her arms up and down excit- edly. "Top shelf, where Mama hides the cookies!"

"Damn." Trav said as he came to a stop at my side. "I didn't think she'd get it. You put a lot of smoke behind it."

"Sure fucking did," I said with pride. "That girl has spunk."

"Just like her mom." He said, skating around in front of me and nodding to the bench behind me.

I glanced over my shoulder and found Frankie's glowing stare aimed directly at us, though she was far enough away that I couldn't tell which one of us she was staring at directly. Which only amped up the excitement of it all for me.

Looking back at Trav and the uncharacteristic smirk on his dark face confirmed that he was thinking the same thing. "Wanna make a bet?" I asked.

He rolled his eyes but didn't skate away, "You never win those."

I scoffed and skated backward away from him and toward my target. "First one to get her alone wins."

Trav looked over at Frankie, and then his grin darkened. "What's the prize?"

"We let her choose." I winked, and my body heated just thinking about finally getting her alone again.

"Game on, brother." He called, and I skated off toward the boards, turning to Frankie and finding her coming down the steps to the opening by the bench.

"What are you two up to?" She asked instead of a greeting with a skeptical look in her eyes.

"Nothing honorable." I replied with a smirk, and her lips parted at my bluntness. "Tell me something," I leaned on the boards, and she quickly looked around at the other parents milling around, but they were all too far away to overhear anything I said. "Were you a good girl?" Her chest heaved, and she quickly licked her lips, eyes darting to Travis on the ice. "Don't look at him, look at me." I demanded, and her eyes snapped back to me. "Were you a good girl the other night?"

She steeled her spine and crossed her arms over her chest, "I was *something*, the other night. Though I'm not sure anyone would classify it as good."

Fuck.

Her words went straight to my dick.

"Did you kiss Travis like I told you to?" I urged and her cheeks pinked even more.

"Yes." She whispered, glancing around us again.

"Did you like it?" I pushed, gripping the top of the boards, begging her to play my game with me.

"Elliot," She warned and then took a deep breath when I didn't waver. "Yes."

"More than you liked my kiss?" Cocking my head to the side, I challenged her even more, "Or do you need a refresher so you can decide?"

"You're trouble." Frankie hissed, glancing over my shoulder again and then back to me before she took an almost invisible step forward. "Maybe I want a refresher."

"After practice is over." I started firmly.

"The kids—" She shook her head, like she was shaking off the spell that weaved around us.

"Leave it to me." I said and gave her a quick grin. "I'll be seeing you then."

Skating back into the chaos of Tiny Tot's hockey, I held her gaze until I had to give my attention back to the kids. Glancing up at the play clock on the wall, I started making plans as I counted down the last twenty minutes of practice.

Twenty minutes.

Then Frankie Blake was going to get a taste of a Net Crashers double team.

7 - FRANKIE
Trial Run

THEY WERE UP TO SOMETHING. I probably should have run for the hills after Eli's dirty warning in the middle of practice, but part of me was waiting to see if he was kidding or not. Part of me didn't want him to be, but the sane part of me knew he was. Or at least knew he should be.

Something was seriously wrong with both infuriatingly sexy hockey players, and the longer they acted like they were okay with the fact that I kissed both of them in the same night, hell, the same hour, I worried about their mental stability.

It wasn't normal.

People labeled women terrible things for even talking to two men at the same time, let alone kissing them. God knew I didn't have time for any more small-town talk and gossip about my name. I'd earned enough of that years ago when I showed back up after leaving without a backward glance, this time with two kids on my hip.

No way was I going to welcome any more talk.

Even if Eli and Travis were just tempting enough to pause long enough to contemplate it.

Nope, I couldn't do that either. Because then I'd start wondering. And wondering would lead to longing. And longing would lead to temptation. If I made it into temptation, I'd sink into the need burning in my belly since they both touched me the other night, and I'd be stupid enough to give in to it.

But as I stood in the lobby of the rink after Tiny Tot practice, as most of the other families walked out for the night, I noticed Eli up to no good. He slipped something to Coach Rick, paired with a whispered message.

It wasn't subtle.

Neither of them was exactly trying to hide the extra-large coffee in a brand new corny mug that Eli always sweetened Rick up with. This one said, *"Practice like you've got Rick's blood pressure on the line."*

Paired with a crumpled-up twenty-dollar bill, Rick was grinning like a man who'd just been handed front row seats to the Stanley Cup Finals.

I narrowed my eyes as Eli sauntered across the lobby to me. "What did you just do?"

Eli balked, innocent as sin. "Who, me? Nothing. Just making sure the kids have some post-practice entertainment."

"Entertainment?" I asked, crossing my arms.

"Arcade, Pizza. Friendly competition," he said, giving me that golden-boy smile that made my knees wobble and my self-respect scatter like pucks on bad ice.

Rick clapped his hands, shouting for the kids still around.

"Toby! Emmie! Round up the team—we've got a shootout showdown and bubble hockey championship to see to. Best-of-three!"

The kids exploded in cheers, not even bothering to give me a glance as they ran off to gather the rest of their friends.

Eli winked at me, and my pulse raced. "Looks like you're suddenly free for the next twenty minutes."

And that's when I felt him—Travis.

At my back.

Close enough, I could smell that sawdust and leather mix that was intoxicating paired with whatever sinful aftershave he used that always made me forget how to work my tongue.

His hands ghosted over the swell of my hips, "Come with me."

It wasn't a question.

Eli's sexy grin distracted me long enough, and before I knew it, my hand was in Trav's big rough one, and he was pulling me back down the stairs toward the ice.

He didn't stop at the ice, or even the bleachers, instead, he kept walking until we hit the last locker room in the strip, and he pushed the door open. It was empty, and the squeak of the door echoed off the tiled walls as the overhead lights dimmed to their usual off-hours level.

The door thudded shut behind us, and suddenly the air felt ten degrees hotter.

Travis didn't waste time, pulling me around the tall lockers to the last row, backing me up against the cold metal surface. With one hand on my hip, the other on the back of my neck, he pinned me with his massive body and didn't stop until his lips met mine.

Damn.

I was hoping I'd made it all up in my head, somehow imagining that he was as good a kisser as I remembered. It was. His kiss was hot and hungry, unrelenting as I clung to him, weaving my fingers through the short hair at the base of his neck, digging my nails in.

He bit my bottom lip, and I gasped, which was all it took for him to deepen the kiss even more, pinning his hips against mine. Embarrassingly, I moaned and rocked into him, but I couldn't stop.

"You kissed my best friend just like this." He growled against my lips.

"I know." I panted.

"You liked it," he said as his fingers skimmed above my jeans, finding the soft flesh of my side and sliding under my sweater.

I didn't deny it as I nodded.

"Good," He whispered, dipping his lips to my throat and sucking on the skin until I moaned for him. "But I'm going to make damn sure you like kissing me even more."

His tongue licked a slow line across my neck, and I whimpered—*actually whimpered*—as he pressed his thigh between mine, grinding just enough to make my body light up like a fire alarm.

"Trav—" I breathed, but I wasn't stopping him. God help me, I was begging him.

His other hand found the hem of my sweater, and then both of his big hands were touching me under it as I melted into him. I leaned my head back against the locker behind me as he slowly kissed his way down to my stomach, falling to his knees. Mouth hot on my skin, worshiping me with reverence that made my eyes roll back and my knees shake.

"Do you know how long I've wanted this?" He murmured, "How many times I've pictured having you right here, begging me for more?"

"Jesus." I gasped, clawing at his hair as he flicked the button of my jeans open. "You're not fighting fair."

"I'm not fighting at all," he growled, "Not with you. Not with Eli."

He blew a breath against the bare skin above my panty line, and then Eli's voice echoed through the room, behind Trav, smooth and unbothered.

I gasped and jolted my eyes open as the grinning playboy let his eyes roam over my exposed stomach to his friend's head at my waistline. "Looks like you owe me five bucks, Hayes."

Travis didn't even flinch, just turned his head enough to meet his best friend's smug smile.

"How?" Trav asked, standing up to his full height, "I'm the one that got her alone first."

"Yeah," Eli said, stepping closer with a burning heat in his eyes. "But I made it happen."

I stared at them both, breathless, clothes twisted and my body pulsating with something I couldn't quite name but hadn't felt in years. Maybe ever.

"You made a bet?"

Eli smirked, "A friendly wager. The winner got alone time with you."

I blinked at him, "And the loser?"

Eli stepped in, brushing my hair over my shoulder, "Gets to watch. Or join. Your call, Black Cat."

"Jesus fuck." I should have been offended. Or enraged. Instead, my legs wobbled, and my body buzzed as the name of the feeling finally came to the front of my mind. Hunger. "You two are unbelievable," I muttered.

Eli's voice dropped low as the smile melted off his face, "And we haven't even made you come yet, either." I clenched my teeth, but the moan still escaped through them, and his eyes fell to my swollen lips. "You're beautiful when you're falling apart."

Travis's fingers stroked up the inside of my thigh. "Let us break you a little more, Shade."

"Shade?" I gasped, locked in on the word that felt like a caress from his lips, and those lips turned up into a gentle smile beneath the stubble of his beard.

"You're so full of shadows. Your dark beauty and your black cat energy give me a place of cool quiet to rest in."

"Damn." Eli groaned, drawing my gaze back to his like I was stuck in some weird game of tug-of-war and I was the flag in the center of the two macho men pulling on me. "That's deep. And here I thought Black Cat was going to win me some brownie points."

My knees buckled, and Travis caught me, anchoring me to the lockers again as Eli weaved his fingers in my hair, unbothered by Travis's proximity before kissing me.

God, I was so warped in the head because I let them.

Eli's lips on mine, Travis's on my neck as his hands held me upright so they could keep going. And I let them.

Both.

Hands. Mouths. Touches that built and built until I was practically shaking between them, every nerve ending lit with want and every ounce of logic gone. But then I pulled back, just enough.

"Wait," I gasped, heart slamming against my ribs. "This can't be real. I can't just—have both of you."

Eli tilted his head, "Why can't you?"

"Because people don't do this. Because I'm a mom. Because it's not *normal!*" Panic was building with each excuse I threw their way.

Travis leaned in and rested his forehead against mine, once again showing me the depth to his quiet soul, "Screw normal. We don't want you to choose. No one else needs to have an opinion on it."

"We want you," Eli added, kissing my neck and making me moan into Travis's mouth. "Both of us."

"I don't think I can do that," I whispered.

"Don't think then," Travis said, "Just try for now."

My heart thundered. My thighs clenched and my entire body screamed yes in a way that left me positive it'd shrivel up and die for good if I denied it what they were offering.

"Okay," I breathed. "Trial run. No thinking. Just—see where this takes us."

Eli grinned, "That's all we're asking of you."

And then they gave me a taste.

I moaned into Eli's mouth as Travis's fingers slid beneath the band of my panties, slowly, as if to give me time to tell him no. But fuck it. I wasn't stopping.

I spread my thighs around his massive tree trunk leg, granting him access, and his fingers found my clit in no time.

"Mmh, baby." Travis groaned, burying his face in my neck as Eli sucked on my tongue. "You're soaked for us."

"Fuck." I whimpered, "Fuck. Fuck. Fuck." I rode his hand shamelessly as Eli bit my earlobe, whispering filthy things to me, and within seconds I was biting the back of my hand to stifle my screams as I came on Travis's fingertips.

I gasped, drawing ragged breaths into my lungs as if it was the first time all day long while Travis looked at his friend.

"Feel how wet she is for us."

Eli didn't hesitate, but when Travis didn't move his hand from my pants, Eli pushed my jeans and panties down to the top of my thighs, making enough room, and then I moaned in absolute shock as Travis used two fingers to spread me open so his best friend could run his fingers through the wetness of my orgasm.

"Oh God," I moaned when Eli pushed his finger into me. Not once had Travis penetrated me that whole time, using just my clit to get me off, and now as Eli started stroking one long finger in and out of me, Trav went back to circling my clit again. "Please."

Eli chuckled, and Travis stared deep into my eyes as I clawed at his chest, rocking against their hands. "You want more, Shade?" I nodded, biting my lip as Eli sucked on my earlobe again. "Then use your words to beg us."

"God," I gasped, trying to get my brain to work to form coherent words. "I want to come again." Licking my lips, I closed my eyes and focused harder. "No, I need to come again. Just like this. From both of you."

"Good girl." Eli growled, biting my neck and fingering me deeper. "That was so fucking sexy to hear."

Travis pinched my clit between his two fingers and stared into my eyes the whole time he played with me. The quiet man loved his eye contact, apparently, so I gave in to it and held his gaze as they both played me in perfect harmony until I was crashing over the edge of my second orgasm again. This time Travis used his lips to silence my screams, and I clung to him as I came again.

When my world stopped spinning on its axis, I felt embarrassment trying to take root in my gut as they both towered over me with smug and sinful looks on their faces.

"Jesus." I whispered, pushing my hair back off my face as Eli pulled my panties and jeans back up, buttoning them like they hadn't just wrecked me together so effortlessly.

"That was just a preview." Eli said, noting my embarrassment and kissing me again. "Wait until we really have the time to make you feel everything."

I scoffed as Travis lurked just out of reach, finally I forced myself to look up into his dark face again, because somehow his quiet nature made me feel even more embarrassed now that the high of my orgasm was crashing.

At least, I felt that way until he slowly lifted his fingers to his lips and sucked them clean, all while staring directly at me.

"Fuck." I gulped and sagged into the lockers. "I think you broke my brain."

Finally, he grinned, and part of me relaxed a little. "Wait until we're inside of you at the same time, Frankie." He said it with such conviction, there wasn't any question of whether it would happen, but it felt more like a question of when. "Then you'll be thoroughly changed."

I didn't reply, as Elliot and Trav sauntered away from me, leaving me trembling and questioning every single thing about my life in an empty locker room.

Wanting more.

"Jesus, Frankie, get your head on straight," I whispered to myself, staring at my reflection in the mirror above a sink. "Just go out there and act normal. Act cool. Act like you didn't just let two men finger-fuck you at the same time in the locker room."

I snorted, rolling my eyes at myself.

Piece of cake.

8 - TRAVIS
Sudden Death

I OPENED a new chat on my phone, adding Frankie and Elliot to it, and typed out a message.

ME

> I hear you switched your shift around to work now, so you'll be off tonight. Any particular reason why?

Rick texted me with that random, unnecessary info like he knew I'd want to know it. Which would be weird if it were anyone else, considering Eli was the one who paid him off to entertain the kids last night after practice. But it was Rick, and nothing got past him.

Last night's memories flooded back through my body as I

sat in the front seat of my truck waiting for a reply. It played like a movie as I pinned Frankie on the lockers in the dark and empty locker room after Tiny Tot practice. Her moans echoed in my ears, vibrating through my soul as she bit my lip, climbing me like a tree.

I had no idea she'd be so passionate with a little attention, but watching her let her guard down enough to show me and Eli just how badly she wanted us—damn.

The way she begged us.

The way she spread her legs for us to play.

Fuck.

I reached down and palmed my hard dick in my jeans as I got even more excited, remembering how it felt to work with Eli to get her off.

That had been something I hadn't expected to enjoy either. We'd slept with women together before, usually both so drunk off our asses neither of us did a good job on our own, anyway. And never during those nights did we give two shits about the women's pleasure or comfort.

Last night though, last night had been monumental. Even if we both left with the worst cases of blue balls in history.

It had been worth it to focus on Frankie and her needs only, giving her a taste of what it would be like to be with both of us. And she had agreed to it. She agreed to let it play out and see where it went, without worrying about all the reasons she shouldn't.

Which meant we were going to work even harder to prove to her how we could make it work.

Because when I tasted her pussy on my fingers after she came twice for me, I knew I wasn't going to get enough of her in just a short fling.

I wanted it all.

My phone buzzed, pulling me out of my daydream, and I read Frankie's reply.

FRANKIE

My kids are at the zoo with my mom today, so I figured I'd make the most of my day. That's all.

ELI

So it's not so you can sit on the bench and watch us play tonight, ouch baby. Break my heart.

I snorted and watched as Frankie's text bubbles popped back up and then disappeared a few times before her reply came through.

FRANKIE

I mean I could probably be persuaded to stick around after I get off.

ME

If you stick around, I can make sure you get off, real good.

ELI

Same.

Same, times two.

Extra same.

I chuckled, and Frankie sent a laughing emoji at his ridiculousness.

ELI

What are you wearing to our game tonight?

Instantly, the energy changed as we played with fire. I knew she was at work, and I was still sitting on a job site I'd stopped in on to check some things, but Eli was off until Monday. Which meant he was probably home alone and horny.

Coordinating three people together, especially one that had two kids, was going to be difficult to master. But I was willing to try.

ME

Please say nothing. I'm dying to see more of you.

ELI

Rude. I was going to say something tasteful and supportive like, "That ACDC shirt with the hole in the sleeve you wear when you're stressed."

FRANKIE

That's only mildly creepy.

ELI

I was going for romantic.

FRANKIE

It's that too.

ME

So, are you going to watch our game and cheer us on? Or abandon us knowing we can't give chase?

FRANKIE

I never watch your games as a spectator. Won't that draw attention?

ELI

So? Let them stare, baby. I don't care.

ME

Do you care, Frankie? Do you want to hide this?

I asked, but I wasn't sure I was ready to hear the answer. What if she said yes? Would it change how I felt about her?

No.

But it would damper it a little.

I didn't want to hide.

Obviously, I knew the possibility of a relationship between the three of us wasn't the norm, especially for Cedar Bluff, but it wasn't the weirdest thing either.

FRANKIE

I don't want to hide. I'm tired of spending every day living for everyone else. I just want to be selfish tonight.

ELI

Good, because I've been thinking about the noise you made when Trav slid his hand into your panties all damn day. And I want another hit of that high.

ME

What a damn good noise it was too. I can't wait for more.

FRANKIE

Tell me more about getting more. You know… for science.

ELI

Do you want the details now or do you want me to whisper them into your ear from the penalty box?

ME

If I score tonight, I want a reward. Locker room. Door Locked. Hands on the wall as soon as we walk in.

ELI

> If I get a penalty, I want a reward too.
> Preferably something involving my mouth
> and absolutely no interruptions.

FRANKIE

> Are you two going to fight each other on the
> ice just to get my attention?

ELI

> I won't say no.

ME

> You're worth the bruises, Shade.

She didn't reply right away, but I wasn't worried because she was at work after all. The point of the whole conversation was to make sure she knew we were thinking of her. And to keep her thinking of us.

If we didn't, the chaos of her life would steal her away before we could convince her to let us take some of her burden.

THE ICE WAS the only place in the world where my brain would turn off. It had been that way since I was a kid, looking to escape the expectations and opinions of everyone else.

Cold air, the weight of the gear, the thud of the puck against my stick, it gave my body something to do when my mind wouldn't shut up.

Tonight though? Nothing shut off.

Not with her in the bleachers.

I spotted Frankie the second she got to the landing at the top of the stairs, looking down at the ice as we hit our warmups. Her sage green dress was the same shade as her witchy eyes, and it looked like it was as soft as a cloud, hugging her lush curves with sexy brown buttons running down the front of it.

Buttons I was going to rip open with my teeth.

She had undone two at her chest, revealing the top of her cleavage, and she had undone a few at the bottom, which created a V at her knees. All it did was lead my eyes to that prize between her thick thighs, above her thigh-high brown boots that disappeared under the hem of the dress.

Fuck.

I was hard, and my athletic cup was seriously cramping my dick up.

Her pretty lips curved when she found me staring, she knew how damn good she looked. With grace and sex appeal I didn't know she had, she walked down the aisle like she owned the whole damn rink. None of us were even worthy enough to breathe the same air.

And all I could think about was how her pretty thighs trembled around my hand when I rubbed her clit in slow, lazy circles while Eli pushed his finger deep inside of her.

I fumbled a puck passed to me and cursed under my breath.

Eli skated by, smirking, "Eyes up, Saw."

He'd seen her too. Of course, he had. We didn't share much in life, not in personality traits, or wardrobe styles—hell, we didn't even like the same teams in the NHL. But Frankie?

She was in both of our systems now.

I took another lap, slammed a shot into the boards harder than I meant to, and let the thrum in my chest tighten until it felt like it might crack open. Eli took a cheap shot against my shoulder, catching me off guard once again, and laughed as he skated away.

I didn't want to fight him.

But I'd bury him in the ice to get to her first.

The game started, and the entire first period passed by in a blur. I barely even registered the score as I skated around, knocking guys on their asses for the fun of it.

Frankie sat in the middle of a row tucked behind our bench with her legs crossed and that look on her face. The one that screamed how hard she was trying not to be obvious.

But every time I hit the boards, she looked at me. Every time Eli stole the puck and raced by her to go shoot on goal, she watched him.

It was torture, and heaven.

Midway through the second period, we got a line change, and I didn't hesitate to make a move. I skated straight to the glass and pressed my glove against it, locking eyes with her. "Having fun yet?" I mouthed.

She bit her lip and nodded slowly.

Fuck.

Two shifts later, Eli did the same, leaning over the bench to mutter something through the gap in the glass right in front of her. I didn't catch the words from the ice, but I saw her reaction.

Flushed cheeks.

Shaky breath.

Thighs slowly shifting under her.

She was breaking. Slowly. Gloriously.

And as soon as our game was over, we were going to ruin her all over again.

9 - ELI
Locker Room Secrets

THE FINAL BUZZER SOUNDED, breaking us free of the torment we'd endured all game. We won, but just barely. Rick was yelling something obscene from the bench about our poor excuse for skilled plays, yet I couldn't care less.

The second we hit the tunnel, I pulled off my gloves, yanked my helmet free and turned to Travis, who eyed me. "She's mine tonight." He said hungrily, the need behind it was visible enough to almost make me question if he'd let me near her.

Almost.

I just grinned, "You scored, but I sat my ass in that penalty box for her. You think I'm not coming? I'm at least going to watch."

Twenty minutes later, fresh from the shower, we walked out together, bags forgotten and left in our lockers. Frankie stood outside the back hallway door, waiting for us. The loud noise from the bar up in the lobby echoed through the hall, but the locker rooms were empty this time of night and as if on cue, the second she saw us, the lights on the ice dimmed, signaling the shutdown for the night.

She crossed her arms, but her eyes revealed her true emotions - wild, filled with nerves and longing.

"I thought you were going to kill each other out there." She murmured.

I stepped in fast, crowding her against the opposite wall and pinning her with my hips. "We still might," I said low with a growl. "We're both high on adrenaline and testosterone."

Travis came up to her side, running a hand over her hip, and she licked her lips, glancing between the two of us. "Are you ready for that reward, Shade?" he asked, letting his fingers drift to the edge of her dress. "I watched you all night, hoping you'd spread these pretty thighs just enough for me to see if you had anything on underneath for me."

I groaned, and she panted when my cock jumped against her stomach. "Are you ready for us?"

Frankie nodded, breath hitching, lips parting just enough for me to see that tiny tremble in her chin.

"But I have one rule." She pushed me back with a hand on my chest, and I backed up, just enough for her to slide out between our bodies.

Sensually, she tossed her long hair over her shoulder and turned, slowly walking backward toward the locker room door.

"Name it." Travis demanded, taking a step after her.

Slowly, she undid a button at her chest, revealing a peek

of black lace hugging her lush tits. "I'm not getting fucked in a stinky locker room." Her fingers dropped and pushed another button free, and the skin beneath her bra came into view. I nearly swallowed my tongue, and her words should have iced me out until she finished it up with, "That doesn't mean I won't let you get me off in one again before you take me to bed though."

God damnit.

Her back hit the door, and she pushed it open, hooking her finger for us to follow her, and we both bolted. A girlish squeal slid from her lips when I got to her first, elbowing Travis out of the way and picking her up. The lush weight of her curves in my hands for the first time made my dick throb even more as she wrapped her legs around my waist and leaned in, so her tits were right in my face.

"Don't mind if I do." I said before kissing the swell of one in the opening of the fabric.

She giggled and moaned when I pushed my tongue under the lace cup of her bra. The sound made my blood go dark and hungry.

"Door's locked." Travis said from behind us as he followed me into the small room on the edge where team doctors could set up shop to tape up players before games. It was private and perfectly equipped with a large, sturdy, padded table.

The perfect place for the first course of the night.

Frankie shimmied out of my arms and pulled another button free, opening her dress to the feminine slope of her stomach as she backed up against the table. She wasn't afraid or timid and I fucking loved that. I didn't want someone whom I needed to coax or convince.

No, our girl was ready for us, eager for everything we'd give her.

"Are you sure?" I asked quietly, because I needed to hear

it in her voice, not just see it in the wild, aroused flicker of her eyes.

She didn't flinch or hesitate as she lifted herself up onto the table and slowly spread her thighs, showing the tiniest scrap of black lace covering her pussy. My mouth watered, but she held up her finger, stopping us before we could move. "I'm sure. But this—" She undid the last two buttons and opened her dress, revealing her entire sexy body to us. Travis groaned at my hip, and I licked my lips, hungry for more. "This is just a preview. You want more? Take me home. Treat me as more than heat and want tangled up with curiosity. You need to earn what's under the surface."

Travis stepped up to her, standing at the edge of her spread knees with a tight jaw. "We already are. We have been. But I won't hold it against you that you haven't seen it. We'll just do it better."

I nodded, "This isn't about claiming your body, Frankie. It's about letting you feel how wanted you are. Every inch of you with every inch of us."

Her breath caught, and her spine arched as I stood between her legs. Running my hand up her calf slowly, reverently, as Travis kissed the side of her neck, pulling her dress and bra strap off her shoulder.

She gasped when my hands slid up the back of her knees. He groaned when she dug her nails into the back of his neck, pulling him in for more as he turned his head and kissed his way down the front of her chest.

Frankie was already trembling before he pushed the cup of her bra down and sucked her nipple into his mouth. Watching him do it hit me with a physical rush of pleasure as her moans filled the air, even though I wasn't doing it myself. "Perfection," He growled, letting it pop from his lips.

"Table's sturdy," I said, pressing my palm to the pad next

to her thigh. "We'll be gentle with it, but I can't say the same for you."

Travis chuckled, low and dark. "She doesn't want gentle."

"No," She whispered. "I really don't." Reaching up, she pulled her bra down, tucking both cups under her full breasts, and I growled at the perfect image of sexual prowess she gave off, leaned back with her thighs spread, wearing a thigh-high pair of boots and longing. "I want to feel the high of adrenaline and testosterone touch my skin tonight, boys."

Travis moved behind the table and pulled her back into his big chest, instantly running his fingers over her tits, playing with the offered toys and making her rock in his expert hold.

I couldn't hold back anymore, not when she was offering herself to us, like a Goddess.

Dropping to my knees, her bright green eyes watched me from above before fluttering closed when Travis pulled on her nipples. I kissed the top of her thigh above her boots, soft and then firmer, covering every inch of exposed skin between her lace panties and the leather of her boots.

She writhed between us, rocking and clawing her nails into whatever she could reach. Her thighs shook and her hips rolled forward, desperate for friction, for me.

"You smell like sin," I murmured, nuzzling my nose against the lace covering her core. Hooking my finger in the band, I pulled the fabric aside, revealing the most sensual sight I'd ever seen before. Frankie Blake, wet and pink, desperate for me and Travis, open and eager for whatever we'd give her. Dipping my tongue through her wetness, I shook with delight, "And you taste like a fucking promise."

She moaned loudly, and Travis hooked his fingers around the front of her throat, tipping her head back so he could kiss her upside down, absorbing them. If she screamed, it would echo off the tile walls, and someone could hear. The idea of being caught, while simultaneously knowing the door was locked and no one would see what was ours, spurred me on.

It was my mission to make her as loud as possible.

I licked her like a man drowning with deep slow strokes. Deliberate circles and flicks that made her arch off the table and beg through her teeth.

The whole time, Travis kissed her, playing with her nipples and toying with her.

Team effort.

He released her lips, and she dropped her gaze back to me, burning with need as she watched me eat her pussy like she'd never seen something sexier. I lifted her thighs and spread them wide as she rocked against my face.

Travis reached down the front of her body and pulled her panties to the side, giving me better access before using his fingers to spread her pink lips open for me just like he did last night. I attacked her clit, sucking it into my mouth as he pinched her nipple and held her open for me.

"Eli!" She gasped, shaking between us. "Just like that. Don't stop. My God, don't ever stop!"

And then she came. Hard.

Messy and wild. Gasping a broken sob on a moan muffled against Travis's lips as he kissed her again. I kept going, pushing my tongue into her to taste her orgasm as she sank into his hold, slumping against his chest with boneless flushed skin.

"More." She whispered, reaching for me with a desperation that nearly undid me.

"Not here." Travis said, his voice rough with arousal, "We promised you a bed."

"And I want more than one round," I added, standing up and wiping her wetness from my mouth before leaning down to kiss her.

When I pulled back, she smiled, wrecked yet radiant, and swallowed, "Well then, what are you two standing around for then?"

We didn't answer her. We just buttoned her back up, helped her off the table and led her to the parking lot where my truck was parked next to Trav's. "Take your pick, princess." I nodded to the trucks. "His place or mine?"

Her green eyes flicked over the two options, and a devilish grin kissed her lips. "I don't care whose truck we take, as long as I finally get to see what one of you is packing in those jeans on the way there."

Fucking hell.

10 - FRANKIE
The Loft

THE SECOND I jumped up into Eli's lifted truck and slid into the backseat, I knew I had made a mistake. A calculated, filthy, absolutely worth it kind of mistake. Eli's truck smelled like his turnout gear and smoke, and the combination had me clenching my thighs before the door even shut.

Travis got in beside me, spreading those thick legs and dragging a palm over his beard like he already knew what I was thinking. The black fleece flannel he wore matched his dark gaze, and the tightness of his jeans made my mouth water, even though I had just come a few minutes ago.

Eli slid into the driver's seat, glanced in the rearview mirror once and shook his head like he was regretting saying that he wanted me in his bed tonight, which meant he had to drive.

"You two behave back there," he warned, voice rough.

I smiled.

"Silly boy."

The truck pulled out of the rink's lot, tires crunching over the ice-packed gravel, but I wasn't cold. My skin was burning with excitement and need. I felt alive for the first time in years. When we hit the first red light, I made my move. Leaning into Travis, I brushed my hand down his thigh.

Casual.

Slow.

Deadly.

His breath caught, and I saw the muscle in his jaw twitch as he turned to look at me. "Frankie." He said low and ominously.

"Yes?" I asked sweetly, fingers finding the button of his jeans.

He swallowed hard, but he didn't stop me. My chest rubbed against his side as he lifted his arm and put it over my shoulders. Silently granting me access to his body.

God that was such a turn on.

"You're going to get us killed," Eli muttered from the front, his knuckles tightening on the wheel.

"I'm not doing anything," I said, feigning innocence while sliding Travis's zipper down.

Still, he didn't stop me or try to warn me off. He simply growled when I slid my hand inside his jeans, finding the hard, hot length of his cock through his silky briefs and wrapped my fingers around it. "Jesus," he hissed.

"You're so thick." I purred, stroking him slowly, watching the way his lids went heavy, and his chest rose sharply under his shirt. "What do you think, Elliott?" I turned and found his best friend's gaze in the mirror. "You've felt how tight I am, do you think he'll fit?"

Eli cursed and one hand left the wheel, and I watched as he gripped his own cock, stroking it through his jeans.

Travis turned my jaw back toward him, "You're trouble."

"I thought you said I was the peace you found in the shade?" I pouted, squeezing him harder.

"You are both of those things."

"Do you want to tame me?" I questioned, dipping my finger in through the opening of his briefs and rubbing one fingertip over the leaking tip of his cock, gathering his pre-cum. His eyes were ravenous as I lifted it to my lips and ran it over my tongue. "Mmh,"

"No," He said through clenched teeth, "I want to lose control with you."

A groan came from the front seat.

"Eli." Trav warned.

"I swear to God, if I crash this truck—"

"Then you'd better keep your eyes on the road, Fireman," I purred, working my hand again in long, lazy pulls.

"Frankie," Eli barked, but it was strangled—desperate. "You wanted us all in bed tonight, but you're going to have to settle for the one you left soaked in the locker room if you don't stop."

He was on edge, and I felt bad for him, so I played nice. Kind of.

I dragged my hand out and sat back in my seat with Travis's arm over my shoulder, tucking me against his side as I rubbed my palms over my thighs and stomach, wiping the heat of him off. "Guess you'd better drive faster, then."

The air in the cab was thick enough to cut with a blade for the few minutes left before he pulled the truck into a parking spot in a private lot next to a warehouse.

Eli hardly stopped the truck before he jumped out, ripped my door open, pulled me from Trav's arms, and kissed me wildly.

Both men kissed so differently, and I wouldn't have been able to pick a favorite if there was a gun to my head. So quickly, I became obsessed with both. Eli carried me up the metal stairs to a nondescript steel door at the edge of the industrial strip lining the edge of downtown.

It was the kind of place that looked abandoned from the outside, but it pulsed with warmth the second he opened the door and carried me inside.

Exposed brick walls. Black steel beams. Concrete floors polished to a mirror shine. It was so perfectly Eli.

Setting me down in the open living space, he kissed me again before pulling back and kicking his boots off. He looked so damn good in his tight dark wash jeans and white henley, but I wondered what he looked like under it all more than that.

Forcing my eyes away from him, I admired his home. On the side of the massive room with tall ceilings was a staircase, leading to an open loft above, and my eyes tracked the steps, wondering if that was where his bed was. Could we go right up, or would they drag it out to tease me more?

I couldn't remember a time when I had ever longed for another human being the way I did for Eli and Travis.

And the way they hungered for me in return, I could almost trick my dark soul into thinking maybe they wouldn't hurt me in the end like another man had.

Travis's boots echoed behind me, and when I turned, both of them were watching me like they were starving.

"You sure?" Eli asked, his voice low and rough.

I nodded. "I need more than stolen moments in the dark," I leaned down and unzipped one of my boots, stepping out of it. "I want to *feel* it. The weight of this. The reality of it." Stepping out of the other one, I pushed them to the side and stared at my men.

Because they were fucking mine. I could feel it.

Travis moved first. He kissed me as if I were oxygen, as if the hours since he dropped me off on my doorstep had nearly done him in. His hands were big and rough and so damn reverent it nearly broke me open.

He lifted me with one arm under my thighs, walking me backward until my back hit a steel pillar in the middle of the room. I gasped, kissing him deeper as Eli slid behind me, shielding me from the cold hard metal and pressing me between them. His fingers worked in front of me, undoing the buttons on my dress until he pulled it free of my body, leaving me in my bra and panties in Travis's arms still.

"I want you to know what it's like," Eli whispered against the back of my neck, "to be ruined by both of us. Not for fun. Not for power. But because you're ours."

If I had been standing, my knees would have buckled. And I knew they would have caught me.

"Bed." I cried, as Eli's teeth sank into my shoulder and Trav's fingers slid under the crotch of my panties, rubbing me with the rough pads of his fingers. "Now, please!"

They moved in unison, carrying me up the steps and I pulled away from Travis's delicious lips long enough to look at the massive king-size bed in the center of the loft, the headboard against a gigantic wall of windows overlooking the town below with the streetlights casting a warm glow through the mismatched glass. "God, it's beautiful."

It wasn't a bachelor pad. It was a den, his sanctuary. A place built to handle the weight of things that weren't allowed out into the daylight after his shifts.

It was perfect.

"Yes, you are." Eli said, and I turned my attention back to them as Travis set me on my feet at the end of the bed.

"Are you sure?" I asked, parroting Eli's questions earlier as I looked at each of them. "You're best friends. What if this changes something?"

Travis shucked his flannel off with those steady eyes that never wavered in the face of uncertainty and then pulled the hem of his shirt up over his head, revealing his massive abdominals, coated with a layer of manly dark hair.

What was I saying? Damn.

"I hope it *does* change things." Travis said, staring at me. "I hope it means the start of something powerful for all three of us."

"You're sure?" I asked, looking at Travis, who nodded surely, to Eli, who gave me a grin.

"We're sure." Eli said, pulling his shirt off by the back of his collar and tossing it into the pile of clothes on the floor. "Now what do *you* want from us?"

"Mmh," I moaned, looking from his smooth, ripped eight-pack to Travis's manly barrel chest. "Strip."

Eli grinned with his pretty-boy smirk and pulled the button of his jeans open as Travis did the same.

They weren't shy as they each stripped; they didn't even pretend not to look at each other as they pushed their briefs down and stood naked before me for the first time. It was so surreal to see their level of comfort with each other and their hunger for me in one.

And holy mother of God, they were both packing glorious dicks, and I was in massive trouble. The second I saw them both, I longed to take them both at the same time, but I knew that would take time.

Time I didn't know if I would have the patience to wait for.

"Lie down." I said, putting a hand on each of their chests and pushing them back onto the bed. Standing before them in my best pair of black lingerie, and with confidence I didn't know I possessed anymore, I prayed I'd stay upright before I fell to my knees and begged them. "You both have played, now it's my turn."

Both men leaned back on the pillows at the top of the bed and watched me with hungry gazes as I slid my bra and panties off and kneeled on the bed between them. Never in my life had I taken two men to bed, and part of me was intimidated by the idea of trying to please even one of the magnificent men in front of me, let alone both of them.

Instead of letting that fear stop me, I leaned into the arousal and need it had created in my core and followed my urges from that.

Laying one hand on each of their thighs, I slowly trailed my fingers up their muscles to the prizes they held at the top. Trav's cock was so thick, built just like the rest of his body with veins and ridges along it that would tease me with every thrust. He groaned when I stroked him, pulling more pre-cum from the tip. Then I finally got to feel Eli against my skin. He wasn't as thick, but he was long, and I knew he'd go deeper than any man had ever been when I took him.

"I don't think either of you has any idea how happy I am that you're both so big." I grinned, leaning over Eli's hip slowly while holding his stare as I kissed the tip of his cock. His hips thrust and his body tensed when I traced the tip of my tongue around the swollen head. "I still would have fucked you both even if you had small dicks, but I would have blocked you after."

Trav grunted, and I tightened my hand around his cock, using his pre-cum to lubricate my strokes. I watched his eyes darken even more as I started sucking Eli's cock, holding Travis's gaze.

There was something wicked about the way both of them hardened even more, leaking for me as I pleasured them both. It wasn't right, but I couldn't care less about that as my body got hotter for them.

"God, baby." Elliot groaned, threading his fingers into my hair and pushing it back to see me as I started sucking him deeper, taking him as far as I could before gagging and doing it again. "You're incredible."

"You should be rewarded." Travis said as he slid down the bed and got behind me on the floor. His big hands pulled me over Eli's leg until I kneeled between both of his muscular thighs, and Travis pushed my shoulders down and pulled my ass into the air.

"I agree." Eli moaned, "Make her come while she sucks me off."

I didn't have time to say anything in response before Travis spread my cheeks with his big hands and then his face was pressed against my pussy, licking me from clit to ass and back like a man possessed. I moaned around Eli's cock as I spread my thighs wider, giving Travis more access as he tongue-fucked me.

"Jesus, baby." I moaned, stroking Eli's cock with one hand as I reached back and dragged my nails across Travis's scalp, pulling him in more. "God."

He was so fucking good at it; I was star-struck as I tried to keep pleasuring Eli, but quickly lost track of my moves as I careened into an orgasm, coming all over Travis' face and beard.

"I need—" I gasped, hanging my head between my shoulders as Travis kissed his way up my spine. "More."

"You want me?" He whispered, laying his big body

against my back, and his hard cock nudged between my thighs, and I pushed back, trying to get him inside of me in my desperation. "Who do you want to go first?"

"Fuck." I moaned, nearly coming again from his words. "I don't care. Just fuck me."

"I got the first kiss." Eli said with a wicked grin, leaning up and kissing me deeply, stroking my tongue with his as Travis reached around my body and tweaked my nipples. "I also felt your mouth on my cock first." He said, leading my head down, and I eagerly sucked the head of his cock into my mouth again, playing his game. "I think it's only fair that Travis gets to take that pretty little pussy first, don't you?"

"Please." I moaned, wiggling my hips as the head of his cock brushed against my wet lips again. "I'm desperate here, guys."

Travis wrapped his hand around the front of my throat and forced me down onto Eli's cock again, pushing it so deep I could feel the pressure of his hand against the head through my skin. "Be a good girl and ask me nicely."

My first reaction was to snark back at him, throwing some sort of challenge his way to keep power in my hands, but before I could even form that thought completely, the words he wanted fell from my lips.

"Please, big guy." I mewled, "Please let me feel you stretch me open. It's been so long, I need it. I need to get fucked."

Travis groaned, and Eli smirked, tracing the head of his cock across my lips.

"Good girl," Travis murmured in my ear, and then the heat of his body was off my back and the head of his cock brushed against me again. "Are you on birth control?"

"Damn." Eli groaned, staring me in the eyes, "Please say yes."

"Yes." I moaned, pushing back as Travis held the head of his cock against my opening. "I have the implant. I'm good."

The first half of the head of his cock started stretching me open, and I moaned at the delicious burn I got from it. "You want me to take you bare, Shade?" Travis asked, hands gripping my hips tight enough to bruise. "You want our come left inside of you so you can feel us all day tomorrow, reminded of what you begged for tonight?"

"Yes." I moaned.

"Good girl." Travis said, pushing forward until I felt the whole mushroom head of his cock slide in and then he pulled out again. He spat and then his soaked cock pushed back into me again, and I groaned an animalistic cry of delight when he gave me more of him. "Don't forget about Eli, Shade. Let him push his cock deep down your throat while you take mine in this tight pussy."

The way they both held me as Travis gave me every inch, holding me like a secret worth spilling between them—the way they grounded me as I shattered. I'd never recover.

And I didn't think I wanted to.

11 - TRAVIS
The Weight of Want

I HAD one hand splayed across the small of her back, the other gripping her hip like a fucking lifeline. Frankie was on all fours, between us, body slick and shaking, with her mouth wrapped around Eli's dick while I took her from behind.

And nothing—*nothing*—had ever wrecked me like it.

The sounds.

The *fucking* sounds.

Her wet, messy moans as Eli fisted her hair and pulled her down onto him again.

His low groans as he whispered her name like a prayer. The slap of skin on skin every time I thrust back into her tight body. She was wild about it. Starving and unashamed of the pleasure and fulfillment we were giving her.

Mine.

Ours.

"Goddamn, Frankie," I growled, teeth gritted as I dragged her hips back against me. "You were made for this. You feel that?"

She whimpered around Eli's cock.

"You're so fucking tight," I kept going, voice breaking. "So full of us, you don't even know which one's going to ruin you first."

She moaned again, long and guttural, and Eli hissed, hand tightening in her hair.

"She's close, isn't she?" He said, breath ragged. "She wants to come with both of us filling her up."

"Not yet." I groaned, laying my palm across her lush ass and watching it ripple and redden. "Not until she's taken us both."

"Trav," She cried, pushing back and meeting me thrust for thrust. "Please!"

I pulled out, even though it was the very last thing I wanted to do. "On your back, Shade."

She protested, glaring at me over her shoulder as I flipped her around and slapped my fingers over her clit. "Fuck!" She cried, spreading her milky thighs wide as Eli got off the bed. I took his spot, kneeling at her side and brushed her hair off her damp forehead.

"You're being such a good girl for us tonight, Shade." I licked my lips and leaned down to kiss her. Her nails dug into my neck, pulling me in deeper before she suddenly hissed and rocked under me.

I looked down her body to find Eli buried inside her with a feral look in his eyes as he pulled out and gave her every inch of his long dick again.

She moaned and looked between us to watch Eli fuck her,

and my dick twitched watching his work her up into a furry. "Come here." Frankie grabbed my dick and stroked me, still wet from her body, and pulled me to her mouth.

"Damn," I groaned as she spread her lips wide and took me into her mouth while Eli fucked her.

She couldn't move much on her back, so I leaned over her face, rocking my hips to fuck her mouth, and she dug her nails into my ass, pulling me deeper each time.

"Jesus, woman." Eli cursed, lifting her legs up to kiss the inside of her ankle. "You're fucking perfect."

"Mmh," She moaned, stroking my cock with a smirk. "Then let me come."

I grinned, sharing a look with my best friend. "I think she's earned it, don't you?"

"I do." He growled, biting the arch of her foot, "How about a helping hand, Trav?" Eli winked and spread her legs wide around his shoulders as he slammed back into her.

"On it." I slid my fingers over her wet lower lips and then started stroking her clit in time with his rough thrusts as she sucked my cock like a pro. We were a tangle of limbs and skin, working each other over to see who would crash first.

With an echoing scream, Frankie beat us to the finish line. Her back bowed as I slapped my fingers down against her clit while Eli cursed and switched angles, fucking her even harder as she came. I knew my best friend wouldn't be able to hold off for long, no doubt feeling her silky pussy strangling his cock as she came on and on.

"That's it, baby." I mused, looking down at her as she shattered, "Milk his cock, make him come with you. Feel him deep inside of you."

"God," She gasped, opening her green eyes to look up at me as she stroked my hard cock from root to tip as Eli roared and gave her a few more thrusts before burying himself inside of her and leaning forward on her legs. "Fuck, that feels so good, Eli."

He groaned and pulled out so he could crash on the mattress next to her as I gently kept playing with her clit. Dipping my fingers down into the swollen flesh of her pussy, I felt his release and reveled in the combination of her wetness and his.

I wasn't repulsed by the mess he left; it fucking turned me on to feel her claimed by him, while she simultaneously still sucked me.

"Come for me, big guy." She purred and ran the tip of her teeth over the head of my cock. "Fly high with us."

I threaded my fingers in her hair and lifted her head so she could take me deep again and groaned when her throat tightened. "This what you want?" I growled, pulling her on and off me at my will, and she nodded, staring up at me with watery green eyes as she rolled my balls in her fingers. "Then be a good girl and take what you demanded. Take my come and don't spill a drop."

Fire spliced my spine, and my balls tightened as I started filling her mouth and belly with come and she kept her neck moving, bobbing up and down on it, taking every single drop I gave her.

"Suck him good, Black Cat," Eli praised, wrapping himself around her side and playing with her nipples as I growled with the last of my orgasm. "Such a good girl."

"The best." I sighed, pulling my cock free of her lips as she let it go with a pop. Her pink lips were swollen, matching her lower ones, and I ran my thumb over them as she laid back on the bed with a sated smile. "So, fucking perfect."

Frankie reached above her, stretching like a satisfied kitten with her eyes closed, and Eli grinned like a sneaky little playboy. "Stay tonight," He said, pulling the blankets from the end of the bed and covering her up. "I don't want you to leave yet."

She opened her eyes and looked up at me where I stood at the side of the bed, watching her. "Will you stay too?"

"Is that what you want?" I asked, nodding to the bed. "Because if I get in that bed, I'm not getting out without feeling you wrapped around my cock at least once more."

Her grin deepened, and she licked her lips, flicking the blankets open on my side, "Then get in, because I'm already imagining all the ways I can take you both at the same time."

"Fuck," Eli chuckled, laying back against the pillow with an arm over his head, "Marry me."

Frankie giggled as I climbed in beside her, pulling her ass in against my dick and breathing her in as Eli rolled to face us. "Let's get some sleep, and then you can tell us all the ways you want to take us deep."

"Mmh," she moaned, snuggling in and kissing Eli with a satisfied sigh. "You've got yourself a deal."

12 - MYSTERY
Watching

SHE DIDN'T GO HOME.

I watched, parked a block down from her place, waiting for her to show up after her weird afternoon shift at the rink.

I waited.

And waited some more.

I knew the schedule. I'd done the math. I knew how long it took her to get home from the rink across town. Normally she'd work until midnight on Saturday night, but for some reason she switched things around and worked earlier.

Yet she still didn't come home. Not tonight.

Tonight, she left with *them*.

Not one.

Both.

I went back to the rink and waited for her to leave and saw her come out a little after eleven with two men on each side of her. Not as coworkers, or friends. They sandwiched her close and possessive, like they already knew what she wore under her dress.

And from the way she leaned into them, like she was aching to be claimed, I knew exactly what was happening.

They touched her as if she were theirs. She fucking let them, too.

So, I tailed them, two stoplights behind. Headlights off.

They didn't notice me, too wrapped up in whatever sick and perverse little game they were playing in that truck.

When they turned off onto the warehouse strip, my stomach rolled. I knew that area. No one lived there except the firefighter. I'd seen him there before, the pretty boy with the hero complex and the perfectly white teeth.

When I first found Frankie, I did research on everyone she interacted with. And I'd pegged the firefighter as a problem from the start.

I should have taken care of it then.

Instead, I was forced to sit parked across the street in my tinted truck, engine off, watching her climb him like a ladder as he picked her up out of the back seat. Her dress was half undone, her hair wild and worst of all, she laughed as he kissed her.

He pulled the top of her dress open and kissed her chest as he climbed the stairs, two at a time, while the big carpenter climbed out of the other side of the truck. The fucker adjusted his dick in his jeans as he shut the doors and gave chase.

Son of a bitch probably had her on his dick on the ride home.

Whore.

I watched them all go in.

And I waited.

And waited.

Yet she still didn't fucking come out.

Not for hours.

Not even by sunrise.

Just after seven, she came out of the same door they all disappeared into last night. Her hair was tied up on top of her head, and she wore a baggy hoodie over a pair of sweatpants that weren't hers.

She looked smug. Like someone who'd just had the best night of her life. The two half-wit hockey players followed her back down to the truck. One of them kissed her neck while the other one slapped her ass.

And she smiled—at both of them.

She never fucking smiled at anyone.

They all got back into the truck and pulled out like she hadn't just shattered the last thread of dignity I'd let her keep.

That's when I knew.

She was never going to do the right thing.

She was never going to stop being a fucking whore.

So now?

Now I had to fix it for her.

I'd been patient.

I gave her space. Time.

But she wanted to make a spectacle of herself? She wanted to be shared like a toy?

Then she'd learn what it felt like to be broken and thrown away for real.

She was mine first.

And I wasn't going to let her forget it.

13 - ELI
Desperate Phone Call

I LAY in the tiny single bed at the fire station, staring at the dark ceiling. It was the same thing I'd been doing for the last hour, even though I should have been sleeping. Monday nights were notoriously slow for our station, like it was the world's way of giving us all a break after a chaotic weekend.

I was the lieutenant on staff for the shift, which meant I got the single room, avoiding the common bunkhouse, but part of me actually wished for the familiar noise and awful smells of that compared to the solitude.

With nothing around distracting me, I couldn't help but think of Frankie.

Of our perfect night together on Saturday. Of how right it

had felt to share her with Travis. Of how much I fucking missed her since then.

She had her kids, and Travis had work, and now it was my turn to work, and it all just felt—meaningless somehow.

Nothing else mattered but her.

And in turn, Trav. God, I was fucked in my head over the whole thing.

I was flat on my back in the dark, one arm under my head and the other still curled around my phone. I'd just finished reading Frankie's goodnight text for the fifth time when it lit up again.

Incoming Call: Frankie <3

I didn't hesitate. "Hey," I answered, voice low.

There was silence on the other end for a beat, then a breath. And something in me tightened.

"Are you okay?" I asked, sitting up slightly.

"Yeah," She whispered. "I just—missed your voice."

Fuck.

That did something to me I wasn't ready for.

"Yeah?" I murmured, stretching my legs out slowly. "Were you thinking about me?"

She exhaled, quiet and shaky, and my body tingled from the noise. "Mmh."

I smiled into the dark. "What do you need, baby?" My voice was thick, and I hoped she could hear what she did to me. "Tell me what you need."

"You." She whispered. "Trav." Followed by a groan. "I'm just being a whiny girl, ignore me."

I chuckled and relaxed into her honesty. "What are you wearing?"

Another pause, but I could hear the rustle of fabric on the line.

"A tank top." She replied.

"What else?" I asked, licking my lips as I imagined her in bed,

"Nothing else."

I groaned softly, rubbing a hand over my chest. "Frankie." Even I could hear the need in my voice as I called her name. "I have half of my shift left."

"I'm sorry." She chuckled, "I couldn't sleep," She whispered, "I don't normally have that problem thanks to exhaustion, but tonight, I just kept thinking about you."

"What part of me?" I urged, seeing how far she'd take it.

Her shaky breath echoed through the line, "Your mouth." She replied honestly, "The way you looked at me after—"

"After what, Black Cat?" I challenged.

"After you tasted me on that exam table the first time." She moaned, "And then again sometime in the middle of the night in your bed."

I groaned, remembering how she tasted with both of our scents on her body. I'd woken up, hungry for more, and couldn't resist. "You mean after we made you come so hard you forgot your own name?"

A small, breathy laugh escaped her, "Yeah. That."

"Are you touching yourself right now?"

Silence echoed back, then— "Yes."

Christ.

I swallowed hard, my cock hardening against the waistband of my shorts. I knew there would be no stopping it, so I didn't even try as I reached down to adjust it, stroking myself slowly.

"Talk to me," I rasped, "Tell me how."

Her voice was almost silent as she whispered, "Fingers. Just two. I'm already so wet."

"Of course you are," I said, closing my eyes and dragging my hand up my cock. "You're always wet for me, aren't you?"

"Yes." She moaned.

"Lay back, Frankie. Open your legs real wide for me." A sharp inhale echoed from her lips, and I could hear the rustling of fabric again as she shifted, doing what I told her to. "Now circle those pretty fingers just how you like. Slow. Draw it out."

"Are you—" She shuddered, "Are you alone?"

"Completely," I replied, and moaned as I pulled my cock free. "Except for you and your phone-sex voice."

She chuckled, "Touch yourself with me."

"Already am, baby." I assured her. "I'm rock hard and ready, I just wish you were here."

"What would you do to me if I was?" She asked, and I loved the sexual goddess she was for me.

"I'd get you on my lap, taking my cock nice and deep, and then I'd lay back and watch you ride me." I licked my lips and stroked the head of my cock in a tight fist. "I'd watch your perfect tits sway with each thrust and then I'd hold your hips and fuck you, making you take every inch of me." I groaned, arousing myself more than I needed to as I imagined it. "That's my biggest regret from the other night, I never got you on top of me."

"Next time." She panted, "Promise?"

"Oh, I promise," I replied, "But only if you promise to let Travis take your mouth at the same time."

"Fuck," She moaned, breathy and desperate. "Elliot."

"I miss the way you moaned my name when I was between those pretty thighs, Frankie. I need to hear it again."

"Oh God," She cried.

"I'm not there, baby, so you've got to make this last, don't rush it. Wait for me."

"I—I can't," She whimpered.

"You can. You want to come for me, right? Just like you did in my bed."

"Please," She moaned, spurring my own orgasm closer. I fucking loved when she begged.

"That's it, pretty girl." I stroked faster. "Beg me."

"Please, baby," She gasped, and I could hear the slick sound of her fingers when she whimpered my name like it physically hurt to hold back.

"Don't stop, then. You need this, right? You deserve to feel worshiped, even if it's just my voice in your ear. Even though I'd kill to be in your bed right now."

She gasped, broken and breathless now, unable to respond with words. But I didn't need them, I knew where she was.

"That's it," I said, voice dark with heat and need to match hers. "You're doing so good. You're so fucking perfect for me. I want you to come with me, Frankie. Right now, I'm going to come too."

She came with a sob, stifled, but I still heard her cries, wrecked and shaky through the speaker. And it was the most beautiful fucking sound I'd ever heard.

I shot off, covering my abs with come as I moaned her name, blinded with pure ecstasy as she kept calling mine.

And then there was only our breathing, blanketed with silence. Her breathing slowed, so did mine. I stayed exactly where I was, heart racing hard and aching.

"Eli?" She whispered after a while.

"Yeah, baby?"

"I wish you were here."

God, me too.

"Soon," I promised, staring at the ceiling like it held the answer. "As soon as I can. I want to wake up next to you."

"Me too." She whispered.

"Call Trav." I said, feeling the need to push her into his arms, since mine weren't available. "Let him take care of you."

"No," She whispered, "Not without you. Not yet."

"Why?"

"Because it's new." She answered, and I could hear the uncertainty in her voice. "And I don't want to make either of you jealous or worry or anything like that."

I chuckled, "What do you think he's going to feel when I rub it in that I made you come on the phone when he was alone in his bed right down the road, baby girl?"

She sighed, and I could hear the smile, "Don't worry about that, I already have plans to keep things even."

"Oh, do you?" I laughed, "Tell me more of your plans."

"Well, you see I was thinking of stopping by to see him in the morning after I dropped the kids off at school," She started with that silly tone to her voice she only let free every once in a while, "He's working on a job in the middle of nowhere— very secluded atmosphere."

"With about twenty men working around him." I pointed it out, and she chuckled.

"I don't know what you think I plan to do with my visit there, Sir. I just wanted to stop by and tease him as I told him about this call."

"Or you could let him make you feel good. Play a game with him, and try not to get caught."

"Are you sure?" She asked hesitantly.

"Do me a favor, Frankie." I said as my eyelids finally started to get heavy.

"Name it."

"Blow his fucking mind," I smiled to myself, letting my eyes close. "And maybe send me a picture or two while you're at it."

She chuckled sleepily and sighed gently. "You got it, Sunshine."

14 - FRANKIE
Good Morning Saw

I WOKE UP SMILING. Not because I had gotten a full night's sleep, I didn't. And not because the kids magically learned how to dress themselves or pack their own lunches, they didn't.

I woke up smiling because I woke up feeling *wanted*.

And not in the manipulated way I was used to. There were no strings attached to the desire, there were no rules dictating the availability of it.

It was just there.

I was still wrecked from last night's midnight phone call with Eli, still flushed from the sound of his voice and still very much aching in the best way from everything that happened Saturday night with him and Travis.

Every single inch of me hummed with satisfaction and the addictive little thrill that came from knowing two incredible men wanted me like that.

Not just for a night.

Not just for the fun of it.

But fully, wildly, and maybe even a bit dangerously.

It made me want to lean into it and embrace it. So, I fucking did.

I curled my hair with the fancy little tool that I used more in the last week than in the last three years and even put some mascara on again. The bra that made my boobs sit a little higher than necessary worked perfectly under my black cropped sweatshirt that just *happened* to fall off one shoulder when I moved the right way.

Paired with my blood-red skinny jeans with rips in them and my Doc Martens, it was a whole vibe.

And I was buzzing with excitement from just feeling confident.

When I walked into the kitchen, both kids paused and stared at me like I'd grown a second head, though.

"Whoa," Toby said, holding a toaster waffle in one hand and a dinosaur in the other, "Are you going on a date?"

"No," I replied, pouring cereal like I hadn't already planned out how to climb a carpenter at a job site.

Emmie narrowed her eyes, "Then why do you smell good?"

"It's perfume, Em." I deadpanned, "I always wear perfume."

"No," She argued back like a stubborn mini-me. "You usually smell like chicken fingers and beer."

"Okay, wow. We're done with this conversation," I said, grabbing her hairbrush before she could hide it. "Sit. Brush. Eat."

As soon as I was done with her hair, stupidly I turned my back and tried to pack their lunches, fooled into thinking they'd stay on track doing what I asked of them.

That was when I heard it.

The sound of a hockey stick dragging across the tile floor. I turned just in time to see Emmie wielding her mini goalie stick like a sword, spinning through the kitchen in her socks while holding Toby's metal lunch box like a puck.

"Emmie Blake—"

"It's stick-handling practice! I need to improve my agility in confined spaces! Saw said so!" She dropped the lunch box and started passing it back and forth.

"You're going to improve your face planting when you crash into the dishwasher!" I snapped with my hands on my hips.

Too late.

Her socks slipped, her balance wobbled, and down she went. The lunch box flew across the kitchen like a twirling top, sending Toby's day-old goldfish spraying across the floor like confetti at a parade.

"I regret nothing," she yelled as she hit the ground, completely unbothered.

Meanwhile, Toby sat calmly at the table, spooning cereal into his mouth like it was all just another Tuesday morning in the Blake household. Glancing over at me, he shrugged and said, "I think she's going to make it to the pros."

WE FINALLY MADE it to the car with only one meltdown, mine; one time-out, Emmie's; and a full outfit change, Toby's, after Emmie flung maple syrup at him with a spoon for being a *dweeb*.

Heaven help me, I wasn't going to survive the teenage years.

By the time I pulled into their elementary school drop-off line, I felt like I'd run a triathlon in high heels, and the sunshiny confidence I'd felt when I woke up was fading.

Fast.

I reached back to check that Toby had his backpack as Emmie jumped from the car with barely a *see ya later*, but he surprised me and grabbed my hand, holding it tight.

"Hey, Mama?"

"Yeah, baby?" I turned to look at him in his booster seat, all gap-toothed grin and syrup-sticky cheeks.

"You're really pretty today." My heart cracked wide open, and my shoulders relaxed as his warm eyes held mine. "And you look happy too."

I blinked hard, "I do?"

He nodded, "I think it's because you're letting people help you. Like for real. Not just pretend stuff. You should keep doing that."

I blinked again, harder.

"Where did you learn to say things like that?" I whispered.

He shrugged. "You." He opened the door and started to climb out, then paused. "I'm glad you're smiling again."

Then he was gone; backpack bouncing, shoes untied, hoodie crooked, and I sat there for a full minute, staring through the windshield with tears prickling the corners of my eyes and something *huge* blooming in my chest.

I was wanted.

Seen.

And my kids were seeing the difference in me without even knowing the cause. Which only gave me the confidence I needed to make sure I kept my guard down and my heart open. Because I'd do anything for my kids.

I had already survived the worst to make them happy; I could do this.

Halfway to the bakery in town, my phone buzzed with a text, and I glanced at it when I stopped in the parking lot.

TRAVIS

Still thinking about the way you moaned my name. Good luck getting through your day, Shade. Think of me at some point too.

I smirked so hard I almost looked like a clown as I walked into the shop, instead of a moody, aloof black cat.

Weird.

Twenty minutes later, I pulled down the long driveway to the mansion on the lake, tucked back into the woods that he was building. He didn't know I was coming, that was the fun of it.

As soon as I saw the monstrosity, I was mesmerized by Travis's talent in crafting such a beautiful masterpiece by hand. The oversized beams and floor to ceiling windows were breathtaking.

Forcing myself to be braver than I felt, I parked behind a flatbed truck, balancing two boxes of coffee and a tray of bakery goodies, praying my boots wouldn't get stuck in the mud.

The second I stepped out around the truck, I found my target out of the dozens of other bulky men on site. Travis was up on scaffolding, flannel sleeves pushed up, tool belt slung low on his hips, and sawdust clinging to his hands like glitter.

Man glitter.

He didn't see me at first, too focused on leveling the beam on his shoulder, so I silently watched the show. His forearms flexed as he hefted it into place, his strength an insane wonder to watch.

God, he looked good enough to ruin.

The job site had gotten quiet around us, and he clued in, looking down from his perch and finding me instantly. And when he did—the look on his face was *primal*.

He hadn't expected to see me, but now that he did, there wasn't a chance in hell I was leaving untouched.

"Morning, Saw," I called up, lifting the tray and coffee. "Thought you could use a pick-me-up."

He stared at me for a second, down to the coffee, then right back up at me, but slower this time. "You're the pick-me-up."

My thighs clenched involuntarily as I glanced around at the men watching on in open fascination.

He climbed down, all slow and deliberate moves of power and strength, stalking toward me. Sweat glistened at the temples, barely touching his dark hair under his ball cap, which only added to the rugged manliness of his appearance.

The look in his eyes was obvious as he approached me.

Trouble.

Delicious, sawdust-covered, six-and-a-half-foot tall trouble.

"Are you coming over to say thank you?" I asked, biting my lip.

He didn't answer.

Travis took the burden from my hands, set it on the open tailgate next to me and backed me up against it in one smooth motion.

"You came all this way just to tease me?" He asked, voice low and menacing.

"I came because I couldn't stop thinking about you. Your text just solidified my plans."

Travis leaned in, nose brushing mine, lips so close I could feel the heat of them. "I have ten minutes."

My breath caught. "I doubt I'll even need that long."

15 - TRAVIS

Sawdust and Sin

AT FIRST, I thought I was hallucinating, too much caffeine, not enough sleep, and a steady buzz in my blood since Saturday night. But then she spoke, and the mirage of Frankie disappeared, and the real damn thing took its place.

Now, she was backed up against my truck, lips parted, and cheeks flushed as my men all looked on. She was all curves and confidence, baiting me into letting her do exactly what kind of damage she came here to do.

I knew what she had come for.

Her red jeans looked painted on, and her black hoodie showed me glimpses of her tummy below the cropped hem. When I pinned her to the truck, it slid off her shoulder, giving me a glimpse of the lush swell of her breasts beneath and the matching red strap of her bra.

Damnit.

I was rock hard.

Her hair was perfectly loose and wild, like she'd just gotten out of someone's bed. While I would have preferred it to be mine, I wouldn't have been mad if it had been Eli's.

Frankie smiled as I got close, that slow teasing little thing she did with her lips when she knew the power she had over me. I pushed my thigh between hers and pinned her harder to my truck bed, and her smirk fell into something more needy. That smirk that said *I know what I did to you, and I know you want me to do it again.*

"You just passing by to deliver caffeine to random blue-collar men now? Hoping for a ten-minute fuck on the way out?" I asked, teasing her and tempting her.

"Only from the sweaty, grumpy, six-foot something ones with shoulders for days and an attitude problem."

"You're playing a dangerous game." I argued.

She rocked her hips forward, rubbing against my thigh. "You chastise me for telling you what I want, whereas Eli simply gave me what I needed when I called him for a little phone sex last night," She sucked on her bottom lip condescendingly, "Interesting."

I didn't give in right away. Instead, I looked at her, really fucking looked at her, and my chest caved in from her beauty.

Her cheeks were flushed. Her eyes were bright. She looked happy.

That did something to me. Twisted my insides into knots and made me feel like I'd waited my whole damn life for her to look at me like that.

So, I gave in because she was right. She was here to get something from me, and I'd be a stupid fool to deny it when it was the only thing I'd wanted since I watched her drive away Sunday morning.

I kissed her hard, greedily, using my tongue to sweep past her lips without any hesitation or permission. She moaned against my lips, and I swore I saw stars. My hands slid down to cup her ass, pulling her tight against the thick line of my cock behind my jeans.

"Miss me?" I rasped against her mouth.

"I woke up aching for you."

"Say that again," I growled.

She licked her lips as her eyes darkened, and everyone around us disappeared. "I missed you, Travis. I missed the way you touch me. Missed the way you need me."

I groaned, dragging my mouth down her throat, sucking a mark just above her collarbone before she could stop me. It'd be impossible to hide.

"What if someone sees?" She whispered, breathless, but she wasn't talking about the mark.

"Then they'll know who you belong to."

She whimpered, and fuck, I was going to make a mess in my jeans if I didn't get her somewhere.

I grabbed her wrist, "Come with me."

I didn't wait for a response, lacing my fingers with hers and dragging her around the side of the house, through a partially framed garage, into the only finished room on the property.

It was a storage room in the back of the garage that we stored tools in at night, and it was going to have to work because I was too desperate for her to get any further away from prying eyes.

The only things inside were a saw, a stack of plywood and me—losing every shred of self-control I had.

Slamming the door shut behind us, I pushed her up

against it. The lock was on the outside, which meant I had to stop someone from walking in like this.

"Travis—"

"Did you come here to tease me?" I demanded, pinning her back against the rough surface, "Looking like sin, talking like you wanted me to snap?"

She bit her lip but didn't deny it.

That was all it took.

I undid her jeans, and she shimmied them off one leg before she climbed me, wrapping her legs tight around my waist as I dropped my tool belt to the ground with a thud.

"I've been hard for you for *days*, Frankie."

"Show me." She panted, "Use me."

Her breath hitched as I thrust my fingers into the heat between her thighs, groaning at how wet she already was.

"You want fast?" I rasped, "Or do you want to be ruined?"

She gasped, grinding against my fingers, "Both, baby."

Fuck me.

I undid my jeans, gritting my teeth and lining myself up, pushing into her slowly just to hear that sharp inhale.

The one that made me feel like a fucking God.

"Travis—oh my God."

"Shh," I whispered, kissing her neck, her jaw, her lips as I started to thrust. "You're going to get us caught."

Her nails dug into my shoulders, "I don't care."

I didn't either. Not when she was that tight. Not when her breath stuttered against my ear and her thighs clenched like, she never wanted to let me go.

"You came for Eli on the phone last night?" I questioned her as I slammed into her, rattling the door on the hinges.

"Yes." She moaned, digging her nails into my neck as she stared right at me, making the sexiest eye contact of my life. "And he came for me too."

"Damn," I growled. "That's hot."

"You don't hate it?" She leaned in and licked my neck before biting it, leaving an impression of her teeth. "You aren't jealous that I called him and not you?"

"No," I slammed into her hard enough to make the door creak like it was going to give way. "Because it's not a competition, Shade. He's not my rival. He's my best friend."

"God," She moaned. "You guys are crazy. And I love it. He told me to blow your mind the next time I saw you, and you're fucking my brains out even as I talk about how he made me come last night. Wild."

We moved together as if we'd done it a thousand times.

Rough and perfect.

Frantic and filthy.

She told me how she played with her wet pussy for Eli on the phone and got soaked hearing him jack off in return, and my balls tightened, imagining how good she looked laid out and open, being dirty for my best friend.

The slap of skin echoed in the room, punctuated by her moans and my growls.

The creak of wood tempted us.

Her whimper when I whispered how good she felt on my cock pushed me on.

It didn't take long.

Her body went tight around me, every muscle shaking as she came, biting my shoulder to keep from crying out. I followed right after, cursing, spilling into her with a growl that rumbled deep in my chest.

We stayed locked like that for a while, breathing hard, sweaty, spent.

Then I slowly set her down, tugging her jeans back into place and brushing her hair from her face as she smiled up at me like I'd just rearranged her entire nervous system.

"Next time," she whispered, brushing her lips against mine, "I want you somewhere with a door that locks so I can make you beg me for mercy before, during and after."

"Next time," I said, pulling her in for a gentle kiss, "I won't stop until your knees give out."

She left a few minutes later—satisfied, flushed and walking with a slight limp.

And I went back to work with a hard-on for her laugh, a memory of her moans, and zero fucking regrets.

16 - MYSTERY
Lost Keys

SHE THOUGHT I wouldn't notice.

That she could fuck around with any man, let alone two of them, and I wouldn't care.

But I noticed.

I always noticed.

It took nothing to get into her backyard. The gate latch was already busted. I didn't even need gloves or a tool. I just slid it open, stepped through it, and took a slow walk around her pathetic little life.

The flowerpots were dead. The back porch light flickered. The kids left toys everywhere—like she couldn't be bothered to keep shit clean.

I stood in the shadows for a long time, watching the sun go down behind her house and the light in her bedroom click on at nine.

She was alone. But she wouldn't be for long. I could tell.

She was getting reckless.

Wearing her hair down, smiling like she had nothing to be afraid of, walking through town as people started talking about seeing her with one of them, and then the other. It was like she wanted people to see what kind of whore she'd become.

That was the part that pissed me off the most.

She looked happy.

Like she didn't even feel guilty for what she'd done. For how she'd abandoned her place, forgetting where she came from. Forgetting who had already claimed her.

She was mine.

She'd always been mine.

And if she needed a reminder—well.

I'd leave one.

I didn't go inside. Not yet.

That part would come later.

But I took something. Just one thing.

Her spare set of keys, hanging stupidly from the hook in the unlocked shed.

She'd notice that they were gone.

Not right away. But soon.

And when she did?

She'd know.

She'd *feel* it.

That someone was close.

Watching.

Waiting.

Breathing down her neck without ever making a sound. The first step always had to be the softest. The one that didn't leave a mark. The whisper before the scream.

And I was so fucking close.

17 - FRANKIE
On Edge

I LIVED AT A CIRCUS. A full-on, multi-tent, traveling side acts circus. I just couldn't tell if I was the ringleader or the poor sap that followed the elephants around scooping up the poop.

Toby had gotten yogurt all over the inside of his backpack at school, which was a freaking wild mind trip considering I didn't even pack him yogurt today. Emmie had given herself bangs with safety scissors in art class. And I showed up to the pick-up line late thanks to my one afternoon class at the community college two towns over running late.

Typical Wednesday.

By the time we got home, I just wanted five minutes of

silence, a hot shower, and maybe a ten-minute nap before my shift.

Instead, I got—"Oops. Mom! I locked the keys in the car."

I turned around mid-step, holding Emmie's backpack and a grocery bag, to stare at Toby like he'd just confessed to burning the house down.

"You *what?*"

"I was trying to help grab the milk," He pointed at the back seat where I could see the last of the groceries and the ring of keys, I asked him to carry to go unlock the door. "You were frustrated, and I was being pro-*tactive.*"

I didn't correct the misuse of the big-kid word and moved past it, "And now we're locked out. Which isn't *proactive.*"

He paused, "Okay, yeah. When you say it like that—"

I exhaled slowly, and Emmie watched me silently, like she was waiting to see if my head would pop off my shoulders and roll across the grass so she could hit it with her hockey stick.

"It's fine," I said, sitting down the heavy burden in my arms, keeping the mental burden on my shoulders and not theirs, as I counted to ten to stop myself from screaming off into the void. "I'll go get the spare."

Jogging around the house to the back gate, I reached for the latch when I noticed something strange.

The gate was already open.

Not just unlatched—but swinging gently with the breeze.

Weird.

I was positive I had closed it the other day after getting rock salt from the shed. It always stuck unless you yanked it hard to open it, so it hadn't blown open. Shaking it off, I stepped into the shed, scanning the hooks inside the door.

But there were no keys hanging on the dusty wall.

I frowned and checked again. Moved the old rake, and

then the random junk lying on the floor. I even checked the bucket of random screws and bolts.

Still, no key.

A slow trickle of unease worked its way down my spine.

A familiar sense of foreshadowing that used to control my life.

The keys were always there. I kept them in the same spot, hung on a hook beside the box of sidewalk chalk and broken Halloween decorations. Simply because we used them so often thanks to both kids' insane ability to lock us out all the time.

No one else even knew about them, except for my mom, and she hadn't stepped foot in the shed since a snake "rattled" at her once a few summers ago.

I stood there in the still silence for a second too long, chewing my bottom lip and listening to the wind.

The yard felt *off*.

Like it had been looked at.

Like someone had been there.

But that was ridiculous. Right?

Maybe one of the kids moved them. Maybe I grabbed them and forgot to hang them back up last time. Maybe I was just exhausted from too many shifts, too many stolen kisses in the dark, too many feelings I didn't know how to process yet.

Still, I double-checked the gate on the way back to the front yard, closing it firmly behind me. Pulling my phone from my back pocket, I called my mom.

"Hey," I said when she picked up. "Any chance I can drop the gremlins off a little early?"

"Of course," she replied, "Hot date?"

I scoffed. "Yeah sure. Life's just hectic. You know."

I didn't mention the keys. Or the gate. Or the way my

stomach hadn't quite unclenched since I walked out of the shed.

Because what was I even going to say?

That I got spooked by a missing key?

That I felt like someone was watching me?

No, I couldn't say that. I couldn't tell her that. Because then she'd zero in on the fear behind those statements.

The fear that I thought I buried years ago.

No, I'd just pretend that the chill tingling up my spine was nothing.

I wasn't that kind of woman, anyway. I was a bartender, a single mom, a black-cat energy baddie who didn't scare easily anymore.

Still, I glanced over my shoulder once before I left, and I *swore* the hairs on the back of my neck stood up.

I COULDN'T FOCUS.

Not on the drinks I was pouring, not on the small talk from my regulars, not even when Coach Rick made some crude joke about playing *just the tip* with the puck.

I laughed and shook my head, because that was what I did.

But it didn't reach my eyes.

Ever since I found my backyard gate swinging open and the spare keys gone, something felt off. Like I'd left the door unlocked to a nightmare, and it was breathing through the cracks in my walls.

I didn't tell anyone, not even my mom.

The fear and anger my past had caused her last time

nearly gave her a heart attack. I couldn't do it again. If I lost her—because of him—I'd never survive it.

I didn't tell anyone else either, because I didn't want to be the girl who jumped at shadows. I didn't want Eli to worry. And I didn't want Travis to go full caveman, patrolling my backyard with a sledgehammer like some kind of hot suburban vigilante.

The second they walked in for practice, I knew I wasn't hiding it well. We were in uncharted territory too, and that didn't help ease the feeling of being off-kilter either.

It was their first practice since we crossed every invisible boundary and got together. I had already heard whispers about my visit to the job site while I was walking around the grocery store earlier.

Some guy on the site told his wife, and she told a friend, and so on and so forth. It was big news when a new couple got together in Cedar Bluff, but the rumors were saying that it wasn't just Travis and me together, and that people saw us leaving the rink with Eli the other night too.

I needed to get my head on straight to deal with that mess, on top of the one currently controlling my anxiety meter.

Eli came behind the bar when he got there, grabbing a bottle of water from the team cooler, sliding up behind me and kissing my temple without missing a beat. I could feel the team's eyes on me as he put our relationship out there in the open. When I turned to him, his eyes locked on mine and narrowed.

"You okay?" He asked.

"Fine." I lied.

He didn't push it, but I could feel his penetrating gaze as he stood at the end of the bar, opening his pre-game beer with the others while I stocked the cooler.

Travis—God, he was even worse.

He leaned on the counter, looked me over like I was glass he couldn't quite see through and asked plainly in front of everyone, "What happened?"

I swallowed, feeling my skin heat and blush at the attention. "Nothing."

He tilted his head, "Frankie." It felt like a dare to defy him.

"I said I'm fine." I snapped, with more vigor than I intended and cringed when I turned my back to ring out a customer.

"You don't lie worth a shit," he muttered darkly, and I caught his gaze in the mirror behind the cash register and shivered involuntarily.

I didn't reply because he was right. I was failing miserably at convincing them and myself that I was fine. The tension followed me around like smoke as they left the bar and got on the ice for their practice.

They were on the rink along the edge of the bar, and I could feel the heavy smoke every time one of them looked over. I could hear it in the short snaps of their conversation during practice. Like they were both holding back and itching to call me on my bullshit.

But I held it together.

Because that was what I did.

It's what I had always done.

That didn't mean it didn't hurt a little when I realized they both left without saying goodbye after practice. I didn't blame them; I had pushed them away after all.

And even though every part of me wanted to run after them, to say, *Please stay, please help me, please see me*, I just smiled instead.

When Coach Rick left, I turned the lock on the front door

and turned the lights off as I went through the empty building on my way to the ice.

It was late.

The rink was empty.

Everyone was gone.

Or so I thought.

I stepped out onto the fresh sheet of ice, smooth from the Zamboni, and exhaled. It was supposed to be my quiet place to escape with my secrets and shortcomings.

But before I could take more than two strides, a voice echoed through the rafters.

"Frankie."

A scream ripped through my lips as I stumbled, wobbling on my skates spinning towards the boards.

Eli and Travis stood there at the bench—waiting.

Eli had his hoodie pushed up to his elbows, hands in his pockets with a serious and unreadable expression on his normally easygoing face.

Travis looked like a goddamn nightmare—hat low, arms crossed, jaw tight, eyes burning a hole straight through me in the dim light.

"I thought you left," I said as my breath caught in my throat.

"No," Travis said, stepping onto the ice in his work boots without hesitation. "*You shut down.* So, we gave you space."

"But we're done with that now," Eli added, walking beside his best friend toward me.

My throat tightened. "I told you I was fine."

"You're not," Travis said, calm but hard. "You're anxious. Distracted. Looking over your shoulder like a monster is breathing down your neck."

Eli stopped in front of me and took my hand in his, blanketing it with his softness and warmth. "Tell us what's going on, Black Cat."

I shook my head, swallowing the lump in my throat, "I don't want to make a big deal over nothing. I'm just tired and paranoid. It's nothing."

"Those are two things you're allowed to be," Eli said, voice soft, but I didn't miss the steel edge to it. "But don't shut us out."

"I'm not—"

"You are." Travis moved behind me, his voice in my ear, low and dark. "And I'm trying really hard not to pin you to the boards and force the truth out of you with my hand on your ass."

My knees buckled a little at the growl in his voice, and for the first time in hours, something besides fear filled my senses.

"Tell us," Eli said again, squeezing my fingers, "Right now. Or we'll make you talk."

I tried to play into the chemistry between us, "Are you going to double-team me again if I don't?" The joke fell flat, even to me.

Travis leaned down, breath hot at my neck, "No, Shade. The opposite. We're going to withhold any physical touch or pleasure until you give in and let us inside that head of yours."

I shivered.

Not from fear. But because I'd never wanted someone to see through me this badly before.

I stood there, caught between both of them, and my body screamed yes, my heart whispered not yet, and that flicker of unease still coiled tight in my gut.

They didn't know about my past.

But they were going to. They weren't going to let me run anymore.

"I just," I shook my head, "It's been a long week. With work, and the kids. I haven't had time to breathe."

It wasn't a lie, but it wasn't the truth either.

Eli searched my face as if he could see straight through the cracks. "You sure that's all?"

I forced a smile. "Unless you're volunteering to babysit and clean my house, yeah."

Travis grunted, unimpressed. "You're full of shit."

"Maybe," I said, grabbing Eli's sweater and pulling him closer. "But I'm hot, tired, and standing between two men I can't stop thinking about. So maybe we can deal with my hormonal emotions after one of you makes me forget my name for a while?"

They exchanged a look, one of those quiet ones.

And just like that, the air shifted again—back to that safe zone, filled with lust and lacking fear. But even as Travis bent to whisper dark promises in my ear and Eli kissed the smirk off my lips, I felt the lie sit in my chest like a stone.

And I knew I'd have to tell them, eventually. Just not today.

18 - ELI
Handymen

SHE LIED.

Not outright, not with words. But I saw it in her eyes. The way she shifted, dodged, spun herself in circles trying to say everything except what she was actually feeling.

Something was wrong.

She was too quiet, too tense, and when Travis asked her straight up what happened, she gave him a tired smile and a half-assed excuse about work and kids.

"I just need a win today," She sighed, grabbing me and pulling me closer.

Travis didn't let up right away, but when she looked over her shoulder and kissed him, slow and deep, fingers tangling in his shirt, he caved. We both did.

Because we were starving for her.

Maybe it was easier to fuck through the questions than force answers out of her that she wasn't ready to give us. Maybe we hadn't earned them from her yet.

But later, as she drove away into the night toward her house and there was nothing but that quiet still darkness surrounding us, Travis turned to me and said exactly what I'd been thinking all night.

"She's hiding something."

I nodded, tossing my duffel into the back seat of my truck. "You felt it too."

"Yeah, and it wasn't just stress and kid chaos."

"She was different tonight. Guarded."

"Afraid." He looked over at me, his expression sharp. "You think it has anything to do with why she left town back then?"

That hit me like a punch to the chest.

Because the truth was, none of us ever really knew why Frankie Blake left town in the first place. One day she was the fierce, sarcastic girl with wild eyes and more bite than bark. Then, she was *gone*.

No goodbyes.

No explanations.

Just gone.

"I think it might have more to do with why she came back." I said with a sigh, staring off where her taillights had disappeared. "She acts like she's been surviving a war no one else can see. Like she's been carrying shit alone for years, and now someone's offering to carry it for her, and she doesn't know how to let us."

Travis exhaled hard. "You think someone hurt her?"

I didn't answer right away.

Because, yeah, I did. I'd seen it in the way she flinched around loud noises when she thought no one was looking. In the way her eyes tracked every exit. In how she laughed only in tough situations, using it to change subjects too fast.

She was soft with us, but not safe.

"If someone did—" I said slowly, feeling something coil around my stomach, "then we find out who. And we make sure they don't ever come close again."

Travis nodded once, jaw ticking. "I want her to trust us. Enough to tell us at least."

"She will."

"When?"

I looked down at my boot and shrugged, "When she stops waiting for the other shoe to drop."

He grunted, "Then maybe it's time we showed her we're not going anywhere. And that this is more than just a nighttime thing."

WE DIDN'T TELL her we were coming.

Travis called me first thing in the morning and said, "You busy?"

"Why?"

I wasn't, but I never volunteered for his shenanigans without giving him a hard time first.

"Frankie's house needs shit."

That was it. That was the whole plan.

He picked me up with his truck bed full of tools and an energy drink already in hand for me. I didn't ask how he knew what size lightbulbs to buy, or why he had new hinges without ever stepping foot in her house to know what was wrong with it.

Truth was, houses were his love language, and working on them with his bare hands was his passion.

And she deserved a house that didn't reflect how hard life had turned out for her.

Mrs. Blake gave us a spare key the second I flashed her a smile and told her what we were up to. At first, she glared at me like she'd heard rumors about what we were doing with her precious daughter in the dark of night. But then she relaxed her shoulders and gave me one of her warm, affectionate gazes.

She supported the idea of us in her daughter's life, even if she didn't understand the dynamic exactly.

We let ourselves into Frankie's quaint little rental house next door to her mom's through the back, and we both took it all in, seeing her place on the inside for the first time.

The kids were at school; the place was silent. Frankie was starting a shift at the rink cafe.

And the house? Yeah, it needed us.

The back doorknob spun in my hand like a roulette wheel.

Half the lights in the kitchen had burned out, some could be easily fixed by replacing the bulbs, while behind the box, some had fried electrical wires.

The bathroom towel rack fell off the second Travis leaned on it. He caught it midair and glared at me with an *I told you so* look.

"Add it to the list," I offered, taking a mental inventory of what needed to get done and in what order.

"Nah," He said, tossing me screws as he pulled his drill out like a weapon, "We'll do it. All of it."

And we did.

We moved through her house as if we belonged there,

tightening screws, swapping bulbs, testing windows, patching the loose step at the bottom of the stairs before it could send one of the kids flying.

Even through all the repairs and the obvious things that were broken, the thing I saw the most inside her four walls was love. There was so much damn warmth and love, literally beaming off every wall and surface in the photos, kids' art, and homemade trinkets.

Frankie loved her kids and gave them the very best she could, which was more than enough in reality. But Frankie herself deserved more.

And that was where we were going to take over.

We didn't talk while we worked, but it wasn't quiet either. There was a rhythm to it, something easy between two best friends with decades of history. It felt like we weren't just fixing her house, but we were staking our claim.

Hours later, the front door opened, and Frankie walked in with a scowl on her face. We sat at her dining room table, both sweaty and satisfied, holding court like kings. She froze in the front foyer, staring at us.

Travis cut her off as she opened her mouth, no doubt to yell at us, and beat her to it. "Nice of you to join us."

"What are you doing here?" She asked, dropping her bag and crossing her arms over her chest. Damn that delicious chest. She looked good in a white Budweiser shirt over a black thermal, dark jeans and a tan beanie on her head with her dark locks framing her face beneath.

"Being manly," I said, standing up and wiping my hands on the rag over my shoulder, "Your place was crying for help."

"You—" she turned on her heel, looking around her space with fresh eyes. "You fixed my door?"

"And the porch step, and the towel rack, and the drawer." I said.

"Drawers." Travis said with a pointed stare, "Almost every single one of them. In every room."

Her mouth dropped open slightly. "You two broke into my house to—do maintenance?" She stumbled over the thought, "Wait, did you use my spare key?"

"No," I watched her closely as her face gave something away I couldn't quite place. "Your mom lent us hers." I closed the distance and stared down at her with a smirk. "You know I'm a big softy for Mrs. Blake."

She looked around again, over at Travis, with a slow, quiet appraisal. Like she didn't know what to say.

Then she swallowed hard and met my gaze. "No one has ever done that for me."

I brushed a lock of hair behind her ear, "Get used to it. Because your mom is onto us, and I'm afraid if we walked away now, I'd break her heart. And I can't stomach the thought."

She poked her knuckles into my stomach and let me pull her in close. But I didn't miss the sudden gloss in her eyes, as she tried to blink it away before burying her face in my shirt.

Travis joined us, coming up behind her and kissing the top of her head, before adding, "Next time we'll start upstairs."

She laughed just a little, and I kissed her lips, feeling her melt into me. Because I couldn't not. Not when her heart was soft like clay and I wanted nothing more than to leave my fingerprints on every piece of it.

Frankie melted between us like butter on warm skin. One moment she was standing there, still stunned from the repairs, heart cracked wide open and eyes blinking like she didn't think we could see her tears.

And then the next, she was under me on her couch.

She giggled when I pinned her down, and Travis locked the front door. "How long until the kids get home?"

"Uh," she licked her lips as I pushed her shirt up over her head, revealing a black lace bralette thing that made my mouth water. "Um."

"Frankie." Travis said dominantly from behind the couch, undoing the buttons on his flannel. "What time do they get home, baby?"

"Fuck," She cursed and moaned when I bit her nipple through the lace. "What day of the week is it? Thursday?" She panted, "Five. They go to after-school art camp on Thursdays until five. A friend drives them home."

"Mmh," I groaned, glancing at the clock over the television. "You mean we get you all alone for hours? Damn, the things I can do to this sexy little body in that time."

"God," She arched her back, feeding her lush tits into my hungry mouth and reached for Travis's belt over the back of the couch. "This was not how I was planning to spend my afternoon."

I chuckled, kissing my way down her stomach, spending time at each mark left in her skin from growing her babies until I got to the button of her jeans, and flicking it open. "Is this an okay alternative?" I asked, laying a wet kiss at the top of her panties.

She nodded, breathless, "Yes."

But that wasn't enough. I looked up at her, green eyes burning, flushed cheeks, wild hair falling over her shoulders. "I need to hear it, sweetheart."

Her eyes locked on mine, fierce and tender. "I can't imagine a better way to spend an afternoon," She traced her fingers over my cheek before turning her attention up to Travis as he pulled his shirt off. "I regretted leaving you two behind last night."

Last night, we forced her to practice skating like she had intended, and then let her go home alone, even though that was the last thing we wanted to do when she had an empty house waiting for her. But the invisible barrier she had up between us last night kept us from following her home and using her body against her to get what we wanted.

Today was a different story though, because we were using our dedication to caring for her as a weapon to earn her trust as well as our bodies to pleasure hers.

"Please." She purred, eyes widening with each moment that passed, "Please, Eli."

Fuck, that *please* lit me on fire.

Travis leaned over the back of the couch and kissed her hard, as I pulled her jeans off her flared hips. "You don't have to beg us, Shade. Not unless you *want* to."

"I kind of do," She whispered.

And we lost it.

I tore her jeans and panties off the rest of the way as he kept kissing her, pushing his big hand under the fabric of her bra and tearing at the delicate stitching as she writhed against it.

I kissed every inch of skin I could reach, mouthing it like it held secrets I was desperate to hear. Her moans came in soft waves when I pushed my tongue against her clit and tasted her for the first time in what felt like ages.

Her first orgasm ripped through her without warning, coming fast and out of nowhere. She was arching, gasping, and grabbing for us both like she needed something to tether her to reality.

"Let go," I whispered. "We've got you."

As she came for us, I slid a finger into her, then two, slow and steady while Travis flicked his tongue over her nipples, sucking them until her hips rolled into me with reckless need again.

"You feel that?" I murmured, "Do you feel how wet you are for us?"

She whined, grinding into my hand.

"All for us," Travis growled, reaching over to lay his hand on her stomach right above mine, "This is ours now,"

She came again with a strangled cry, hips shaking, nails biting into my shoulders.

But we weren't done, not even close.

"My turn," Travis kicked his jeans off and stalked around the couch. "I want you to ride my face."

"Dear God," She panted with a wild look on her face, "I don't know if my legs can hold me up right now."

I wiped my hand over my jaw as I stood up next to him, "You're going to be sitting on his face, Black Cat, you don't have to hold yourself up."

She rolled her eyes and glared at me defiantly.

The age-old argument between men and women about face riding. God.

I leaned down and picked her up, throwing her squealing, flailing body over my shoulder as Travis laid down on the couch with a sinister grin.

"Right here, baby." Travis said as I put her down, straddling his head so she was facing the end of the couch as he pulled her down flush to his waiting face. "Perfect."

"Oh my God," She groaned, leaning forward on the arm as her eyes rolled into the back of her head. "Fuck, Trav."

"Good girl," I moved to the end of the couch and stripped out of my clothes as she started rocking and moaning with his moves. "Tell me how it feels."

"So damn good," She cried, tearing her bra off and tossing it across the room. Her large tits swayed heavily between her braced arms, and I palmed them, flicking her nipples. "Fucking intense."

Frankie's green eyes fluttered open as she arched her back and looked up at me with parted lips and a drunken gaze.

"Be a good girl," I tilted her jaw with my hand, pulling it down and opening her mouth, "Stick your tongue out for my cock."

"Mmh," She hummed and seductively pushed her tongue out flat, ready and waiting as I stroked my cock in front of her. Her eyes fell to my dick and then fluttered back up to me. "You want to fuck my throat, Sunshine?"

I slapped the head of my cock against her tongue when she stuck it back out, and she sloppily sucked on it when I pushed it deeper. "That's it." I threaded my fingers through her wild hair, holding her still as I thrust into her mouth. The whole time, she held my stare, looking at me up through her lashes as she rocked on Travis's face with my cock in her mouth.

Damn.

I pulled out and wrapped my hand around her throat, holding her still, and kissed her so I wouldn't blow already from just the way she looked.

"I'm coming—" She gasped, pressing her throat into my hand tighter. "FUCK!"

Her scream echoed off the walls around us as she shattered in our arms. We worshiped her with tongue, teeth, and fingers until she was dripping and wrecked, begging for more. I picked her up off Travis, and he wiped his hand over his lips with a wicked grin as he sat up on the couch to make room for us.

Sitting down next to him, Frankie straddled me while I kissed her hard and lined my cock up with her soaking wet hole. Slowly, she lowered herself onto me with a look of wonderment on her face. "God, you're so deep, Elliot."

Hearing my full name on her lips, tinted with ecstasy and pleasure, made my balls tighten. "Damnit girl, you're going to make me come before you even get off." I cursed, leaning forward and taking both of her breasts in my hands, sucking, biting and playing with them as she moaned and rocked up and down in my lap.

"Hear that, Shade?" Travis leaned over and kissed her neck, biting her ear. "Your pussy feels so good, you've got Sunshine already on edge."

"Good," She moaned, dragging her nails down my chest. "I want to feel him filling me up."

My balls tightened and my skin felt like it was being sliced off my muscles, I couldn't remember another time I'd been so close to blowing so fast, not even the first time I sank into her lush body. What the fuck was wrong with me?

Her eyes were molten fire as she watched me losing it for her. "Come for me, Elliot." She purred, "Fill me up and come deep for me."

"Fuck!" I hissed, and Travis wrapped his big hand around her throat, as my hips started thrusting up into her lush body on their own. "Take it, baby. Take my cock." She screamed as her face reddened under his hold, and it just made it even better for me. "Take every fucking inch of me."

Her tits rocked with each punishing thrust, and her nails dug into Trav's wrist as she clung to him. I came as blood pooled under her black-painted nails like a brand on his body as I claimed hers from the inside.

"Yes!" Her pussy clenched tight around my dick, and I cursed, fucking her harder even after I came to make her orgasm last until it felt like my lungs were going to explode and my body crashed out against her couch. Travis let go of her neck, and she sagged into me, collapsing as she took ragged breaths in. Her body twitched with aftershocks neither of us could control.

I sensed Travis move, and then her hips lifted until my cock slid out of her wet body, but then the sultry heat of her pussy landed against the underside of my spent dick, and she moaned harshly, rocking against it.

I opened my eyes and watched as Travis mounted her from behind, even as she still lay in my lap, sliding his fat cock into her body. She smiled against my neck and arched her back, giving him better access as her clit rubbed against the oversensitive underside of my cock with each of his harsh thrusts.

"Damn," I groaned, gripping her thighs to rock her in time with him, pleasuring all three of us. "Fucking hell, man."

Trav grinned like a wild animal over her shoulder as his hands tightened on her hips, and he slammed into her harder, making all of us moan. He changed angles and wrapped one arm over her shoulder, the other on her hip as he drove into her.

"Don't stop," Frankie begged, reaching back to grab his thigh as she rubbed her clit up my dick, which was hard again in no time. "Fuck, this feels so good."

Trav and I had fucked women together before, but never *together* like this. We took turns, lending a helping hand and what not, but not like this.

This felt shared.

This felt like it *should* feel wrong.

I shouldn't be taking pleasure from him fucking her, but at the same time, I didn't want to take another breath without feeling the high he was giving me. And Frankie, dear God, she was mewling, moaning incoherent pleas as she gave it as good as she took it.

"That's it, Shade." Travis growled, and then I watched as he spat on her ass and started rubbing his thumb against her asshole.

My vision darkened when she begged him to do it, pushing back against his thumb as she stroked my cock with her wet lips and took his cock into her pussy.

Lines were being crossed, body parts were touching, and fire was exploding into my soul each time his thighs brushed against mine as he fucked her harder.

I distracted myself, pulling her head back by a handful of her hair and looking into her eyes as I neared a second orgasm, even as I sat completely still. They were pleasuring me together, and I wasn't ready to wrap my head around that just yet.

It was as if Frankie could sense the panic inside of me and laid her hand against my chest, right over the rapid beating of my heart. "You feel so good, baby." She purred, pressing her pussy against my cock harder, and Travis followed her, putting one knee on the couch next to mine. The change in angle sandwiched her between us, and each time he thrust deep into her, I could feel it through her body right against my cock. She gasped and dug her nails into my pec, "Oh God," Her eyes closed, and her lips parted. "That's it, don't stop. Don't ever fucking stop."

"Fuck," I groaned, losing my hold on my sanity when Travis' sack grazed mine.

"Look at her, Elliot." Travis growled, and I forced myself to finally make eye contact with him over her shoulder, and the intensity in his eyes blew me back. Damnit, he knew what he was doing. What I was feeling. "Look at what we're doing to her."

Tearing my gaze from his as he grabbed the back of her neck, pulling her chest up off mine, I focused on her.

And he was right.

Fucking hell, she was in absolute ecstasy, sandwiched between us.

"I'm—" She gasped, opening her eyes as her pussy soaked his cock so much it dripped down onto my cock beneath them. "Yes!"

"Take it, Shade," He growled, "Open her up, Elliot. Let me see where she's taking me," and I gave in to my urge to throw every reservation out the window. Reaching around her body, I pulled her lush cheeks apart, lifting her hips a fraction of an inch so she pressed against my dick harder. I walked my fingers in until I pulled her pussy lips wider, even if I couldn't see it directly, watching Travis stare at her pretty pink pussy wrapped around his cock and her ass around his thumb drove me wild.

And then I took it one step further when she screamed again, coming harder. I lowered my fingers and played with the wet inner part of her lips that were spread wide around his fat cock.

With the quickest brush of his cock against my fingertips, he cursed, throwing his head back in what looked like pleasure. I knew it wasn't from me, but my lust-filled cock didn't care. In the next second I started coming, coating her pussy lips with it each time she rocked up and down against it, and then Travis was following us off the cliff.

He came with a roar, body tight and strong against her back, cock brushing against my fingertips with each thrust and when he buried himself deep inside of her and didn't pull back out, I tore my gaze from her wrecked face to glance up at him.

And instantly regretted it.

The fire.

The intensity.

The—anger.

Fuck.

Too far. I pushed too far, fueled by lust and hormones. I crossed a line.

Fuck.

"Oh my God," Frankie sighed against my neck, laying soft kisses there, and I could feel her satisfied smile against my skin as I closed my eyes and tried to ground myself to it.

What the fuck did I just do?

19 - TRAVIS
Lines We Cross

I SHOULDN'T HAVE PUSHED it. I shouldn't have liked it either.

But I did.

It should have felt like a victory, the whole day, not just the sex, yet I was in some warped alternate reality, and I couldn't find the surface. Damn, I didn't even want to.

We snuck in, fixed Frankie's door, her stairs, her porch light, the rack in her bathroom, and a hundred other little things that needed attention. And then we gave her the attention that she needed.

Actually, we wrecked her in the best kind of way, laid out on the couch like a goddamn offering, and we both showed her just how *not alone* she was anymore.

And then she invited us to stay for dinner with her and the kids. It was the first step of hopefully many towards proving to them that we were here to stay too.

But now?

Now Eli wouldn't look me in the eye.

The kids had come bursting through the door half an hour ago, backpacks slung sideways, Emmie was yelling about wanting a granola bar, and Toby was holding a hand-drawn picture of a dinosaur wearing a tutu. Frankie kissed them both, asking about their day with that sweet, dedicated energy that made her mom of the year even on the edge of burnout.

And the best part was, neither of them hardly even blinked twice about us being in their home.

They rolled with it as if it were totally normal.

Maybe even excited to have us. Emmie was for sure, throwing down hockey stats from the games she watched this week. Even Toby was instantly climbing on my shoulders like his very own jungle gym in the middle of his living room. And I liked it.

I craved the feeling of being wanted by them, in their space, in their life.

But Eli? He'd vanished into the kitchen shortly after they settled down to do homework.

And me?

I silently watched from a distance as he gripped the edge of the counter like it might hold him together the second he thought he was out of view.

I should have known something like this would happen, I should have expected it, even. He was my best friend, not my fucking experiment.

But something about that moment earlier—both of us with her, touching her, pleasing her—had cracked something open inside of me I hadn't even known was sealed.

And then he touched me.

Just a graze at first. Fingertips. *That was it.*

It wasn't accidental, like mine had been at first. To be honest, mine hadn't stayed accidental for long.

And it had been hot as hell.

And I'd liked it. God help me, I fucking liked it.

Not in a sexual way—I didn't think. But in a connection way.

A deep-rooted sense of linking between us as she cried our names.

But he hadn't said a word since.

Not about her. Not about us. Not about the fact that our friendship had turned into something blurred and raw, and he was looking at me now like he wasn't sure if I was going to swing on him, or hug him.

Somehow, he managed to continue avoiding me, and I could accept that. I could accept his cold shoulder, as long as he didn't give Frankie or the kids one.

Which he didn't. But what they didn't see was what it was costing him to keep up the act. Which gutted me.

I was chopping bell peppers in the kitchen when he finally passed behind me, grabbing the skillet off the stovetop.

"Need to find the oil," He muttered.

I nodded, trying to keep it casual. "Cabinet above the microwave."

He didn't answer.

He didn't touch me either as he leaned around me to get it. I could tell he was intentionally trying to avoid it too.

And I felt that shit like a vacuum in my chest.

Frankie walked in a second later, barefoot, wearing an oversized hoodie and shorts that hugged her ass like a pair of hands. She looked domesticated, and happy. Almost like she belonged there in the doorway with a soft smile on her face. Like we all did.

"Dinner smells amazing," she said, pulling her hair up into a messy bun and blocking a grinning Emmie from the doorway as she once again tried to sneak in for a snack. "Toby asked if you two were moving in." She said when Emmie left, leaning her shoulder on the doorway and crossing her arms and ankle.

She was so at ease, and it calmed something inside my chest.

I laughed, or at least I tried to. "He told me I take up too much space on the couch."

She chuckled, glancing over her shoulder at her son. "If you keep playing trucks and dinos with him, he might start packing your stuff for you."

Eli gave a tight smile but didn't say anything.

I looked at him.

He looked at the food.

THE KIDS WERE FED, their homework was done, and thanks to Frankie's smarts and Eli's diligence, Emmie even managed to complete the next two days' worth of math problems that were troubling her. They had baths and were upstairs getting ready to go to sleep, with Frankie running command from the landing between their bedrooms.

So, I took my opportunity when it presented itself and followed Eli out onto the back porch. He glanced over at me as I stepped out after him and sighed, annoyed. Handing him a beer I grabbed for us, I hoped he'd at least take it and stick around long enough for me to figure out how to fix what was wrong.

"You mad at me?" I asked, leaning back against the railing.

He glanced up at me and held my stare for a second with a scowl before dropping it and cracking the top of his can. "No."

"You've been avoiding my eyes since before the mac and cheese hit the oven."

He sighed again, long and rough, and leaned against the railing next to me, looking out over the dark yard. "I don't know what I'm feeling."

"That makes two of us."

He glanced at me again, and I held his stare, unwavering. "I touched you." His voice sounded haunted, and the fear in his eyes was noticeable enough that I couldn't ignore it.

I swallowed, "I know."

"And you didn't stop me."

"No," I said quietly, taking a sip of my beer, trying to figure out how to tell him what I was feeling. Communicating wasn't my strongest skill, but it had never been a problem with Eli before. And the idea of something breaking the open honesty we'd always shared, scared the shit out of me. So, I had to give it if I wanted to get it in return. "Because I didn't want to."

Eli's throat worked around a dozen unsaid things as he stared at me. "You were pissed afterward." He accused, looking away again. "I saw it in your eyes when we were done."

"You're wrong." I held fast, turning to face him. "I was fucked up about it."

"I read it wrong," He deflected. "Things before that. I messed it up."

"What things?" I asked, urging for more insight into his brain.

But he shook his head and stayed silent.

"You mean the way I was taking her?" I pushed, "Against you. Using you at the same time to please her. Because that was intentional, Eli."

He whipped his head my way angrily, "No, dude. Because I was fucking enjoying it too!"

There it was.

I grabbed the back of his neck, holding him still because he looked like he was ready to bolt the second the words left his mouth. "So was I."

"Fuck." He groaned, pulling away from me and crossing the deck. "You don't get what I'm saying!"

"Then say it clearer!" I barked back, on edge and hoping he'd spit it out before Frankie returned. We had to get our heads on straight before she thought any of this was because of her

"I could feel you!" He hissed, taking a step back toward me like he wasn't even aware of it. "Through her. Against me. Your dick." He clenched his jaw, "Your sack on mine, man."

"And?" I scoffed.

"And I got hard from it!" He snapped.

It all started making sense, and my shoulders deflated. I leaned back against the railing as he paced, avoiding my gaze completely. And I let him, as I articulated all of my feelings in my head before I started.

I couldn't fuck this up with him. He deserved for me to get it right.

So did Frankie.

"You weren't the only one who liked it, Eli." I said evenly, but he still didn't stop moving. "I pushed into her body, knowing parts of us were going to be touching. But I didn't care, because Frankie was the focus." Reaching out, I grabbed his arm and forced him to stop. "I wouldn't have been into it if she wasn't there. But she was, and I felt so goddamn connected to both of you in that moment I didn't care! And neither should you!"

"I'm not gay!" He cursed, glaring at me. "And neither are you!"

"I know that." I let go, and he didn't take off, "That's what this is about though, isn't it?" Instantly, I remembered the rumors that flew around our town when Eli got out of the fire-fighter academy. "They said you were too pretty to be straight. People you'd known your whole life, made jokes and picked on you about it. Like it would matter even if you weren't."

Finally, I could read him again clearly. I could read his fear.

All those years ago, the rumors had been mostly just ball busting from guys, but some of them seemed to hit Eli harder than others. It was also the same time he went on a man-whore bender, fucking any chick within ten miles like he was trying to prove something to them.

To himself.

"I'm not gay." He repeated, "I'm not even bi. I'm not into guys."

"I know that." I reiterated, "I'm not either. But we're best friends, Eli. We're on a tricky road right now, dating the same woman. Focusing on working together and making her happy. Maybe that's why it felt so powerful. But either way, I felt it too. And I'm not at all stressed about what it means, other than I want to do it again. Because we all fucking liked it."

He dropped his shoulders and thought it over before finally replying, "So what do we do now?"

I looked through the sliding glass door and saw Frankie picking up some toys off the coffee table. "We go inside. We continue to lead with our hearts, and keep open lines of communication along the way." I held my hand out to him as a form of an olive branch. "We talk through what we're thinking, in real time, and work through it."

He scoffed, though it felt forced, but I could tell he was trying to relax into what I was offering him. "You sound very mature all of a sudden," He took my hand and shook it, but didn't release it right away. "You're good for her."

That felt like a gut punch because I could feel the words he wasn't saying after it. "And so are you." I forced him to hold my stare. "We're both good for each other too, so don't even think about walking away now. I won't let you. We keep showing up for her. And them. Maybe for each other, too."

He pushed me and took a sip of his beer, "As if I'd let you have her all to yourself," He smirked, looking past me to where Frankie was inside. "I'm kind of obsessed."

"Same," I turned and watched her brush her hair off her face and then look for us, finding us both in the window. "Fucking obsessed."

20 - FRANKIE
Uncharted Heat

THE HEAT in their eyes made something in my stomach clench. Something low, somewhere that had gone dormant over the years of loneliness. To feel their desire so aggressively after feeling so unwanted for so long, fucked with my good sense.

"What were you talking about?" I asked, hoping they'd tell me the truth, tell me what had been building between them all evening in silence.

Travis looked at Eli before walking to me and kissing me. It wasn't soft or chaste, but for him it was short. All too soon, he pulled away and sat down on the couch, spreading his massive tree-trunk thighs as he settled into the cushions.

"Tell her." Travis stated, and I shot a quick glance over at Eli in question.

Anxiety built in my gut, crowding out the desire I'd felt moments ago as something gnawed at me.

Eli smiled at me, but it didn't warm me the way his smiles usually did, and my own fell. God, was this the end of everything? Already?

"Something happened earlier," Eli said, taking a deep breath, and my own shuddered in my lungs. "Something when we took you together on the couch."

"What?" I whispered, confused, playing the whole encounter back through my head trying to remember everything that happened. "Did I do something wrong?"

"No," Travis inserted, and I looked over my shoulder at him, and his penetrating stare did what it always did—made me feel like he could read my mind. He wrapped his big hands around my waist and pulled me into his lap, kissing my temple and holding me close. "Something between Eli and me."

"What do you mean?" I stammered, "I was there, I don't understand."

"I touched him." Eli blurted out and then scrubbed a hand over his face and circled the coffee table to sit down on it, facing me. He ran his hands over my bare knees, and I threaded my fingers through his as I tried to ground myself with them around the fear in my gut. "When he was fucking you." Eli closed his eyes and shook his head, squeezing my hand. "It felt like I crossed a line, and I thought he was mad, and I got in my head and fucked with my own thoughts and fears until I was on the edge of throwing myself off a cliff in embarrassment." He smiled, but it was sad. "So, we were talking about it."

"I don't understand." I whispered again, looking over my

shoulder at Travis and then back to Eli. "What do you mean you touched him? We were all touching," I chuckled lightly, trying to add some humor into the tense room. Travis's hands rubbed up and down my hips as I talked. "That was the point, wasn't it?"

"I could feel him," Eli said, pushing on even though I could tell he was uncomfortable. "Every time he bottomed out inside of you, I could feel him against my dick. And I didn't hate it. And I also didn't understand it, but I got wrapped up in it all and then I—"

"You—" I worried, "You what?"

Eli swallowed but didn't answer.

"He touched my dick," Travis filled the gap, "When I told him to spread you open for me."

I thought back, in the height of my ecstasy, to Travis telling Eli to show him where he was fucking me. I remembered the way his fingers pulled my pussy open while Travis drove me over the edge time and time again.

"Which crossed a line." Eli said shamefully.

"It also pushed me headfirst into a massive orgasm." Travis stated plainly, and Eli groaned, dropping his head.

"Not helping, man."

"I'm man enough to admit it," Travis shrugged, and I smirked at him and the supportive way he was handling his best friend's feelings. Watching him take care of Eli warmed my heart in ways I didn't know was possible.

"You liked him touching you?" I asked in surprise. When I shifted to look at him, my thighs clenched, and a jolt of excitement rushed through my clit. Damn, did I like the idea of them touching?

"I liked that we were all enjoying ourselves," Travis said, staring up at me smugly. "I liked that I was making you both feel good." He leaned forward and kissed me. "I liked that each of us was involved. Connected."

"I liked that too," I admitted, turning back to Eli, who still looked like he was teetering on the edge of bolting from the house altogether. "And there's something else," I slid from Travis's lap and slowly sank to my knees in front of Eli, running my hands up his thighs as his warm eyes tracked my face like he was looking for something hidden on it. He sat up when my hands found their way into his lap and I leaned up to speak against his lips, "I wish I had seen you touch him. Or known what was happening as I used both of your cocks for my own selfish enjoyment, because damn." I purred, "That sounds sexy."

"Fucking hell, Frankie." Eli groaned when I ran my nails over the bulge in his jeans. He wasn't hard, just so damn big there was no hiding it from me even when he was soft. Within seconds though, I felt him stiffen beneath my hands. "I'm so on edge right now. I'm raw. Be careful."

"Then let me help you." I put my best effort into tempting him with seduction, and he watched me with feral eyes. "Sit next to Travis on the couch."

The tension was thick enough to chew. And I was feeling ravenous enough to try.

Eli hesitated before standing up over me and throwing himself down on the couch next to his best friend.

Close to Travis.

He could have sat down at the other end of the couch, but he didn't.

And that made me fucking wet.

I crawled over to them, kneeling between their legs with a needy grin on my face. Slowly, I ran my palms over one leg each of theirs until I got to their belts. "What do you say, boys?" I purred, pulling Eli's belt free and then reaching over and opening up Travis's. "Can I play?"

Travis growled, flexing his hips when I pulled the button of his jeans open and then slowly lowered his fly. Turning to Eli, I did the same, and the heat from his stare nearly melted me right there.

Teasingly, I pulled my baggy hoodie off over my head, knowing they were going to love what I was wearing underneath it.

Nothing.

Tight black booty shorts, and warm skin—all for them.

Eli sucked in a deep breath, and Travis palmed his dick through his jeans. "Help a girl out and take off your clothes." I demanded, leaning back as both of them didn't waste a second to do as I said.

Having both of the men, cut in their prime, deliciously sexy, sitting on my couch, aching for me, excited me more than anything else in the world.

Travis, with his massive muscles and thick black tattoos that matched his dark penetrating stare. And Eli, with his tanned, golden skin that moved and flowed over his incredibly cut muscles and divots perfectly paired with his warm dimpled smile.

I wasn't worthy of either of them, but I'd never let them know that.

"Good boys," I bit my bottom lip and looked from one drool-worthy man to the other. I fisted both of their hard cocks and stroked them, dragging moans from their lips. It was intense, watching their bodies react to my touch.

Almost every other time we played, it was them pushing me through every wild limit and forcing me to lose myself in my own needs and pleasures. But now—I was captivated watching their bodies flex, pupils dilate, their lips part and jaws clench.

God, it was erotic.

Empowering.

Heady.

Leaning up on my knees, I bent over Eli's lap and started taking him in my mouth as I kept the same tight strokes on Trav's cock. Eli's moans caressed my confidence as Travis praised what I was doing to his best friend.

"Good girl," He growled, low and intense as he pushed my hair back over my shoulders, holding it back for me as I sucked Eli off. "Make him feel so damn good, Shade."

I moaned, going deeper and gagging on Eli's long cock as Travis's heavy hand pushed me down further gently.

Fuck, that was so hot.

It was exactly what Travis said he enjoyed earlier.

The mutual pleasures.

Eli's abs flexed and his hips jerked when I got closer to the base of his cock, but he never pushed himself deeper. He was too polite.

Travis wasn't though. "Take him all the way, Shade." Trav demanded, pushing my head deeper, and I moaned as I came up, gasping and locking eyes with Eli as I went back for more. "You're making him feel so good."

I gasped, fighting for control of my own need as Travis praised me straight toward an orgasm. Turning to him, I spit on his cock and aggressively sucked him deep, pulling a curse from his lips as he leaned back against the cushions in shock and awe.

Eli chuckled, putting his hands behind his head and watching, all of his delicious muscles on display. "That's it, baby."

"Shh," I moaned, teasing them as I lowered my lips to Travis's full balls and sucked one into my mouth, making him curse against his fist as he bit it to stay quiet. "Can't wake the kids."

"Fuck," Travis growled, no longer joking and teasing as I pushed him toward ecstasy. "You're so good with your mouth."

"I'm good with all of my holes," I tempted, scraping my teeth up the underside of him before switching back to Eli.

"Tell me more about that," Eli demanded, gathering my hair as I slid between his knees so I could really work on taking all of him. "You liked Travis's thumb in your ass earlier, you begged for it."

"Fuck that," Travis hissed, pushing the coffee table away and kneeling behind me, covering the back of my body with his hot one, hard cock nestling against my ass. "She demanded it, didn't you? You pushed back on it the second I touched you there."

"Mmh," I moaned and smiled up at Eli and flicked the end of my tongue over his cock. "I can't wait to feel you both fuck me there."

"Dammit," Eli groaned, and Travis bit my neck, rubbing his cock against my ass like he was so turned on he didn't care that I still had clothes on. "You're so damn good with that mouth. I can't wait to feel you take my cock in your ass for the first time. When was the last time you took something there?"

"I've never taken a real cock there," I admitted, and then grinned and looked at Travis over my shoulder as his hands tightened on my hips. "But I have toys. And I like filling both of my holes when I have the house to myself and don't have to be quiet."

"Fuck," Travis growled, and then his big hands were in

the waistband of my shorts, pulling them down to my knees, and his fingers were parting my pussy lips and pushing in deep from behind.

"God!" I cried, arching my back and pushing back on them. "I'm so close already."

"Look at Eli," Travis demanded at my shoulder, pushing my chest forward as he lifted my hips to give himself better access to my lower half. "Look how feral he is for you."

He wasn't lying either. Elliot's eyes were nearly black, blown wide open as he watched me suck his cock while Travis played with me.

He was close to blowing too, his balls were tight and his muscles were clenching in time with my strokes.

"Will you let me try something?" I purred up at him, biting my lip and then spitting on his already wet cock. He didn't say anything, but he didn't stop me either as I leaned forward and pushed his cock between my breasts. "Will you fuck my tits, baby?" I asked, lifting my shoulders and letting his cock slide in and out between them. "It's something I've never done."

"Goddamnit." Eli growled, throwing his head back and flexing his hips to push his cock up into my chest. "You want me to fuck these pretty tits?" He asked and pinched both of my nipples around my hands and pulled on them.

Bingo.

I knew he was a tits man.

Travis was all about my ass, and Eli was obsessed with my tits. What a dirty combination they made.

"That's it, Shade." Travis said, and then his big hands were covering mine, squeezing my tits around Eli's cock. There was that edge of taboo in the scenario, a man stroking his best friend off with his girlfriend's tits. But I'd be lying if I said it didn't make me dripping wet all at the same time. "Make him feel good."

"Yes, Sir." I purred, and his cock pushed between my thighs, rubbing right against my pussy, making me moan in sync with Eli. God, he was good at this whole pleasuring everyone thing. It unlocked a new kink in me. "Mmh, put it in." I challenged, glancing at him as I kept my chest moving up and down on Eli's cock.

"You're not already balls deep in her yet, man?" Eli hissed in a hushed tone, scowling at the man teasing us both. "Fuck her. What are you waiting for?"

Travis chuckled, and arched his hips until the head of his cock nudged into me and I froze, testing the stretch as I no longer stroked either of them. But Eli wasn't having any of that.

"Eyes on me, Black Cat." He took my chin between his fingers and lifted his hips, rocking me on his cock and, in turn, pushing me back onto Travis's in one slow, complete thrust that made us all moan. "Good girl, take that fat cock."

"Jesus," I moaned, digging my nails into Eli's thighs as I started moving again, every move forward pushed Eli's long cock deep between my tits. Every move backward, pushed Travis's monster cock deep inside of me. "I'm never going to be the same."

Eli chuckled and pushed his thumb into my mouth, pushing against my bottom teeth and holding me how he wanted as I fucked them both. "That's exactly what we're counting on."

"Take me to bed." I begged, staring up at him. "I want you both in my bed."

Travis pushed his hips forward, pinning me to Eli's waist, and wrapped his hand around the front of my throat to turn me to face him. "Only if you show us these toys you told us about."

"Only after you make me come." I challenged, and Eli smirked, looking like his old self more and more with each minute of ease between us.

"Deal."

Tentacles and Chill

BREATHE, *Eli*.

Just fucking breathe.

If I screwed up and came before I was ready for it, I'd never forgive myself. Not with so much on the line.

"Show us." I demanded, desperate to see what she did with the pretty orange and blue toy in her hand that looked suspiciously like a small octopus tentacle. Did she pick those colors specifically, or was it just a coincidence that they matched our team jerseys?

Frankie bit her bottom lip and nodded to the armchair in the corner. "Hand me that round pillow."

I looked at Trav, who gave me a shrug, and then I picked

up the pillow she motioned to. It was about the size of a loaf of bread, rock hard, and covered with a girly pillowcase.

She took it from me and laid the toy on it, before pulling two straps I hadn't seen out of the bottom and tightening them around the pillow.

"Damn," Trav groaned, leaning forward as she set the toy in the center of the bed and then grabbed a bottle of lube from the same drawer she got the tentacle from. "Tell me you can take the whole thing."

The man was feral.

He was literally salivating as she crawled up on the bed, thighs spread, kneeling over the toy, while she seductively poured lube on it before rubbing it in.

"That depends on which hole you're talking about."

"Fuck." I hissed, stroking my cock. I couldn't help it; I needed to come as she took that toy in whatever hole she wanted it in. I *had* to. "Show us."

She lifted one leg and hovered over the toy, ribbed with fake suckers like an authentic tentacle. The thing wasn't overly long, but it got wide at the base, and grooved all the way down as if she didn't even need to put it inside, but could simply grind on it.

"Can you handle it, Sunshine?" She purred and flicked a button on the base, and the entire thing came to life. Humming. Buzzing. Rotating. "You look like you're going to blow."

"All over your tits." I clapped back, never taking my eyes off where she let the tip of it tickle against her clit as she hovered. "In no time flat."

She chuckled and then started lowering herself down onto it. And then all the jokes and smiles faded from the room.

All that was left was carnal need, coursing through our

veins, with the impending need to stay quiet and controlled hanging over our heads.

Slowly, Frankie took the toy into her body, lowering herself onto it and then lifting up. Her rosy red lips, still swollen from sucking us off, were parted, and her eyelids were heavy over her lust-filled eyes. Soft moans slipped from her as she worked herself down the toy until it was inside of her, and then she dropped her other knee to the bed and leaned forward, taking ragged breaths like she was celebrating a victory.

Her victory or ours, I didn't know.

"You're so sexy, sweetheart." I groaned, unable to stay put any longer as I climbed up onto her bed and pulled her face up to mine. "Do you have any idea how incredible you look right now?"

She smiled with a haze in her gaze and started rocking her hips. "Tell me more, I apparently have a praise kink around you two."

"I'm imagining how you're going to look stuffed with both of us." I admitted, "Filled to the brim with our cocks. Unable to move because you're so full as we give you every inch until you're melted into a puddle."

Travis joined her and put his hand on the base of the toy behind her so that every time she rocked backward or lowered herself back onto the toy, his knuckles brushed against her ass.

The man was obsessed with her ass.

The same way I was about her tits.

"Tell us something, Shade." He leaned over her shoulder and bit her neck, covering her mouth with his free hand when she moaned loudly from it. "Are you coming home with us after our game on Saturday?"

Frankie mewled, rocking faster against her toy, and I stroked my cock as she watched. "Yes," She gasped, chest falling as a blush grew up her neck. "If you make it worth my time."

I chuckled and started playing with one of her hard nipples. I watched her face as I pinched it lightly and pulled on it. I watched what she liked and what she loved.

"You're going to love every second of feeling us both in your body at the same time."

"Oh God," She moaned, closing her eyes and laying her hand against my abs as Travis popped the top of the lube open ominously behind her. "You're going to tag team me?"

Fuck. Those words on her lips.

"Only if you're a good girl." Travis said, and even though I couldn't see it from my angle, I knew the second he started playing with her asshole. "You're going to come with this toy in your pussy, then you're going to show us how far you can take it in your ass so we know if Sunshine will fit Saturday night."

"Oh God," She cried in a whisper. And then those glowing green eyes opened, and she stared right at me as she started coming, orgasming all over her toy as Travis fingered her ass. The whole time, holding my stare like I was the only thing tethering her to the ground. "Kiss me, Eli." She begged in a hoarse voice.

I didn't hesitate, leaning in and silencing her cries as she clung to me. "Good girl," I praised, playing with her nipples as she took ragged, shuddering breaths on the other side of her orgasm.

"That's it, Shade." Travis praised. "Now let's loosen this ass up."

We moved as one, lifting her feet under her and pulling her up off the toy until she squatted above it and then Travis pulled her back against his chest, angling her hips so I had a perfect view of her entire body and swollen pink pussy lips. That was all it took for me.

She started lowering herself down onto the toy again, this time taking it into her ass, and I squeezed my cock one more time before I cursed in climax.

"Yes," she cried, digging her nails into my arm. "Cover me with it. On my tits like you promised."

Quickly I jumped to my feet, stroking my cock as she leaned back on Travis's chest with the toy in her ass and his fingers strumming her clit, and I erupted in ways I didn't know were possible.

I cursed, blinded with pleasure, and coated her entire chest with come as she cried out, orgasming in sync.

"Good girl," Travis praised, holding her up as she came on the toy and his hand. "That's so fucking hot. You pushed him over the edge, so he couldn't help himself."

I collapsed backward onto the bed in a heap as she bit the back of her hand, silencing her cries and pleas. My cock never even softened all the way as I stared at her incredible body, covered in my come glistening in the lamplight.

"Holy fuck," She leaned back into him, but my friend wasn't going to let her go that easily. "I'm shaking."

"You're dirty too." Travis said, and then I watched in absolute rapture as he rubbed his hand across her chest, rubbing my come into her tits and down her belly. "Don't worry, I'll clean you up before I bend you over for my turn."

"Mmh," She melted into him even more and then hissed when he leaned her forward onto all fours and took the toy away from her. And in the next moment he was buried balls deep in her pussy and tipping his head back in a silent growl. "Mmh, yes." She cried out, biting the blanket as she sank down onto her elbows, presenting for him. "God, harder, Trav."

He grabbed her hips and slammed into her hard. The sound of skin was loud, but I knew he wouldn't risk the volume unless he was close enough to keep it quick. I got up on my knees and lifted her off the bed, holding her and kissing her cries as he fucked her savagely. The moment she started coming, so did he, and I held her through it, bracing her so he could fuck her as hard as they were both desperate for.

She crawled away from him, and I eagerly picked her up, laying her across my chest so she could catch her breath after the wild shenanigans of the night.

Of the whole day.

What a wild trip my days had turned into.

"Thank you." She whispered against my neck as Travis went to get a wet washcloth to clean us all up with.

"For what?"

She smiled against my neck and kissed it before responding. "For staying tonight even though you were mentally at war with yourself."

"Hmm." I thought about it as I stared at the ceiling. Thank God I hadn't left earlier, even though I had contemplated it a dozen times as the night went on.

Look at all I would have missed.

"Thank you for wanting me to stay, even though I was at war."

"We all have fears, baby." She said, and then yawned. "We just have to trust each other with them."

"Careful what you try to preach to me." I ran my hand down her spine, "Because we both know you're still holding your fears to yourself and not letting us burden them with you."

She stayed quiet, and Travis walked back in, giving her an out to keep from acknowledging the truth of what I said. And I let her. For now.

22 - MYSTERY
Lights, Camera, Action

SHE WAS MINE. If she was going to refuse to acknowledge that, then I'll make *them* understand it.

She thought she was safe. She thought I had forgotten. She thought I had moved on.

She was wrong.

I stood in the darkness outside her sliding door, the open curtains mocking me, daring me to watch her be a whore. I watched her drop to her knees, and suck them off. I watched her do things to them she never did for me.

And those two big bastards thought they were good enough to touch her, to take from her.

To fuck her dirty little cunt like it was theirs.

It wasn't!

It was mine.

It had always been mine.

It would always be mine. And if I wasn't the one having it, no one would.

She used to beg me to wreck her, like she did for them now, but in the end, I'd wreck her for good. I forced myself to stay and watch her entire show, moving to the window outside her bedroom and staring through the slats in her broken blinds as she fucked herself on a toy. Then she let the big one, the construction boss, fuck her harder than she ever let me.

All the while, her annoying ass kids slept upstairs.

What a shit excuse for a mom.

And luckily, I had all the proof I needed to prove it on my camera roll now.

But I wanted more. For my own enjoyment.

So, I sat and waited, watching her leave the house Saturday night for her shift at the rink, dropping her brats off at her mom's like the irresponsible parent she was. Then I let myself into her space.

The key slid in the lock like butter, like it wanted me to get inside the whole time. Like I belonged there.

Which I did.

Though if she had been a decent wife, she never would have ended up back in her shitty little hometown in her junky little rental.

I slowly walked around, looking at everything, and made my way to her bedroom. It still reeked of sex, both men stayed and fucked her on and off all night before they snuck out before the rascals woke up and caught them spit roasting dear old mommy.

Disgusting.

I shoved her pillow off the bed onto the floor and opened the drawer at the top of her closet, where she pulled that disgusting toy from that she used to defile herself for their pleasure.

My blood boiled with disgust, and my hands shook as I palmed the huge thing, testing the weight of it.

Whore.

I hated her. But it didn't stop my cock from throbbing, remembering the way she sounded when she came on the tip of it last night for them while they watched. I stood there too long, caught between that hate and temptation before giving in to what I needed.

I pulled my dick out and stroked myself as I stared at the ribbed toy, imagining it sinking deep into her pussy and her ass. Instead of remembering the sights from last night, I made up new ones in my head, where she bent over in the center of our bed and let me shove the toy into her body deep and roughly.

She wasn't moaning in pleasure as I did it though; she was crying.

And her tears made my dick weep.

I imagined her screams as I fucked her with it before slamming straight into her ass with that toy buried in her pussy, and then I came. My orgasm spilled all over the silicone toy, dripping down the ridges of it like an oath to her.

I'd fuck her again.

And when I did—her tears would fall just like they did the last time I saw her.

I laid the toy on top of her nightstand and left it for her to find.

A message only she'd understand.

The camera went up next—high in the corner behind the edge of her curtain that she never closed. I'd get every naked inch of her body on recording as she walked from the bathroom to her closet and then to her bed, doing whatever depraved things I allowed before I made my move.

Each second of recordings would just add to the bank of proof I was gathering. To prove she was unfit.

Two more cameras went up in the living room, one on the bookshelf tucked between the two school pictures on the shelf, and the other stuck to the underside of the television they stared at all the time.

Next came the little touches.

Her favorite coffee mug went into the freezer.

The matches from the decorative drawer on the hutch that she used to light her candles every day—gone.

Her slippers moved from the front door, where she kicked them off each time she left the house, to the back porch.

Tiny things.

Things that would make her second-guess herself.

By the time I left, I came twice more. Once on her toothbrush and another as I sat on the couch, exactly where the fireman had last night as he fucked her big, lush tits.

Another thing she'd never done for me, though that would change once she realized she had no other choice but to start begging me to take her back.

23 - FRANKIE

Stalked

I SANG along to the Joan Jett song blaring through my speakers as I rushed back across town. There was absolutely no time to spare on my impromptu little field trip back home on my lunch break.

I should have just done what I wanted to before I left the house to go to the rink for my shift, but I'd let fear talk me out of it.

Embarrassment.

I was rushing home to grab the Net Crasher Jersey that had hung in my closet for the last two years since Rick got it for me for Christmas. I had never worn it. It was too embarrassing to wear the jersey of my secret crushes like some horny teenage girl. But now, I didn't just have a crush on a player. I was dating him, both of them.

The whole idea of wearing their jersey tonight was stupid, childish even. But the thought of walking in tonight wearing their team logo on my chest had been gnawing at me since Wednesday's practice. The thought of what they'd look like when they saw me in it was reason enough to risk the embarrassment.

For them, I'd do just about anything.

Never mind the idea of them tag teaming me after the game, filling me at the same time, pushed me into it.

The other night, had fulfilled sexual fantasies of mine I never even admitted in the daylight before. They were ravenous for me, watching me, helping me, urging me to give them more.

And I wanted to give them this in return.

The second I put my car in park, I ran to the front door, chased by the cold front moving in, and slammed the door shut behind me to ward it off.

I was doing a mental countdown of how many minutes I had until I was expected back behind the bar, slinging beers to drunk players and fans as I rushed through the house to my bedroom.

Straight to my closet, pushing past all of my other clothes to grab the feminine cut orange and blue jersey I had loved from the first second I saw it in the shop at the front of the rink.

Turning with it in my hands, a smile on my lips, I froze when I caught sight of something out of place.

My nightstand.

Or better yet, on my nightstand.

My sex toy, that I used for Travis and Eli.

My head cocked to the side as I slowly walked toward it,

perplexed. I remembered washing it in the bathroom sink after the guys left and putting it away back in the kid-proof drawer at the top of my closet before Emmie and Toby woke up.

My mind screamed as I tried to figure out how I had somehow put it back out in the wide open.

But I knew I didn't.

When I picked it up, something wet touched the tip of my finger, and I dropped it back onto the stand in disgust.

"No," I bent over and clicked the lamp on above it, and saw the half-dried opaque mess all over it. "What the fuck?"

My stomach turned, and every hair on my skin prickled and rose.

Someone had been in my room.

In my home.

My pulse was in my throat as I scanned the rest of the room. Nothing looked stolen, everything was still there. Nothing was overturned or broken.

But the air felt wrong.

Heavy.

Like the walls were falling in on me, leaning against them-selves, telling me that I wasn't alone inside.

Travis.

Eli.

Call them.

The thoughts raced through my head as my stomach clenched in fear. But I couldn't. They were already at the rink by now, changing and warming up for their game.

I couldn't disrupt them.

Besides, what was I supposed to say? That I found some-thing gross on my nightstand and that I was scared?

I was a single mom; I didn't get to be scared. I always had to be brave. With shaking hands, I lifted the toy by the base and shoved it in the trash in the kitchen, burying it under paper towels and other trash sitting on top.

And then I pulled the jersey on and left the house, calling my mom as I got back in my car.

"Hey, Honey." She said in greeting, "Is everything okay?"

"Yeah," I swallowed, driving through the winter darkness back to the rink. "Is everything good there?"

"Here?" She asked with a chuckle, "Yes, we're fine. The kids are watching a movie, and I'm reading. Why?"

"No reason," I said, forcing myself to take a deep breath. "I just wanted to make sure before I went back in for the rest of my shift."

"Are you okay?" She asked, and I could feel the shift in her voice like a physical change in direction. "You sound winded."

"Yeah, I'm fine." I raised my voice to sound more upbeat.

"Franny," She warned, "I don't want you overburdening yourself." I groaned silently, fighting the urge to hang up before she could talk about the worst time of my life. "The last time you burned out so hard you—"

"Mom." I snapped. "I'm not burned out; I just had a few minutes to get stuff done. Nothing more."

"Are you sure?" She pushed, "You're dating. Not just one man either—"

"Mom." I turned my car off as I parked in the rink lot next to Eli's truck. Travis's truck wasn't around, but I tried not to worry about that. "I am actually loving life right now, thriving and happy and not at all worried about all that other crap, okay? Now I have to get back inside before Rick tries to play bar-back and ruins my night."

She chuckled, like she was letting it go, "Okay fine. Have a good night. I'll bring the kids over after church in the morning. So, sleep in and get some rest."

"Okay." I swallowed, already anxious over the idea of going back to the house, but pushed it down as I got out. "Love you."

"Love you too, sweetie pie."

I rushed inside, fighting the urge to look over my shoulder at the door. The rink was buzzing with people, the locals all loved the Saturday night Net Crasher games. As I rounded the lobby, I spotted Travis and Eli at the near end of the rink working through warm-ups, but they both noticed me immediately.

The way Travis's mouth curved when he saw me in the jersey momentarily mesmerized me, and then again by the way Eli's eyes lingered on its logo across my chest.

For a moment, I almost forgot about my fear.

Until Eli's gaze narrowed, head tilting slightly, reading me like he always did.

"You good?" he mouthed, and I gave him two thumbs up with a forced smile.

Could he tell it was forced from the ice?

Nothing's wrong.

I swear.

Eventually, maybe I'd convince myself.

24 - TRAVIS
Brake Check

WARMUPS WERE SUPPOSED to clear my head, get my mind focused on the game and the job at hand. But tonight, they didn't.

Not when Frankie walked into the rink wearing our jersey for the first time. I caught Eli's eyes go wide before I'd even finished my slow drag down her body.

The town was talking about her dating both of us, and this just solidified it. She was proving to us that she was committed to it.

To us.

She looked—fuck, she looked good.

Like she was ours.

But when the shock of that wore off, I noticed something

else. Something about the way she moved—tighter, smaller, made the back of my neck itch.

I took a couple of laps, trying to shake it off, but it didn't work.

Every time I caught a glimpse of her from the bar upstairs, she tried to smile like nothing was wrong. And maybe it worked for everyone else, but not for me. Not for Eli either. I could see it in the way his jaw ticked each time our eyes met across the ice.

By the second period, I wasn't watching the puck anymore. I was watching her.

We won, but I barely felt the rush of it. Eli hardly smiled in the handshake line.

Frankie tried to avoid us at the bar when we got showered and changed, acting like the customers at her bar were going to stage a mutiny if she didn't give them all of her attention.

"Shade." I warned as she came near the end of the bar and pulled her around the side to the walk-in cooler. Eli was right behind us, standing guard at the door like he expected her to bolt. "What's wrong?"

She blinked and swallowed, "What do you mean?"

"The fake-ass smile you've been wearing all night," Eli pointed out, "You don't ever smile at those fucks at your bar, let alone with a fake one. You think we can't tell something's wrong?"

Her eyes darted between us, "I'm fine, really."

"Bullshit," I said.

She hugged her arms around her stomach, fingers tightening into the jersey, "It's—nothing. I just—" She sighed, "It's nothing."

I stepped closer, crowding into her space until her body heat mixed with mine, as I brushed a lock of hair over her shoulder, exposing her neck. "If it's nothing, then why is your heart beating a drum solo right here?" I grazed my finger across the pulse point on her neck.

Her breath caught, but she stayed silent.

Eli joined us, leaning against her side. "You don't have to tell us here, but you are telling us."

She shook her head, that stubborn streak flashing, but I could see the fear beneath the bravado. The kind she couldn't hide or brush off.

And whatever put it there, I was going to rip it to shreds.

"COME ON," I said, sliding my warm hand through her cold one, lacing our fingers. "You can ride with Eli and I'm going to drop your car off at your place."

She hesitated, and then nodded. "Is that why your truck isn't here?"

"We didn't want your car sitting here all night."

"Okay," she said and gave me a small smile. It was tiny and hardly made her cheeks bend, but it was real. The first real one all night.

I got in her SUV and tried not to get jealous as she jumped up into the shotgun seat of Eli's truck and followed me out of the parking lot. We were dropping her car off at home and then going to my place for the night.

The only thing keeping me sane, battling whatever it was that was fucking Frankie up, was the knowledge that she would be in my bed tonight.

Safe.

Happy.

Cared for.

Just as we turned off the main road and came up to a

curve in the road, I tapped the brakes to slow down. But nothing happened.

My stomach dropped as Eli's headlights flashed in the mirror behind me. I pressed harder on the brakes, still nothing. The pedal went straight to the floor.

"Shit—" I cursed, gripping the wheel as the car jerked and veered into a slide. I fought it, but the corner was too sharp and the car was going too fast. All I could do was aim for something that wouldn't kill me.

The tree came at the hood fast. Way too fast.

The impact rocked my entire body, clanking my teeth together as the airbags exploded in my face and pain ricocheted across my chest as the seatbelt locked me into place for the violent ride.

The engine hissed and clanked before the car died as everything came to a stop with the smell of burned rubber in my nose.

My car door ripped open, and Eli forced his way through the side airbag, yelling my name. "Trav, talk to me!" He leaned in through the gap as I tried to sit up from where I landed, leaning over the console. "Trav!"

"I'm okay," I hissed, sitting up and clenching my teeth as my chest burned. My ears rang violently.

"Travis," Frankie screamed, pushing past Eli with eyes wide and wet as she gripped my face in her hands.

"I'm fine," I groaned, clicking the seatbelt off and trying to bend my legs through the mangled dash to get out. "Shit."

"I thought—" She broke off, trembling so hard her hands shook against my chest as I got out, "I thought I was about to watch you die."

Once I was out and leaning against the hood of Eli's truck as he hung up with 911, I watched silently as Frankie's gaze kept flicking back to the mangled car.

There was something in her eyes, sharper than fear.

"What happened, man?" Eli asked, putting his hand on my shoulder, "Did you even touch the brakes?"

"Slammed them." I stated, glancing at Frankie, "The pedal went to the floor without slowing me down at all."

She cringed slowly, glancing back at the car.

"Frankie," Eli urged, picking up on the tension in her mind. "What's going on?"

"I don't know." She whispered, rubbing her hands over her arms even though she wore Eli's thick winter jacket.

"Bullshit." I snapped, angry that I almost just died, but even angrier that it was almost Frankie behind that wheel.

She looked down at where the car sat crumpled against the tree. "What if the brakes didn't just fail?" The air went still between the three of us. "What if it wasn't an accident?"

"What do you mean?" I asked with lethal calmness in my voice, because I was already following her thought path.

Turning to look up at me, her green eyes were haunted. "What if someone cut them?"

I stepped closer, voice low. "If you think someone is trying to hurt you, or hurt us, you tell me everything. No more secrets."

She swallowed, eyes flicking between me and Eli, "I can't shake this feeling." She whispered, "I don't think it was an accident."

Eli put his arm around her, and she instantly sank into his hold as tears fell over her eyelashes again. "Then we don't take anymore chances. You're safe with us."

No hesitation.

No argument.

We'd figure it out when we got there. But first, we were getting Frankie somewhere safe.

25 - ELI
The Cabin

FRANKIE HADN'T LET GO of Travis's hoodie since the crash. Not when the police and EMS arrived at the scene. Not when the tow truck came to load up her car. Not even once we jumped into my truck—Frankie in the middle of the front seat between us.

Her shoulders were drawn in, her hands trembled, and her tiny fist gripped the fabric of his hoodie, as if he might vanish if she released it.

Trav refused to go to the hospital, which I was not surprised. And thankfully, I knew the EMS crew on shift and knew what to keep an eye out for overnight just in case. The police ruled the crash an accident, blaming the ice and weather, and the three of us stayed silent as they loaded the car and towed it to the garage. I'd call Lenny, the head mechanic, in the morning and make sure he looked at the brake lines.

I kept my eyes on the road, one hand on the wheel, and the other on her thigh. Not enough to start anything, but enough to let her know that I was still there.

Luckily, we had already planned to go to Travis's place instead of my loft or Frankie's rental. Even if we hadn't though, he would have insisted upon it, and so would I.

He needed to get her some place that he could control every inch of. Somewhere no one could get close to without him knowing. We drove into the woods; the headlights catching the pine trees like shadowy figures stacked to the starry sky.

Frankie glanced out of the windows, brows pinched together, like she wasn't sure where the hell we were going.

"You'll love it," Travis said, kissing her temple as he gingerly put his arm around her and pulled her against his chest. "I promise."

We turned down the gravel lane, and then it came into view. I watched her out of the corner of my eye as she laid eyes on Travis's life work.

His cabin.

His home.

His masterpiece.

He had worked on it for years, building it piece by piece with me right alongside him. But this was *his* hard work.

It was two stories tall with a wide wrap-around porch and a massive stone chimney along the side, puffing smoke up into the dark night sky. Windows on both floors glinted with warm light from within, and it looked like something out of a Christmas movie set against the snowy hills behind it.

Honestly, it was the perfect family home.

The kind of place that Toby and Emmie deserved to grow up with Frankie inside, warming the wood with her love and nurturing.

When she climbed out of my side of the truck, she paused, waiting for Travis to join us.

"Trav—" Her voice was soft, like she didn't want to disturb the surrounding serenity. "You built this?"

She looked up at him, and I swear something in his eyes shifted, changed even, something deep. Like maybe he could imagine her inside it like I could. "I did." He announced proudly. "Eli and I have worked on it for years."

I stood back when we got inside and watched her take it in. The inside was all smooth lines, warm wood and coziness. The foyer opened into a large living area and open kitchen with butcher block countertops and a farmhouse sink overlooking the wide treelined backyard.

A stone fireplace sat along the edge of the living room, and Travis went over to it and turned it on, letting warmth billow out and hit us.

Frankie walked around the space, dragging her fingertips across the counter and the back of the couch that never got sat on. "You don't live here, do you?" She asked.

"No," Travis leaned back against the wall of smoothed logs, shined up and warm.

"Why?" she asked with a slight scowl.

"Didn't feel finished," he shrugged. "It wasn't done until recently, but even then, it didn't feel right."

"And now?" She whispered as her green eyes caught the firelight.

"Now it's starting to feel like it's the right time."

She looked between us as if she could feel the weight in the air. All the things that still needed to be said hung between us, yet she wasn't making any progress toward saying them.

"Let's start with the most important thing to discuss," I said, dragging my knuckle down her cheek. "Do I need to go get the kids and bring them here? Could they be in danger somehow?"

A haunted, defeated look filled her eyes as she shook her head. "No."

"How do you know?" Travis asked, turning the lights on and urging Frankie to sit down on the couch close to the fire. He took a seat in the chair on the other side of the coffee table, and I covered Frankie with a blanket from the back of the couch before sitting on the arm. I wanted to be close enough to catch her if she bolted, but she needed enough space to open up to us.

"Because the person who did this has never cared about the kids." She brought her knees to her chest and hunkered in on herself. "He wouldn't start now."

Something cold twisted in my gut, "*He?*" I repeated, my voice tighter than I intended it to be. "So, you know who it is. You know that it was in fact intentional."

She flinched, just barely, as the words escaped accidentally. "I didn't say that."

"Enough," Travis growled, leaning forward with a slight grimace. "Just stop, Frankie. For the love of God, just stop. You've been looking over your shoulder all week. Just be honest with us."

She fingered the edge of the blanket, curling it in her fists. "It's not that simple."

"The hell it's not," I barked, and she flinched, making me regret it instantly. I sank to my knees in front of her and held her hands in mine, trying desperately to control myself. "Please, Frankie."

"I have no proof." She cried, widening her eyes as tears misted behind them. "That's his M.O.! He never leaves proof that I can hold on to and use against him!"

"Who?" I asked, lethal grit in my voice.

The tension grew between us as she stared at me before her shoulders sank again. "Danny."

"Danny?" I asked, trying to grasp who she meant.

"The kid's father." Travis growled from the chair, and the hair on the back of my neck stood up.

"Yes." She whispered. "I think he stole my spare keys and broke into my house too."

"Jesus." Trav got out of the chair and came over to the couch, pulling her into his arms as she linked her fingers with mine and pulled me up on her other side.

"I'm sorry." She cried, letting the tears fall over her eyelashes. "I don't know why he's back, and I've been ignoring the signs for so long. But this—" She shuttered, looking up at Travis. "I can't ignore it anymore. You were hurt because of it. You could have died!"

"I'm just glad it was me." Trav said powerfully, pulling her in and resting his forehead against hers. "Because if you had gotten hurt because of him, I would have lost my goddamn mind."

"I don't know how to stop him." She sniffed. "Last time—" She shook her head, letting her eyes close as a memory assaulted her. "It almost killed me."

My blood ran cold as Travis met my stare over her head. "It won't this time." I stated firmly. Assuring her of our commitment. "We're here. We have you."

"It's not that simple," She looked from him to me. "I have the kids to think about."

"We." Travis said firmly with a scowl. "We have your kids to think about. We knew your dynamic when we each made our move on you, Shade. We know you're a package deal, you're not alone anymore."

"Look around you, baby," I said, motioning to the home Travis wouldn't even think of moving into until he had a family. A house big enough for everyone. "Don't fight what's already in motion. Let us take care of you."

"I don't know how," She whispered. "It's been so long."

"Start with this," I leaned in and kissed her, instantly welcoming her whimpers as she deepened it like the adrenaline and stress of the night was trying to seep out of her through our kiss. "Good girl."

It wasn't frantic, or greedy, it wasn't even powerful. It was soft, but needy, filled with silent desire and a connection I couldn't label. Because if I did, I might put a name on it I wasn't ready to scare her away with yet.

I kissed her back, my hand sliding to her jaw. That was when Travis leaned in, his lips brushing over her temple and down to her neck. She gasped, and I smiled as he chuckled, pulling his teeth back far enough to show me the bite he gave her.

"Monster," She moaned, dragging her nails over his scalp and leading his mouth back to the spot where her neck met her shoulder, and he did it again, this time she moaned and rocked forward like she needed something between her thighs.

I met Travis's gaze, and he held mine as he kissed his way up her neck while she nuzzled into mine. "Bite her again," I demanded, and my best friend pulled her jersey to the side and latched down on her shoulder and then sucked on it, leaving a hickey in the center of his teeth marks. "That's so hot."

"You like him branding me?" She teased, pushing her icy hands up under my shirt to my abs.

"I do." I replied, and Travis ran his hands over her hips and ass, hugged tightly in her dark blue jeans.

"Maybe I'll tattoo my name on your ass cheek and then the whole world will know you belong to me," He threatened, shaking the thick flesh with a growl. "Damn, my cock just jumped at the idea."

She purred as I pulled my shirt off over my head so she could nuzzle in against my bare chest, "What about you, Sunshine? Will you tattoo my name on your skin somewhere if I ask really nicely?"

"I don't have any ink," I said and nibbled on her finger when she ran her fingers across my jaw. "But I'm not opposed to the idea of your name being my first."

"Damn," She moaned, and then shifted, throwing her leg over mine and straddling me. "I like that idea. A lot."

26 - FRANKIE
My Anchors

FEAR.

Adrenaline.

Exhaustion.

Burn out.

All of those emotions had rushed through my body earlier, consuming me and threatening to pull me back under, into that black void I sank into after Toby was born. Yet straddling Eli's lap, with Travis's hands tracing every inch of my body from beside me, I couldn't feel anything but need.

It was like my body instantly let go of everything else when they touched me, and all I was left with was a physical cry for more.

I should have been worrying about every single possible

thing that could go wrong, knowing that my past was back to haunt me. But I couldn't.

Not when they were so effectively committing themselves to me.

To my kids.

To make this a real-life fairy tale.

"You don't have to be strong anymore," Eli urged, clued in to how my body and brain were battling each other, even as I rocked in his lap, teasing us both.

"I don't know how not to be."

"Let us show you." Travis said, voice tender, as he stood up and pulled my shirt up over my head until I sat in Eli's lap in just my lace bralette and jeans.

And then Eli's lips were on mine again, deeper, more urgently as Travis's strong hands massaged my shoulders from behind.

"You promised to do something extra special tonight," I whispered, looking at Travis over my shoulder. "But then you got hurt, and my body won't slow down, even though I know you need to rest."

Travis scoffed and lifted me off Eli's lap, cradling me against his big barrel chest as he started walking through the house. "Tonight isn't the night for that, but it's for something deeper. Something more permanent." He vowed, as Eli nodded his agreement as he followed us, "Tonight, we make this real. We make this everlasting. We make this forever."

I swooned at his words, trying to convince my brain to believe them.

"Tonight is the first night of the rest of forever." Eli affirmed, clicking switches as we walked into a dark room, and a soft glow emanated from lamps on two bedside tables on each side of a massive bed. "Tomorrow, we start making changes to how we all live. Tomorrow we become one unit."

God. I was eating every word up like a desperate bitch, needy for their devotion and commitment.

"Prove it."

And then I was surrounded by them.

Their touches.

Their scents.

Their words of devotion and longing.

For the first time in years, I believed it too. In the dark warmth of Travis Hayes's secret home in the woods, I became theirs.

No more doubt.

No more thinking it was too good to be true.

I made love for the first time in my life.

To not just one man, but two best friends.

Two of my best friends.

And I'd never be the same.

I DREAMED OF COFFEE.

And maple syrup.

The warm combination of the two melted into something more sensual as warmth built in my belly as if Travis's hand was still there, against the soft spot below my belly button he seemed to obsess over touching when we slept.

But when I rolled over, the soft morning light filtered in through my lashes, and the sheets were cold where his big warm body had been all night. In pure stubbornness, I refused to open my eyes and accept that my time in the warm, cozy cabin was coming to an end, so I reached back toward the side that Eli had snuggled me from all night. Yet the same cold void met my fingertips, and I growled in discontent, forcing my eyes to open.

It hadn't been a dream, that much was clear until the room came into focus. Travis's room.

It was bare except for the freshly sanded wood and white walls surrounding the bed and end tables. But it was perfect.

And I hated how I could already envision the things I'd do to it if I had any say in decorating it. In turning it from a house into a home.

Trav and Eli insisted that was exactly what was going to happen, but I still felt like it was too far gone to believe. Especially in the morning light without their bodies distracting me.

For a long moment, I just lay there, staring at the slant of sunlight spilling through the wooden shutter blinds on the windows, listening to the low sounds coming from the grand living space beyond the open bedroom door.

Pots clinking, and a soft hum I recognized as Travis's.

It felt—domestic. And that felt dangerous.

I eased my body out of the cold sheets and pulled on my Net Crashers Jersey that had somehow materialized from the living room where I left it last night. As soon as it fell over my skin, however, I realized it was far too big to be mine; the fabric fell to my knees, and the sleeves hung far past my fingertips.

I walked into the bathroom and turned my back to face the big mirror hanging over the sink and smiled to myself when I read the name above the logo.

Hayes.

This man.

Of course, Travis would leave his jersey for me to wear in his dominant, manly way.

I padded barefoot from the bedroom, heading for the smells and sounds that beckoned me like a siren on a shore.

Travis was standing at the stove, shirtless, wearing a pair of low-slung jeans that showed off the delicious muscles of his massive body as he flipped pancakes. The hand towel slung over his shoulder further pushed that vibe of domestication through the air.

His hair was damp from a shower, curling slightly at the ends above the tattoo that ran up the back of his neck.

Damn, my body tightened from simply ogling him in the warm morning sunrise.

"Good morning, Shade," He said without looking back at me. "Coffee's on the counter. Thought you might need it after last night."

I arched a brow. "You mean after you two kept me up all night long with that terribly slow, and boring sex?"

He glared over his shoulder at me and then his lips curved, "Kept you calling out our names and begging for more until three o'clock this morning."

I poured a cup of coffee, trying to hide the way my cheeks heated. "Where's Eli?"

"Getting the kids."

I froze, coffee halfway to my mouth. "He's what?"

Travis glanced at me, plating the last pancake from the built-in griddle taking up half of the massive industrial-size range, his eyes warm and steady. "We figured they'd like to see where their mom was hiding out. And maybe eat a pancake or two with us."

Seconds later, the sound of a truck pulling up the long gravel driveway reached us, and my chest felt too tight to breathe.

"Your pants are on the back of the chair," Travis winked, and nodded to the door. "Go welcome your babies into my home."

I stepped onto the porch, moving on autopilot with my

pants firmly in place, thank God, as Eli came around the side of the porch. Emmie was on his shoulders, and Toby clung to his hand, chatting a million miles an hour about how tall Eli's truck was. The three of them looked like they'd been making that walk up the path every day of their lives, as if it was the most natural thing in the world.

Like just maybe, it was something that could actually be mine.

I couldn't move.

I couldn't breathe.

If I did, I felt like it would all disappear like a mirage in a desert, too damn good to be true.

"Mama!" Toby cheered, jumping up the steps and flinging himself into my arms. "Sunshine says we're having pancakes for breakfast! Grandma was going to make us eat oatmeal again," He grimaced and stuck his tongue out, "Pancakes are so much better!"

I chuckled, kissing his cheek as Eli winked at me, sliding Emmie off his shoulders. "They sure do smell good too," I kissed Emmie's forehead, pushing her hair out of her face. "Let's go in where it's warm."

The kids raced through the front door, cheering about syrup and how awesome Travis's home was. Eli wrapped his hands around my waist and pulled me into his chest as he laid a kiss on my neck. "As good as you look in a Net Crasher's jersey, I'll make sure it's mine next time."

I leaned into him, welcoming his warmth and fresh scent of his aftershave as we watched the kids jump up onto the stools at the counter. "I'll wear your things anytime."

"Mmh," He growled as we walked in the front door. "I think I like it better when you wear nothing at all."

"Fiend." I hissed and then shook off the cold as he closed the door behind us and kicked off his boots.

Joining the kids at the island, Emmie immediately hassled Travis, who had put a shirt on, for the biggest pancake on the platter while Toby tried to negotiate with him for chocolate chips.

And the big, burly man handled them like he had been doing it for years. Eli joined, moving around the kitchen with easy confidence, pouring juice, handing plates to Travis to fill, and even catching Emmie as she almost toppled off her stool in excitement.

Something somewhere in my chest started to take root. Something soft, something warm.

For the first time in a long time, I didn't feel like I was just surviving.

I felt like I was finally *home*.

27 - TRAVIS

Home

COULD the smell of a house change simply because it became inhabited?

The rooms of the house used to smell of cedar and fire, something raw and sturdy around me, yet tonight, it smelled like linen and the pork we ate for dinner. There were bits and pieces of Frankie and the kids sprinkled around the vast home after we made a trip to her house to get the necessities they would need to stay the night and go to school in the morning.

And I couldn't help but finally understand the difference between a house and a home, because of them.

All three of them.

The fireplace threw a low orange glow across the beams

I'd set by hand, reflecting off the polished floorboards and the dark windows.

My house. My cabin. My damn sanctuary I'd spent years building plank by plank when I thought I'd be alone forever, leaving it untouched by the warmth of a family that it had deserved.

Yet now—Frankie was curled up on the couch like she'd always belonged there, the kids sat on pillows on the floor around the coffee table playing a board game, and Eli watched on from the chair next to the couch, a soft smile on his face.

I silently crossed the room and lifted Frankie's shoulders from the cushion, sitting down and pulling her against me as the kids laughed at Eli's impersonation of some reindeer from a movie they knew.

Frankie smiled up at me, and I kissed her forehead before she settled her cheek on my chest to watch them again.

My knuckles still ached from gripping the steering wheel when the brakes gave out in her car last night. My chest burned from the seatbelt bruise I tried to ignore. And my gut simmered with what should have been fear from the whole ordeal, but the truth was, the only thing that rattled me over the whole thing was the look on Frankie's face when she ran to me afterward.

Her pure fear.

Not for me—but of losing me.

That shit hit me harder than the tree did.

I hadn't been able to stop staring at her since. Every laugh she gave the kids. Every cautious glance she threw at me and Eli throughout the day, like she was daring herself not to collapse under the weight of what the hell this was all becoming.

Last night, Eli asked the hard question—if the kids were in

danger. Her answer had chilled the blood in my veins, but she pushed it aside like she always did. Like she thought she had to carry it alone.

We just had to keep showing up for her until she realized we weren't going anywhere. Then she'd finally let us in—all the way.

Into her heart.

THE KIDS WERE PASSED out in one of the rooms upstairs on an air mattress, even though my gut screamed at me for not having proper beds for them.

Yet.

They acted like the whole thing was the best adventure of all though, chatting on about how fun it was to sleep over, and how they wished they could do it every night.

Little did they know, that was exactly what was going to happen. I wasn't spending a night apart from them now that I had them here. It would feel like losing part of myself if I did.

Eli was leaving for his shift at the firehouse, and I was giving him and Frankie some privacy for their goodbye on the porch. If I sat and thought about it long enough, I might start wondering why I didn't get the least bit jealous when Frankie gave her attention to Eli, or why I wasn't threatened when he made her the center of his world.

Maybe it was because we'd been best friends for decades, or maybe it was just because for the first time I genuinely cared for someone else's needs and desires, leading me to not care how she fulfilled them, as long as she included me in the mix.

It was wild, but I was loving it.

Plus, I had her alone all night in my bed while he slept at the fire station. Clearly, I was winning.

My phone buzzed in my pocket, Lenny, the mechanic at the garage we had Frankie's car towed to, was calling me.

"Yeah?" I muttered low, ducking into the privacy of what would one day be my office in case Frankie came back in.

"I got your girl's SUV up on the lift," Lenny said, voice clipped. "This wasn't an accident, Travis. Her brake line was cut clean. It wasn't frayed. It wasn't rusted. It was cut with a blade or pliers. Whoever did it knew what they were doing."

The blood roared in my ears as I forced words out, "You're sure?"

"Dead sure. If she'd been going any faster, or if there'd been another car, well, you can figure out what would have happened."

I swallowed hard, jaw locked tight. "Thanks Len. I'm not telling her yet. I'll handle it with her when she's ready to face it."

"If the kids had been in the car, man—"

"I know." I snapped and then took a deep breath. "We're handling it."

Hanging up, I shoved the phone back into my pocket as my chest felt like it would explode into little shards of broken glass if I didn't find a way to soothe it. To calm the anger.

Frankie had almost died. Because of him—Danny. Because the sick bastard wanted to terrify her.

Without thinking, I stalked through the silent house to the front door and opened it. I found Frankie sitting on the porch steps, staring out at the dark tree line like she could see something I couldn't. Her mug was empty of the tea Eli had made her as he got ready for work, but her fingers clenched tight around the porcelain. She looked breakable, like she was teetering on the edge of something.

Something dark.

"Frankie." I said, low as I sat down on the step next to her.

She didn't look at me, just pulled the blanket tighter. "You okay?" She asked finally, looking over at me. I could only imagine what she saw when she did.

No, I wanted to say. Your stalker cut your brakes. You and the kids aren't safe.

But she was already brittle, already teetering on the edge, and dropping that weight on her tonight would crush her.

So instead, I forced a deep breath into my lungs and slid closer to her. "Not really," I admitted, because the truth had to leak out somewhere. "But I'll be better if you talk to me. Tell me the whole story."

Her breath hitched as she reared back slightly, as if my words physically affected her.

But then her lips parted, and then her words started coming.

"Once—after I had Toby, *I broke*. I couldn't sleep, couldn't eat. Someone—*Danny*—was already circling me, showing up when I was alone, leaving little things behind to tell me he'd been there. I thought I was losing my mind. But that was what he wanted. He wanted me to go insane so he could control me again. And it worked. I ended up—"

Her voice faded, and I slid my hand over the back of her neck, soothing her. "You ended up what?"

"Hospitalized." She whispered. "He had me committed. At the time we were still married."

The word hit me like a punch. Hospitalized. She kept going before she lost her urge.

"And he used it. Later. To try to prove that I was unfit. He threatened to take the kids away if I didn't play nice. If I didn't keep quiet."

Her shoulders curled inward, and I couldn't stand it

another damn second. I cupped her face, turning her toward me, and her green eyes shimmered with unshed tears in the porch light.

But they were fierce and terrified all at the same time.

"Quiet about what?" I whispered.

"The abuse." She admitted with a haunted gleam in her eyes. "The physical, emotional, and—" she shook her head, letting her eyes close as she tore herself open. "The sexual abuse."

My chest felt like it was going to explode again as her tears fell.

"He does not get to break you twice." I growled. "I won't let him. Eli won't let him. You're not alone anymore, Frankie, you hear me?"

Her lips parted, trembling, and I kissed her.

Hard.

Messy.

Desperate.

Like I could press my promise into her bones. She whimpered against me, clutching my shirt, and that sound alone tore me in half.

The blanket slipped from her shoulders as my hands found the heat of her waist, her legs moving until she straddled me right there on the porch. It was raw, frantic, not careful in the slightest, like we both needed to prove she was here for good with our touch.

Her nails dug into the back of my neck as she rocked in my lap, deepening everything with her desperation, and I took it. I took every fucking drop of it until she was begging me to give her more.

And I did.

God, did I fucking give her everything. I always would.

Carrying her inside the home I built, I locked the door behind us and went straight to my bedroom.

Our bedroom.

We weren't talking anymore.

We weren't thinking anymore.

We were burning.

I stripped her out of the jersey she still wore for me, and undid the clasp of her bra as she ripped it off until the warmth of her skin filled my palms while I laid her out in the center of my bed.

She laughed shakily between gasps as I kneeled between her thighs and tore my shirt off over my head, staring down at her.

"Wait." She whispered, running her fingertips down my abs. "Eli."

I groaned, lying down flat against her and her sexy flesh. "Don't tell me I can't have you if he's not here." I growled, kissing the thin skin covering her collarbone and grinding my erection between her thighs that pulled me closer. "I won't if that's what you want. But be prepared for me to pout."

She chuckled softly again and ran her nails over the back of my scalp. "You can have me. But we still have to share with him. So he doesn't feel left out."

"How?" I kissed down her chest, palming both of her lush tits before sucking on one nipple and then the other. Quickly scraping my teeth over the hard nub of her flesh, she moaned and pushed her chest up toward my mouth again. I repeated it, sucking and then biting each of her sensitive nipples until she was humping me from beneath.

"Video." She panted, riding me, rubbing her hot little pussy against my body. "He wants a video of us. Of you fucking me."

"Fuck," I growled, pressing my cock hard into the bed as the idea excited me. "He told you that?"

"Yes," She nodded, biting her bottom lip almost shyly. "When we were on the porch. He said he wanted to watch it while he stroked himself tonight if he couldn't be here with us."

"Damn," I buried my face back in her tits, biting them harder as she bucked under me. "Do you want it of this?" I looked up at her, taking in her lust-filled eyes, "Of me feasting on your perfect tits? You know how obsessed he is with them."

She moaned and chuckled, "A picture of that couldn't hurt."

I grinned, loving the fun, naughty side of her that was coming through the haze of all the turmoil. If I could make her forget for a little while, using my body to distract her, I'd do it.

I pulled my phone out of my pocket and kneeled between her legs again. She instantly crossed her arms under her chest, pushing them together with a dirty look on her face as I snapped half a dozen photos. Some with my hand on her, pinching her nipple and making her gasp, some of her playing with them for Eli, some of her just staring up at the camera, fucking him with her eyes.

"Send them to him." She purred, and I distractedly tried and failed twice to get them off through the cyber ether to her other boyfriend. Finally, I watched the pictures pop up on the screen and turn from sending to sent.

"Done." I said, "You're a goddess." I tossed my phone down next to her and devoured her again. Her legs wrapped around my hips and pulled me up her body until my hips were pinned between hers.

"Mmh," She whispered, rocking against me. "I love how you feel on top of me." She dragged her nails over my shoulders and arms. "The weight and bulk of you against me," She moaned, "Fuck I'm so close already."

"Think I can make you come like this?" I pushed her into the bed harder, and she moaned against my neck, muffled so the kids didn't hear her, though I knew there was no chance with how far away they were. But the sound of her breaking open for me carved its way into my chest like a permanent brand. "Again," I demanded, rocking against her, "Moan for me again, Shade."

Her teeth latched into the cords of my neck as she clung to me, meeting me thrust for thrust until she cried out, coming in my arms like a perfect sex goddess. "Fuck yes," she cried, melting into the bed as my phone pinged on the mattress next to her. With a wicked grin, she picked it up and swiped it open and gasped, biting her bottom lip.

I nuzzled her neck until she pulled the phone away far enough for me to see, and then I chuckled, burying my face back into her neck, kissing and sucking. "Ew."

She giggled and shrugged her shoulder. "I think that's hot as fuck."

I glanced back at the picture of Eli's hard dick, hand wrapped tight around the base in what looked like a bathroom stall. Below it was a message from him.

ELI

Now give me a video of her taking you deep,
so I can come before I get a call.

I growled, reaching between us to slide my hand under her tight leggings. "Now this I can do."

She giggled again and then moaned when I sat up and pulled her leggings and panties down and chucked them across the room. Pushing my jeans down and off, I picked my phone back up and stared down at her sinful body.

"God, you're perfect." I praised as I started a video from my POV. She ran her hands through her hair, fanned out on my pillow as I laid my hand flat on the soft flesh of her lower belly, the same flesh that held her babies, growing and nurturing them with her perfect body. Slowly, I slid my thumb down to her wet pussy, rubbing the pad of it over her hooded clit, before pushing it down through her wet lips, thriving on the wet noise it made when I pushed my thumb into her and pulled it out. Her arousal and the wetness of her orgasm coated my skin, and I held it up for Eli to see through the camera screen. "She's already come once, Eli," I said out into the room and rubbed my wet thumb over her clit, making her gasp and spread her legs wider as she arched into it. "How long do you think it will take until she comes all over my cock?"

"Fuck me already," she purred, "So we can find out."

I fisted my hard cock and slapped the head against her exposed clit, making her moan before I dipped it down into her dripping wetness and then notched it against her opening. "Pull your legs back, Shade. Show Eli right where my cock is going to go. Show him how I fill you up."

She wrapped her hands around the backs of her knees and pulled her legs back wide, making sure to shimmy until her lush tits were perfectly on display between her thighs. "Like this?" She bit her bottom lip and shimmied again, so her flesh jiggled enticingly.

"Fuck yes," I growled, lining my cock up and pushing the head into her until her lips parted in response. "Just like that. Take my cock like a good girl."

"Damn," She moaned, laying her head back onto the pillow as she pinched one of her nipples while I fed her more of my cock and pulled out, to do it again. "You're so thick like this. You're stretching me open, giving me no choice but to take it. I fucking love that."

"That's it, baby, you're doing so good. You're absolute perfection." I pushed in until my balls pressed against her ass cheeks, and we both moaned. Using my thumb, I circled her clit as I slowly pulled all the way out, her arousal dripping from her wet hole in the absence of my cock, and I stroked my finger into her, coating it and playing with her. "What do you think, Eli?" I asked out loud. "Tomorrow night I think we should take turns pushing into this tight little pussy. I'll give her a few thrusts, stretching her out, and then you can push in deep, until you knock the bottom out of her."

"Yes," She moaned, and then she brought her dainty black-painted fingertips to her clit and slapped it as I pushed my cock back in hard. "Just like that." She begged, fighting the urge to scream as I fucked her hard. Her tits jiggled with each thrust as she rubbed and slapped her clit until she started coming. Leaning forward, I covered her mouth with my hand as she lost her hold on her ecstasy and screamed into my palm, biting the flesh as she came on my cock.

"Good girl," I praised, keeping the camera on her face as she pushed through the aftershocks, finally opening her eyes and staring up at the screen.

"I want that." She whispered as her eyelids fluttered, "I want to feel you both, just like that."

"You'll have it." I assured her, sitting back up on my heels to show Eli where her hungry pussy was still clenching around my cock. "Now be a good girl and play with yourself again for Eli to see while I fuck you. Come for us again."

She moaned and brought her fingers back to her clit and did exactly as I said, putting on a show for the missing piece of our triad to enjoy.

And I fucked her hard through four more orgasms for him

to see before I finally tossed my phone away and fucked her just for me.

I made sure that she knew it wasn't just sex for me; it was a vow. Each thrust was a promise that she was safe, that I wasn't letting go. Her nails dug into my shoulders, her moans muffled by my skin as she lost control because of me.

When it was over, she lay curled against me, sweat cooling on our skin, her breath uneven. And I held her tighter, because I knew it wasn't just lust anymore.

It was something far deeper.

28 - ELI
Expectation v Reality

THE DINER SMELLED like butter and coffee; the low hum of conversation filled the space around us as we walked in. Frankie sat across from me in the booth, her chin resting in her hand, pretending to be unimpressed as I stole a drink off her milkshake for the third time.

But I knew the truth.

She was loving every second of our alone time.

It didn't happen often, and that was okay, but when we could make it happen, it felt extra special.

It was the luxury I had of being off during the week, so I could steal Frankie away for a little lunch date in between her crazy schedule.

"Tell me something I don't know about you," she said, her green eyes sharp like she was testing me. Maybe expecting something bad in response.

I leaned back, smirking, "What do you want? Embarrassing stories about me puking on my first date? Or the fact that my mom still sends me holiday pajamas?"

She rolled her eyes, but I caught the smile tugging at her lips. "Fine, your real life. Before I met you as an adult. I know the firehouse stories, and the hockey stories, but what about *you*? What about your childhood?"

"You're going to hate me for saying it, but I had an amazing childhood, and still talk to my parents a couple times a week. My mom was a stay-at-home mom when I was growing up, and our house always smelled like cinnamon rolls and warmth. She baked every morning during school, making something hearty and filling for me and my sister. My dad worked in finance, crunching numbers for big companies and making it home for dinner every single night. He never missed a game either."

She blinked, "That's disgustingly wholesome."

"See," I laughed, scratching the back of my neck, "I told you that you'd hate it. My parents moved south a few years ago. They're obsessed with their life in Arizona, and I can't blame them. They swear its paradise for retirees. They come back up here a few times a year, but when they do, my Mom still insists on cooking for me, and Dad still tries to out skate me."

She shook her head, "So you really did grow up with the perfect family."

"Pretty close." I leaned forward, brushing my hand over hers on the table. "And that's why I knew I wanted this. With you. With Trav. With the kids. It's not just about finding a partner, it's about building a home. The kind I grew up in, only—louder."

She snorted, squeezing my hand. "We've got the louder part down." Leaning back on her side of the booth, she took a deep breath. "My childhood wasn't like that at all."

"What was it like?"

"It was—" she looked down at the table and tilted her head a little as if she was lost in a memory. "Sad." Taking a deep breath, she blinked it away and looked back up at me. "My dad left when I was little, and my mom was on her own. Which, to her credit, she rocked at. She taught me at a very young age that a woman didn't need a man to survive. She could do it on her own."

"But," I pressed gently.

"But she wasn't happy. She never had true support from anyone, and I saw that. So when I was a teenager, I started looking for it. I didn't realize it at the time, obviously, or I would have picked a better," she paused, "I would have picked better."

"You were a kid." I reassured her, "And you didn't know his true colors until it was too late, Frankie. That's not your fault." When Travis told me what Danny had done to Frankie in the past, it all made so much more sense to me.

The hidden truths, her inability to trust, and the obsessive need to take care of everything, all on her own.

"Maybe not," She hummed, leaning forward on her elbows and looking me right in the eye, "But I'm doing it better this time around."

I grinned, leaning toward her, "Is that so?"

"I think so." Her green eyes tracked their way from my eyes to my lips and back. "I feel like I've hit the jackpot. Even if a big part of me feels like I don't deserve it."

"Then I guess I'm going to make sure that you understand just how much you do deserve it. From now on. Travis and I both will."

"I'm happy to let you." She smiled and then leaned in to kiss me.

It was one of the first times she had initiated any affection in public outside of the rink. But I was here for it.

Leaning my head to the side, I slid my hand around the back of her head, deepening the kiss until she melted into me.

"Eli," She whispered, pulling back just enough. "Think we can get our meal to go?"

I growled, leaning back in my seat, catching the hunger in her eyes. Without another thought, I raised my hand, flagging our waitress down, "Can we get our food to go, please?"

"Sure thing, sugar." The old lady said with a wink, "It's just coming up now."

As she walked away, I watched Frankie shift in her seat, eyes blazing and a soft blush on her cheeks.

"What are you thinking, Black Cat?" I asked, watching her.

"I'm wondering if you can drive safely if I give you road head on the way to the cabin."

"Jesus," I groaned, running my hand down my face. "Yes. Yes, I can."

"Good," She stood up slowly from the booth, running her hands down her thick thighs as she stopped at the end of my booth and leaned over me. "Because I plan to let you have me however you want me until Trav gets home from work. Then it's his turn. And we both know I love watching you both lose control around me."

"Fuck, baby." I hissed, standing up and pushing her back as our waitress brought our containers over. I threw down more than enough money to cover it and took them from her with a smirk. "Let's get home."

Frankie chuckled as she all but ran out of the diner with me hot on her trail and the waitress cackled behind us.

"Young love is so damn cute."

29 - DANNY
The Monster Returns

EVERY GODDAMN TIME I tried to follow her out into those hills, I fucking lost her. The road twisted like a snake, and she slipped through my fingers, vanishing into the trees with those two bastards without fail.

Every single time.

I couldn't see where they took her, but I knew she was close.

I couldn't find the house she was hiding in.

But I would.

I was good at that—at finding Frankie Blake when she tried to hide from me.

She thought she was safe, playing house with both of those Neanderthals like the perfect little slutty housewife taking both of their dicks every night as if it was normal and sane.

Bullshit.

Frankie thought she could disappear with them, and I'd stop looking. Stupid. She was mine. She had always been mine.

I remembered the sound of her voice the night I took her virginity years ago. She was sixteen, and I had pushed drink after drink into her hand at that party, loosening her up after she dragged me along for weeks, keeping those pretty little thighs closed tight like a little tease.

But not that night.

No, that night she had fallen onto her back and spread her legs for me like the perfect little slut I wanted her to be.

She was perfect that night too. God, she felt so good wrapped around my dick each time.

It was the start of my obsession with her. One I never grew out of, like I thought I would. So, I made sure she never left me, not like her mom wanted her to do when she graduated high school. Not like her friends begged her to when they realized she was cutting them off for me.

Instead, I convinced her to leave with me. To run away somewhere far away so that no one could try to rip us apart.

Somewhere we could be happy and alone together.

We made it a few years before she started threatening to leave. Before she started telling me everyone had been right about me the whole time.

Before she started fighting me off her when I tried to fuck her after she picked a fight.

Damn, but those nights were almost better than the nights that she came to me willingly.

The sound of her voice when she cursed and spat her

venom at me. And then the way her voice would break when she fought against me.

She was so beautiful like that—weak, desperate, trembling under my hands as I fucked her. She never understood that I was her only lifeline, everyone else abandoned her when she left. I fed her. Clothed her. Paid for everything she had until she had nothing but me.

And all I wanted in return was her body. Her loyalty.

Until she fought me so frequently that I only started wanting her when she screamed *no* while I fucked her.

She was so good at it too. She'd cry. She'd fight. She'd scream like a brat, like saying no would ever mean a damn thing when she was mine.

When she *belonged* to me.

Stupidly, she got pregnant. Again. I hated it when she was pregnant. She stopped fighting me when she was growing an alien inside of her. Instead, she just lay there and let me do whatever I wanted to.

Even though she still felt good as sin wrapped around my cock, I needed the fight back from her. That was what I craved.

So, I went elsewhere for it, and she didn't even care. I fucked whoever I wanted while she stayed at home, sucking me dry of money and patience, raising the girl while she grew the boy like it protected her somehow.

It wasn't like she had anyone; I kept her so locked down for years, she didn't have anyone in her life to turn to. No one to tell. She didn't have friends or family; she didn't even have freedom. She had only me.

I should have seen her submission for what it was, though. She was buying time to run.

To flee from me like a fucking coward. She checked out of the hospital early after having her son and ran.

Bitch.

I knew where she had gone, of course. The only place she'd go was back to Cedar Bluff. So I followed.

And instead of dragging her back by her hair, kicking and screaming as was my right, I fucked with her. And holy fucking shit, it was hot.

Her fear got my dick harder than her anger ever did. Harder than her slutty willingness ever did.

No, fucking with her mind was my favorite.

And I did it so well she broke like a porcelain dish falling off a shelf.

Suddenly, she was in a million pieces on the ground, and then I didn't even have her fear. They doped her up with so many meds; she was numb to everything. I hated that version of her. So, I left. I had to work after all to make money to keep my toy on the hook.

I waited, watching from afar as she regulated and got comfortable in her life back in Cedar Falls again. Until she stopped her meds. Until she started going out again.

And then I started messing with her again.

Unfortunately, she decided to start being a whore for the hockey team around the same time, messing up my plans.

But I wasn't going to leave empty-handed this time. I'd waited long enough. I perfected my plan for a reason.

So that when I finally made my move, she'd be my perfect little toy to control again.

God, she was going to cry so prettily the first time I fucked her again.

And it was time for me to make my move. Because those kids—my kids, no matter what lies she told them about me, were my way to get her back. I'd used them before without her noticing.

This time, all it was going to take was one phone call, one

whisper to the right people, and suddenly the world would see her for what she was.

An unfit whore in a mental health crisis.

Unstable.

Unsafe.

She cracked once, had her little mental breakdown when she almost killed herself, and I made sure it was on the record. This time, the courts would believe me with zero effort.

This time she wouldn't escape.

She thought she could play house with those two douchebags and keep her body away from me; she was wrong.

She'd have no choice but to come crawling back to me.

I'd find her. I'd break her. And then I'd remind her what it meant to be mine.

She could fight. She could scream. She would cry.

But regardless, she would break.

Again.

30 - FRANKIE
Meet the Parents

WHAT A HIGH. Life was starting to really feel like a sunny, bright, optimistic daydream, instead of the dark and ominous heavy cloud it had felt like for years. I wasn't stupid enough to doubt that the shift had something to do with Travis and Elliot coming into our lives.

Even though I was a million percent against attributing anything good happening in my life to a man, out of spite from my past, I couldn't deny it though.

Trav and Eli were just too damn—perfect to deny.

Last week we officially moved in with Travis. We packed up a few boxes of things from my rental and stopped off at the furniture store and bought new beds for the kids to match their new rooms. I moved on autopilot, with tears in my eyes, threatening to fall and ruin my eyeliner, as I struggled to keep myself composed.

One look from either of my kids, their happy-go-lucky smiles and excited squeals of delight as we decorated their bedrooms, silenced all of my spite.

Erased all of my doubts about Travis and Eli.

Watching Eli carry boxes of his own into the house, a sheepish look on his face as he hung clothes up in the massive closet in the primary bedroom, that did something else to me too.

Somehow, Travis had perfected a home for all of us, without even knowing we were the ones he would share it with. But now that we were, it was hard to ignore how perfect it was for all of us.

But my anxiety was high as I blew my bangs back from my face, trying not to mess up my subtle and soft makeup look as I mixed yet another pie dough together.

The first one I made ripped, and the apple pie filling exploded out of it in the oven. Which just would not do, given that Travis's parents were coming over for dinner, to meet me and the kids, and it *had* to be perfect.

"Mmh," Eli hummed, leaning over the pie explosion, "This looks delicious."

I huffed with a snort, "It looks like a volcano."

"I bet it tastes delicious." He pushed, and I cracked a smile, already tracking his motive even as his warm hands danced over my hips as he pressed his body against mine, leaning as far as possible to get near the pie-splosion cooling on the windowsill.

I tried desperately to ignore how I was wearing a thin cotton bathrobe under my apron, desperate not to mess my outfit up while baking before Mr. and Mrs. Hayes arrived.

It meant there wasn't much fabric between his warm

hands and my flushed skin. But I had other things on my plate to handle, and I couldn't give in to my body's need for a quickie to settle my nerves.

Besides, even though I knew Eli was teasing me with his touch, he was really after something else entirely.

He was hungry.

He was *always* hungry.

"Go for it." I shrugged.

He rubbed his hands together like a fool and then took a large forkful of the concoction and ate it without hardly chewing it.

"Hey!" A shrill cry echoed from the loft railing overlooking the living space where the kids' rooms were. "Mom said no snacks!" Emmie cried with outrage.

"If you hurry, I'll save you a bite." Eli tossed over his shoulder as he took another large forkful. Her little feet echoed across the hardwood floor as she flew down the stairs. My little girl could out eat any of the boys in the house, and she sure tried to most days. "God," Eli groaned, "This is nearly as good as your pu—"

"I'm here!" Emmie cried, silencing the indecent thing Eli was about to say, and I shook my head with a chuckle. "Gimmie, gimmie, gimmie!" She pushed a step stool over and dug a fork into the pie.

"Careful, darling." Elliot composed himself in time to hold her long brown curls back before they fell into the sticky apple filling. "Can't mess up the hair your mama spent so much time on."

"Mmh," Emmie groaned with a satisfied little smirk on her chipmunk-filled cheeks as she looked at me. "Your pies are my favorite. But don't tell Grammie."

Eli laughed and leaned on the counter with the fork in his

hands, "Your pies are my favorite too." He winked at me over Emmie's head. "Cream pies, to be exact."

I pushed so hard on the dough with the roller it almost broke again, and I glared at him.

"Cream pies?" Toby's innocent little voice popped up out of where and I jumped, "Like chocolate cream?"

"Exactly like that." Travis droned on with a pointed glare Eli's way as he followed my youngest in from the backyard. They both wore flannel shirts and jeans, covered in mud and dirt.

"You're both a wreck." I deadpanned, glancing at the clock on the stove. "Your parents are going to be here in twenty minutes. What on earth were you doing out there?"

"Splitting logs!" Toby piped up excitedly, "With axes."

My hands froze, and I turned to Travis, "You gave my four-year-old an axe?"

Travis glared at me defiantly as Eli chuckled and lifted a complaining Emmie from the stool, scooping one last fork of apple into her mouth.

"Go wash the apple off your face while Mama yells at Trav." Eli joked, and Emmie grinned, grabbing Toby's hand and pulling him from the kitchen.

"C'mon Tobe, let's get dressed. There are some things we shouldn't see." She said.

Travis held my stare with a powerful intensity that always tried to make my knees weak and my back cave under the pressure of it. Most of the time it did, but the idea of Toby swinging an axe—my Toby, the boy who racked up ER visits like reward points at the coffee shop—left me riddled with anxiety and pent-up frustrations from the whole pressure filled day.

"Answer me." I glared at him with one eyebrow raised.

"What good could come from giving him a weapon! He's a baby! With a perpetual addiction to jackass-ery."

Travis unbuttoned his flannel slowly and methodically before taking it off and tossing it over the bar top chair at the island. I clenched my jaw the second his massive, manly chest was on display for me because I could not let my traitorous body distract me from the conversation at hand.

He gave Toby an axe, for fuck's sake!

"He's a boy." Travis growled back in that smooth way that didn't push me down with his dominance, but caressed me with it like it was trying to take something off my hands. "He's a boy who needs to learn boy things."

"He's—" I opened my mouth, and Travis tilted his head to the side, watching me as he stalked to the sink and washed the mud and dirt off his hands. "It's dangerous."

He dried his hands off with a towel and turned to face me again, "I was with him the whole time."

"Travis." I sighed.

"Do you not trust me to take care of him? To keep him safe?" He asked, and the vulnerability was clear as day in his gruff voice. "If you don't, then what's the point?"

Shit.

"I do!" I argued, getting worked up even more as shame burned on my cheeks for even making him think I doubted him. Fuck. "I don't trust him," I hissed in a whisper. "You know how he can be."

"He's a little boy, babe." Eli offered, standing in solidarity next to Travis against the counter with his arms crossed. "You have to let him risk stuff from time to time. And you have to trust us to keep him safe."

My shoulders deflated, and tears burned behind my eyes. I hated knowing they were disappointed in me and my reaction to the situation. I hated that I made Travis doubt how I felt about his place in the kids' lives.

I turned and lifted the pie dough into the pan, waiting for my replacement pie. "Never mind. I'm sorry." Words I perfected in another life, bubbled out before I could stop them.

I felt like my skin was going to rip from my flesh with each second that they stared at me, scrutinizing and analyzing me as I once again let my own bullshit past cloud my present.

My nose prickled with the tears I refused to let fall as I started scooping filling into the pie, and then I felt Travis move.

I didn't have to turn around to see him; he didn't make a sound for as big as he was, but I felt him coming to me.

I felt Travis's energy engulf me as he came up behind me, the warmth of his skin breaking through the thin fabric of my bathrobe seconds before his scent surrounded me.

Masculinity shouldn't smell so fucking good, but from Travis it did.

I could taste his testosterone, and my body heated, softening and causing my needy and traitorous inner feminine urges to react to his proximity. My thighs clenched, and I barely stifled a moan when my bare thighs rubbed together against my bare pussy under the robe. He hadn't even touched me, yet my body was getting wet, preparing itself to let him in.

It felt like the three of us had been together for lifetimes, wordlessly learning each other in the mere weeks that we'd blurred lines.

"Don't," I whispered, closing my eyes as my hands shook, holding the spoonful of filling over the pie like I was too scared to move. Too scared to breathe. Because if I did, then I'd fold and beg for him to reset my frazzled brain and needy body. The way they could make my entire world stop spinning out of control, with just their touch—it was scary.

"Don't what?" he murmured as he dipped his face to the soft skin of my neck and let his breath warm the skin and cause goose bumps in its wake. "Don't take care of you?"

I whimpered almost silently as my body melted from just the mere mention of him tempting me with relief. The heat of his naked chest burned my back when I leaned into him, tilting my head to expose my neck to his lips.

Vulnerable.

Offering myself to him.

Desperate for what he could give me if I just let him.

"You've been a ball of nerves since I told you my parents were coming over for dinner." He spoke against my neck, and his beard teased my skin, but he didn't actually give me what I wanted.

I wanted his touch.

His lips.

His kiss.

His bite.

His power.

I wanted to submit to it.

I needed to get out of my head.

"Trav," I moaned, and then his fingertips were on the front of my thigh, right above my knee. My eyes closed, and I froze as they silently rose to the spot between my thighs that dripped for him. "The kids."

"Shhh," He whispered as his rough fingers pushed through my pussy lips and instantly pressed against my clit. The wet lubrication paired with the rough calluses of his fingertips made my knees weak. "I'll take care of you." His lips finally touched the skin of my neck as he rolled my clit. "I'll always take care of you."

"Please," I arched my hips, widening my feet so he had more room.

I was a shameful slut for both of my men, and I didn't even care. I was too raw and on edge, desperate for release. Desperate to calm my fears and anxiety about meeting Travis's parents for the first time.

"Give me these." Eli spoke from my side, and my eyes flew open in shock as he took the bowl of filling and spoon from my hands, setting them down on the counter as his dark eyes dropped to the top of my robe that was straining against my free breasts thanks to my arched position against Travis. "Show me my favorite toys, and then go let Trav loosen you up."

I moaned, melting further into Trav's big chest as he undid the waist ties of my half apron, letting it fall to the floor.

My ears were frantically searching for any noise of the kid's arrival from upstairs, but they were singing some ridiculous pop song in the upstairs bathroom with the water running.

I had too many things to do before our dinner party in an hour, but I desperately wanted to let them take the edge off.

Eli's fingers parted the edges of my robe, effortlessly revealing my heavy breasts to his hungry eyes, and I watched entranced as he swallowed and licked his lips, like he could barely refrain from leaning in and taking a bite. "Good girl." He ran his thumbs over my hard nipples, and I whimpered again, biting my bottom lip as the two men turned me into an indecent puddle in the middle of the kitchen with just a few words and a dozen stolen touches.

Eli's dirty grin morphed into something needier as he bent and sucked on one of my nipples, biting it as he pinched the other one. I gasped, and Travis covered my mouth with his free hand while his other hand pinched my clit harder, working me in tandem with his best friend.

"Do me a favor, Love." Eli murmured, kissing his way up my chest and to my neck, before hovering right above my lips. "When you're done coming for Trav, skip the panties you have laid out to wear under that sweet little dress you're wearing tonight."

"Eli," I moaned in shock, and Travis pushed one thick finger up into my pussy, rendering me speechless as Eli kissed me, pushing his tongue into my mouth aggressively as Travis held my jaw still with his hand against my neck.

Eli's fingers kept playing with my nipples, as his tongue fucked my mouth like his cock had done last night in our shower as I fell to my knees for him after the kids went to bed.

Travis worked his finger inside of me, curling and pushing against the secret spot that no one had found before these men proved they were the best I ever had.

Eli pulled back, and Travis rocked his hard-on against my ass as he slowed the thrusting of his finger down until he simply held it inside of me, as if he was claiming that spot as his.

"I want to know that Travis's come is coating your bare pussy lips all night long, while you sit mere feet away from his parents and the kids, knowing it's only a matter of time before you find yourself bent over with my cock so deep inside of you that you can't breathe." Eli's words felt like a threat, and the darkness in them made me gush around Travis's finger, turned on by the blunt words of my usually sweet and tender lover. "Because as soon as the world goes dark around us, and the people in our life leave us alone, you're mine. And I'm going to make you cry with pleasure like never before. Tonight, you're going to feel our brand on your body until the shortcomings of your past lovers have no space left in your mind, or your heart."

"Fuck," I whispered, "Yes. God yes, please!"

"Go take Trav's cock like a good girl and tonight when I catch you alone in the hallway or in the pantry or somewhere else and I push my fingers under your skirt, make sure you spread your thighs so I can feel his come coating your pussy lips. Don't tell me no, or double-guess if it's safe to let me feel, just give in to what I want and do it. Understand, Black Cat?"

"Yes, Sir." I moaned and spread my thighs further as his fingers joined Travis's under my bathrobe and I bit my lip to stop from screaming in ecstasy as Eli pushed a finger in beside his best friends, and then they both thrust a few times, giving me a taste of both of them.

The water upstairs turned off, and Toby called out from the bathroom, "Mama! I need help with the soap! I got mud in my ears!"

"Go," Eli commanded, pulling his finger free and licking it inches in front of my face as Travis pulled me away toward the privacy of our bedroom, hidden from sight in case the kids came to the loft railing. I watched as Eli's gaze left my exposed tits and stared at his friend over my shoulder, "Fuck her good for me."

"Always," Travis growled, "Thanks for helping warm her up."

Fucking hell, there was no way I was going to survive the whole night with these two men, tempting fate and pushing me on sexually the way they were.

But then again, I wasn't sure I would survive if they didn't distract me with pleasure and temptation like they were either.

"Don't make a sound," Trav growled in my ear as we got to our bedroom, and he pushed me up against the door as he closed and locked it behind us. I laid my forehead and my palms against the door as he undid the sash around my waist and pulled my robe off, tossing it onto the floor in a pile, leaving me naked against the cool, smooth wood. "You're going to come on my face, and then my cock." He declared as if he were so sure nothing would stop him from making that statement true, "And then you're going to tell me why meeting my parents has you so twisted up."

"Trav." I whispered, arching my back and leaning up on my tippy toes as he spread my ass cheeks, dipping his fingers in against the wetness of my pussy from behind.

"Not a sound, Shade." He demanded, and then he bit my shoulder, hard enough to leave a mark, but I swallowed the scream as my pussy dripped on his fingers at the same time. "Good girl," he kissed his way down the slope of my spine, and I panted when he laid kisses on the small of my back before pushing my cheeks wide again. His teeth latched onto my ass cheeks over and over again as he pushed one, two and then three fingers into my soaked pussy from behind. I was dizzy with need and arousal, desperate to scream, but more desperate to orgasm, and I knew he'd hold back if I broke his rules.

I pushed back onto his face the moment his wet tongue found my pussy and bit my lips so hard to stay silent as he dragged it up to my ass and rimmed it as he pushed his fingers in and out of my pussy.

"Good girl," he praised again, "I can feel how close you are. How desperately you want to come for me. For Eli. Just how he told you."

"Please," I whispered, digging my nails into the wood when he pushed his tongue into my ass. "I'm going to—" I froze as my orgasm broke over me like a tidal wave. I cried out silently as my skin burned and my pussy tightened around his fingers, desperate for something deeper.

Something harder.

"More." I demanded in a harsh whisper, looking over my shoulder as he stared up at me from his knees. "Cock. Now."

He growled and stood up, lifting me off my feet and throwing me down onto the bed and mounting me from behind as he spanked my ass. The sharp sound of it echoed off the walls around us, but I couldn't care as he pushed his jeans down and was buried deep inside of me in seconds flat. The bite of his belt buckle pressing into the back of my thighs with each thrust just added to the high of it all.

I gripped a pillow that smelled like Eli and bit it as Travis changed angles and straddled my ass, fucking me harder, inching me up the bed with each thrust. And it was exactly what I needed.

Exactly what I craved and relied on him for. What I needed him for.

"I want you to milk my cock," He stated, wrapping his hand around the front of my neck and arching my back so my head was bent back staring up at the ceiling. "I want to feel your pussy draining me, taking every drop of my come deep into your body. I want to feel your tight little cunt flutter and spasm around my cock as I give you what you need."

"Please, yes!" I cried out, hoarse around the pressure of his hand on my neck and then his fingers were under my hips, and circling my clit as he fucked me, pushing me headfirst into an orgasm bigger than the air in the room.

My eyes rolled.

My heart stopped.

And my pussy tightened down on his thick cock, just how he wanted, and I came all over him. The only noise in the room was the wet noise my pussy made with each thrust and I should have been embarrassed, but I couldn't care less as he once again, found that spot on my shoulder that called to him and he bit me, to smother his own growl of pleasure as his cock erupted inside of me.

I stayed still, reveling in the feel of his come filling me up with each jerk of his cock until his hips stopped thrusting. The aftershocks of my orgasm kept tightening down around him, and he whispered in my ear with each one.

"Good girl."

"That's it."

"Again."

"So perfect."

"So fucking perfect."

And for the first time, I actually believed them.

31 - FRANKIE
Found Family

MRS. HAYES WAS GOING to know her son's come was coating my nether bits, free of even a decent pair of panties to keep the mess contained, I just freaking knew it.

Travis's parents pulled in the driveway a moment ago, and I ran my hands over the hand towel again, anxiously turning to make sure the entire house was in perfect condition for their arrival.

I was a ball of nerves, even with the multiple orgasms Travis gave me an hour ago, I was a wreck. But as I took a deep breath, forcing my shoulders to drop from my ears and my mask of calm, cool and collected fell into place.

"Don't worry, Mama," Toby tugged at my hand and gave me a sheepish grin as we headed toward the front door as a family. "I'll tell them I can burp the alphabet. That'll impress them."

My shocked gasp was swallowed up by Travis's deep laugh as he came into the living room from the kitchen. "Honestly, kiddo, that might seal the deal with them."

And then the knock came.

I had imagined a million different scenarios every time I thought about the moment, I would meet Trav or Eli's parents, and part of me imagined stern faces, disapproving stares, judgment even over the children clinging to my legs, shyly watching Hal and Maggie Hayes enter our new home.

But what I got instead was two of the kindest smiles I'd ever seen before. Travis's dad, Hal, wrapped his son in a back-slapping hug, a man worthy of the feat considering he was a massive as my lover was, and his mom, Maggie, pulled him in like he was still a boy who needed a licked thumb wiped across his cheek to clean him up.

And my heart melted just a tiny bit more, letting the soft gooey stuff in the center get even closer to sliding out and over the edge of my ice walls.

Maggie somehow balanced two casserole dishes like she worked at a fifties carhop diner on skates. And Hal followed behind her with a six-pack of root beer tucked under one arm and a vase of the most beautiful flowers I'd ever seen.

Eli helped Maggie set her dishes down and then grinned as she fussed over him like he was still sixteen and crushing on the older, Mrs. Hayes. Travis's shoulders eased as Hal squeezed Eli's shoulder on his way to the counter to set his own loot down.

Trav's parents didn't just welcome Trav and Eli equally, they were loved and claimed without hesitation.

"Well now," Maggie said with a grin that immediately made my nose prickle with stupid emotions, "You must be

Frankie. I've heard so many incredible things about you from both my boys. It's such a pleasure to meet you." She pulled me into an affectionate hug that felt like one my own mother gave me on hard days, and I struggled not to melt into it.

"It's so nice to meet you." I managed as she pulled back with an affectionate brush of her fingers against my cheek, before she turned to the two shadows hiding behind my legs. "And these little sugarplums must be the grandbabies I've been learning so much about."

Emmie gasped and looked up at me with wide eyes. "Grandbabies?" She stumbled over her words in shock. "Mama! They think we're theirs."

Before I could figure out some sort of explanation to fit my kids' maturity, Maggie crouched down, tucking her long flowing western skirt between her knees so she was on Emmie's level, eyes twinkling. "Honey, anyone who belongs to Trav and Eli, belongs to us too. You're our family now, as long as that's okay with you."

Emmie, wide-eyed, leaned in closer to Trav's mom and whispered, "Do grandmas always bring casseroles? Because my grandma can't cook to save her life."

Hal snorted, and Eli grinned from behind Maggie, cutting in to defend my mom's honor, "Hey, Mrs. Blake might not be able to cook, but that woman makes the best baked goods." He rubbed his belly for dramatic effect.

Maggie booped Emmie's nose with a wink, "Sounds like your other grandma and me will be the perfect match made in Granny-land then! I'll do the cooking, and she can bake because I can't make a pie to save my life!"

"Neither can my mom!" Emmie cheered excitedly! "Eli and I ate half of her first experiment earlier!"

"Oh, my lord," I groaned, and Maggie rose to her feet with a good-hearted chuckle.

Toby, not one to be outdone, puffed his chest out and stepped out around me, "I can burp the alphabet, want to hear it?"

"God help us," I whispered under my breath.

But Hal threw his head back and laughed, a sound so warm and genuine it filled the whole cabin, "Boy, if you can do that, I'd be mighty impressed. But maybe after dinner?"

My boy was so happy to have found his part in the conversation that the kids ran off into the living room to sit at the coffee table, where their extreme game of Go-Fish had been paused before as the adults moved into the kitchen.

"These are for you," Maggie said, sliding the vase into the center of the island, fluffing the bow. "Eli said you were a sucker for sunflowers."

I glanced over at Mr. Sunshine himself with his schoolboy smile and gave him a thankful grin back. "I am, thank you so much."

Trav moved behind me, rubbing his hand across my back as he put the root beer in the fridge while Maggie started laying out the side dishes, she insisted on bringing to dinner, and I took a deep breath, letting their easy comfort ease my fears.

How had I been so scared just a few minutes ago of these lovely people?

We all gathered around the long wooden table Travis had built with Eli last year, and I could feel the pride shining through his eyes as he took his seat at the head of it, watching us all share a meal around his hard work.

Maggie kept slipping extra helpings onto Toby's plate, telling him he was a "growing boy who'd out skate them all someday," while Hal teased Travis about the changes that a "woman's touch" had on the home he built.

Somewhere between the laughter, the buttered rolls, and

Emmie climbing into Maggie's lap to whisper secrets, I realized my kids weren't just comfortable. They were thriving.

We all were.

Toby leaned over into Hal's bubble, looking up at him with complete trust. "Are you going to teach me to fish like Travis said? He swears you're the best there is in the whole world."

Hal ruffled his hair, "You better believe it, buddy. As soon as the ice melts, we'll all head out."

Toby whooped loudly in excitement, but as I looked at Hal sitting across from me at the table, the emotions on his face were shining so brightly, it threatened to make the ooey gooey stuff in my chest even worse.

Pride.

Excitement.

Love.

"Can I call you Grandma too?" Emmie asked Maggie, cheeks pink with excitement. "Just sometimes, if you don't want it all the time. My Grandma Blake says I say her name too much sometimes."

My throat closed as Maggie chuckled, hugging Emmie tighter. "You're Grandma is a saint for having you both all to herself for the last few years without reinforcements!" Maggie said and then winked at me over my daughter's shoulder, "But we're here now to help. And you can call us whatever your little hearts desire."

My kids had never known this kind of unconditional acceptance from people that weren't related to them by blood.

Hell, even the other half of their bloodline had never even accepted them like this.

We belonged here.

LATER THAT NIGHT, the kids were curled up in a fort made of quilts and sheets in their new play area in the loft, bellies full, eyes heavy and laughter echoing down through the railing as the evening wound down.

Eli ducked upstairs a couple of different times to check on them as Travis cleaned up the last of the dishes that he and his dad had hand-washed together.

Maggie slid onto the couch beside me with two steaming mugs of tea, as Hal lowered himself down into the chair opposite us, his big hands folded over his knee, watching me with a kind of quiet patience that made me fidget.

"You did good with those two," Maggie said, her chin dipping to the railing where Emmie and Toby's squeals of laughter sang out. "They're polite, funny, full of spirit." She patted my knee, "That's no accident, sweetheart."

Heat rose to my cheeks, compliments had always been hard to take, especially about my kids. Thanks to always feeling like I wasn't enough for them. "They're a handful most days," I admitted softly, "But they're good at their core."

Hal chuckled, the sound low and rumbling. "The best kind of handful there is." His gaze shifted, sharp but not unkind. "Travis and Eli—they don't hand their hearts over easily. But I've never seen them look at anyone the way they look at you. Or at those kids."

Maggie reached for my hand, squeezing it, "We want you to know that we don't care what it looks like from the outside; two men, one woman. What we see is love. And that's all that matters."

Her words cracked something open in my chest. For a

long moment I couldn't speak. I stared at the fire instead, blinking against the sting in my eyes. "I don't—I don't know what I'm doing," I whispered, the truth slipping out before I could catch it. "I feel like I'm living someone else's fairy tale, and at any moment I'm going to wake up and they're going to snatch it all back from me." I sighed, taking a deep breath, "This home. These men. It's too good to be true. And I'm scared I'm going to mess something up for the kids now that they're involved."

"Every mother thinks she's going to screw her kids up." Maggie chuckled affectionately. "Every stern word, or lost patience, small injury, or failing grade." She sighed, "The fact that you're worried about it means you're doing better than most."

Hal leaned forward, his eyes warm and certain. "We're glad they've got you, Frankie. We never in a million years imagined this layout for Travis's life, and hell, Eli's been a second kid to us for decades and we wouldn't have guessed this for him either. But now that we're here, and we see it, we're so damn happy for them. Don't let doubt steal what's right in front of you."

It wasn't approval I heard in his tone, which was what I had been hoping for out of the evening. It was acceptance.

And for the first time in a long, long while, I let myself believe maybe—just maybe—we'd found a place to belong.

32 - ELI
Midnight Mischief

FRANKIE DID INCREDIBLY WELL MEETING Trav's parents, but I knew she would. She had been a ball of nerves all damn day, but the moment they showed up, giving her their unwavering acceptance and love, she melted into it.

I didn't realize how badly she wanted to belong until I sat back and watched her finally let her walls down completely for them. Because of them.

Trav saw it too. At one point we locked eyes across the room, and it felt like something hit me straight in the chest.

They were ours.

Frankie and the kids, they belonged to us. Those kids were ours, and they'd never have to go without a father figure in their lives again. Now they had two.

When Hal and Maggie finally went home, Hal practically dragged Maggie out the door when she didn't seem interested in leaving the cozy warm atmosphere in the cabin, Frankie was dead on her feet.

It was as if as soon as the front door closed, her body finally fell out of survival mode and the exhaustion kicked in.

Even as she crawled into bed, wearing a cute little night-gown with a lace edge that barely contained her lush cleavage and full ass, she didn't prioritize herself.

"You were promised things," She smiled up at me sleepily, "You orchestrated things."

"We'll get there some other time," I kissed her nose, pulling the blankets up over her. "Sleep now, though."

She pouted and turned to Trav on the other side of the bed as he pulled a pair of sweatpants on, shirtless, almost like he'd give in to her temptations. But our priority was always her needs, even above our own.

Even if my cock was thickening by the second as her tits jiggled as she huffed and settled on her back. "No fair." She whined.

"Get some sleep," I chuckled, turning off the lamp as I climbed in next to her. "You're exhausted."

"Not that—" She yawned in the darkness, and Trav's deep laugh came from his side of the bed as he climbed in on her other side. "Bad."

"Right," He mused, and she yawned again.

It took her no time at all to fall asleep between us, and I lay there, holding her against my body as Trav's breathing evened out, falling asleep shortly after her. She shifted in her sleep, snuggling in against me, and Travis moved in sync with her, wrapping himself around her back, like we were all one unit.

I stared up at the ceiling, dragging my fingertips over her

spine as she slept with her head on my chest. But I couldn't tempt sleep to pull me under.

Not when all I could think about was diamond rings, last names, and futures filled with childish belly laughs, little feet, and the feminine warmth building a home around us inside these four walls.

Dreams I never thought would come true as friends of mine got married and had kids, leaving me in the dust to wonder if it would ever be my turn.

Now, I had it all, with my best friend, and our girl, and her sweet kiddos.

And even though it had been quiet the last few weeks, with no more instances of the lurking darkness from her ex to be found, I couldn't help but wonder if he was gone for good.

Or if he was just biding his time.

THE SPACE between sleep and consciousness, where darkness was warm and everything felt incredible, held me tight, even as my body floated toward the light, fighting to wake up.

I couldn't figure out what had woken me up at first, but I could feel it.

Pleasure.

Need.

Desire.

Ache.

"Mmh," A gentle voice coaxed me further from dreamland into consciousness as a hot wet mouth teased the head of my cock. "You taste so good, baby."

"Frankie," I groaned in a whisper, forcing my eyes open as

my hand instinctively went to the back of her head, threading my fingers through her loose locks as she took me to the back of her throat. "Damn, baby,"

The bedroom was still pitch black, and I glanced over at the clock on my table, reading the numbers through my blurry eyes.

One am.

I had just fallen asleep sometime around midnight, but I would never complain about losing sleep if it was due to Frankie's sexy mouth wrapped around my cock.

"You were so good to me earlier," She hummed quietly, and I wanted to see her eyes as her tongue traced the ridge of my cock head, so I reached over and hit the dimmer switch on my bedside table before clicking it on, bathing the room in a soft, light glow. It was just enough to see her by, and she smiled wickedly from where she lay between my thighs, both hands on my cock and her lips teasing the shaft as she kissed her way down it. "You knew I was stressed, and you let Trav take care of me."

I glanced over at the other side of the bed where Trav lay on his back with his arm over his eyes, sleeping soundly before looking back down at her. "And this is my reward?"

She chuckled seductively, and pushed my cock back down her throat, making me groan, and then she pulled back off. "No, this is just the warmup."

"Hmm," I hummed and flexed my hips as she started deep-throating me, pushing her lips down my cock until they brushed against the base and I cursed. "Fuck yes, baby."

Trav groaned and rolled over toward us, and we both froze as his eyes popped open, sensing the light and the gap between us in bed.

"Nothing here for you, go back to sleep." I grinned and then flinched when Frankie pinched my inner thigh as Trav sat up on his elbow, instantly interested in what she was doing.

"Rude." He growled and then palmed his own dick that was hardening in his sweats.

"Don't worry, baby," Frankie purred, and patted the space next to me where she had been sleeping. "I have plans for both of you."

He slid his pants off and moved over next to me, elbowing me in the ribs as he slowly stroked his cock. "Tell me more."

"This is my wet dream." I complained goodheartedly, and Frankie took her wet hand and started stroking Trav with it as she pulled her lips off me.

"But I get so much wetter when I have both of your cocks to play with." She teased, and we both groaned at her dirty words.

"Prove it." I pulled her body up mine to kiss her lips, "Let me taste how wet you are."

She squealed when I flipped her around, lifting her thick hips up until she straddled my face.

"That's it, Shade." Trav directed, as I leaned up to swipe my tongue over her wet clit. "Sit on his face, don't fucking hover. He wants you on his face."

"But—" She argued and then moaned when I wrapped my arms around her hips and pulled her down flush to my face. "Fuck yes."

"Good girl," Trav praised as I started eating her pussy, tasting the flavor of her arousal and letting it flood my senses as she moaned and rocked on my face. "Mmh, good girl."

The muffled sound of her moans, paired with the way her body rocked over mine, let me know she was busy sucking his cock, but she kept her palm wrapped around mine.

Fuck, it was hot having her between us both, everyone getting and giving pleasure.

I arched my neck and licked my way up to her ass as she spit on my cock and stroked me. "Eli," she moaned when I pushed my tongue into her tight hole. "That feels so good."

I fought off an orgasm as her tight fist pleasured me perfectly, before she dropped her palm to my balls, stroking them just how I liked. I was intent on losing myself in her body when I came.

"I need you," She gasped, sitting up and putting her hands on my abs as I tongue-fucked her ass. "Right there, I want your cock. Right. Fucking. There."

I growled as she scrambled down my body, wiping my hand over my mouth as she kneeled on the bed facing us, nipples hard under the fabric of her tight black nightgown and skin flushed with desire. "Where were you?" Trav asked with a smirk.

"Ass." I replied in a deep ominous growl as I rose to my knees as she slid the straps of her gown wide so her big tits could be free as she tweaked her nipples. "You want my cock in your ass tonight, Black Cat?" I hardly recognized my voice as she nodded eagerly.

"I want you both." She purred, sliding her fingers under the hem of her gown and showing us as she spread her lips and played with her clit. "I want to be so fucking full." She reached forward and grabbed my hard cock, stroking me. "I want you in my ass." And then she grabbed Trav's slick cock, "And you in my pussy."

"Fuck yes," Trav pulled her forward, so she was straddling his hips as he leaned up and bit on her nipples as she stroked us both. "Our dirty girl wants to take us at the same time? Finally?"

"Yes," She purred, looking at me as she rocked her hips up the length of Trav's thick cock. "But more than that, I want you both to feel each other." She moaned at her own words, dragging her nails up the length of my cock as she locked eyes with me, "I want you to feel Trav's cock from inside of me, rubbing against yours."

The growl that vibrated out of Trav's chest was pure beast, and my cock jumped in her hand.

It was that taboo, undiscussed boundary we toyed with weeks ago, but hadn't touched again.

I hadn't been brave enough to push for it, even though we all talked about it happening, eventually.

But now, she was demanding it, and it seemed Trav was as desperate for it as I was.

"You heard her, Sunshine." Trav commanded, "Get her ready to take us both."

I moved as if I'd been struck by lightning, getting the lube from the top drawer of my new dresser and returning to the bed as Frankie really started grinding on Trav's cock, using him to tease herself.

I threw every reservation I had about boundaries and perception out the window and focused on the need I saw in both of their eyes as I straddled Trav's legs right behind Frankie's plump ass.

"Hold still, Black Cat." I commanded as I poured lube down her ass crack, letting it coat her ass and pussy, dripping down onto Trav's cock. The visual stimulation was almost too much for me to handle as my own cock dripped with need. "You want us both, then we need to make sure you're ready to take both of our big cocks into your tight little body."

I rubbed my fingers down her crack, collecting the lube and pushing two slicked-up fingers straight into her ass. Her body relaxed instantly, trained to take things there, and she pushed back on my fingers, eagerly taking me as deep as she could.

"Talk to me." Trav demanded, fisting her hair aggressively

as he lifted his hips, rubbing his cock through the lube and her wet pussy lips. "What's he doing to you?"

"Fucking my ass with his fingers." She purred, arching her back so his cock rubbed across her clit. From my position, I could watch it all, and I ached to feel it. "Feel him." Turning her chin, she looked at me over her shoulder, "Put his cock into my pussy."

I clenched my jaw to keep from coming from the filthy things she demanded, but I didn't hesitate. I wrapped my free hand around the base of Trav's cock and lifted it up like the perfect little toy for her to lower herself onto, but she wasn't done destroying us yet.

"Make sure he's good and lubed for me." She purred over her shoulder. "I want his cock to slide right into me. Rub it in for me."

Trav's hand clenched on her hips and his dick twitched in my hand as I slowly slid my fist up the thick veined shaft of my best friend's dick and his curses filled the room, spit out through clenched teeth as he pushed his hips up, sliding it through my fist faster as I went slowly. "Fuck yes," He growled, and I leaned forward to rest my forehead against her back as my world exploded around me

"Good boy," She purred seductively, and I raised my head to stare into her bottomless eyes as she arched her back, hands flat on his chest, and presented herself for me. "Fill me up with it now."

"Frankie." I growled, scissoring my fingers in her ass as I angled his cock toward her dripping wet, silky pussy and then pushed him into her. Never in my life had I touched another dick, and here I was feeding my best friend's cock into our girl, pushing my fingers against it through the thin wall of her asshole. "I'm going to come."

She moaned, lowering herself onto his fat cock and lifting

herself off as I kept my hand still, so she was taking us both in and out of her body at the same time.

"Elliot!" Trav growled, "Fuck her ass. I'm not lasting long at all."

Turning my wrist, I hooked my fingers in her ass and poured lube on my cock before holding it hard and still behind her so on her next down thrust I pushed in against my fingers, letting her control the pace.

Her breath shuddered as a primal moan, deep and guttural, escaped her lips as she slowly but steadily pushed down on both our cocks until we were both buried balls deep inside of her.

"Holy fucking shit," She rocked her hips, testing it out and moaned when Trav leaned up to suck on her big tits dangling over his face.

"Lucky bastard." I growled, pulling my fingers from her body and grabbing her hips.

"Lower, Eli." Frankie begged, reaching around her ass to direct me until I was sitting on Trav's thighs, legs spread over them. "Mmh," she purred, using her fingers on my balls and rubbing them against Trav's before she gasped. "I'm coming. Don't move. Don't fucking move, either of you."

I gripped her hips so tight there would be bruises left in the morning as her ass clenched around my cock and Trav's cock got tighter against mine.

Her moans and pleas filled my ears as her pussy fluttered, until she finally relaxed around us, sagging a little. "Jesus Christ," She gasped. "I literally felt your balls touching each other and came so fucking hard I couldn't think straight."

"You like us bending the rules for you, don't you?" Trav asked, and she didn't hesitate for a second with her response.

"I know neither of you are into guys." She panted as she rolled her hips, testing out moving on our cocks. "But I know you get pleasure from him touching your body, don't you?" She challenged him. "You liked the way his hand felt on your cock, didn't you?"

"Fuck yes," He growled without hesitation, and my chest tightened at his confidence while I shook with uncertainty. "Feeding my cock into your tight pussy," He growled, "I nearly came in his hand."

My hips flexed, pushing my cock into her ass all the way, and then I pulled back, stroking against his cock and making them both curse and moan. "I have to fuck."

"Fuck us." Frankie licked her lips, looking at me over her shoulder again. "Give me that long cock and rub it against Trav's. Make us all come."

"Every inch, Eli," Trav demanded as he rocked his hips just enough when I was buried deep inside of her again. "Let us feel every fucking inch of you."

I wasn't gay.

But, fuck if I wasn't going to blow my load as my best friend talked about my cock.

Was I bi?

"Harder, Eli," Frankie begged and pushed back on me. "Fuck me so hard, please. I want to feel you for days."

"Hold on to him," I said, leaning over her back so the angle changed, and her hole got even tighter as Trav's cock pressed up against mine through her. "Take me deep, like a good girl, Frankie. Beg for it."

"Please, Eli," She gasped, digging her nails into Trav's chest as she laid her head on his pec, "I'm going to come so hard on your cock. You're fucking me deeper than anything has ever been. You're the longest cock I've ever taken, and I'm obsessed. I'm fucking obsessed with how good you're making me feel."

"I'm—" Trav grunted and then his hips were moving, lifting her with each of his thrusts. "I'm coming."

Time ceased.

My vision darkened.

Blood roared in my ears over Frankie's muffled cries of pleasure as she bit Trav's pec to stay as quiet as possible. And then Trav's hand was on my thigh, pulling me in deeper as I cursed, blinded by my orgasm as I felt Frankie tighten around us, coming on our cocks.

I thrust into her body, through the tightness of her orgasm and then through the aftershocks of it as she came down, relaxing around us, even then, I didn't stop. My cock didn't go down, my come dripped out around it as I kept fucking her. I couldn't speak, I couldn't stop.

"Oh my God," Frankie moaned in a deep, needy cry as her nails dug into my other thigh, both of their fingers gripping my flesh as I pushed into her body over and over again.

My cock was still rock hard, and through the haze of pleasure, I could feel another orgasm building inside of me.

"Keep going, Sunshine," Trav commanded, and I finally opened my eyes, locking my stare on him as he pulled her head up off his chest with a handful of hair so she could arch her back and take me, meeting me thrust for thrust. "Fucking take his cock, Shade. He needs your body right now. He's going to lose himself in how damn good you feel."

"You both," I hissed, fighting to get air into my lungs as I described the pleasure I was getting into existence, admitting to it and risking outrage from Trav. "Fuck, you both feel so damn good."

"Use us," Frankie pushed back, meeting me, and Trav growled, eyes rolling with pleasure. "Jesus, we're all going to come again. Please, God, come again for me, boys."

"Can't help it," I gasped, and Trav lost his restraint as he careened towards another orgasm. He dug his heels into the bed, lifting his knees up behind me and pushing me into Frankie even deeper as he lifted us both with his strong body, fucking up into her. "God. Fuck. Travis."

"Yes!" She cried out, and I wrapped my hand around her jaw, covering her mouth and holding her still to take us as she came. Her orgasm instantly spurred my own on, and I filled her ass with even more come. Seconds later, Trav's body convulsed beneath us both, and his hushed curses filled the room as his balls jerked underneath mine.

The only noise in the room was our ragged breaths and the wisps of pleasure lingering in the air around us until I forced myself to pull out of her used body, slowly, as she winced.

"Easy," I kissed her shoulder and rolled off the bed to go clean up in the bathroom.

I paused at the sink with only the nightlight illuminating my face in the mirror, and I stared at my reflection. Bracing my palms on the countertop, my chest still heaved like my body hadn't caught up to the fact that it was over.

The man in the mirror looked different somehow. My hair was a mess, my skin flushed, the kind of raw, wrecked look I usually saw in Frankie after we'd wrung her out between us. Except for this, it wasn't just about her.

It was him too.

And me.

My eyes fell shut, replaying it all in my mind. The feel of Frankie shuddering between us, the heat of her body stretched to take us both. But layered over that—Travis.

His legs pressed against mine as we moved in sync.

His hand gripping my hip, steadying me while I drove into her.

The way his body brushed mine, the way the pressure doubled in my chest each time, sharp and electric.

It hadn't been just her making me come undone.

And, fuck, I liked it.

I blew out a shaky breath, staring at myself again. Did that mean I was bi? Was that what this was? The thought twisted in my chest; it didn't feel right. I wasn't—I didn't like men.

I didn't even like Travis.

I didn't crave him when Frankie wasn't there. I didn't picture him when I closed my eyes.

But in bed, in that moment, sharing her, sharing the rhythm, touching him because he was touching her, I hadn't wanted to pull away. I'd wanted more.

I had wanted all of it.

My fingers curled against the porcelain sink, knuckles white. Maybe it wasn't about labels, maybe it wasn't about being bi or straight, maybe it was just us.

Frankie.

Travis.

Me.

The three of us together in ways that made sense only when we were tangled up like that, no rules, no definitions. I wasn't in love with Travis. But I loved him. Trusted him with my life. And if his touch, his weight, his presence lit me up when we were both inside of her, then maybe that didn't need a name.

Maybe it just needed to be real.

Because it felt fucking real to me.

Forcing myself to go back into the bedroom, the adrenaline had worn off, leaving me wrung out. Frankie was asleep on Travis's chest, her dark hair spilling over him like a blanket. She looked peaceful, lips parted, leg thrown over his and tangled, her hand curling possessively over his ribs like she couldn't let him go even in her dreams.

Silently, I kneeled on the bed, and cleaned her up, using a warm washcloth and a soft touch. She stirred a little, but Trav hooked his hand under the knee resting across his bare waist and hiked it up further, opening her up for me to get all the mess we left behind.

When I was done, I pulled the blanket up over her naked body and tossed the cloth into the hamper. My chest felt tight, my skin was too hot with the weight of what we'd done and what it had meant hanging over my head.

Travis looked over at me when I slid under the covers, leaning back against the headboard instead of sliding down and going to sleep. His hand absently stroked Frankie's back as she slept on him, and his eyes met mine in the dim light.

Calm.

Steady.

Always fucking steady.

"You alright?" He asked quietly.

I swallowed, "I don't know."

He didn't press, didn't fill the silence. He just waited. That was the thing about my best friend; he had the patience that I didn't.

I ran a hand through my hair, staring at the ceiling. "Back there, with her. With you. I—fuck, man—I liked it. More than I should have."

Something shifted in his expression, but he didn't flinch. Didn't mock me or look away. "I thought we already squashed this after that time in her living room."

I sighed but didn't say anything else. Because so had I.

Doubt was a fucking dick.

"Are you saying you're into me?" He asked.

"No," I said quickly, maybe too quickly. "It's not that.

I'm not looking at other guys. I don't want that. But with you —" I broke off, shaking my head and then whispered, "When we're with her, when it's the three of us, I don't hate it. I like it. Your touch. The way it feels. It doesn't make sense, but—"

"It doesn't have to," Travis said, his voice low but certain.

I turned my head toward him, the quiet conviction in his tone pulled me in.

"We're not following rules here, Eli. We're making our own. If what we've got feels good—feels right—we don't have to stick a label on it. Doesn't mean you are anything but you. Doesn't mean I'm anything but me. It just means it works. For us. For her." He scoffed a little. "I think it *really* fucking works for her." He grinned.

Something in my chest cracked, a pressure I hadn't realized I was holding.

"And if it ever stops working?" I asked.

His mouth curved again, with the barest hint of a smile. "Then we talk. But until then, stop overthinking and let yourself have this, if it's what you want."

I let out a shaky laugh, rubbing a hand over my face. "Christ, you always know how to make shit sound simple."

"Because it is," He said, tilting his head toward the woman asleep on his chest. "She's ours. We're hers. That's all that matters."

Frankie stirred between us, letting out a soft sigh as she shifted in her sleep. Travis adjusted the blanket over her, his hand still steady against her spine.

"Being with this incredible woman feels amazing." Trav said, "I think we can both agree on that. And if for the rest of my life, I got to please her, fuck her, and give her what I had to offer, without you even being in the room, I'd die a happy man."

"Fuck you," I grunted, turning off the light and sliding down in bed.

In the silent darkness he went on, voice soft and barely more than a whisper. "But if I get to spend the rest of my life pleasing her, loving her, and fucking her, with you wrapped up in it from head to toe, I'd die a happier man. Because it felt fucking right to me, Sunshine. It felt damn fucking good too."

For the first time since I'd stared myself down in the bathroom mirror, I let the knot in my chest ease. Maybe he was right. Maybe it didn't need a name.

Maybe it just needed us.

I turned on my side and slid up against Frankie's back, bending my legs behind hers, and she wiggled back into me in her sleep.

Trav took a deep breath, and the air in the room suddenly didn't feel so heavy.

33 - FRANKIE
No Jealousy, No Shame

THE KITCHEN WAS ALREADY BUZZING when I walked in, hair still messy and one of Travis's massive flannels wrapped around me like a cozy blanket over my jammies. My bare feet soaked up the warmth radiating through the floor, another bonus point in Trav's corner of ingenious things he added to his home that just make life so fucking beautiful.

I was a little disappointed to find both of the guys gone this morning when I woke up to the smell of coffee, normally we rotated in shifts so two of us could sleep in—or do anything but sleep in the lazy early morning light behind a closed door.

Then again, with each step I took as I brushed my teeth and made my way to the kitchen, I felt every single inch of my body that they had commanded last night when they took me together for the first time. Maybe it was a good thing one of them didn't stay in bed with me for round two.

Giggles met me before I made it down the long hall from our bedroom to the open kitchen, and I grinned as I saw the chaos waiting for me.

Emmie sat at the counter, a plastic tiara on her head and one of Eli's favorite hockey jerseys hanging to her toes, with a spoon dangling dangerously close to the edge of her cereal bowl. Toby was mid-lecture about the proper way to pour milk—complete with hand gestures—when he promptly sloshed half the carton across the counter.

"Mom!" He yelped, spotting me, wide-eyed, holding the dripping carton like it had betrayed him. "It has a mind of its own!"

I hung my head to hide my grin as Emmie dissolved into giggles, sliding her tiara onto Toby's head. "Now you're the Milk King!"

"Am not," he muttered, though he wore the pink tiara proudly as Eli swooped in with a towel, laughing as he cleaned up the mess.

Travis, ever the steady one, flipped another pancake onto the growing stack next to a platter of bacon and hash browns, like nothing phased him as he winked at me over his shoulder. "Milk King, huh? Guess that makes me the Pancake Prince."

"Wrong," Emmie declared, spooning a massive bite of cereal into her mouth, "You're the Pancake *Grandpa* because you're old and have hair growing in your ears."

That sent Eli into a fit of laughter so loud I was sure it shook the walls. "He has hair everywhere!" He added dramatically, and Emmie dissolved into giggles again.

Travis only lifted one brow, but I caught the twitch of a smile as he passed behind Eli with the syrup bottle, adding it to the counter. And that's when it happened–subtle, so subtle, but enough to make me pause.

Travis's hand brushed the small of Eli's back as he passed, a light touch, grounding even. Eli glanced at him, smirking and winking as if it were a private joke.

Heat bloomed in my belly.

They'd never done that before.

The kids bickered happily over who got the biggest pancake, and I sat there holding my coffee, trying to act normal while my stomach fluttered with butterflies. Something was different between them.

Last night—God, last night—was it because of that?

The ease with which they moved around each other, the softness in Eli's grin, the quiet certainty in Travis's touch.

It wasn't just me they were sharing anymore.

And damn it all, it made my thighs clench even thinking about it.

HOURS LATER, I felt like my chest was going to explode if I didn't speak the words out into the void.

The cabin was empty and quiet; the kids having left to go to my mom's for the night before my shift at the rink.

The air was finally still around us.

But I was anything but.

I'd been restless all morning, the image burned into my head; Travis's hand brushing Eli's back, Eli's grin when he winked at him. It had been so quick, so casual, but I couldn't unsee it. I couldn't stop replaying it.

I couldn't stop *hoping* for it.

Finally, I gave up trying to process it silently in my own

head. I marched out of the laundry room and found them in the living room, both of them sprawled out on the couch with a hockey game on above the fireplace.

They were joking about something but stopped short when I stood in front of them, hands on my hips, blocking the TV. Travis stared up at me, something unreadable in his eyes. Eli's smile was easy, but I caught the faint flush on his cheeks.

He fucking blushed when he was turned on.

But he was already flushed when I walked in.

Before I could talk myself out of it, the words tumbled out. "I saw you."

Two sets of eyes locked on me, intense and unwavering.

"In the kitchen this morning." I clarified as my pulse hammered when I crossed my arms, trying to hide the way my hands shook. "You touched him," I stared at Travis, "And you," I pointed at Eli, my voice catching, "You winked at him like it was a secret just for the two of you."

Silence. Heat. My heart was in my throat.

The quiet stretched too long, heavy and charged. Travis sat up on the edge of the couch, his eyes burning into me, while Eli stayed sprawled out with his legs spread, looking far too relaxed for the way his jaw clenched.

"And?" Trav drawled on, "I thought you wanted us to touch." He glanced over his shoulder at Eli, "Begged us to touch last night, didn't she?"

"I—" I stammered, my lips parting as Eli cut me off.

"Gushed all over your cock when I fisted you, rubbing the lube all over you for her." Eli deadpanned and then squinted his gaze at me. "So why are you upset about it?"

"I—" I swallowed and crossed my arms as I suddenly felt very off-kilter about the whole situation.

"I thought it turned you on." Trav pushed, and a blush

heated my cheeks. "I thought that's what you wanted. I guess not."

"I didn't say that!" I rushed out and forced myself to take a deep breath, "I do like it."

"You do?" Eli raised a brow at me defiantly, and I kind of hated the smug look on his normally kind and easygoing face. "Because you're all worked up right now."

"I'm turned on!" I screamed at the beams in the vaulted ceiling. "All fucking day you fucking morons have been teasing me! Tempting me! And I couldn't say anything because I'm riddled with guilt and crazy hormones or something, because one minute I'm the fucking center of this out of this world dirty romance book where both of you are solely focused on me and my pleasures and I'm a selfish fucking cunt because I'm into it and totally prepared to be smothered between the two of you for the rest of forever! But today—" I throw my hands up as Travis raises his eyebrows and Eli hides an infuriating smirk behind his hand, "Today you two flip the script and now all I can fucking think about is how badly I want to sit in a cuck chair in the corner and just watch! The fucking things I'd give—" I groan dramatically, "The feral and dirty things I'd give up in exchange to watch you two do something, anything! But I can't think like that because then I feel guilty, thinking maybe you're only doing it for me because I'm a needy bitch who pushes you two to touch when we fuck like we did last night!"

"You think we only touched last night because of you?" Travis said after a beat, interrupting the mental breakdown I was having with that annoying calm he perfected.

"I mean," Eli shrugged, "She's kind of right."

"Ugh!" I hissed, throwing my head back in shame and guilt and utter stupidity, letting all of it rush over me. "I knew it!"

Eli chuckled, and I dropped my chin to glare at him, imagining all the ways I wanted to wipe that stupid fucking grin off his face while I crashed out. "What I mean is," he unfolded himself from the couch and stood up, circling around me like I was some specimen to be examined, and I scowled at him as he paused at my shoulder. "That I never would have figured out how fucking good it felt to give in to those dark and dirty, carnal urges I had toward Trav if it hadn't been for you, giving me the opportunity to act on them."

"You—*what?*" I blinked in confusion.

"Stop blaming yourself," Trav said calmly, standing right in front of me with his arms crossed as he leaned in slightly to talk against my ear, "Nothing is happening that we don't want. Not with you. Not with each other. If we touch, if we take pleasure from it, it's because we choose it."

I sucked a breath in, my chest tight, my body buzzing like a Christmas tree from the day full of teasing and their voices alone right now.

"You—" I licked my lips, "You want to—"

"Maybe." Eli teased, and I fought the urge to throw my elbow into his gut for toying with me in such a fragile state. "Maybe not."

"I hate you." I hissed, backing up to walk away but Travis caught my elbow and pulled me flush to his front, in one smooth motion he had his hand under my jaw, fingers pressed lightly against the column of my throat as he tilted my head back to stare up into his eyes. "Yes." He said firmly. "I want to."

"So do I." Eli spoke from behind me, pressing his groin against my ass, and a moan slipped from my lips when I felt his erection grinding against me. "But only if you're with us. This isn't a Travis and Eli show; it's not for us if you're not there."

"But—" I closed my eyes and dug my nails into Trav's forearm for leverage. "Are you sure? You can't do it if it's only for me! I can't tempt your friendship like that—"

"Shh," Trav whispered, tightening his hand around my neck, and I moaned. "We don't have all the answers for you right now, Shade, but we *do know* that we both really," his eyes closed as he growled, "really, enjoyed last night. And we're going to see where it takes us from here." He loosened his hold and bent to speak right against my lips, pressing the front of his body against mine, "But I will tell you this much, and I haven't even told him yet."

"Please," I begged, desperate for more of the delicious taboo.

"When he lubed my cock up for me last night, so I could slide up into your tight, hot, wet pussy with ease." Trav said, and I melted as Eli blew against the back of my neck, running his hands down over my hips to the front of my thighs, between Travis and me. "I was tempted to make you ride my face while he kept going, just to see how far it would go."

"Fuck." I whined, flexing my hips forward against his hard body as Eli brought his hand right up between my thighs, rubbing me through my jeans. "I need it. I need to—"

"Shh," Eli hushed in my ear, and I gulped against Trav's hand. "Would you lose that pretty little mind of yours if I jacked Trav off while you watched?"

My knees buckled as a need like I'd never felt before pulsed inside of me.

"Too bad you don't have time to find out," Trav clicked his tongue and looked at the clock on the wall. "The rink is calling all three of our names."

"Fuck!" I screeched, melting into a puddle at their feet. Aroused, horny, and so fucking angry to have to go to work.

Travis released me and kissed my lips, gently lingering

against them as Eli kept rubbing me, his hand pinned between my pussy and Trav's thigh.

"Maybe if you're a good girl," Eli bit my earlobe, pressing against my clit, "I mean a very, very good girl," He enunciated, "Maybe we'll find out tonight after our game."

I took a deep breath, and an idea came to mind, bringing a sinister smile to my lips as I pushed away from both of them, leaving them standing only inches apart with a surprised look on their faces.

"Maybe it's time we put some pressure on the game tonight." I adjusted my shirt, pulling it down so the tops of my tits sat right at the neckline again, and both of them dropped their gaze to watch like I was going to slip a nipple out for them.

"What are you thinking?" Trav asked, turning to face me with his arms crossed again.

"I'm thinking," I mused, "That whoever has a better game tonight wins the pillow princess spot in bed when we get home."

"The pillow princess," Eli grinned. "As in the one person who lays back and—"

"And gets serviced." I finished for him, and both of their jaws dropped. "Whoever has the better game tonight gets to lay back and enjoy while the loser gets to help me get the winner off." I licked my lips and took a step back from them, "Loser gets to help me service the winner, however they're comfortable with." I winked at Eli and blew Trav a kiss, "Game on, boys. May the best man win."

I walked out of the room, on shaking legs with a heart that felt like a time bomb nearing detonation, as a wild fucking smile grew on my lips.

Game fucking on, fellas.

34 - TRAVIS
Locker Room Temptation

FRANKIE WAS an evil witch with a delicious game of tease mastered, dragging us along with a voice sweet as sin, and daring eyes.

And I fucking loved it. There was no going back for me. I was all in.

Whichever man played better tonight won *pillow princess* privilege. Christ, I'd never wanted to win something so badly in my life.

By warmups, I was already keyed up, my legs burning with the push, my stick hitting the ice harder than usual. Eli caught my eye across the rink, his grin infuriatingly cocky, like he had already claimed the prize.

"Better bring your A-game, Saw," He called, leaning on

the boards as I skated by, I stopped short, spraying him with ice, but he was unfazed. "Because I'm not letting you lie back and enjoy her while I do all the work."

I snarled under my breath, tightening my gloves as we stood toe to toe, warning him quietly. "We'll see who's flat on their back by the end of the night,"

And then the devil herself appeared at the glass above him.

Hair loose under a knit beanie, lips painted red and that sharp eyeliner making her eyes look dramatic paired with her usual graphic tee and torn jeans. Damn, my cock hardened just looking at her. And then I realized what she was doing.

What she was wearing.

Or better yet, not wearing.

Her fitted graphic tee, thin and worn, leaving it soft and cozy, did little to hide the evidence of her lack of a bra under it. Both of her nipples were hard, and as she came down the steps, her tits swayed heavily under her shirt.

Fuck, I could taste them in my mouth from the ice. How easy would it be to lift her shirt, right there on the bleachers, surrounded by the crowd, and suck one of her perfect pink nipples into my mouth?

That little smirk played at the corners of her lips like she knew exactly what she was doing. She leaned forward, cupping her hands to the glass over Eli's head, who had no idea she was behind him, and my chest tightened when I caught the words she mouthed.

Earn it, Trav.

The puck dropped, and everything blurred into one thing: Earn it.

Every check, every slapshot, every rush down the ice was laced with the thought of Frankie waiting, watching, deciding who got to sink into the bed tonight and let the other man and her hands, her mouth, drive him insane.

Fuck, I wanted to be insane.

Eli played like a man possessed. Every player on our team hooted and hollered with each of his races down the ice at lightning speed, and power shots at the goal. I hated to admit it, but he was faster, sharper than even in his normally great games, every shot snapped with precision. The bastard was feeding off her just like I was.

Halfway through the second period, he slid over during a break, helmet unbuckled, sweat dripping down his temple. He pressed his hip against the boards right where Frankie leaned, spending a lot of her time at the ice to watch us in between customers.

"Hey, Black Cat." He drawled, loud enough for me to hear from the bench where I was sucking air. "How do you want me tonight? Hands in your hair while you take care of me? Or should I make Travis sit in the corner while you ruin me with that mouth of yours?"

Frankie's cheeks flushed pink, her tongue darting over her bottom lip, making my blood roar. I already imagined her red lipstick smeared up the shaft of my cock.

"You're not the only one she'll ruin, Eli," I growled, skating past. "She's gonna ride me first, and you'll be on your knees begging to touch."

Her eyes went wide, the smirk wobbling into something breathless. And damn if that wasn't fuel enough to tear down the rink.

By the last buzzer of the game, everything around us was a blur of sweat, body checks, and Frankie's eyes burning into me from the glass. Eli and I shook hands with the other team before we skated over to her after the ice and bleachers had emptied.

She moved to the bench so she could talk to us freely, and I could almost see the arousal in the blown pupils of her eyes as she looked at each of us.

"Well," Eli urged, "Who won?"

She grinned, and I knew we were both in trouble, about to be victimized by her wicked ways, once again.

"I told the guys that there was a draft sale tonight to the first ten players that make it to the bar." She licked her lips, "Which means the locker room should clear out pretty fast tonight."

"Shade," I growled, tilting my head in warning as her teasing took us further from our prize.

"What?" she whispered with a look of innocence on her pouty lips. "All I'm saying is that you'll have the place to yourself if you want to warm things up while you wait for me to get off my shift. I'll tell you who won when we get home." She shrugged and took a step back toward the stairs. "See you boys in an hour."

"Fuck," Eli groaned, watching her walk up the steps with that confident sway to her flared hips. "I'm going to come in my pants. No fucking way I'm making it home without blowing."

I looked over at him, leaning into our decade's long friendship and trust in Frankie's feelings about the lines we were blurring, while simultaneously trying to set the pace for him to find comfort in since I knew he was more worried about the dynamic than I was.

"Guess you should probably spend your time in the shower wisely, burn off some steam before she gets her claws back into us on the way home." I skated backward towards the tunnel as his eyes darkened.

He looked off where Frankie disappeared and then back at me, skating to catch up. "You think she wants that? Truly?"

I shrugged, because I was sure that was what she was telling us to do. But I didn't know how far she meant it to go.

"I guess we'll see how well her half-off draft sale goes down and go from there."

"Damn." He muttered. "I might come in my pants before we get to the showers."

I chuckled and turned.

He would if I had any say in it.

THE GAME WAS OVER, but my body didn't get the memo. Every single cell and nerve in my body was alight with need.

Carnal.

Feral.

Dying need.

The way she had leaned against the glass and mouthed, *earn it* was like she could already picture us on our knees for her, totally at her mercy.

The locker room was bustling with energy, high off a win thanks to our extra incentive to play like machines. Guys laughed, busted balls as they all stripped their gear off and changed. Eli and I kept our heads down, waiting them out as both of us were too wound up, too tight, to risk anyone seeing what was about to spill over.

By the time the last door slammed shut, it was just us. And I forced my feet into motion before I lost the nerve.

The showers hissed back to life, steam already filling the air from the rest of the guys as I walked into the secluded room at the back of the locker room. I ducked under the spray, bracing my hands against the wall, letting the heat scald the adrenaline off my skin. Maybe I should have turned the water to ice to get my head back in working order before I did something I couldn't take back, but dammit, I didn't want to.

And then I felt it—Eli's gaze.

I left him on the bench at his locker, the ball firmly in his court, but now he silently joined me.

And I could feel his eyes.

Slow.

Heavy.

Lingering.

"You're staring," I muttered without looking at him.

He chuckled low, stepping under the water, one faucet away, and let the water pour over his head before he finally replied, "And you aren't."

I turned my head just enough to catch him through the mist. Drops rolling down his chest, hair slicked back, eyes dark with the same hunger twisting in my own gut.

And maybe it was the steam, or the bet, or just her—always her—but I didn't look away.

He moved first, turning toward me.

Then he gave me what I wanted. A deliberate stroke of his hand down his chest, lower, slow enough that it was meant for me to watch. To see.

He clenched his dick, stroking it while he stared at me. My body responded instantly, my cock hard again like we hadn't just skated a whole fucking game of hell.

"Jesus, Eli," I growled, dragging my own hand down to adjust my cock as it grew to life in response. I couldn't believe I was getting hard watching him stroke himself.

Instantly, I remembered the way his hand felt around my dick last night, one steady stroke up and down to "prep" it for our girl, and then the way it felt when he pushed into her body, right up against me.

I'd stayed still, buried balls deep in Frankie as he fucked

her ass, rubbing his cock against mine inside of her and came from it alone the first time.

"Are you trying to drive me insane?" I grunted, turning to lean back against the wall behind me, spreading my thighs to get the perfect tension in my body as I jacked off.

His smirk curved sharp, "I thought that was her job. Walking around our rink, her tits swayed with each step. Every man in the place could see the point of her nipples tonight." He growled, "But only we get to fuck with them."

"Damn fucking right," I clenched my teeth, imagining our teammates staring at her chest right now, imagining they were the lucky bastards that got to play with those lush tits. No doubt they'd all go home, and jack off to the mental imagery of her body. "God, I'm fucked in the head over that girl."

We were both breathing hard, caught up in the taboo appeal of it, not touching each other, but close enough it felt like we were already crossing lines we'd never go back from.

His eyes fell to my cock as his pretty boy face lit up with a flush he'd probably blame on the steam if I called him out on it. But I didn't.

I'd never tip this in a way that made him feel guilty for it.

Never.

I'd never make him feel uncomfortable if I weren't.

And I was the furthest thing from uncomfortable as we jacked off together.

Every groan, every stolen glance ratcheted the tension tighter.

"I won tonight," he challenged, reaching down with his free hand to palm his balls, and my spine burned with the urge to come. "We both know it."

"And?" I held his stare, quickening my pace as we toed the subject of later.

"And," he panted, "I'm trying to figure out if I should let you off the hook."

I rolled my eyes and stood up taller, "Not on your life." I commanded, and his jaw clenched as if he was surprised. Grabbing my phone off the ledge at the edge of the shower stall, I aimed it at him, and he silently watched me, but didn't stop what he was doing. Through the mist, his cock was red, and the head looked angry as he stroked himself faster while I clicked a photo showing him dripping because of Frankie's wicked ways, head tipped back slightly, lips parted. "Let's make sure she knows what she does to us."

The image would have wrecked me on its own if I hadn't lived it firsthand.

His laugh was breathless as he nodded, snatching his phone off the ledge. A second later, he stared at his screen, snapped a picture of me in return and then glanced back at me.

The group chat between the three of us had two brand-new photos waiting for her with my caption below.

> Just a preview, Shade. So you know what's waiting for you when you get done.

I pushed my phone back onto the dry ledge and leaned back on the wall again as he did the same.

We were at a pivotal point.

Come or don't.

Finish and get some clarity.

Or hold off and go into tonight crazed with the haze of need.

"I don't want to stop," Eli answered my silent hesitation as he slowly twisted his fist over the head of his cock and then to the root with a groan. "I don't think I can."

"So don't," I replied, stroking faster as his lips parted,

Adam's apple bobbing as his eyes closed in pleasure. "Besides," I panted, nearing my orgasm at an alarming rate as I desperately pushed to get him there with me. "I know you won. And I think you're going to look so fucking perfect lying back on that pillow while Frankie and I torture you together."

"Fuck," His chest fell as his eyes snapped open, holding mine as he started coming on the floor at his feet. "Trav."

I growled in response, adding my own release to the tile before throwing my head back into the wall as the urge to collapse onto the floor hit me like a brick.

Silently, we caught our breaths and then showered off the game and the thoughts trying to consume us. By the time the water shut off, we were both wrecked, but nowhere near satisfied. We dressed fast, pacing like caged animals, killing time until Frankie finished her shift in a few minutes.

And when she finally texted that she was on her way out to the truck, Eli looked at me, eyes burning.

"Race you."

And just like that—we were gone.

35 - FRANKIE
Pillow Princess

MY PHONE BUZZED in my back pocket while I was wiping down pint glasses from all the draft beers, I sold in the post-game frenzy that drew the players out of the locker room. I wasn't sure if my horny, harebrained plan would work, but less than ten minutes after the ice cleared, every player from the Net Crashers, Coach Rick included, rushed to the bar to get their cheap beer.

My body hummed to life when I realized that Trav and Eli hadn't joined them. And then my phone buzzed.

Two photo messages, and a text message from Trav.

My knees went weak when I opened it.

The first picture was from Eli, but it was of Trav.

Naked.

Hard.

Hand on his cock and a menacing glare in his eyes as he stared at the camera with the steam of the shower curling around him in the locker room.

"Fuck," I whispered, biting my lip and scrolling down.

The next one was from Trav, but of Eli. His head was tipped back under the spray, lips parted, fist wrapped around himself, the angle showing just how tight he was fisting himself.

My breath caught. It wasn't just them—God, it was them *together*. In my head, the steam blurred them together into one picture, and the fantasy came quick, hot and unstoppable until I was clenching my thighs imagining dirty, depraved things.

Travis stepping into Eli's space, dominating the air like he did with me and silently sliding his hand down Eli's stomach, going lower until he pushed Eli's hand off, stroking his best friend himself. Eli groaning and tipping his head back before Trav wrapped a firm hand around the back of his neck, forcing him to make eye contact as he pleasured him.

For me.

I clutched the edge of the bar to steady myself, heat flooding my skin, my thighs pressing tight as if that would make it stop.

It didn't.

"Yo, Coach," Billy called out, making me jump, "Boss lady's blushing!"

I startled, nearly dropping my phone into the sanitizer sink, and locked it before someone could see my private photos and then went back to work, hoping the team would drop it.

Rick watched me, leaning against the bar with a smirk, his face smug as hell.

"I am not." I lied in a voice a little too high.

"Sure you're not," Rick said quietly, eyes twinkling. "It's been a long time since I've seen that kind of spark in your eyes, kid. Guess you finally remembered you're still alive, huh?"

My face burned hotter.

The whole team knew I was dating Travis and Elliot, they knew we were living together too and were in a weird poly dynamic.

But they didn't know half of it, really.

And it was going to stay that way.

"Maybe I just got warm from running around after all of you stinky fucks."

Rick chuckled as the guys cackled and shot their insults at me through the bottom of their glasses. Some ducked out, heading home for the night, some stayed for another round, but within an hour, I was done and closing the bar.

The second I stepped out of the rink, the cold night air hit me, reminding me that I was a fucking lunatic who didn't wear any layers because I was a cock hungry whore.

The thin, long-sleeve band tee I wore did little to ward off any of the frosty night now that I wasn't running around the bar to stay warm, thankfully, my guys didn't make me stand out in the cold though.

Trav's truck rolled around the corner, idling at the curb as Eli jumped out, looking smug and hungry.

His eyes dropped to my chest as he held the door open. "Naughty little tease." I licked my lips as I passed him, almost faltering when I saw the dominant need in Trav's eyes, sitting behind the wheel. Eli slapped my ass, the sound sharp and the burn melting straight into my clit as I jumped up in, sliding across the bench seat to sit next to him.

Eli climbed in behind me and shut the door, turning the cab light off until we sat in the warm darkness.

My nerves were buzzing, desperate to get home and crown the winner of tonight's bet, but Trav didn't put the truck in gear.

"What?" I asked, looking between the two of them, confused.

The lot was mostly empty, and the lights were bright enough to see that no one else was around. But they weren't expecting to—no, they wouldn't want to fuck here. Would they?

"Take it off." Trav said dominantly, his voice vibrating through my ear.

My breath caught, "What?"

"Your shirt." He stated. "You wanted to play dangerously tonight, showing all of our friends how perfect your tits were. So, show us."

My fingers trembled in my lap as I looked over at Eli, scanning the parking lot again.

Fuck it.

The heat in Trav's eyes left no room for argument, so I peeled my shirt up over my head, the cool air biting my bare skin. The leather of the seat was cold against my back, and I jumped away from it.

"Good girl," Trav growled deep in his chest, licking the pad of his thumb before dragging it over my nipple and pinching it. "Lean against me so Eli can play."

I turned my hips, and Trav pulled me back into his side, his massive arm slung over my shoulder as he kept one set of fingers pinching and pulling at my nipple. Eli shifted on the seat and pulled my legs over his before leaning down, sucking my other into his mouth instantly, squeezing both of them together and playing.

Damn.

I moaned as they both played with my chest, fully on display as Trav finally put the truck in gear and started driving down the dark streets. There was no tint on his truck windows and the high of being so exposed if we ran into anyone heightened the pleasure of what Eli was doing with his tongue as Trav ran his hand up my throat, pulling my head back to look up at him.

"Did you think we'd deliver on your shower-time request?" Trav asked.

"Mmh," I hummed, adjusting my hips to accommodate the angle he had me in. "Did you touch him?"

"Would you be mad if I did?" He challenged, never looking away as he drove us down the road. It was such a power move, and my body melted even more under the dominance.

"Fuck no," I growled, baring my teeth at him and biting his thumb as he pulled my lip down. "I am going to demand a redo though so I can watch next time."

Eli hissed and kissed his way up my chest to my neck. "We came together."

I whimpered, but Trav wouldn't let go of my neck, so I just rocked against Eli's body even though I couldn't see him. I could feel him.

I could feel his hard cock against the underside of my thigh as he pushed against me. Reaching behind me, I palmed Trav's erection, and his hand tightened on my throat.

Fuck yes, baby.

The truck rumbled down the dark sleepy streets with its tuned exhaust, its headlights flashing over houses and trees, but it felt like a whole other world inside the restored cab.

Eli's lips were hot on me as he moved to my other breast, biting and sucking on it hard as I cried out for both men. Begging, daring them to do something else to make me come.

The thrill of it all, the obscenity and the promise of what was going to happen when we got home left me panting and pulsing with need.

"Dirty girl," Eli whispered when I moaned louder when Trav let go of my neck to pinch my nipple again. I cried out in desperation when Trav held my breast in a tight grip, as Eli lowered his lips to it. I loved when they worked me over together, in sync. "You like this, riding home topless, letting us use you like this, don't you?"

Trav's hand slid lower, over my bare stomach to the button of my pants, Eli pulled it open as Trav pushed his hand down the front of my pants. "She's dripping for it. I can smell her already."

I cried out when his fingers found my clit, pushing through my wetness and then instantly forcing his thick finger up into me. "Fuck yes," I panted, riding his hand.

Eli smirked at me as I watched him still obsessing over my chest. "I want a taste."

The air in the truck crackled with tension as I sat between them, panting and dripping for them. Silently, Trav pulled his finger out of me and held his hand up between Eli and me.

"Lick it clean then," His chest rumbled against my back. My soul left my body as Eli's eyes darkened and flicked from Trav's fingers to my gaze before he leaned forward and sucked Trav's pointer finger into his mouth until his lips touched the meat of Trav's hand and then slowly sucked it clean.

"Fuck." I whispered, and Trav growled behind me, and his cock jumped in his jeans. "I need to come."

"Too bad." Eli winked, taking one last lick of Trav's fingers before sitting up and palming his hard dick. "We're almost home."

"Rude!" I cried and crossed my arms over my chest, but Trav wasn't going to let me deny him access to my body, and he pushed his hand under my arm so he could absently rub his wet fingers over my nipple.

He was edging me.

Toying with me.

Playing with my body and my needs.

And I fucking loved it.

I fucking loved them both.

TRAVIS AND ELI circled me like wolves as we silently walked through the empty and dark cabin. We didn't bother turning the lights on.

We didn't bother with words or idle conversation as we moved straight into the bedroom, locking up behind us.

"You going to tell us who won, Frankie?" Eli asked as I stood in the middle of the bedroom, still topless with soaked panties and a deep need in my core.

"Maybe I don't want to." I purred, sliding my jeans down my body to stand before them in my black panties and nothing else. "Maybe it was a tie."

Trav glared at me, and I could read it clear as day in his clear and concise way.

He knew he had lost.

He knew that he was on the hook to play with Eli and me.

And he wanted me to just fucking say it.

"Eli won," I said, holding his stare before looking over at the winner himself. "Eli wins the pleasure tonight."

Sunshine's grin spread, looking like a starving man who was just served a steak on a platter. "Lucky me."

"Guess that means I get the best seat in the house." Trav said with a low chuckle that vibrated across my bare skin as he came to stand next to me. "Watching you take care of him and letting me help."

Letting.

Not forcing.

Yep, I was obsessed with the two men standing around me.

Heat flooded me, my body already ready to give them both everything. I should have known that even though they were playing the game against each other, they wouldn't let me off easy. As soon as I named Eli the winner, Trav's smirk turned predatory, Eli's grin split wide, and I was caught between them, exactly where they wanted me.

"You heard her, Sunshine," Trav said, glancing at our lover, who stood at the end of the bed, looking perfectly ready to be ruined by the two dark souls in the room. "You get to lie back and enjoy us tonight. And you, Shade," he looked at me, "You get to watch your fantasy come to life."

Need curled through me, sharp and greedy, "Then make it worth watching." I challenged him. "Undress our winner."

Trav's eyes darkened, but he didn't argue. Instead, he turned to Eli, and crossed the room. "Safe words for tonight," Always the Dom, making sure everyone was on the same page. "Red, yellow, green. Understood."

Eli nodded and licked his lips. "All green here."

Silently, Trav started undoing the pearl snaps on the front of Eli's shirt, simply using one finger on each side of his shirt to pull them apart.

Something about the percussive sound each snap made as they came free, felt like a physical tap to my clit.

"Slower," I whispered, my throat tight. "Travis, do it slower."

He obeyed me, and Eli looked over at me as Trav silently slid both hands into the fabric to pull it apart until he got to the end, where it was still tucked into his jeans.

Slowly, he pulled it out, and Eli turned back to look at his best friend as Trav ran both hands over the skin of Eli's chest, pushing the shirt off over his wide shoulders until Eli pulled it off and tossed it aside.

Eli's body was magnificent, cut of stone and smooth. Every inch of his body was crafted intentionally, worked on daily at the gym and through training for work to stay in the best shape possible.

And we got to enjoy it.

Travis silently pulled the button on Eli's jeans open, and a groan escaped our sunshiny lover, a blush covering his tan cheeks and ripped chest as Trav lowered his fingers to his zipper.

My body lit up like a live wire watching them, Trav's rough hands, Eli's shameless surrender as his best friend stripped him for me. It did things to me I didn't know I could feel.

"God, look at you." Eli muttered, eyes cracking open to catch me. "Touching yourself already?"

I was startled, realizing my hand had drifted to the front of my panties without me even thinking as I watched the show. My face burned, but I didn't stop as I slid them lower, to rub my clit through the soft fabric.

Travis's gaze cut me, molten lava eyes and desperate longing in them. "She's dripping for it. Just for us, aren't you, Frankie?"

Eli chuckled and then gasped when Travis pushed his hands down the opening of Eli's jeans to take them off. "Guess we found her new favorite show," he said, biting his bottom lip as Trav slid his hands lower over Eli's thighs, pushing his jeans down to his knees.

"Get on your knees." I commanded, unsure of where I got the guts to tell Travis to do anything, let alone to get on his knees in front of his best friend. My heart was racing, and it felt like I would pass out as I fell into the armchair by the window, the one with a perfect view of the show they were putting on for me. I didn't even try to hide it as I leaned back and spread my legs. "Now."

I watched with rapture as Trav slowly went down onto his knees, staring at me the whole time. I knew he'd make me pay for it later, and I'd take his punishment with a smile on my face, because my fingers slid down the front of my panties and circled my clit as he resumed stripping Eli for me.

His hands grazed Eli's legs, and I had no idea how Eli stayed on his feet as Trav tossed his jeans to the side, leaving him in his tight black boxer briefs, erection growing down the leg, testing the stretchiness of the fabric a mere foot from Trav's face.

I palmed my breast, playing with my nipple as they both turned to look at me, waiting for their next instruction.

Now or never.

Do or die.

I pushed my panties down and kicked them off into the pile before hooking my knees over the arms of the chair to show them my naked body before pushing two fingers straight into my needy cunt.

"Take his boxers off."

36 - ELI
Green for Go

SHE MADE indecent whimpers as she fingered herself, the wet noise and her soft pants were nearly enough to make me come as Frankie stared at us. I tore my eyes away from her fingers disappearing in and out of my favorite hole, and turned back to Travis.

On his knees.

For me.

For her.

Fuck, don't come, Elliot.

He had hardly touched me really, but it was the power of knowing he was doing it willingly, intentionally, that made my knees want to buckle under it all. Paired with the power of knowing how hot it made our girl, I was a mess.

"Color." I grunted out as Trav raised his hands to my waist, seconds before he touched me, and he froze.

"Green." He said effortlessly with that power I envied before we started dating Frankie, and now I craved it. "You?"

"Green." I panted. "So, fucking green."

He smirked with that controlling humor as he slid his fingers in under the waistband of my briefs and slowly—so fucking slowly—started pulling them down.

Was he torturing me or Frankie by going so slow? I couldn't tell.

But I was nearly convulsing as his fingers slid down my groin, on each side of my dick as he pulled them down.

His eyes left mine, and he stared at my body as he stripped me, and when my dick finally sprung free, growing harder by the millisecond now that it was free and aimed up toward my best friend, I nearly came.

"Frankie!" I cried out, and within a second, she was there, sinking to her knees in Trav's lap, her naked body pressed against his fully clothed one as she kneeled at my feet. "Please."

"I've got you, Sunshine," she purred and ran the flat of her tongue up the underside of my cock as Trav wrapped his arms around her lush body, crushing her to him and biting her shoulder like he had been seconds away from losing control like I had been.

I didn't expect Trav to suck my cock. But if he had touched it. At all. Even breathed on it. I would have done something stupid.

Like begged him to lick it or something.

Anything.

"Fuck yes," I growled, fisting Frankie's hair as she started sucking me down her throat. "Just like that."

Trav looked up from her shoulder, breathing through his

nose as he watched, up close, as she sucked on me and I tipped my head back to stare at the ceiling.

If I came while looking into his eyes from this point of view, I'd never recover.

"Deeper, Shade." Trav growled and then Frankie took me all the way down her throat, gagging and holding there like he was—

I dropped my chin to my chest to find his hand on the back of her neck, pushing her mouth down onto my cock with slow, deep thrusts.

"Take his cock all the way down your pretty throat." He demanded, "Make him feel so good."

She moaned, and dropped one hand to my balls, rubbing them the way I loved when I was chasing an orgasm. Frankie pulled off me and gasped, spitting onto my cock and rubbing it in as she stared up at me. "Color?"

"Green." I panted, flicking a glance at Trav behind her as his hands ran down her body to her pussy as she sucked me deep again. "You man?"

"Green." He replied firmly and then bit her neck while pushing his fingers deep into her, making her scream around my cock as she tilted her head and sucked on my balls, making my eyes go cross-eyed. "Teach me."

My knees buckled, but I managed to stay standing barely as she pulled off my cock and looked at him over her shoulder. "Teach you what?"

"How he likes his balls rubbed." He said, looking up at me. "He did it in the shower earlier. I want to know."

"Fuck." I panted, rolling my neck as it felt like they were no longer just pleasuring me, but torturing me.

"On your back." Frankie pushed me back toward the bed. "Before you fall on your ass."

I didn't fight her as I fell onto my back, throwing my arm over my face a millisecond before her lips started their way up my legs from my ankles. Slow, light, wet kisses covered every inch of my calves and knees and then my thighs as she slowed things down, letting me catch my breath.

I couldn't look down at her, or I'd blow my load from just the echo of Trav's words looping through my head.

She could tell. Frankie could always tell what I needed, like she had known me her whole life. "Is that okay with you, Sunshine? Can I teach Trav how you like your balls rubbed when your cock is in my mouth? How you like them squeezed just a little, with a whole lot of rubbing."

"Green." I said, because saying yes felt wrong. I wanted that so fucking badly, but admitting it was too much. So, I gave her the go-ahead instead without looking down.

"Come here, big guy." She purred, and then Trav's hot body was lying on the bed next to my leg. I could feel the skin of his abdomen against my foot, and I fought the urge to see if he was naked, or just shirtless. She kept one wet hand wrapped around my cock as she lay down between my thighs.

I wrapped one leg around her side, anchoring myself to her soft skin and supple body as my best friend laid his hand on my naked thigh, an inch from my balls.

"He likes them rubbed together." She said in a sultry voice that dripped with sex and desire. "Like you've got two ice cubes in your palm, and you're spinning them around."

I knew it was coming, but I still flinched when Trav's rough hand took place of hers, the callouses on his fingertips a stark comparison to the smooth softness of hers, but I didn't dislike it.

Not one fucking bit.

Slowly, and tentatively at first, he started rolling them in his hand as Frankie started sucking me back into her mouth, nails dug deep into my thigh as her hips rocked against the bed in time with her motions. She was as on edge as I was.

But what was Travis thinking?

"Like this?" He asked, and his voice was thick and hoarse.

I couldn't reply, so I nodded in place, but he didn't like that. Quickly, he tightened his grip on my balls, squeezing them just enough to make me jump as a wave of pre-cum filled Frankie's mouth. "Yes," I replied haggardly, dropping my hands to the bed to grab the bedsheets. "Like that."

"Does it feel good," He asked, pushing it further and pressing on the taboo. "Do you like it?"

"Trav." I growled, tensing as Frankie moaned, sucking me harder and deeper.

"Answer me, Elliot." He demanded, and I finally forced myself to look down my body to where the two most perfect people in the world lay on the bed around me. Frankie's eyes were wide and her pupils blown with desire as she pulled off my cock, panting and writhing against the mattress, rubbing her pussy against it as best she could on her belly. Trav stared at me dominantly, his hand working my balls in a way that felt better than anything I'd ever felt before.

"I like it." I panted, admitting something I never imagined feeling, let alone speaking about. "I fucking like how you do it."

"Good," He said, shifting onto his side more, and it was then that I realized he had stripped down before he got on the bed and was naked. And his dick was rock hard, lying against the mattress between him and Frankie, leaving a wet stain on the sheets from his arousal as he pleasured me. "So good, Sunshine."

"Fuck," I growled, throwing my head back as my body tensed with bliss. "Shit."

"Swallow that come, Shade." He instructed, but Frankie was already sucking it out of me as he pumped my balls, rubbing them and squeezing them as they seized, pushing come up my cock and into Frankie's mouth like he had any fucking clue how damn good it felt, how much more powerful it made it all.

"Yellow." I panted, shaking with the intensity of my orgasm, and his hands fell away from my body instantly as Frankie slid up further, sucking me deeper into her mouth and covering my skin with hers. Almost like she could tell I needed the reassurance of her familiar touch in the uncertainty of my post-orgasm mind fuck. "I'm sorry." I covered my eyes again with my arm as my body went lax against the bed. "Fuck, I'm sorry."

"Shh," Frankie soothed, crawling up my body, and I wrapped my arms around her, squeezing her tight as I clung to my sanity. "You're okay. We're okay. Everyone is okay."

I sensed Trav get up off the bed, and guilt washed over me even stronger as I caught my breath. When everything settled, I forced my eyes open, staring at the ceiling as Frankie shifted to the side, still laying over my body but so she could watch my face as I came out of hiding.

From the corner of my eye, I saw Trav sitting in the chair against the window, silently watching me lose my fucking mind, and I wanted to bolt from the room, I wanted to escape the way his stare made my skin feel too tight.

"Talk to me, baby." Frankie whispered, laying a kiss on my shoulder, softly coaxing me into her comfort. "Are you okay?"

I scoffed, an animalistic cry of incredulity as I tried to form words. "I'm sorry. I fucked up."

"No," She stated firmly, running her hand over my chest, "No, you didn't. Nothing is wrong. And no one is angry. Just tell us how you feel. Tell me what happened there."

I scoffed again, but forced myself to take a deep breath, ripping myself wide open to bleed at her feet. "You mean besides the fact that I just had the best orgasm of my life, and I feel fucking guilty and terrible as hell because it wasn't just you making me feel that good?" I laughed humorlessly. "Or the fact that I want to do it again, which isn't fair to you?"

37 - FRANKIE
Blurred Boundaries

"SHH," I whispered, running my fingers through Eli's hair, strumming them as he closed his eyes again and took another deep breath. "I'm not jealous of Travis, Eli." I stated firmly but with a soft voice. "I'm not jealous that you found pleasure in him."

Eli wouldn't open his eyes again, and I could tell how wrecked he was, and I hated that I forced this on him.

Again.

"We won't do it again," I said evenly, "It's okay."

"The fuck we won't." Trav said firmly from behind me, and I whipped my head around to stare at him with daggers.

"Shut it."

"No," He stood up and walked back to the bed, and Eli

rolled away from me to stand on the side of it. They were both naked, I mean damn, we all were, but they were standing there, facing each other with their massively strong and muscular bodies on display and I hated how I ended up getting distracted by it all, again. "We will not shy away from things that make us uncomfortable if it's what we want." Trav turned his disapproving glare my way, "That's your M.O., not mine."

"Me?" I sputtered, jumping up off the bed in frustration, "What the hell did I do?"

"You run!" Trav bellowed and then took a deep breath, hands on his hips in tight fists before he dropped them and his eyes flicked between us. He wasn't angry or mocking, there was only a calm, grounded power there, like he was the only one who saw straight through the mess. "You're both twisting yourselves in knots because of something that isn't wrong. It's not broken. You enjoyed it, Elliot, good. That's the point!"

Eli's laugh was bitter, "The point? Since when is me getting off on your hands the point?"

Trav walked around the bed until they stood toe to toe, and his voice dropped low until it was more deliberate. As if the words should be felt, not heard. "Since we decided we weren't playing the boring game of monogamy. We're polyamorous, I don't know if you two haven't noticed, but we're not dividing ourselves into neat little boxes, forced to stay behind lines that others drew for us. It doesn't mean I'm only allowed to touch her, or you're only allowed to touch her. It means we share. We explore. We find what feels good together. I'm way too fucking old to be limiting myself to what others expect. I did that, and I never found happiness. True fucking happiness. But with you two," He turned and looked at me, "Both of you, I'm happy!"

He wrapped his hand around the back of Eli's neck,

pulling him toward him, in that manly way that always made me weak in the knees. "Monogamy is about exclusivity. One partner. One path. But that's not what we're doing, man." He loosened his grip on Eli and looked at me again. "We're poly. Which means there are no walls here. No one is cheating. No one is betraying anyone. It's the three of us. All in."

My throat went tight as I took a step toward them, "But what if, what if it's too much? What if it changes things? You have to know that there are going to be judgements from the world, are you prepared for that?"

"Am I going to scream from the rooftops that I shot my load watching my best friend stroke his cock?" Trav deadpanned, "No, the same way I wouldn't tell any of the guys on the team that I got so fucking hard knowing they were looking at your braless tits while you secretly cleared out the locker room for us to do that." He held his hand out to me, "It's none of their fucking business what we do behind closed doors. It's ours." When I was within reach, Eli grabbed my other hand, Trav's hold still on his neck. "It doesn't change what we feel, though. It just changes how we show it when we're together. Your body reacting to both of us? That's not wrong. Eli enjoying my touch when we're both ruining him? That's not wrong either. It's just more. And more isn't bad if we're all on board with it."

Eli's shoulders sagged, his breath shaky. "You always make everything sound so simple. Like you aren't self-conscious or worried about anything outside of these walls."

"It's because I'm not." Travis's mouth curved just the slightest. "I've dated dozens of women—"

I growled in a very unladylike way, and Eli chuckled softly, but Travis just pursed his lips at me, unimpressed.

"And I've never felt anything toward any of them like I do when I'm here, with both of you, just like this. We're not rewriting the rules of the universe here. We're rewriting ours. And ours says no guilt. No shame. Only what we want, what we choose, together."

Silence hung thick, but it wasn't heavy anymore. It was settling. Safe.

I let out a shaky laugh, tears prickling my eyes as his resounding strength and belief in me, in Eli, in us hit me in the feels. "How are you always so strong and confident, giving both of us exactly what we need before we even know what it is?"

His thumb brushed my knuckles. "Because love is natural with you two, Shade. Complicated as hell, sure. Some days it feels like I'm managing four toddlers instead of just two." Eli punched him in the gut, and he grunted with a smirk, but I couldn't move as the L word echoed in my ears. "But it's never wrong. It's right."

When Eli finally took a deep breath, his eyes were raw but calmer, squeezing my hand, and I knew Travis was right. We weren't going to break apart under the pressure of the unknown. We were only just beginning to figure out how to fit together as broken pieces coming together as one.

THE STORM HAD BROKEN, but the quiet that followed felt heavier than anything. Our bare skin pressed together as we tangled in bed, with the softness of the sheets covering us in the gentle silence.

Trav leaned up against the headboard with a pillow across his lap, nestling my head, steady and warm, always supporting me. Eli lay across the end of the bed with my foot on his stomach as he absently rubbed it, staring at the ceiling.

It should have been awkward, should have been unbearable after all the things we were all processing, but it wasn't.

Travis made it simple.

No shame, no guilt, just us.

"You said it like it was nothing." I stammered before I could stop myself as I finally addressed the main issue. Eli didn't mention it, and to be honest, I wasn't sure he even caught it at the moment. But Trav didn't say it without meaning to. He never did anything unintentionally. "Like it wasn't—huge."

Trav hummed low, brushing his fingers through my hair fanned out over the pillow, as Eli leaned up on one elbow. "Said what?"

I smiled, closing my eyes as my initial thoughts were proven right by Eli's confusion. "That this is love." The word felt dangerous on my tongue. Fragile even. "Said it like the word itself was easy."

Eli stiffened, and then he laid back down on the bed to stare back up at the ceiling. "It isn't easy. Not for me. I'm not —" He shrugged, and my heart broke for him as his doubt radiated off him like a noxious gas trying to take us all out. Was that how Travis felt when I doubted myself? "I'm not worthy of that. Not from you or her."

My chest tightened, shame rising like bile. "Me either. I've screwed up too much, been broken too badly, too many times. You both deserve someone who—"

"Stop." Travis's voice cut through, sharp but steady, like a command we both leaned into. His fingers tightened in my hair until my eyelids fluttered closed. "Love isn't about who deserves it," he said, voice rough with a conviction I craved. "It's about whom you give it to. And I'm giving it to you. Both of you. Without hesitation. Without doubt. It's not conditional. It's not earned like some damn trophy for your hard work and dedication. It just *is*." I opened my eyes and looked up into his, burning back into me before he shifted them to Eli, unflinching, and I knew Eli was staring back at him. "So quit telling me why you don't deserve it. Quit trying to hand it back. It's already yours."

"Once again," Eli sighed, "You make it sound so easy."

"Because it is," Travis murmured, wiping his thumb over a tear that escaped from my lashes and ran down into my hair without bringing attention to it. "Love's supposed to be the simplest thing in the world, even when the rest is complicated as hell. So let me make this clear to both of you." Travis's fingers tightened again, pulling my head up to face him as another tear spilled onto his abs. "I love you, Frankie Blake, and I can't imagine ever waking up without your warmth and the laughter you've brought to my house with you surrounding me every single day."

"I love you too." I whispered and leaned in to kiss him, feeling the conviction in his touch that my mind wouldn't believe through his words alone.

When I pulled back, I turned and found Eli sitting up on the bed, watching us, and held my hand out for him. He slid behind me, wrapping his arms around my body and his legs ended up pressed against Trav's side.

Our strong and dominant man wrapped his hand around the back of Eli's neck again, holding him steady. "I love you too, Eli." Eli smiled, but I could feel his brush-off coming, no doubt making some joke about friendship and years of camaraderie, but Trav silenced him. "I'm in love with you, the same way I am with Frankie. I can't imagine a day going by without having you here, right here, in this bed, in this home, beside me. We might have started as friends and teammates, building it into some sort of brotherhood, but now, I want more. I want you, Eli."

"Hell," Eli groaned. "I thought I was going insane the last few weeks as this shifted."

Trav smiled that cocky smirk and then leaned in until his face was right in front of Eli's. I covered my lips to keep from gasping like a freaking loser as they hovered, an inch away, a breath apart. "I think tonight proved that this was more than just friendship. I want more than that."

"Prove it." Eli challenged, tightening his arm around my waist even as he shared a moment with Trav that I felt like I wasn't worthy of watching.

Trav closed the distance and kissed Eli.

It wasn't the kiss I'd built up in my head each time I fantasized about this moment. I'd half expected something macho, with chests colliding, teeth clashing, fueled by nothing but testosterone and pride. Yet, it wasn't soft either, not tender or worshipful like when they kissed me, mouths coaxing me open with patience and heat.

It was—hungry. Demanding. A collision of needs neither of them knew how to put into words.

Travis's hand pulled Eli in at the back of his neck, steady and sure. Eli leaned forward as if he'd been waiting years for it, lips moving against Travis's with a desperation that stole my breath. There was nothing delicate about it, just heat and tension, the scrape of Eli's stubble against Trav's beard, the rough sound of two men giving in to something bigger than labels.

And it worked. God, it worked.

I felt the tremor run through Eli's body still wrapped around mine as they pulled back enough to whisper, "I don't know how to do this. But I don't want to stop. Because I love you both too."

"We'll figure it out," I said when they pulled back to look at me, both looking a little sheepish for having a moment without me, but my body and heart was floating on cloud nine as they both got something they deserved for so long. "Together. That's what love does."

For the first time in a long, long time, I let myself believe in someone else.

Two men who broke down every barrier I thought I'd perfected building around my heart and crashed through them like they were never there to begin with.

38 - DANNY

Boo

I FINALLY CAUGHT THEM ALONE. Not her—not Frankie, who couldn't be bothered to raise her own kids. But them—our kids.

Emmie and Toby.

Stupid fucking names that Frankie picked out on her own.

The old woman, who had aimed her finger at my face once, years ago, threatening to kill me and bury me in her backyard, dragged them through the grocery store like she had any fucking right to keep them from me.

My kids.

My blood.

She had no fucking say over them, not any more than I did. Their father.

She paraded them down the aisles, herding them like puppies, stopping to talk to almost everyone like she couldn't tell they were bored shitless.

And I followed a few steps behind with a cart I didn't need.

Toby was taller than the last time I saw him on one of my visits. His face was sharper, older, but he was a mini-me, all the same. He didn't even look twice at me as I pushed my luck and drifted closer in the cereal aisle.

"Toby," His grandmother said as she walked away, "Pick out a cereal and let's go."

"I'm trying." He argued, huffing as he stared at two boxes of sugary food that would rot his brain and his teeth.

I crouched down low a few feet away and pointed to the one between us. "That one's my favorite."

He blinked politely, like I was some stranger making small talk. "Mine too." He said, and then turned back, but instead of grabbing the one I pointed out, he picked up the one with some cartoon hockey player on the front and ran off toward where his grandma paused at the end of the aisle, talking to someone else.

The kid had no clue who I was, technically, he had never met me.

Good. That meant I could teach him. I could teach him respect and the importance of rank.

Emmie though—Emmie knew.

When I tore my gaze away from Toby and stood to my full height, I found her eyes locked on me, peeking from around her grandmother's side. Her big green eyes widened the moment I stared back at her.

Her little hand gripped the cart like she was holding on for dear life. She didn't speak, but her lip trembled as she ducked behind the old woman's coat.

Almost as if I were the big terrible monster living under her bed, the shadow in the dark.

She remembered.

The fear on her face made her look so much like her mother, and my blood warmed with excitement. Frankie poisoned Emmie against me, filled her head with lies about where I was and why I wasn't in their life, but her fear meant she remembered the truth about me.

Silently, I followed them from a safe distance. Every aisle. Every step.

Emmie's scared eyes searched for me around every turn.

I imagined walking up, snatching her wrist and making her face me head on. Making her say my name.

I imagined Toby's confusion, the dawning horror when he realized the man talking to him wasn't just some stranger but the man his mother told him was dead.

A real-life bogeyman.

But not here.

Not yet.

I wasn't sloppy or stupid.

I had waited four years to make my last move against Frankie.

When I finally made my move, it wouldn't be just her on her knees.

I'd make all of them fall to their knees for me.

THE RINK SMELLED how I expected, but walking in made my skin tingle with the closeness to my prize, like being in her space made it more real.

I slid onto a stool at the bar, ordered a beer from a middle-aged man and let my eyes roam the place. She wasn't working; she was in her college classes, finalizing the last few weeks of her degree. It was pathetic that she thought a piece of paper would make her worthy of something.

Part of me wished she was working, so I could catch her behind the counter, watch her pour a drink with that sharp little smile she gave strangers. But tonight wasn't the time for that.

It didn't matter. I had time.

Soon, I'd have all the time in the world to fuck with her out in the open.

The older man next to me nursed a beer, half watching the muted hockey game on the TV above the bar. I recognized him from stalking Frankie—Rick. Rink rat, coach, bartender, Zamboni driver. He was always around.

Always in my way.

I waited until he sighed at a bad play before I broke the ice and spoke up, "This place is kind of a dump, isn't it?"

He glanced over and snorted with a friendly smile, "Some people call this dump home, so watch it."

I sipped my beer, pulling back my lips to smile at him with the same friendliness. "A friend of mine told me to stop by, Frankie. Cute little thing, dark hair, green eyes. Body full of curves and sass. You know her?"

Rick's whole face softened, and he chuckled, shaking his head like he couldn't help himself. "Don't let her hear you describing her like that, she'll knock your lights out. But yeah, everyone here knows Frankie. She runs the place and practically owns it. Strong as they come, hell of a mom. Her kiddos are the heartbeat of this place."

My jaw clenched, but I forced a smile. "Yeah, I bet."

He leaned closer, lowering his voice conspiratorially, as if we were good friends. "She's not working tonight, but you might see her around. I don't know how she does it. Bartending, raising two kids, going to college, and keeping those two idiots on skates in line."

"Two idiots?" I asked, feigning casualness.

Rick laughed, tossing back the rest of his drink. "Her men. Trav and Eli. One's a firefighter, the other one builds homes. Good men. She's got herself a little fan club here, I'll tell you that."

The words hit like a blade to the ribs, twisting in and cutting everything up to pieces. My grip tightened around my beer glass. *Her men.* He said it as if it were a fact. Like they belonged to her.

Like they all belonged to each other.

I leaned in, my smile tightening. "And she just what? Takes up with the both of them? No one bats an eye? Where I come from, the town would run her out with a scarlet A on her chest for being a slut."

The menace in my voice was strong, and I grimaced as Rick's grin faltered.

His brow kit as he studied me more closely, like the air had shifted, "Funny question for a stranger. How do you know Frankie again?"

I pushed back from the bar stool, sliding a few bills across the counter. "Doesn't matter."

Rick straightened, his shoulders squaring, "It does if you're asking about Frankie."

I met his stare head-on, letting him see the truth simmering just under my skin. "Tell her I stopped by. She'll know who I am."

And then I walked out, leaving him with his mouth half open and the unease settling in his gut.

Exactly where I wanted it.

39 - FRANKIE
Dreams that Scream

THE SCREAM SHREDDED through the cabin like a knife, shrill and ear splitting.

I was on my feet before my brain caught up, jumping over Eli's body as the sound of Emmie's wails tore me out of a dead sleep and yanked me down the hall toward her. The guys were right behind me, bare feet pounding up the stairs to her room and crashing through the door to her new room all together as one.

She was curled into a ball in the center of her brand-new bed, thrashing in her blankets and sobbing as her little hands clawed at the air like she was fighting off invisible hands. "No!" She cried, "No, don't! Mama! Please, Mama!"

My chest caved in as I sprinted across the room to her,

throwing myself onto her bed as I wrapped her up, whispering his name over and over, trying to break her free of her nightmare.

"Baby girl," I cooed, trying to hide the fear in my voice. "It's okay, it's Mama. I've got you. You're safe, baby. You're safe."

But she wouldn't stop screaming, even as she clung to me like she would drown if she let go. Her tiny voice hiccupped through the sobs, broken words spilling out. "I—I saw him. I saw the monster. He was here."

The room was silent except for her cries.

I felt Travis's presence at my back, solid and steady as Eli crouched on the other side of the bed, turning the light on. His face was tight and pale in the warm light as he held Emmie's hand in his big one.

The word monster hung between us, heavy and sharp.

I brushed Emmie's hair back, kissing her damp forehead as I rocked her against my chest. But my mind raced, cold dread trickling down my spine until it felt like my heart was going to burst through my ribs.

"Who baby? Who did you see?" I whispered, praying for some fictional villain to be the star of her nightmare.

"Him." She sobbed, "The man who locked me in the closet." Her chest rattled as the memories assaulted her. "The man who made you scream from the other side of the door."

My blood ran cold, and I could feel every single molecule in the air around me as time stood still.

Danny. Her father.

One of the last nights I spent with him before I had Toby was one of the worst nights of my life.

The night I thought he was finally going to kill me for good. He had locked Emmie in the closet when she wandered from her bedroom and found him on top of me, choking me. I had been so pregnant I couldn't fight back, even if I was stupid enough to try.

But then he locked her in our closet, and I couldn't get to her as he beat me. I couldn't ease her fears and cries as she clawed her little fingers under the door, screaming for me.

What if she didn't just dream it?

What if somehow, someway, Danny got close enough for her to see him?

It didn't fit.

That wasn't how he worked. He was a coward who slithered in the shadows and played games. But the way she screamed sounded like recognition, not just fear.

"I've got her," I whispered, holding Emmie tighter as I looked from Eli to Trav. "I'm staying in here."

Travis didn't move, standing over us with his sweatpants on and his big bare chest rising and falling with power and strength. Eli's soft voice was low but lethal. "Lockdown starts right now." He held my stare. "The kids don't go anywhere without us. Ever again."

I looked at him and shivered from the fire in his stare. It matched the power radiating off Travis's hot skin. They meant it.

Finally, Travis spoke, his voice quiet like a growl. "This isn't just some bad dream, Frankie. We can't keep brushing this off. If that bastard is circling closer, we need to put this on record. We need to go to the authorities and tell them what's happening."

I wanted to argue, to tell them they're overreacting—but Emmie's cries broke through my skin again, raw and terrified. My little girl saw something, maybe someone.

Even if she doesn't remember her father, she could have recognized him in person if she had seen him.

Silently, I tucked her against me, laying back on her

pillow as my heartbeat stuttered, rocking her through the echoes of her fear. One thought clawed its way through the chaos, one I didn't have the bravery to say out loud.

If Danny really showed himself, then he wasn't just after me anymore.

He was after all of us.

I WORKED ON AUTOPILOT, stuck in my head, the same way I had been since Emmie woke up in the middle of the night, screaming about the monster in her nightmare. Eli had gone to work for a half shift to cover someone else, and Trav stood at the front door at six thirty in the morning, like he couldn't quite convince himself to leave, to leave us.

But we couldn't live like that.

I had to be strong.

For my kids.

For them.

Which meant I finally had to go to the police. I had to file a report and give them all the things I had to start building a case against the father of my kids. It would be hard, and people would doubt my word, and second-guess my integrity and my character, and I'd have to convince them I was a good mom before they ever treated me fairly.

It was all the things that kept me from going to the police any of the other times Danny abused me when we were together. Or any of the times after I finally left when I felt like the walls were closing in around me because of his little games.

But I had too much to lose to just be complacent in his abuse any longer.

The rink bar was buzzing the way it always did on a Wednesday night, beer league guys swapping chirps, locals hooting and hollering at the TVs as hockey played out across the country. Rick poured drafts, living his best life as I wiped down the bar top, ready to start kicking people out so I could go home.

Home.

The serenity I found in the beautiful cabin in the woods, tucked into bed between Travis and Eli, with my kids tucked into their beds upstairs, happy and safe.

Safe.

Even thinking the word left anxiety crawling across my skin.

Trav and Eli were sitting at the bar with their friends, pretending to stick around to watch the game, instead of heading home like they usually did after practice. When in reality, they were waiting for me.

Watching me.

Waiting for me to crumble.

So they could catch me.

I was so distracted by my own thoughts that it took a second to notice that something had happened around me, the noise in the bar cut out like someone hit the off switch on a speaker. Glancing up from the bar, I watched as everyone in the place turned and looked toward the front door, at the newcomers standing there looking over everyone.

A man and woman, wearing dress clothes and matching jackets with some sort of badge on the breast pocket I couldn't make out from across the room. Each of them had file folders in their hands, as if they were ready to conduct some sort of official business.

Clearly, they had the wrong place if they were looking for something official. There wasn't an official in the place.

Or at least that was what I had thought until three uniformed police officers walked in behind them. Two I recognized as locals, the third was the chief of police himself.

Shit.

Something was wrong.

My skin prickled as I wiped my hands on a rag as the chief pointed toward the bar and the two officials headed our way.

My way.

"Franchesca Blake?" The woman asked, voice echoing too loud in the silence.

Every eye in the place swung toward me, and my stomach dropped.

They were close enough now that I dared to glance at the emblem on their jackets.

The badge.

The title.

Department of Children and Families.

"Right here." Rick said, stepping up beside me, placing his hand on my shoulder in solidarity as I fought to speak like I had suddenly forgotten how.

The man didn't even flinch as he pulled a thick envelope out of the folder and laid it on the bar in front of me. "My name is Agent Andrews, of the Department of Children and Families. You've been named in a petition, and we're here to conduct a full investigation into the criminal charges claimed against you."

The air left my lungs as Rick tightened his hold on my shoulders. "For what?" I whispered.

"Child neglect. Child Endangerment. And Child abandonment." The woman next to him said with a haughty sneer as my world crashed down around me, with every eye in the room staring at me like I hadn't been friends with everyone in the room for the last three decades of my life.

"There has to be some sort of mistake." I said, grabbing the envelope and ripping it open.

But there in black bold ink on the first page were the allegations and words I never wanted to read about myself.

Unfit mother.

Neglect.

Abandonment.

Risk to minors.

My hands shook so hard the paper rattled.

"Bullshit." The growl came from beside them, making both agents flinch across the bar.

Travis.

Stepping up so fast, his stool screeched across the floor. His chest rose and fell as if he were holding himself back by a thread.

Eli wasn't holding back at all. He was already behind the bar, slamming his fist down on the bar top, "You walk in here, in front of the entire fucking town, and you throw this at her. Who the hell would make up these claims?"

"Sir, we're just—" The man in the official jacket that mocked me held his hands up, stepping backward toward the armed guards they brought with them for their late-night visit.

"No," Travis's low, lethal voice interrupted him as he came to my other side, "You're not doing this here. Not like this."

"Now, Travis," The chief of police, a man my mother went to school with, stepped forward with a fatherly tone dripping with authority and disappointment, "Let the agents do their job. They have to investigate the claims; they're too compounding to be brushed off."

"I don't understand," I cried, closing my eyes as tears

welled up in them. I felt like I had landed in some alternate universe and couldn't get my feet underneath me. "What exactly is being claimed against me? By whom? My kids aren't neglected. I haven't abandoned them."

"Where are your kids currently, Ms. Blake?" The female agent asked, raising one unimpressed eyebrow at me.

"At home. Sleeping." I answered.

"And who's watching them?" She fired back instantly, "While you're here—" She eyed up the massive crowd.

"Working." I clapped back in anger. "While I'm *working*, they are at home, in bed, with my mother watching them until we get home."

"We." The man said, flipping through his file. "Would that include a Mr. Travis Hayes and a Mr. Elliot Torres?" He looked up at the two men flanking my shoulders with open disdain, like he was counting the marks against me and just found two more.

"Yes." I ground out through my clenched teeth. "Is that against the law?"

The man tsked, and Eli's hand settled on my back, like he was trying to offer some sort of comfort under the man's blatant judgement. "It is if you're subjecting your children to depravity and indecent behavior."

"Oh my God," I whispered in horror. "It's Danny." Trav looked at me with murder in his eyes as Eli's hand tightened around my back. "We should have—" I felt despair trying to pull me under into hysterics as I realized just how fucked I was. "He went to them first, which means they'll never believe me."

"Shh," Eli pressed his lips to my temple as I fell into his support. "He's not going to win this."

"So, help me God, if you believe the blatant lies of Danny Masters over this whole situation, you're as dumb as you fucking look walking in here and throwing this bullshit at Frankie. She's an incredible mother, and you don't even know the half of the shit that piece of trash has done to her!" Trav roared, losing his normal grip on his control and dissolving.

"Ma'am," Agent Andrews ignored Trav's outburst and glared at me, "As part of our investigation, we'll be placing the children," He opened his file again, "Emmaline and Toby Blake into protective custody."

"No!" I broke, falling completely into Eli's arms. "You can't take my kids! That's insane, you can't take them! Based on one person's claims? That's absurd! They need me!"

"Then why aren't they with you?" The woman scorned me, and I felt every shred of humanity slip from my body as I realized I was already guilty in their eyes.

"Ma'am," Andrews interrupted again. "We're going to let you go with us to collect the kids, but we're placing them in the care of their father under an emergency custody ruling until this investigation is complete."

"Please!" I sobbed, "No, you can't! Please don't give them to him! Please!"

"Over my dead body are you placing those kids in the care of the man who beat and abused Frankie for years." Eli pulled my face into his neck and held me tight as he yelled at the agents, ripping open my secrets for the entire bar to hear, hoping to save my kids. "You say that the allegations against Frankie are too severe to leave anything to chance, then those are my allegations against him. He beat her. He abused her. And when she finally got away and ran home to be safe here in Cedar Bluff," He sneered, like he was speaking to the Chief himself, "Where outsiders don't get to come into our community and fuck with our people, he followed her! He has been stalking her, breaking into her home, stealing items from her belongings, and terrorizing her children. He cut the brakes on her car trying to hurt her for fucks sake!" He roared, "And if you don't believe me then ask Lenny," He waved his hand out to where the mechanic sat, drinking a beer with his wife and his friends. Then he looked at one cop standing behind the agents, "And don't fucking just stand there silently while this shit all goes down, Johnny Hallstead, because you were at the crash that night. Time to talk! These aren't just my allegations; there are others who have seen the shit that Danny's been doing to Frankie and her children. He's terrorizing them! You can't honestly think for one second that they're better off with him!"

"He's right," Lenny stepped forward instantly, "A few weeks ago, Frankie's car was towed to my shop, with front end damage after Travis lost control while driving it. There was suspicion behind the crash because of the way the car responded during the incident, and when I looked into it, the brake lines had been cut. Not all the way through so the line would bleed instantly, but in a way that would let them bleed with each press of the brake until suddenly there would just be no resistance at all. Travis sustained injuries in the crash.

"We responded to that crash," Officer Hallstead piped up, giving the Chief a pointed look. "There were no skid marks, backing the claim."

"Did you report any of this?" The Chief asked, looking at me directly.

Shrinking, I grimaced as I shook my head, "We were coming to the station to file a report in the morning."

Instantly, all the credibility Eli had built for me disappeared just as fast. "Please, you have to believe me. I don't neglect my kids. They're my whole life. Every single thing I've ever done has been for them. I work for them. I go to school for them. I have provided for them 100% on my own and have every single second since we moved back here four years ago. Toby has never even met Danny! You can't put them in his care; he doesn't know anything about them!"

The Chief watched the agents share a glance and then stepped in. Maybe it was the long-standing reputation of Travis's family, or Eli's respectable character as a first responder, or maybe even his friendship with my mom, but he stuck his neck out.

"They're right though, report or not, those allegations are too serious to place the kids in his care. There has to be another solution."

"Foster care." The woman agent, who never even introduced herself, said, "We will place them in a temporary housing facility until we can run our—"

"No!" I cried again, banging my hands on the bar as I lost my grip on my control. "You'll traumatize them! You're standing there, judging me for being a working mom, who escaped an impossible situation and has fought for every single thing I have given them, calling me an unfit mother, but you're willing to just throw them in foster care when there are dozens of other solutions!"

"What would you recommend we do then?" She pursed her lips with her hand on her lips, and I wanted to reach across the bar and slap the attitude off her fucking face more than anything else in the world.

"If I'm the problem, then I'll leave. Let them stay in their home, with Travis and Eli, who are good men, loving men who care for them and protect them every single day alongside me, and I'll leave while you do your investigation. Or let them stay at my mom's! Anything but the two pathetic, heartless solutions you've thrown like they don't fucking matter to you! They matter to me! Let me keep them safe!"

She sighed as if the mere mention of my recommendations annoyed her, but the other agent looked more reasonable.

"Please," I implored, "It's late. Let them stay in their beds and in their home."

The Chief stepped forward again and spoke to the agents, "Mrs. Blake, Frankie's mother, is a good woman, the kids would be safe with her if that's what route you want to take, but I think they'd be better staying at home with Trav and Eli. Both are stand-up men, who have never been in trouble."

The woman scoffed, "You have to hear the absurdity of that statement as plainly as I do." She put her hands on her hips, "How long have you *three* been in a relationship?"

"Months." Travis snapped irritability. "And the kids have lived with us for almost as long thanks to Danny's tormenting. They moved in with us to be safe."

"Fine," Andrews sighed as he closed up his folder. "But we'll be conducting a formal search of the home, and we'll need you to come down to the office for questioning."

The words sounded so far away as I blinked in disbelief. I tried to find relief that the kids could stay with Trav and Eli, but I couldn't get past the part where I wasn't free of the whole situation.

"You are not to return to the home until you've been cleared, *if* you're cleared. You're also not permitted to have any contact with the children. No phone calls, no visits, no bumping into them at school pickup. Nothing." The woman stated firmly and then laid a card down on the bar top. "You can follow us to the office now to begin your interview."

"Yes, Ma'am." I whispered, haunted inside and shamed.

I couldn't go home.

The agents turned and walked away, as if they hadn't walked in ten minutes ago, destroyed my entire sense of security and happiness, before leaving for the night.

The Chief and his officers lingered longer, coming up to the bar. "Frankie, I'd like you to come down to the station tomorrow to start the paperwork on these other incidents."

"I—" I stammered, blinking away the tears. "How—" I suddenly felt like I was going to collapse.

"Shh," Trav kissed the back of my head as Eli pulled me into his chest again. "Eli will go with you, and I'll go home to the kids." I turned and looked at him, shaking my head in absolute defeat. "We're going to clear this all up, I promise you, Shade. No one will take those kids from us. No one will touch them, I promise you."

"Go on," Eli said, squeezing Trav's arm as he turned us to all walk out. "Rick, close up."

"On it." Rick said, patting me on the shoulder as Eli pulled me from the bar, taking the back door to his truck with Trav following us.

"I'll pack you some things and send them home with your mom." Trav said, pulling me into his arms and squeezing me so tight my bones creaked under pressure. But I never wanted him to let go. "I love you, Frankie. I promise you I won't let anyone take them from us. Those damn kids are ours."

I cried again, melting into his strength and crumbling under the fear of Danny getting his claws into my kids because of me. He'd destroy every good part of them, every inch of innocence inside of them that believed in right and wrong. They'd never heal from the venom they found in him.

When Travis turned the wheel of his truck toward the opposite side of the rink, taillights glowing red against the dark on his way home, to be with the kids, to a place where I wasn't allowed, something inside of me broke.

It didn't matter that he was going to the kids. It didn't matter that he was protecting them, the only thing that was important right now.

All I saw was distance. Him driving away from me.

I felt it.

The familiar ache in my chest as I realized what Danny was doing to me all over again. The alienation. The isolation. The distance he forced between me and everyone that mattered in my life.

He was doing it again. And he was going to get away with it if I didn't find some way to prove something I didn't believe most days myself.

I was a good mom.

But there was a hollow ache of knowing I couldn't be their mother and a partner to anyone but Danny.

He'd never allow it.

Eli touched my hand on the console, murmured something steady, but it barely cut through the roar in my head. Because in that instant, I realized DCFS didn't need to prove I was unfit. I already felt like I was.

I had to walk away from Travis and Eli if I ever wanted this to end.

I had to choose my children over myself if I had even the barest chance of keeping them safe from the monster that fathered them.

40 - ELI
Screaming into the Void

THE OFFICE SMELLED of stale coffee and ink, the kind of place where lives got shredded and filed away in manila folders. Frankie sat beside me in a stiff chair, her shoulders tense, papers clutched in her lap. She looked smaller than I'd ever seen her.

The walls were closing in on her, like she was already braced for the worst, and it gutted me.

All I wanted to do was pull her into my arms, snarl at everyone in the building that she was a damn good mother, better than anyone I'd ever known, and drag her out.

But I couldn't, not here.

Trav was blowing up my phone, obsessively inquiring about what was happening and how Frankie was doing. The kids were asleep, and her mother had broken down the moment he told her the news.

There was nothing we could do to quell their fears; we could simply support them as we let the process run its course and hope that justice prevailed.

So, I sat still, jaw tight, trying to be steady when she glanced at me. Because if I lost it, she would too.

The agent across the desk shuffled through the report, every word another knife twisting in my gut.

Unfit. Neglect. Exposing minors to an unsafe environment. Unsupervised time.

My fists curled on my knees. Neglect? I'd seen Frankie skip meals so her kids could eat. I'd seen her stumble in exhausted from late-night shifts and early school drop-offs but still make it work to do homework and bedtime stories simultaneously while going to school for her own degree.

I'd seen her carry the weight of the entire world alone and somehow never let it crush them.

If that was unsafe, then I didn't know what the hell safe was anymore.

Frankie's voice cracked when she finally spoke up, cutting through the silence as the agent prolonged the suspense, scribbling in her notes. "I love my kids. They're my life. I'd die before I let anything happen to them."

The agent didn't even look up, as if Frankie's heart bleeding on the table didn't matter.

I reached under the desk, found her hand, and squeezed. She squeezed back, so hard it hurt, but I didn't let go.

She was breaking in front of me, and I couldn't stop it. I couldn't shield her from this. I could only sit here and hold her while strangers decided if she got to keep the two people who mattered the most to her.

And I swear in that moment, I hated Danny more than I'd ever hated anything in my life.

The agent's pen scratched across the form as if she were already writing the verdict when she finally cleared her throat and started the *investigation*.

Interrogation was more like it.

"Ms. Blake," she said without looking up, "do your children often spend evenings at the ice rink unsupervised while you're working?"

Frankie's voice shook. "They're never unsupervised. The players, coaches—"

"Are not parental supervision." The woman cut in, cold as steel.

"But I am," I cut in just as powerful. "Travis and I are parental figures in their lives as their mother's partners. Therefore, we qualify as parental supervision when they're at the rink. And they're never there without us. So no, the answer to your question is no, they do not spend evenings at the rink unsupervised while Frankie works."

The woman's eyes squinted in indignation slightly before she looked back down at the papers. "Ms. Blake, your petition shows a pattern of neglectful behavior." Looking back up at Frankie, she pushed on, "The elementary school they attend documented four instances this year alone when you've been late to pick them up."

I could hear Frankie swallow, but she replied through her fear. "Never more than a few minutes. The doors were always still open; I wasn't that late. It was just a few minutes."

"Were you spending that time with your lovers?" The woman cut making my skin crawl.

"No," Frankie answered firmly, "I was at college, attending classes to get my business degree. Those four instances were when my class ran over, and I was stuck arriving a few moments late. That's all."

"How many sexual relationships have you been in over the last four years?"

"Are you kidding me?" I roared, and Frankie flinched, the accusation laced with enough venom to bruise her.

"None." Frankie replied firmly, "I don't date. I don't go out. I don't have friends. I don't do anything but work, go to school, and take care of my kids, taking them from hockey practice and art camp and every other extracurricular activity I can afford because I want them to be well-rounded individuals." She took a shuddering breath and pressed on. "Until I started dating Travis and Elliot, I hadn't been with anyone since my children's father."

The agent turned her gaze to me. Sharp. Too sharp.

"Mr. Torres, correct? You and your friend—Mr. Hayes. You're both romantically involved with Ms. Blake?"

Frankie inhaled sharply, shame burning her cheeks. This was her worst fear come true.

I squared my shoulders, meeting her stare head on, "Yes. Both of us. And if you think loving Frankie makes her an unfit mother, then you've never seen what real parenting looks like. It doesn't matter if there's one or two of us, the dynamic in our household does not differ from any other single parent dating and introducing their children to their partners."

The pen stopped scratching across her notes, and the room got colder almost instantly. "Are the children exposed to your—relationship?"

The question was acid in my gut. What the fuck did she think we did in front of the kids?

"They're exposed to love. To safety. To two men who would lay down their lives for them, same as their mother.

That's what they see. They're loved by a woman, and two men, who are finally giving them the good male influence in their lives that they've been lacking since their father beat the shit out of their mother so badly, she ran for her life and returned to Cedar Bluff."

Frankie broke then, tears spilling as she buried her face in her hands. "They're my *babies*. I would never hurt them. I would never put them at risk."

With a mask of impassive power, the agent wrote something else, and I felt my control slipping with each stroke of her pen. My voice dropped, low and dangerous.

"You're twisting her life into something ugly because her ex fed you lies. You want to investigate? Fine. But don't sit there and act like you already know the end of the story. You don't know her. You don't know us."

The agent didn't flinch, didn't even acknowledge the fury radiating off me. Just opened the folder next to her on the table and pulled out something.

"What do you have to say about this?" she asked, laying down a dark photo on the table in front of Frankie.

"Oh, my God—" Frankie's voice broke on a startled sob as she flipped the photo over, disgusted by the image.

"Jesus fuck." I growled, ripping it from her hands and crumpling it. "Seriously?"

"Well," The agent asked, raising one brow. "You tell me what that is, because to me, it looks like you're engaging in a sex act in the middle of a public parking lot. Topless in the wide open, not even trying to hide it."

"You can't throw out nude photos of a woman and hold them against her when she didn't consent to them being taken!" I roared.

The agent didn't even blink. "The security camera footage from the outside of the rink had them. We didn't invade any privacy to obtain them. If you wanted privacy, perhaps you should have had your orgy behind closed doors."

"You listen here—"

"Elliot, please," Frankie cried, pulling me back to my seat as I rose to my feet, towering over the infuriating woman. I fell back down into the chair, my body coiled tight like it would snap at any moment. "My children were nowhere near that situation, Ma'am. I would never do something like that around them. And I wasn't in the wide open, I was in a personal vehicle."

"No, they weren't around that night, Ms. Blake." The woman stood up, gathering her paperwork, "Because once again, someone else was taking care of them for you while you frolicked around doing whatever you damn well please." She walked away from the table. "We'll be in touch. In the meantime, no contact with the minors involved."

Without another word, she left the room, leaving a shattered and broken Frankie in her wake.

THE TRUCK RIDE to Lucy Blake's home, in the middle of the night, was a quiet kind of hell.

Frankie sat curled against the passenger door, her forehead pressed to the cold glass, papers clutched tight in her lap. She wouldn't let go of that damn envelope holding all the cruel and untrue things they claimed against her.

She had no tears left to cry, no words left to say, she was simply silent. And the silence was so thick it pressed in on my chest, making it hard to breathe.

We should be going home, to the cabin, to Travis and the kids, but the agents refused to budge on their order for no interaction, and Frankie was being forced to stay at Lucy's for the time being.

I just prayed it wouldn't be for long, because a part of her was dying inside with each minute separated from her children.

I wanted to fill the silence, promising her it would be okay, that we'd fight it, and that the department created to protect children wouldn't succeed in destroying a happy home based on lies fed to them by a monster. But every word felt like a lie when she looked so broken.

So instead, I reached across the seat and wrapped my hand around hers. She didn't move, didn't squeeze it back, but she didn't pull away either.

I held on anyway.

By the time we pulled into her mom's driveway, it felt like years had passed since I had left the house that morning for work.

How had I lived three lifetimes in a single day?

The porch light outside Lucy's small cape glowed warm, but everything inside of me was ice as Frankie silently slid from the truck without making any eye contact with me.

Lucy was waiting in the doorway, wrapped up tight in an oversized sweater, her face pale and crumpled. She didn't ask questions as we walked into her home, she just pulled Frankie into her arms the second she crossed the threshold.

"My baby," She whispered, rocking her grown daughter like she was a little girl all over again. "My sweet baby girl."

Frankie clung to her for a second before she slipped free, her voice hollow and thin. "I can't. I can't be soft right now. Please, just let me go."

With dead eyes, she turned to me, like the fight had already been drained from her soul. "Eli," She whispered, swallowing down as emotions tried to make her crumble,

"Take care of them. Please, just—tell them I love them and that I'm sorry." She broke, shoulders crumbling under it all as she sobbed, "Tell them how sorry I am."

The bottom dropped out of my world as I took a step toward her, "Frankie, no—"

But she backed away, moving down the hall and disappearing into the dark of her childhood bedroom, the door clicking shut behind her with finality.

I stood frozen in the entryway, Lucy's hand clutching mine, her eyes wet and pleading. "Don't let her give up, Eli," She begged, "He can't win. She won't survive it."

All I could do was nod, heart splitting wide open because I knew her words were the truth. Frankie wouldn't be able to exist on this earth if she was kept from her kids, they were her world. "Don't let her out of your sight," I murmured, taking a deep breath and forcing my shoulders to stand firm and strong. "We have to be sturdy when she can't be, but we have to keep her safe."

Her mom nodded, knowing how fragile our black cat was at that very moment, and squeezed my hand. "Go home to Trav, I've got our girl."

I backed out of her home, back out into the icy cold night even though I wanted to push my way into Frankie's space, and hold her tight while she fell apart so all the broken pieces of her soul would have a safe place to be stored until she was ready to let me put them all back together again, but I couldn't.

Not at the moment.

Instead, I pulled out of her driveway and headed toward home.

I couldn't help Frankie right now, but I could help the kids to feel as little of a ripple as possible while we all lived in limbo.

With my very last dying breath, I'd take care of those damn kids like they were my own, because at this point, they were.

They were ours.

And so was their mom.

We'd prove it.

41 - TRAVIS
Reinforcements

WE KEPT the kids at home.

It didn't matter that it was a school day; it didn't matter that I was supposed to be on a job site, or that Eli was supposed to be at the firehouse. After last night, there was no way in hell we were letting those kids out of our sight knowing that Danny was trying to get them in his custody.

So, I made breakfast, Eli kept the cartoons rolling, and when Toby asked why Mom wasn't there, I gave him the first lie I could stomach.

"She's got a really nasty stomach bug, bud. Grammie Blake is taking care of her for a few days so she doesn't get anyone else sick."

He frowned, suspicious in that sharp way of his, but

nodded slowly. Emmie just clutched her stuffed goalie bear tighter and asked if she could call Frankie to see how she was feeling.

I swallowed down bile as I gave her a smile and told her we'd call her soon.

Eli and I were able to keep them entertained and distracted for a few hours before they started getting suspicious. Eli tried to referee a hockey scrimmage in the living room using couch cushions as goals, but when Toby launched himself across the coffee table, I knew we needed backup.

So, I called my parents.

Mom and Dad showed up within the hour, arms full of board games and cookies, love beaming out of them bright enough to hold my brittle smile together.

My mom swept Emmie up into her lap, cuddling with her on the couch like she'd been waiting her whole life for that hug. Dad set up Candy Land with Toby on the coffee table, letting the boy cheat just enough to win every round.

The house felt lighter with them there. Softer. Like maybe we could shield the kids from the storm brewing outside our walls. But every time I caught Eli's eye, I saw the same thing I felt in my chest; the weight of what we weren't saying.

Frankie wasn't here. She was at her mom's, broken and alone, fighting a war she should have never been thrown into.

It didn't help that she wouldn't answer any of our calls. She sent a few texts, mostly asking about the kids, asking how we were doing, but anytime we asked about her, she deflected.

She was firmly back behind those walls that Eli and I had worked so hard to break down. And it fucking gutted me to the core, I felt like at any moment, my insides were going to fall out onto the floor, and I'd have a moment to recognize the impeding pain and death heading my way, but I wouldn't be able to stop it.

I hated the doom lingering in my chest.

As much as I smiled for the kids, as much as I held Emmie's hand and gave her unlimited cuddles on the couch when she missed her mom, and high-fived Toby's "hockey goals," and eased his worries, my gut burned with the truth.

We were holding the line. That was all it was. One day at a time. One step at a time.

We would keep the kids safe, we would keep them loved, until Frankie came back to us.

But God help the man who thought he could rip them away from her.

Because if DCFS didn't see the truth of who she was, I'd carve it into the world myself.

After lunch, Emmie lay down in her bed to watch a movie, and Toby passed out on the couch after one too many chocolate chip cookies from my mom's loot, leaving the house quiet.

I stepped into the kitchen, hands braced on the counter to breathe, I just needed to catch my breath and then I'd go back in.

Eli followed, sliding a hand over my shoulder as he leaned against the counter next to me, and not long after, my mom and dad joined us. It was the first kid-free moment we'd had all day.

My mom's eyes were wet, her voice low so Toby didn't hear from the couch. "How bad is it?" When I called them this morning on an SOS, I gave a very condensed version of what was happening, but they deserved to know the truth.

Eli and I shared a look before I answered, my throat felt like glass shards had taken the place of my tonsils as I spoke.

"Bad. They are claiming neglect and abuse. Things that hold the weight of felonies if she's found guilty of them, let alone the fact that they'll take the kids in a heartbeat over them. All because her ex is a psychopath."

My dad's jaw set, his rough, weathered hands curling into fists on the counter, "That bastard's been poison since the day I met him. If he thinks he can take those kids, he'll have to go through us too."

Mom reached for my arm, squeezing hard. "Travis, Eli— you're not in this alone. And neither is Frankie; we'll stand with her. Publicly, if that's what it takes, we'll tell anyone who asks what kind of mother Frankie is. How those kids light up when she walks into a room. How they're thriving because of her, not in spite of her." Her voice cracked, but she straightened her spine and stood strong, mirroring the brave woman I'd admired my whole life. "And if they try to take them away from her, from you both, then they'll have to look me in the eye while they do it."

Something in my chest loosened for a moment. It didn't feel like just me and Eli holding the line with my parents here. It felt like a family.

I nodded steady, "Good, because we're going to need every ounce of strength we can get."

Dad clapped me on the shoulder, his eyes hard with the same determination I felt in my gut. "Then it's settled. Whatever storm's coming, this family weathers it together."

I glanced back into the living room, at Toby's sleeping frame on the couch, echoed by Emmie's sweet musical playing from her bedroom upstairs, and my throat burned again.

Together.

That was the only way we were going to win this.

THE KIDS WERE TUCKED into bed, sleeping soundly. We managed to hold them off on yet another request to call Frankie when Eli set their imaginations free as he described how bad her stomach bug was. There was just something about kids and poop, they loved talking about it.

My parents left, lingering as long as possible, making us both promise that they could come back in the morning, maybe even take the kids to their house for the day so we could support Frankie.

I was hesitant to let the kids out of my sight, but I desperately ached to be there for Frankie too. She refused to let us come to her.

And I tried—fuck, I was trying so damn hard—to respect her wishes and let her keep some of her power over the situation, but I was unraveling the longer I didn't have her in my arms.

Eli wasn't weathering it any better than I was, and my pressing need to console him, since I couldn't get to her, was overwhelming me. He sat slumped at the end of the bed in our room, hands fisted in the blankets as he stared off blindly at the fireplace across the room. His broad shoulders slumped as if the weight of the world pressed down on him.

I leaned against the doorframe, watching him for a moment, the knot in my chest pulled tighter. I was a provider, a protector, and so was he, but right now it was obvious he needed something.

He looked how I felt. Broken. Useless. Adrift.

I crossed the room and dropped down beside him, and for

a long stretch of time, we didn't say a word. We simply sat there, breathing in sync, the quiet was thick with everything we couldn't fix or change.

Finally, Eli muttered, "She begged me to take care of the kids. Like she thought it was already over." His voice cracked, raw. "I didn't know what to say, I still don't."

I turned, pressing my shoulder into his until we leaned together, solid and steady, and he leaned back into me. "You said enough by being there. She needs to know we'll catch her when she falls apart. That's all she's asking for."

His hands scrubbed over his face, "And if she doesn't come back from this? If they take—"

"No." The word came out sharp, and absolute. "We don't think like that. She's coming back. And we'll fight like hell until she does."

He looked at me then, eyes red-rimmed, and for once there wasn't anything cocky or bright in him. Just raw, desperate need for comfort.

So, I did the only thing I knew how; I reached over and gripped the back of his neck, grounding him the way I always did, pulling him close until our foreheads touched. "We've got her. We've got them. And I've got you." I murmured.

His breath shuddered, and his hand came up to grip my wrist, holding on tight like he was afraid to let go. For a moment, there was no noise, no fear, no Danny Masters. Just us. Leaning on each other. Borrowing strength we didn't have to spare.

And God help me—it was enough to keep me breathing.

Neither of us moved, Eli just breathed hard, like he was drowning, and I was the only solid thing left to grab. I held him there, my hand firm on the back of his neck, my thumb brushing against the tense line of his jaw.

Then he exhaled, sharp and ragged, and it broke something in me. His shoulders sagged, his whole-body folding toward me like he'd been holding it all in for too long.

So, I let him.

I tugged him forward until his face was buried in my neck, his chest shaking against mine, and wrapped my arms around him tight, letting him pour all that hurt out.

"This is killing her," he muttered, his voice raw. "And I can't fix it."

I tightened my grip, my chin resting on the back of his head, "We don't fix it for her, Eli. We fight beside her. That's enough."

His fingers curled into the back of my shirt, knuckles white. He was strong, always so damn strong, running into the scariest situations to save other people, protecting and supporting them on their worst days, but in that moment, he leaned on me like he didn't know how to stand on his own.

And I realized I didn't mind carrying him, not for a single second did it feel any different than it did when I supported Frankie.

He lifted his head after a moment, eyes red-rimmed, his mouth locked into a hard line. Our faces were too close, breaths mingling in the quiet. Something flickered between us, fear, need, maybe even hunger. I didn't overthink it, I just leaned in, slowly, giving him time to pull back, but he didn't.

Our lips brushed once, tentatively, clumsy almost without the desperate lust driving us like last time, but God, it felt right.

It wasn't about lust; it wasn't even about curiosity. It was about not being alone in this. About holding onto something solid when the ground kept crumbling.

And when he finally kissed me back, soft, shaky, filled

with desperation I recognized, I knew this was a line we weren't coming back from. And for the first time in days, that didn't scare me.

The kiss ended as fast as it started, but it knocked me sideways all the same.

Eli pulled back first, eyes wide, chest heaving like he'd just sprinted a mile. For a second, I thought he'd bolt and run away from what he felt growing between us, but he didn't move. He just stared at me, caught between panic and relief, like he wasn't sure if he should apologize or beg for more.

I didn't let him do either.

I kept my hand at the back of his neck, grounding him. "Don't," I said quietly. "Don't make this into a mistake."

His throat bobbed, "Trav—"

"I mean it." My voice was rough and low as I fought to control myself. "We've been holding Frankie together, holding the kids together, but who the hell holds us? We do. And I fucking needed that. And there's nothing wrong with it."

He slumped forward again, his body trembling like a coiled spring finally breaking loose. "I didn't even think about you." He groaned painfully, "I've been so preoccupied with my own feelings and the pain, and stressing over Frankie and the kids and I—"

"Don't," I said again, giving him an out as I stood up, forcing myself to put space between us. "It's okay. I just needed a second."

I wasn't ashamed of it. Not of the kiss, or the closeness. Hell, I wasn't even ashamed of admitting that I was weak for a moment. Frankie opened a door between us, one I hadn't seen coming, and I wasn't about to slam it shut because of pride or fear. Not when I'd felt how right it was.

"Go to her," He said, rising to his feet and stopping right

in front of me. "Sleep at Lucy's with her, give her what she needs, and get some of this tension out of your body. Settle it by making sure she's okay. I know you're going nuts inside there," He put his hand on my sternum, "not being able to ease her pain right now."

I groaned, "I don't want to leave them, I swore to her I wouldn't."

"You aren't," He reassured, using the pressured dominance I used on him and Frankie all the time. The same dominance they craved from me, and it was weird to be on the other side of it. But I didn't hate it. "I was already planning to sleep up on the couch in the loft in case they need me, so you might as well go sleep next to her. I know she needs you, even if she won't ask for it."

"Are you sure?" I hesitated, and he nodded firmly.

"Let me take it all from you," He said with a small smirk before he leaned in and kissed me again.

It was new.

And he didn't linger more than a second or two, like he was testing out if it was an appropriate time to use the move or not, but when he pulled away, I had to fight the urge to pull him back for more.

But he was right. Frankie needed one of us, and even if she wouldn't ask for it, we could divide-and-conquer right now, taking care of her and the kids.

"Okay," I backed away toward the closet to pack a bag for the night, "Thanks, Eli."

"It's kind of nice being the boss," he said with a cautious chuckle.

"Don't get used to it," I chided good-heartedly.

And within five minutes of kissing my best friend for the first time in a private moment just the two of us, I was rushing out the door to go to our girl to take care of her.

For the first time since the nightmare started yesterday, I didn't feel like the world was tearing us apart; I felt like maybe it was pushing us all closer together.

Or at least that was what I was going to make sure came of the whole ordeal in the end.

42 - FRANKIE
Shadows

THE HOUSE WAS QUIET, too quiet. It mocked me. The shadows lurked around me like judges of the night, standing over me and finding me unworthy.

I curled up on the old bed in my childhood room, the same one with the floral wallpaper and creaky floorboards. The same one Emmie slept in when she stayed over with her grandmother.

It should have felt safe.

It should have felt like refuge.

But it didn't, no matter how hard I buried my face in the pillow that smelled like my daughter's shampoo and sobbed so no one would hear the noise.

No one could hear me break.

They'd tell. They'd surround. They'd pity.

And then they'd agree that I was too fragile to keep my kids.

I pressed my fists to my mouth to keep the sobs in, because once they broke free, they wouldn't stop.

All I could hear in the quiet silence of the house was the echo of that woman's voice as she read my charges like my last rites on the gallows.

Neglect.

Risk.

Abuse.

Unfit.

Each word pounded against my skull until they blurred into one sentence.

They're going to take your kids.

And then the memories came, uninvited and merciless, assaulting me all over again like I was back in that house, married to my tormentor.

Danny's voice attacked my mind, like he was in the room with me again. I remembered a time when his voice was once a noise I fell for, a smooth honey sound that promised me the world, speaking louder than the doubts that everyone else had when we were young and in love. I loved him with an innocent love that couldn't fathom how it would ever be anything but sunshine and rainbows and perfect.

I thought I'd get a white picket fence around a house in a sleepy little town, a husband who worked with his hands and came home at the end of the day, with a bouquet of wildflowers and a smile, happy to be home.

That wasn't at all what I got, though. And I couldn't even remember how many times I wished I could go back to that day that we left Cedar Bluff, on his motorcycle with just a few changes of clothes with us, so I could run far, far away from him and his lies.

His voice slurred in my ear all over again like he was right here in this very room, his fists pounding the wall around my head. The sting of his grip on my arms, the way he'd shove me back against the floor when I tried to fight him off. The nights he staggered into our room, smelling like whiskey and smoke, forcing himself on me no matter how hard I screamed for him to stop.

Begged him for mercy.

I remembered the time he locked the door with Emmie crying in her crib on the other side, forcing me to endure him while I begged to go to my baby. I could still remember how scared I was when she finally went silent behind that door as he continued to abuse me. I prayed to the heavens that she simply fell asleep and didn't choke or suffocate in my absence.

The worst part of it all was how my body remembered him even when I tried to get my mind to forget. It had been over four years, but the panic still curled in my chest, the shadows in my too familiar room made me feel like I was back there, trapped, helpless.

He was a monster that just would not die and leave me alone.

I just wanted him to leave me alone.

Guilt gnawed at me until I could barely breathe, threatening to pull me under completely. What kind of mother would let this happen? Again? What kind of mother brought danger back into her children's lives by daring to be happy? By daring to want love, want touch, want something more than survival bad enough to risk it?

I risked too much!

I thought about Travis's steady strength, Eli's warm smile,

the way the kids had laughed in their arms. And it only made the guilt sharper.

They deserved better than me.

The door creaked open softly, and I saw my mom's tiny silhouette framed in the light from the hallway. Her shoulders were hunched, and I could hear the tears in her voice as she stood there holding an extra blanket in her arms like she wasn't sure if she should come in.

"Baby," She whispered, "You don't have to do this alone."

I shook my head, curling tighter into myself and rolling over to face the wall. "Yes, I do. I'll only drag you all down with me. Please, Mom, just—please let me fall apart in peace."

There was a long pause, and then the blanket was set down on the end of my bed, "I'll be right downstairs."

When the door clicked shut again, the silence roared back in her wake, and I buried my face in the pillow, choking on sobs until there was nothing left but emptiness. And still, in the back of my mind, Danny's voice hissed like a curse.

They'll see. They'll see what kind of mother you really are.

Hours passed, darkness mocked me through the window to mix with the darkness in my mind, but still I didn't get out of bed. What was the point when all that was left inside of me was despair? I dreaded the sunrise, another day without my kids, without Travis and Eli. Even though I spent all day at the police station, filing reports and giving the proof I had of what I did, I still had no hope.

There were times when I felt like the Chief was going to say *I believe you, we got it wrong.*

But he didn't. He just kept taking notes and compiling my reports, ending the day with a passing, *We'll be in touch.*

Limbo.

Purgatory.

Hell.

That was where I was. Stuck waiting for everyone else to get their shit together so I could go home to my family.

If they still wanted me.

The door creaked behind me again, and I stiffened. My mom was an angel, but I couldn't face her. Coming home four years ago, broken and desolate, had been hard enough on her. Watching her break for me, feeling my pain in the way only a mother could, was too much for her. I couldn't hurt her that way again.

A deep voice filled the room, low and steady. "Shade."

My breath hitched as I turned over, and there he was. Travis. Like I'd conjured him from longing alone, big, broad and steady, filling the doorway like he was built to hold the whole world up.

I sat up fast, clutching the blanket to my chest. "What are you doing here? Are the kids okay?"

"They're fine," he said, closing the door behind him, encapsulating us in darkness. He crossed the room in three strides, crouching at the edge of the bed and gathering my shaking hands in his warm, strong ones. His eyes were softer than I could stand, because in his softness, I'd crumble. "I couldn't let you go another night thinking you're alone in this."

The knot in my throat tightened until I could barely speak, "They need you."

His hands slid up to cup my cheek, and I selfishly leaned into it, desperate for his touch, "They still have me. I tucked them in, they're asleep, and Eli is sleeping on the couch outside of their rooms. They're fine." I sobbed again, leaning into him as he went on. "They laughed today, baby. They ate too many of my mom's cookies, made Eli referee a hockey game in the living room and brushed their teeth at bedtime. They're safe. They're happy. Because of you."

My chest shook as I tried to breathe, "Because of you," I whispered, "Not me. I'm the reason—"

"No," His voice sharpened, firm enough to cut through the spiral. "Don't do that. Don't give him his victory. You're their mother. Their anchor. The reason those kids shine the way they do is because of you and your sacrifices. No report, no agent, no son of a bitch can rewrite that truth."

"Then why don't they see that!" I cried, falling forward, crashing into him with my fists clutching his shirt. He wrapped me up without hesitation, lifting me onto his lap like I weighed nothing, holding me until the sobs shook free.

We sat there in the dark, the old house creaking around us, his heartbeat steady under my ear.

When the silence finally stretched, he leaned down, whispering against my hair. "The world just needs to do its due diligence to make sure. We're going to fight the whole time until they do, though. All of us, Me, Eli, my parents. Hell, the whole damn town if we have to. You're not carrying it alone."

I nodded against him, too broken to argue anymore. For the first time since the papers hit the bar, I felt the smallest thread of hope. Travis was here, and he wasn't letting go.

He still wanted me.

He never let go, physically or mentally, as he shifted us both up onto the mattress, pulling the blanket up around me like I was something fragile, on the edge of breaking. My head stayed pressed to his chest, his heartbeat steady under my ear, the warmth of his body wrapping around me like armor.

"You should go," I whispered, though my voice cracked even as I said it. "You should be there when they wake up."

"I'm right where I need to be, baby." He murmured, his hand smoothing over my hair, down my back in slow, steady strokes. "Right here, right now, I'm here with you. And tomorrow, they're going to my parent's house to be carefree kids on a farm, with all the fun they can find there. But I'm with you, we don't leave each other behind, Frankie, not anymore. I'm here."

The tears came again, softer this time, quiet against the fabric of his shirt. He didn't flinch; he didn't press me to talk or pull me tighter than I could handle. He just stayed solid and unyielding.

I forced myself to rest. I forced myself to find some solace in his arms long enough to make the noise in my head fall silent.

"Close your eyes, Shade. I've got you."

And I did.

The memories still lurked, the fear still sat heavy in my chest, but with his arms around me, the edges dulled. For once, my body didn't feel like it belonged to Danny's shadow. It felt safe. It felt like it was mine.

Somewhere in the quiet hours, sleep finally dragged me under, the last thing I heard was Travis whispering into my hair, words meant more for me than for himself.

"You're not losing them. You're not losing us. Not while I'm breathing. I love you too fucking much, Shade."

And with that promise, I let the darkness take me.

43 - ELI
The Truth

I DROPPED the kids off at Hal and Maggie's place for a day on the farm. Both kids were nearly salivating at the chance of doing farm chores and playing on all the fun machinery Hal collected instead of going to school for a second day.

They were less impressed with me when I told them Frankie was sleeping, so they'd have to call her later at some point. I was going to have to get more creative with reasons why they couldn't speak to her if this went on for any longer.

They were like bloodhounds and knew I was stretching the truth.

Plus, I hated lying to them.

But for the moment, they were safe, laughing, blissfully

unaware of the turmoil coursing through the family at the moment. Which was exactly how I planned to keep them.

Now I needed to see to my own selfish needs, the desperation clawing inside of me to be near Frankie again. I needed to hold her, and care for her, and remind her how fucking much we loved her.

As soon as I pulled into Lucy's driveway though, my skin prickled with trepidation as I parked behind a police cruiser that had pulled in right before me.

Chief Weller stepped out, hat tucked under his arm, with a grim look on his face that meant bad news, or worse truths.

"Morning, Elliot," He said low, "I'm here to see Frankie, you coming in?"

My gut tightened, but I nodded. There was no way in hell he was going in without me.

Travis must have seen the cruiser pull in, because he met us at the door, an impenetrable force of protection standing between Frankie and the world, ready to hold the line, no matter the cost.

I nodded to him and moved around him to where Frankie stood in the living room, wringing her hands together, swallowed up in Trav's sweater and with worry etched into every line of her tired face.

"Take a deep breath, Black Cat." I murmured, kissing her temple and pulling her against my side as Lucy welcomed the chief in.

I didn't miss the respect in the chief's eyes as he greeted Trav and came in behind me. Trav joined us, taking Frankie's other side, unified and steady.

"Ms. Blake," Weller said gently, "I need to ask you some more questions about the alleged break-ins."

Her throat worked, but she nodded. "Okay,"

I pulled her back to the couch and the three of us sat

down, instantly, Travis and I both put our hands on her, his arm over her shoulders, my palm flat on her leg, and she curled into both of us even as she bravely faced the man in front of her.

Chief Weller opened a slim file, flipped to a page, and my stomach churned from all the different vile things we'd heard read off papers identical to that one the last few days.

"In the DCFS report, there's an allegation that you leave," He cleared his throat and looked at me briefly then back to her, "adult items out in the open. Around your kids."

"Adult items?" Trav snapped.

"Toys." Weller clarified, and I could feel Frankie stiffen in my arms.

"That's a lie." She replied.

"I believe you," He said quickly, holding his hand up as Trav leaned forward in outrage. "But here's what doesn't sit right with me. The report is specific. I'll save you the absurdity of the terms used by the source, but it references something being left on your nightstand." His eyes narrowed. "Yet in your interview, you told me you haven't seen the father of your kids in years. So tell me, Frankie—how the hell would he know about something sitting on your nightstand?"

Her breath stuttered, tears flooding her eyes, "Because he—he put it there."

Travis's hand shot to hers, steady and grounding as he barked, "You knew he was in there?"

Her voice broke as she stared forward at the Chief, "He took it from my closet and left it on the nightstand. He—touched it. Violated it. And he left it for me to find. To mess with me."

My fists clenched so tight I thought my bones would snap. Rage burned through me like fire, but the chief's eyes only hardened.

"When was this, Frankie?"

She swallowed and took a deep breath, and I hated how it made her shoulders shake. "A little over a month ago," She cleared her throat, "The day that my brakes were cut." She turned to look up at me with watery eyes, pleading with me. "I forgot at first after the crash. And then—" She shook her head slightly, "I didn't want to believe that he was back, and I buried it. I'm sorry. I should have told you. I should have told you both, but I was so scared."

"Shh," I leaned forward, pressing my lips to her temple, sending a very pointed and crystal-clear message to Travis on her other side, where his anger was radiating so powerfully she was bound to think it was at her. "It's okay."

"It's not." She crumbled a little more. "If I had told you guys that he—you would have made me go to the police way back then. And maybe we could have stopped him before it got to this point. Before I was the guilty one!"

"Ms. Blake," Chief Weller interrupted her, "I believe you. But that means that Danny has been inside your home. And if he's been inside once, odds are he's been there more than you realize."

Travis turned to the man, eyebrows pinched in anger, "What are you saying?"

"I'm saying," Weller replied, taking a deep breath, "I want to walk through your old rental next door. Yesterday, Ms. Blake, you said you still have belongings there, that you haven't moved out completely yet. You said there was still furniture and other things there. I believe that if he was bold enough to leave his DNA evidence on something, he may have been bold enough to leave more than just that behind."

We didn't waste any time, moving as one, all of us walked down the driveway to the rental next door that we hadn't made the time to clean out yet. When we moved in together over a month ago, we packed clothes and the kids' special toys but left everything else. We had three households worth of furniture, and nothing Frankie had in the rental was anything she wanted to bring with her. The cabin was a fresh start for all of us.

Our black cat trembled the whole way over to the house, sandwiched between us. No matter how tight I held her, or how reassuring Travis was with his words and affirmations, she couldn't stop shaking.

The moment we stepped through the front door of the rental we had fixed up for her, I could tell he had been there after all. It didn't feel warm and inviting like it had when she lived there with the kids, the air now felt wrong.

Cold.

Violated.

We stood off to the side, watching the Sheriff walk around and look at things as if he was looking for something. But none of us had any clue what he was hunting for.

Until he found it.

Under the television.

A small pinhole camera, tucked under the light bar for the screen, pointed right at the couch. Then another one in Frankie's bedroom aimed directly at her bed.

Frankie crumpled, hand over her mouth as she realized how violated she had been. Trav caught her before she hit the ground, but the damage was done.

Weller cursed under her breath, ripping them both free and shoving them in an evidence bag. "Jesus, Frankie, he's been watching you. For God knows how long."

The bile rose hot in my throat, but underneath it, something else stirred. Something that felt like hope. It wasn't just Frankie's word against Danny's anymore. There was the proof she needed to confirm everything we'd been screaming into the void.

"Now what?" I barked as I mentally replayed every single conversation, every touch, every moment of passion that we shared in the fucking house, angry that we ever exposed Frankie to them under the watchful, sadistic eye of her ex.

As Weller snapped the bag shut and handed it off to an evidence tech as we all watched. Behind the weathered and professional mask he wore as he did his job, I could see the anger on the man's face. I respected him as Sheriff and worked several cases with him during my time in the fire department. And I hoped that this would help me regain some of the respect I lost in him, watching him stand by as someone destroyed the woman I loved.

"This isn't just harassment anymore," He said, "This is stalking. This is criminal. This is dangerous." He glanced at Frankie, his voice softening but firm. "And it's enough to open doors that your claims against him alone couldn't."

Frankie clutched Travis's sleeve, her eyes glassy and hollow, "What does that mean?"

"It means," Weller said, "I'll be updating DCFS with this evidence. They need to know you're not the problem—you're the victim of a predator. It changes everything."

Frankie's breath hitched, a sob choking her throat, but she pressed her lips together to smother it before asking the question we all wanted to. "Does this mean I get my kids back?"

The chief shifted, squaring his shoulders, "By the end of the night, you'll all be under the same roof. I just need some time to get the paperwork squared away." He said, and Frankie sagged into us with relief. "I'm also calling Danny in for questioning. We'll get him in a room, put pressure on him, see how his story holds up against the cameras we found. If he's stupid, he'll slip. If he's careful, we'll keep tightening the noose until he cracks."

Travis's voice rumbled low beside me. "And in the meantime?"

Weller turned back, his gaze steady. "In the meantime, you live your life. You go to work. You keep your head high and let the people who know you see that you're not hiding. That's the best thing you can do—for yourself and for your case. The news will break soon enough that you're the victim in all of this."

Frankie's head shook, "But he's out there. He's watching me."

The chief's jaw flexed, "Not for long, Elliot was right last night when he said people don't come into my town and fuck with my people," Then his tone gentled, "We'll increase patrols near the rink and by the cabin. You're not alone in this anymore. I'll get to the bottom of it, Frankie. I promise you that."

She clutched my hand with her trembling one, holding on like I was a lifeline as Travis kissed her temple, tucking her into his side, the three of us locked together with fresh hope burning inside of us.

44 - DANNY
Fuel on the Fire

THE SHERIFF MADE it sound easy. A quick signature, some paperwork and formality shit.

Custody papers. Then I would finally get what I deserved, what had been mine all along.

Her kids.

And with them, Frankie.

She could fight, cry, scream all she wanted, but once I had the kids in my hands again, she'd come crawling back. She'd have no choice.

The thought lit me up from the inside, that familiar rush, that power burned, and I was jumpy with excitement. I'd been patient, careful, biding my time. Now, it was all falling into place.

I could almost taste the high I'd get when I pushed into her writhing body again for the first time in almost five years.

Five years without my favorite little fuck doll to play with.

My dick hardened even just thinking about it as I stood at the gas pump, filling my truck to make sure I had everything in place to get the fuck out of this hellhole the moment she was back with me.

I wasn't going to stick around long enough for the dumb and dumber twins to convince her to fight me in the long game for the kids.

I didn't have the patience for that; I'd snap and shoot them between the eyes.

Which would complicate things, but I wasn't against the idea altogether.

They'd get what was coming to them eventually, after I got Frankie locked away and secure.

"Did you hear the big news," A voice said from the other side of the pump as a woman got out of her car, talking on her phone a mile a minute.

Small towns made my skin crawl, and she was a perfect reason why.

"No," She went on, popping her gum like a teenage cheerleader, and I rolled my eyes as I leaned back against the truck, watching the numbers rolling on the pump roll even slower as she started pumping her own gas.

Cunt.

"The shitshow that Frankie Blake's life turned out to be!" She hissed.

My ears sharpened at the sound of Frankie's name.

Now that—that was a story I could get behind gossiping about.

"I know! The whole town's buzzing about the rink the other night, but get this—the Chief found creepy shit in her house. Cameras. Like stalker-level stuff! That loser she dated back in high school? Turns out he's been messing with her the whole time. Wanda said her husband, who works as a cleaner down at the station, told her they tricked him into coming in and they're planning to nail him."

My blood ran cold as my heart rate lowered, thumping forcefully in my chest the way it always did right before I snapped and lost control.

"That's what he gets," the woman said. "Coming around and screwing with her like that. Shame she wasted her good years on him, but at least she's finally got herself a real man like Travis now to make up for all that lost time."

The woman giggled, the noise like nails on a chalkboard as I stared down at the nozzle in my hand. She kept going.

"Well, two men. God, that Elliot—mmh, in that fire gear? I'd set a garbage can on fire just to get him to my place one night." She chuckled, still running her mouth. "And to think Frankie's the one underneath both of them each night. Way better than that scrawny skater boy her ex was."

Scrawny. She was talking about me.

My knuckles whitened around the nozzle, fury and something darker twisting hot in my gut.

This stupid cow was laughing at me like I was some kind of joke.

Frankie was laughing at me.

The cops were laughing at me.

The carpenter and the firefighter were laughing at me.

But they didn't know me. They didn't know what I was capable of.

Frankie did.

And now the fat cow running her mouth would too.

"Hey," I barked, leaning around the pump.

She startled, her gum nearly falling out of her mouth. "What—"

I squeezed the nozzle in my other hand, spraying gasoline all over her stupid fucking face. The reek filled the air instantly, sharp and acidic, biting at my nose. She screamed, stumbling back, swatting at her face.

Her screams cut through the quiet gas station, raw and panicked, and it was beautiful. If I'd had a lighter, she'd be ashes by the time I pulled out thanks to flames licking over her cheap clothes and ugly face.

Instead, she just flailed, gas burning her skin like acid, eyes wide with horror as if she could already feel the fire crawling up her.

Pathetic.

She thought the gas was bad now, she should thank me for not lighting her on fire.

I stepped back, letting the nozzle drip, watching her scramble. The fear in her eyes was pure and raw. And it should have satisfied me.

But it didn't.

Because it wasn't Frankie.

No—the one who needed to scream like that, thrash like that, cry out for help until her throat bled—was Frankie.

Frankie, with her new life. Her new men.

Climbing back into my truck, my heart hammered with dark satisfaction. That little show proved it.

I was still in control. Still capable of making anyone crumble when I wanted, and the cops would know that when they showed up.

And Frankie? She was going to feel it too.

I'd make sure the next time she screamed; it would be for me.

45 - FRANKIE
Ashes of Me

GO ON WITH LIFE, *as normally as possible.*

Keep moving forward.

We'll have it all settled as soon as possible.

Chief Weller's promise rang through my head on repeat as I tried to do what he said. Part of me was doubtful, unable to trust anyone anymore, pushed down by cynicism put there thanks to life's cruel ways.

I kept telling myself that I *did* have to keep moving forward, though, because I had worked too damn hard to let the whole ordeal steal my progress. Which was why I was sitting in a lecture hall, two weeks away from finishing my degree and being done with school altogether.

It was the last place I wanted to be, but I had to at least

show up for the notes, even if I understood nothing my professor was saying over the manic thoughts running through my head.

Chief Weller had called Travis and told him he had called Danny in for questioning an hour ago. With each clock tick above my professor, I waited for a text from Travis to tell me the whole fucking thing was over.

We got him.

He's in jail.

You're free.

That was what I needed to hear so that I could finally feel like I could breathe again. Never mind the fact that I needed to hug my kids. God, my eyes watered even thinking about how badly I ached to see them, how badly I missed them.

My nose burned even as I forced in a few deep breaths, trying to keep them from falling in the middle of my class. The last thing I needed was to start sobbing in Professor White's lecture, he already hated me.

Feeling the edge of a panic attack curling its sharp claws into my mind, I got out of my chair, making a silent exit out of the lecture hall so I could get myself under control. Thankfully, the hallway outside was empty as I walked toward the emergency exit to get some fresh air.

Again, I was so over everyone watching me. The lurking stares, hushed whispers, and snide comments were enough to make my skin crawl. I just needed a few minutes of silence to get my panic under control.

Then I'd go back to living my life as normal as possible.

After I took a few minutes for myself.

The skin on my neck prickled to life as I got to the end of the hallway, a millisecond before I felt the weight of eyes on my back. Glancing over my shoulder, my breath caught in my throat when a pair of eyes from my past stared back at me, from only a foot away.

"No—" I gasped as Danny slammed his fist into the side of my head, disorienting me. I crumpled in the next heartbeat, my body going numb from the sheer power behind the punch to the soft part of my head behind my ear.

Fuck.

My brain felt like I was looking through the water in a pool as I rolled over onto my back, looking up at the ceiling.

Danny's sadistic face blocked my vision, his smile stretched too wide, too sharp. "Miss me, baby?" He hissed as his hands gripped my hair, pulling me across the floor toward the exit.

No.

No!

My voice was stuck in my chest, paralyzed with disorientation as I tried to grab at the door frame he pulled me through. His sick chuckle, with the edge of mania lacing it, assaulted me as I saw a black truck idling at the curb a foot away.

Fight, Frankie! For the love of God, fucking fight!

I knew what would happen if he got me into his truck without anyone seeing. The emergency exit he pulled me through was at the back of the building near the faculty parking lot, which was almost empty by this time on a Friday afternoon.

Fuck.

Fear gripped my heart so hard I thought it would stop beating completely as he opened the back door and lifted me into it, shoving me face down on the floorboard behind the front seats. He was so much stronger now than he had been before, and even then, he beat the daylights out of me every chance he had.

I was in serious trouble.

Finally, my body reconnected to my brain, as fear took over and I kicked my feet out at him, fighting to get my body out from the cramped space, but I was still sluggish.

"No, Danny. No!" I screamed as something wrapped around my ankles, and then they were bent toward my ass and within the next second both of my wrists were shackled to it, hogtying me.

His body pressed against my back, and his hot breath hit my neck, making me freeze with fear as nightmares assaulted me from times in the past when he would immobilize me like this. "Mmh, I missed you, baby. I missed you so fucking much. But you've been so bad. So fucking naughty. A whore. A slut." His hips pushed against my legs, and I could feel his hardness, making bile rise to my throat. "I'm going to make you pay for it." I screamed again, right before he shoved a rag into my mouth and then duct taped it there, muffling my screams to near silent grunts. "Every single thing you did for them, you're going to do for me. You're going to make it up to me, Frankie. You're going to make this right."

I sobbed against the rag, flailing against the floorboards as he pushed his dick into my leg again and then chuckled.

"I can't wait to feel you break for me again. It's been too long."

With that, he got off my back and shut the door with a resounding thud that sounded a lot like a gunshot, ending my life.

He had me.

And I was utterly fucked. Hopelessness clawed at my throat as he started driving, pulling away from the school and racing down streets I couldn't see to a destination I didn't know.

If he took me, if he got free with me like this, I was dead.

I'd never see Emmie and Toby again.

I'd never feel the warmth of their hugs, or hear the joy of their giggles again.

Days ago now, I walked out of our home, waving goodbye, blowing air kisses at them in the window as I drove away to go to work, and I didn't know at the time that those were the last memories I'd have of them.

I didn't know those were the last hugs and kisses.

I would have held on tighter.

I would have made it last longer.

I would have memorized every single freckle on their perfect faces to hold me over, had I known.

Had I known then what I knew now, I would have told them how much I loved them more than the automatic reply I gave them on my way out the door, worried about work and life and everything else I had to do that day.

I would have meant it more.

Because it was the last thing they had from me.

I was terrified as Danny rushed through curves, hardly slowing down at turns before speeding off. I tried to pay attention, mapping out the path he took as he raced through the drive, but I couldn't see anything from the floor, and I couldn't break through the ties around my ankles and wrists. Yet I never stopped trying. The ties dug into my skin, burning the flesh, but still I fought.

He muttered to himself in the front seat, spitting menace my way as he slammed his fist into the steering wheel.

"You thought you won, huh?" He sneered, looking over the center console at me, "The police, DCFS, your new boyfriends? None of them matter!" He screamed, slamming his fist into my head again, even though I didn't do anything, I couldn't do anything but take it. "You're mine! You've always been mine! From the first moment I fucked your virgin body, you were mine!"

I tried to scream, to fight, to break free. I couldn't just stay still as he drove me further from my life, spiraling out of control with every mile he drove. As his rage grew, the insults he hurled my way became more vile. "You ruined everything, Frankie!"

I fought against my binds, feeling the hard outline of my phone in my jeans pocket, fumbling with numb fingers from the tight restraints as I finally worked it free.

I knew if he looked back over the console at me, he'd see me with my phone, so I tucked it between the seats the best I could and swiped my finger over the fingerprint. It vibrated in my hand, signaling that I got it unlocked.

I took a deep breath, forcing my brain to work as I used muscle memory to open the phone app without looking. I had no idea who I had called last, but pressed the call button twice to dial it, hoping it was one of the guys as I turned the volume all the way down so Danny wouldn't hear the feedback.

Chancing one glance at the screen, I nearly screamed with relief when I saw Travis's name with the timer started above it, meaning he picked up.

I forced the phone back into my pocket with the microphone up so he could hear everything. Even though I couldn't hear his strong voice, I instantly felt brave knowing he was hearing me.

Hearing Danny scream obscenities at everyone around us as he drove, ranting his sick plans for me.

The truck made a quick turn, and I slammed my head into the door, making my neck burn from the impact, and then it came to a stop. The first full stop since we left the college.

Danny got out of the truck, and then the door behind me opened, and he pulled me by the ties on my ankles, ripping me from the truck and throwing me into the snow on the ground.

Instantly I recognized the worn paint on the back porch of my rental, and I looked around to see that he drove through the open gate as he stomped over to it, swinging it shut, locking us away behind the tall privacy fence.

I rocked, trying to roll over on my side to see my mom's house, but the fence was too high from my spot on the ground. The cold wetness of the snow seeped through my clothes and soaked my skin, freezing me to the bones as Danny stomped back over to me, dragging me by my elbows.

I screamed, hot searing pain shooting through my shoulders as they bent in the wrong direction and then the wind was knocked out of my lungs when he threw me across the floor in the living room, slamming the glass sliding door behind him and locking us inside the house.

Earlier in the morning, I had stood in the same room, watching Chief Weller discover Danny's hidden cameras with Travis and Eli's warmth and strength around me, comforting me.

Now I was freezing cold, paralyzed with fear as he started destroying the place in his anger.

"You made me look like a fool!" He screamed, ripping open cabinets, pulling bottles down, throwing glasses across the room to shatter against the wall, yanking papers off the fridge and walls, ripping up memories as he spiraled.

His madness was everywhere, infecting the walls.

I got my body up on the side again, backing up to the wall as Danny destroyed the home I spent years building for my kids.

"You think you're better than me now?" Danny snarled, flipping the kitchen table over into the wall, the catastrophic noise echoing through the silent house as I screamed against my gag. "Parading around with those big-shot heroes, like they can give you something I didn't? You forget who made you, Frankie! You forget who taught you how to use your body for a man. Whose name you wore before you fucked anyone else with a body that belongs to me!"

He ripped the tape off my face, and I screamed from the sharp pain, even as I stared him down, letting go of my fear thanks to my anger. "I didn't forget!" I rasped, throat burning from screaming into the rag, "I survived!"

He grabbed me by my hair and turned me over onto my back, twisting my legs and arms into a painful angle as he wrapped his hand around my throat, his smile stretching into that sick mocking grin I hated, "Survived? No. You belonged, baby. You still do. To me. Those kids? They're mine. You? Mine. You've just been playing house, and you've got the whole town fooled, but I see you. I know you."

"Let me go, Danny—"

"You don't tell me what to do!" His voice cracked, rage bubbling through. "You spread your legs for them. Both of them." He stood up, chest heaving, "Right here on this fucking couch." He grabbed a knife from his pocket, and my blood ran cold as the metal flashed, "I watched you through the fucking sliding door as you let them fuck you like a dirty cheap whore. I watched you throw your head back and pretend you liked their touch on your body." He swung the knife around as he walked to the couch, stabbing it into the cushion and ripping it wide open. "But I know the truth, baby. You only like it when you have to fight. You only come when you're screaming and fighting me off. I know the truth."

My stomach turned, but I forced the words through my shaking lips, trying to help Travis find me, praying the call was still connected. "So what? Why bring me here if you hate my house so much?"

His angry glare came back to me, and I instantly regretted speaking at all. But if I had a prayer of getting free, I had to help Travis find me. I had to get help.

"To erase it." He sneered, stomping back over to me. He cut the tie between my ankles and wrists, but my limbs were still bound to each other as he pulled me up to my feet. "To erase every single touch. Every kiss. Every fuck. You belong to me!"

The slap came sharp and fast, the sound ringing in my skull as I staggered on my bound feet, but he yanked me upright again, laughter spilling harsh from his throat.

"There she is." He sneered, "The fighter. The cunt who knows how to take a hit and come back swinging. I missed that part of you. It almost makes my dick harder than when you go back to breaking for me." He groaned, leaning in and biting my ear as I shook, trying to get him off me, "I love it when you cry for me, Frankie. I love when you beg."

"Fuck you!" I sneered, refusing to give him my fear if that was what he liked best. "I hate you! You're pathetic!"

He laughed, the sound was sick and twisted as he shoved me down onto the floor again, standing over me. "You'll break for me again. Just like before. I'll strip you down until there's nothing left but the girl who begged me to love her."

"Never." I spat, tasting blood on my tongue from his hits. "I never begged you."

His laugh was raw and cruel. "Oh, you did. For those fucking kids of yours you did." My heart seized in my chest as he cocked his head to the side with a sneer, "And when I get the girl back, I'll use her against you just like I used to until you're on your knees for me again."

He walked away from me, going from room to room, destroying what was left and I inched my way across the floor, trying to get to the door with my hands and ankles tied behind me.

Suddenly, his sick, twisted laugh came from the kitchen, and I dared to look over my shoulder at him as he pulled something out from under the sink, walking back over to me.

He held a can of lighter fluid, shaking it like a prize. "New house, new men, new life—you thought you could erase me. But I'll erase you. If I can't have you, then no one will. I'll burn it all down until there's nothing left but me."

My blood froze.

"Danny—don't."

His eyes gleamed, fever-bright. "This is what it takes, Frankie! Wipe the slate clean. I have to burn the lies, burn their fingerprints off you, burn their touch from this place. When it's ash, it'll just be you and me again."

He opened the cap and sloshed it across the counter, the sharp chemical stink stinging my eyes as he coated the kitchen. It dripped down the cabinets, puddled on the floor, soaking into the papers under his boots.

I went back to fighting to get out of the house, crawling across the floor toward the front door, flopping from side to side as the fear of burning alive fueled my adrenaline.

He worked behind me, spraying it over every surface of the downstairs, trapping me in the ring of death as he went on with his threats. "You'll watch it all burn, and then you'll thank me when I take you from this place. If you're a good girl, I'll leave those fucking cock-twits alive when I take you and our girl from here. I'll let them live their pathetic lives, taking care of your stupid son. I should take him too, just to ruin you completely, but I hate the idea of you having any other man to love. I'll rip them all away from you until you only have me."

I jumped to my knees, bracing my shoulder against the front door as I climbed to my feet, and then I heard it.

The strike of the match.

I looked over my shoulder as the tiny flame flared in the dark, reflected in his eyes like madness itself.

"No—" My voice broke, raw with panic.

He grinned, "Yes. Finally." He moaned, taking a step toward me. "There's that fear I crave."

Then he dropped the match.

Fire roared to life in a heartbeat, racing across the fluid-slick floor, licking up the walls and consuming the couch in a single breath. Heat blasted my face, the air turning thick with smoke as my numb fingers fought with the dead bolt, finally flipping it free.

Danny's triumphant laughter filled the room, unhinged and awful.

"See?" He shouted over the crackle, with his arms spread like a conductor. "This is what freedom looks like! No one can take you from me now!"

The smoke clogged my lungs, searing and choking me as I twisted the knob and pulled the door. I screamed as it snagged; the chain catching it, giving me only a few inches of fresh air. Hope faded as fast as the flames grew behind me when the chain held the door shut above my head. With my hands tied behind my back, I couldn't reach it to free it, and I screamed as the heat nipped at my skin, turning my mind crazed with fear.

I turned my face into the gap, screaming out into the fresh air, sucking oxygen as I tried to rip the door open. "Please help me! Please, someone help me!" It was pitch black outside, darkness fell quickly in the wintertime, but the orange glow of the fire reflected off the snow all around the house. It was burning—fast.

Danny stomped across the floor toward me, stumbling through the flames, still laughing, but the fire moved faster than he did, and it caught him by surprise. It licked the laces of his boots and then climbed his jeans in a single heartbeat.

His manic eyes found mine through the smoke, and for the first time in all the years I knew him, I saw fear looking back at me. So many times, he had broken me, beating me, terrifying me, tormenting me, and usually there was sick obsessive pleasure in his gaze when he did so. Sometimes, early on, there had been remorse in them after a fight, but not in many years. Seeing the fear in his eyes, and then the pain, broke something in my chest, even though he deserved it.

He fucking deserved it and so much more.

But I was human, and I couldn't celebrate his pain like he always did mine.

Still, I couldn't look away from it, so I froze, watching it consume his body in half the time it took to engulf the whole house. His screams echoed through my ears, horrible and ragged, sounds that ripped through me even as I screamed my own.

I felt like my skin was melting, my flesh scorching as the flames danced across the ceiling. My lungs burned from the smoke, and I coughed hard enough to break ribs, but still I found no relief from the pain.

I wasn't going to make it out of the house.

That single thought raced through my mind as I collapsed to my knees, searching for reprieve from the choking smoke and burning heat.

I wasn't going to survive Danny, after all.

I fell back against the wall as I watched him fall to the ground, no longer screaming as the flames swallowed him whole.

At least I was going to die knowing that he was dead too.

At least he could no longer torment anyone, even if it cost me my life.

Fire nipped at my feet, burning through my shoes and pants, and I watched helplessly in some sort of dissociative state as the flames danced across my jeans.

I smiled grimly as Emmie's giggle filled my mind, a calming balm on my soul as I neared death. Toby's silly baby-tooth smile flashed in front of my eyes, covered in chocolate and chaos.

I felt Travis's rough hands on my skin, tender and slow in that special combination I craved in the darkness of our home. Then I heard Elliot's warm voice, calling my name in ecstasy, shouting for me.

The door beside me exploded into the house, and the flames danced higher from the fresh air that kissed my face.

Still, I couldn't move to embrace it the way I wanted to. My mind locked up, so I couldn't feel the fire's pain anymore.

Movement through the door caught my attention, and then a massive body crashed through, in full firefighter gear. I watched with a sense of separation, as if I wasn't inside of my own body anymore as the masked firefighter turned and grabbed my body, lifting me onto his shoulder as if I weighed nothing at all and carried me out into the cold crisp winter air.

"Frankie!"

I fought the fog in my mind when I realized Eli's voice was coming from the man carrying me out into the dark night.

"Eli—" I coughed,

I saw Elliot's face in my mind, his smile and dimples, the view easing the pain in my heart.

Ice-cold pain engulfed my body, a stark contrast to the searing heat that had been killing me as I fell onto my back in the deep snow.

It was the shock to my system that I needed, and then

suddenly I was staring up at the night sky as a scream ripped from my lips, the pain coming back to me in full force.

The impact of me falling to the ground ripped the ties off my wrists, and I swung my arms at the flames burning my body.

Eli ripped his helmet and mask off as he covered my body with snow, burying my burning clothes in it with desperation as I thrashed, clawing at him wildly with hands black with soot and smoke.

"Easy, baby," He drawled, as other firefighters surrounded me, helping him put out the flames on my legs and cover my skin with the blessedly painful snow. "Don't move, baby!"

A loud screeching of tires echoed over the sound of the fire engines and their sirens as Travis's truck bombed through the snow, sliding to a stop in my peripheral vision before his massive frame raced around the vehicle, falling to his knees at my side.

Another scream ripped from my lips as my brain felt like it was going to explode in my skull from the pain as he helped Eli hold me down in the snow.

"Shh, Shade." Travis stared at me with a broken look in his eyes. "We've got you. I'm so sorry, baby. We've got you now."

I fell back into the snow, sinking into it as my screams felt like they were still ripping through my throat, but I could no longer hear them. All I could do was stare up at the two men I loved more than I could have ever hoped for, as darkness started to pull me under.

Damnit.

I was still going to die, my heart raced so fast in my chest there was no doubt in my mind that it would eventually give out, right before their faces vanished completely.

Life was really fucking unfair, but at least now I felt no more pain or fear. Just darkness.

46 - TRAVIS
Bound by her Cry

MY HAND RAN over the wood beam, the smooth strength familiar under my skin as I tried to focus on work. But my mind was elsewhere.

With Frankie at her afternoon class, nearly broken with worry but forcing herself to keep focused.

Waiting for the Chief to call me with the good news of Danny's arrest.

Wondering how Eli was handling it all and hating that he was in the middle of a shift at the firehouse.

I took a deep breath, forcing the worry from my shoulders as my phone rang.

Frankie.

I hit accept and lifted it to my ear, hoping for good news, when I got only chaos through the speaker.

A scuffle. Tires squealing.

A muffled cry.

"Frankie?" My voice cracked, and everything froze around me.

Her sobs bled through the line, muffled and frantic. Then Danny's voice, sharp and menacing, filled my ear as he roared his rambling threats, incoherently slurred words of vengeance and violence.

Ice sliced through me.

I didn't think as I grabbed one of my guys' phones off the bench where they were taking a break. "Timmy, call 911 and tell them to patch through to this phone!"

My guy just stared at me, my crew falling silent, "Trav—"

"Do it!" I roared.

And then I was running. Out of the shop, into the truck, my keys shaking in my hands as I jammed them into the ignition. My tires squealed, gravel spitting in my wake as I tore down the road.

I had no idea where to go. But I listened to Danny's sick voice telling her all the vile things he was going to do to her.

Her screams kept echoing in my head, rattling my bones, louder than the engine of my truck as I sped toward town, louder than the pounding of my pulse.

I opened the second phone and called Eli, praying he'd answer. "Sup, Timmy?"

"He has her." I barked.

There was a slight pause on his line as I put Frankie's phone on speaker with his, holding the phones together. "Trav?"

"She called me—" My voice cracked, "The line is open,

and it's on speaker. He has her, Eli. I can hear him. I can hear her crying."

"Jesus Christ." The roar of his pained voice echoed out as another scuffle happened on the line, and Eli and I both went silent. Listening to a car door slam, and then a struggle before Frankie's clear scream ripped through the air.

"Frankie!" I hissed.

"I'm tracking her," Eli spoke, clicking through his apps to locate her. It felt like a million years passed as we listened to Danny throwing stuff and destroying things around her, Frankie's cries in the background. "The rental!" Eli yelled, "They're at her rental!"

"I'm on my way!"

"Me too," He yelled, directing orders to his men, and then the roar of the fire engine filled the speaker. "We're not far."

I couldn't tell where Frankie's phone was, but there was rustling, and we couldn't make out what Danny was saying, just her replies and soft cries until it cleared up again, like she moved, getting the phone in a better position.

"Danny—don't." She spoke.

And there was something hauntingly calm about her voice. Something I didn't recognize.

Then Danny's sick voice came through clear as well. "This is what it takes, Frankie! Wipe the slate clean. I have to burn the lies, burn their fingerprints off you, burn their touch from this place. When it's ash, it'll just be you and me again."

"Oh my God," I hissed, driving faster toward town as the distinct hiss of flames crackled through the line. "Eli. He lit it —he fucking lit it—"

He barked out more orders and then the sirens of his engine blared in the background, the air horn sounded as they cleared around obstacles to get to her.

"Eli, you have to get to her. Please, Eli. You have to save her."

"911 calls are coming in, Trav!" Eli barked, "Smoke showing from the house!"

"God," I slammed my fist into the wheel. "No! Frankie, if you can hear me, we're coming! Please just hold on, baby, we're coming!"

Another scream ripped through the phone, one that didn't sound human, one that shattered me right down the middle. I almost drove off the road.

"Get her out!"

Frankie's screams echoed through the speaker, a repetitive broken record of horror as she burned, hollowing me out, shattering something I didn't know could break.

I didn't have to see it to know what was happening. I could feel it.

She was burning.

His voice was grim and steady, and it scared me more than anything. "We're here. I'm going in."

His line went dead, and I couldn't hear anything else from Frankie's. She'd gone silent as the noise of the fire burning around her filled the cab of my truck.

"Dear God," I cried, getting closer to town just in time to see the smoke billowing up into the sky from three blocks away. "If you've ever believed in us, in mankind, then please, please save her. Because if you don't, I'll destroy everything around me in her wake. No one will survive my grief."

47 - ELI
On Scene

HER SCREAMS RATTLED me through the speaker, shaking my core and trying to break my mind as we neared the scene. I could see the smoke long before we got to the street.

My training kicked in as I put my gear on as our engine roared down the street. I held onto the handle as we rounded the last corner and saw it.

The inferno.

My stomach dropped as Frankie no longer screamed through the line. Flames poured from the windows, the roof already sagging under the weight of the fire.

"We're here," I said into the phone, "I'm going in."

My boots crunched across the frozen gravel before the engine even came to a full stop.

From the corner of my eye, I saw Lucy running from her house, eyes wide with horror as she saw Frankie's house on fire and Danny's truck parked in the back. The house was a coffin waiting to collapse, smoke pulsing out of every crack in the siding.

"Stop her!" I barked out orders, pulling my mask down over my face and running toward the house.

I barreled onto the front porch and saw the smoke curling out through the crack around the front door. I knew what that meant. The fire inside was starving for air.

My gut clenched hard as my panic rose. The second I broke through the door, the fire would flash. It would burn a million times hotter as it fed its hunger with the rush of fresh oxygen, consuming everything in its wake.

Backdraft.

A firefighter's worst nightmare. The thing that killed more of us than anything else.

But I didn't have a choice, Frankie was in there.

I braced, throwing my shoulder against the door, and the second the chain broke, swinging in, the world exploded.

Flames blasted outward, a fireball rushing over me in a roar, the pressure slamming into my chest like a truck. My mask rattled against my face, my tank straps dug deep into my shoulders.

For a second, I couldn't see anything but orange and black.

And then the fire rolled back inside, clawing for more fuel. Through the smoke, I saw her.

Frankie.

She was on the floor just inside the front door, collapsed, with her legs on fire.

"Frankie!" My voice echoed in the mask as I dropped, shielding her with my body, the heat hammering my back.

I swept my arms under her, lifting her onto my shoulder and running from the house. She was limp as I jumped from the porch and fell into the knee-deep snow on the front lawn.

I flung her off my shoulder and into the snow, using the ice water to extinguish the flames feasting on her feet and legs.

A broken scream erupted through her lips as the wet cold snow assaulted the fresh open wounds of her burns, but it was her best chance at limiting the burns. I had to cool her skin to stop the burns from spreading, even after the fire was extinguished. Her skin was black, covered in soot and ash, and I couldn't see what was actually burned and what was just scorched.

"Easy, baby," I cried, ripping my mask off and dodging her swinging arms as the pain became too much for her to bear. "Don't move, baby."

My team split, half going to contain the fire even though the house was a total loss, and the other half joined me, using the snow to encapsulate Frankie's broken body until EMS arrived.

Sirens blared around us as more fire squads rolled up, dispersing and working around us. I glanced up and locked eyes with Lucy, who was fighting off my Sergent, trying to get to Frankie.

Then Trav was there, barreling his truck directly at the fire and stopping in the snow next to us, racing around his truck to collapse at Frankie's other side. His face was covered in shock as he stared down at our girl, beaten, and broken but alive. Almost as if he was expecting to show up and find her dead.

Not on my fucking watch.

"Shh, Shade." Travis stared down at her with a broken

look in his eyes. "We've got you, I'm so sorry, baby. We've got you now."

The fight in Frankie's limbs lessened, falling limp as the trauma of it all took over her body, shielding her mind from it before she fell unconscious.

"Is she alive?" Trav barked, leaning over to listen for a breath, as EMS arrived. "Frankie!"

"Trav, let them in." I said, letting go of Frankie's hot hand and stepping over her to push him back into the snow when he snarled at the medic like a rabid animal when they tried to get to her. "Let them work. They're her best chance right now."

"I can't—" He gasped, shaking his head, sitting in the snow with my arms around him, I expected him to jump back up the second he was free as the medics started working on her. "I can't lose her." He turned and looked at me, that broken look in his eyes. "We can't lose her, Sunshine."

"I know." I said, grabbing the back of his neck to hold him still as he tried to look around the medic as they started intubating her, forcing straight oxygen into her black lungs. "I know."

And we sat there, watching them do their work until they scooped her body out of the snow, revealing the angry red skin on her lower legs, open and brutal as they laid her on the stretcher.

My team said things that were only partially registering in my broken mind.

Trauma Alert.

Medi-flight.

Flight Surgeon.

And then she was whisked away in a helicopter that landed somewhere nearby, and we were left in the rotor wash of snow and smoke, broken and defeated.

A grim-faced Chief Weller walked over to us, I was still sitting on my ass in the snow, in shock, I think, as Travis paced, watching the helicopter take off, Lucy cried standing next to me with her hand on my shoulder.

The whirl of the rotors faded into the night sky, carrying Frankie away from us, and I felt like half my chest had gone with her.

I just sat there in the glow of the fire trucks; helmet discarded in the snow with ash caked in the snow from Frankie's skin. My lungs burned, but that was nothing compared to the ache clawing inside me.

Travis was a wall at my side, broad, steady, but even he looked hollow. His jaw was locked so tight I thought his teeth might crack.

"They found a body inside," Weller said, his voice firm but measured. His eyes met ours with the steadiness of a man who dealt with tragedy like this all the time. "It's burned to a crisp, but we're assuming it's Danny."

Travis grunted, "It's him. I heard his—" He cleared his throat and took a deep breath, "His screams."

My lungs emptied all at once.

Relief.

Horror.

Disbelief.

They all tangled together in my chest.

"So, it's over?" Lucy asked shakily.

Weller nodded his head, "As over as it can be. We'll wait for the official confirmation from the medical examiner, but yes. It looks like he's gone."

I swallowed hard, a bitter taste coating my tongue.

Danny was dead.

The monster of Frankie's nightmares was finally snuffed out.

Then why didn't I feel lighter? Why did Frankie's scream still echo through me like he was alive and laughing in the fire?

Weller's voice softened as I pulled myself out of the snow. "Let me drive you all to the hospital. You can wait for updates there."

"The kids," Travis sighed, running his hand down his face in agony. I could feel the way he was torn through our connection.

"Will be fine with Maggie and Hal," I put my hand on his back and led him away from the disturbed snow where I buried the woman we loved, trying to save her life. "I'll give Hal a call on our way."

He looked over at me, eyes searching, and for the first time in my whole life I saw such doubt and uncertainty in them. "I don't know—"

"I know." I replied, squeezing the back of his neck as we walked, pulling Lucy with us as she tucked in against my side. "*I know.*"

48 - FRANKIE
Scorched Nightmares

THE WEIGHT on my chest felt like I'd never take a deep breath again, even though I felt the pain in my ribs with each deep inhale.

My breath scraped like sandpaper up my throat, shallow and hot, as if the smoke still clung to my lungs. All I could smell was the smoke. It was overbearing and noxious.

My eyelids fluttered, heavy, the sterile glare of white lights cutting through the haze.

Hospital.

The antiseptic smell hit next, pushing past the smoke, and for once I welcomed that sickening scent. I tried to move, but my ankles and feet felt like they were held down with cement blocks, and wires tugged across my arms as I reached for the railing to pull myself upright.

And then I remembered Danny.

The roar of his voice, the look on his face as the flames took him—

My heart lurched, the monitors beeping to life with warning.

"Black Cat."

My name in his voice instantly soothed the ache in my chest as I turned my head, eyes burning to find him.

"Eli." I croaked, voice broken, reaching for him as he slid his fingers through mine, bringing them to his lips to kiss. He had soot on his face and was wearing his uniform, without his turnout gear on, his eyes were bloodshot but locked on me like I was the only thing in the world.

Travis moved behind him, looming, his face carved from stone but his eyes soft, raw, and wet.

"You're safe," Eli whispered, as Travis stalked around the bed to sit at my hip, lacing his fingers with my free hand like Eli had. "You're safe now."

"He's dead—" I swallowed, trying to soothe my broken voice. "Isn't he?"

Tears stung my eyes as Travis nodded solemnly. "He died in the fire."

"It's not your fault," Eli voiced, drawing my attention back to him. "I know that you're feeling guilty for the loss of his life, even if he deserved it."

I felt tears slide down my cheeks into my hair. "It was horrific." I cried, feeling that familiar, overwhelming sense of panic trying to overtake my body and my mind. "I was so scared."

"I never should have listened to Weller," Travis cursed, lifting my hand to his mouth and holding it there as he closed his eyes to take a deep calming breath. "You should never have left my sight."

"He would have done it anyway." I whispered, shaking my head, "He was crazed with insanity. He would have waited and hurt you if you'd been with me." I took a shuddered breath, "And I wouldn't have survived that." His eyes opened, looking at me, and I glanced over at Eli, leaning on his elbows right next to me to make sure they both understood what I meant. "I survived this, but I would have walked into those flames willingly if he had hurt you to get to me."

Eli leaned over and kissed my forehead, "You barely survived as it is."

I looked down at my body, to the massive white bandages covering my lower legs. "How bad is it?"

"Second degree." Trav replied, wiping a tear off my cheek. "From calf down. But the rest is superficial. And it will all heal. Physically, you'll heal with time."

"I'll heal." I reiterated, coughing a little through the dry ache in my throat, "All of me will heal. Want to know how I know?"

"How?" Eli asked.

"Because you walked through fire for me." I tried to smile at him, but it barely made it to my lips. "You found me," I turned to Travis. "You saved me. And you're here now. Which means I can do anything I want to do. And I want to heal." I forced my lips to keep moving even as my eyelids started to fall when exhaustion pushed against them. "I want to embrace this life we're building, the three of us. I don't want to live with a guarded heart or a skeptical mind. I want to love you. I want you to love me." Trav's hand tightened in mine, and Eli leaned his forehead against mine.

"We do, Black Cat." Eli vowed, "We love you so fucking much."

"I love you too," I found the energy to smile with my eyes closed, and then Travis leaned over, brushing his lips against my cheek.

"I love you both, Shade." He whispered, "Get some rest now, and in the morning, we can start living our fairytale."

"Mmh," I whispered, "Emmie will be so happy to have her knights in shining armor in real life."

Eli chuckled, it sounded brittle, but I was hopeful that it would warm as time went on. "With our luck, Toby will make us kiss frogs to prove our worthiness."

"Don't leave me," I sighed, hoping the words came out clear. "Please."

"We're not going anywhere, Shade." Travis said firmly, kissing my cheek again, and I nuzzled into him, feeling both of their lips against my face and temple.

"Good."

49 - FRANKIE

Home

IT TOOK A WEEK OF BEGGING, borrowing, and pleading to get my release paperwork completed by one very stern-looking nurse. She was the kind of nurse that gave the best care, because she was too scary for her patients to defy and mess around with their own recovery.

She also threatened that if I misbehaved at home, she'd take on the role of my home health nurse, visiting me daily at home for bandage changes, and I shivered at the thought of her standing in my bedroom.

"I'll be the perfect patient," I smirked up at her. "You just wait and see."

She pursed her lips but cracked a smile with a proud nod, "Go home and live your beautiful life, Frankie."

I smiled back, glancing up at Eli, standing behind me, hands on the wheelchair ready to break me free from my prison. "You heard her, let's get out of here."

He pushed me to where his truck waited on the curb, locked the brakes and came around to lift me effortlessly from the seat. I used to worry about hurting my men when they'd insist on carrying me or manhandling me, but now, I simply sat back and let them do it.

They both proved they could carry my curvy ass around, and I was done pretending that I didn't love every second in their arms.

What I didn't love were the burns covering both of my lower legs and feet.

Those were a real fucking bitch that made existing pretty miserable, but I would not complain. The alternative was too crude comparatively.

Besides, it meant that the guys stayed close, taking care of me and spending quality time with me non-stop.

Which my black, dark soul was eating up like an aphrodisiac-laced catnip.

I loved being doted on by Travis and Eli.

"What are you masterminding up in that pretty head of yours?" Eli asked as he gently set me in the front seat of his truck, lingering in the open doorway as I shrugged with a smirk.

"Nothing proper." I mused, and his stare darkened as I winked at him. "I can't wait to be in our bed again, that's all."

"Hmm," He hummed, unconvinced. "Well, don't let those thoughts stray too far, because Travis and I are sleeping on the couches while you heal."

I gasped, making a deliciously dramatic noise, clutching my chest in outrage and slapped his arm. "Don't be so cruel, my fragile heart can't take it."

He snorted, leaning in to kiss me, lingering just long enough to make me melt before he pulled back and winked at me. "Recovery, Frankie." He mused, shutting the door with a resounding thud before walking around to his side, "You heard what the doctor said."

I snorted in disbelief as he pulled the truck out of the hospital parking lot, aiming it toward home, where my babies and Travis waited for us. "Yeah, but that's just what they have to say—"

"No." He shook his head, reaching across the center console, that I hated being down, taking my usual seat in the center, "Not a chance. Six weeks. Minimum."

Now my gasp was more of an outraged gurgle of incredulity, but he wouldn't waver, staring out the front window, while his thumb rubbed back and forth over my knuckle.

Like hell I was going six weeks without sex.

My feet were broken.

Not my vagina.

I didn't argue with him, because it wouldn't do me any good in the truck on the way home, my mind was too distracted with seeing my babies and snuggling with them on our couch instead of in my hospital bed like I'd been forced to do for the last week.

Besides, it wasn't like he was the only one with a dick I could ride in the house.

And he always came around to my wicked ways when I was naked, getting fucked.

I obediently rode home, touching him only on the hand, and he looked at me out of the corner of his eye, as if he was expecting me to keep trying to persuade him.

But I didn't.

I was the perfect and patient girlfriend.

For now.

As soon as we pulled into the driveway, clearing the dense trees and breaking through up near the house, my heart rate sped up with excitement for a different reason.

"Welcome home, Black Cat." Eli smiled, leaning over the console to kiss me once again, teasing me.

"It's so damn good to be here." I said back and then Travis was at my door, opening it up and leaning in, surprising me and making me squeal with laughter.

"Welcome home, Shade." He purred, kissing me, with dominant hands on my cheeks, using tongue just the way I craved from him. I whimpered against his lips, digging my nails into his wrist and moaning for him, desperate for the comfort his kisses were giving me before he pulled back and forced a deep breath into his big barrel chest. "Sorry. I got carried away."

I whimpered again, this time in a pout as Eli chuckled at my disappointment when it was obvious I wasn't about to get railed in the driveway.

Rude.

Travis at least had the decency to look guilty over the tease as he lifted me from the seat, tucking me in against his chest to make the quick walk up the porch and through the front door.

My bandages made pants impossible, so my short pajama shorts did little to ward off the cold, even paired with one of Eli's hoodies that hung to my knees.

As soon as we made it through the front door, the warmth of the fireplace pushed away the cold, and I managed to only stare at the flames dancing in the hearth for a moment before my kid's cries of glee distracted me.

"Mommy!" Toby cheered, leaping off the kitchen barstool,

directly into Eli's arms as he caught him right before he landed on my lap in Trav's arms.

Emmie came barreling down the stairs in dress-up shoes and a jersey. "Mama's home!"

I chuckled, swatting away the guys as they sat me down in the chair next to the couch. "I'm home." I swaddled both of my babies up in my arms, pulling them onto my lap and away from my bandages. "God, I missed you both like crazy!"

The kids snuggled in hard, trying to get under my skin and stay within me, and I welcomed it, smelling their sweet little innocent scents and basking in the cozy warmth of our home.

Hal and Maggie lingered at the edge of the living room, next to my mom and I gave them a little wave as Toby leaped right into a full recounting story of his time at the Hayes's farm the last few days while Travis and Eli doted on me.

It was nice having my men with me in the hospital, both off work for a few weeks to take care of me, but it was even better having everyone at home together again.

The kids visited me each day at the hospital, and we talked multiple times on the phone daily, but it was still so much fun hearing about their times all over again.

Their storytelling skills were really coming in, the recounts were animated and magical, and I lived for it.

I lived.

I was taking nothing for granted ever again, either.

And I sat back, enjoying every second of my favorite brand of chaos.

Mine.

THE CABIN WAS FINALLY QUIET.

The kids were asleep in their beds, exhausted from the excitement of the day, Maggie and Hal had left with my mom, promising to be back the next day to keep the guys from smothering me with their attention.

I should have been asleep too, my body was tired enough, still tender and sore deep in the early stages of recovery. But the words my asshole doctor dared to mutter in front of both Travis and Eli haunted my head like a curse.

No strenuous activity for six weeks.

Six.

Meanwhile, I had two gorgeous men under the same roof who hovered over me like saints yet refused to touch me like sinners.

It was rude as hell.

Earlier, I had tried to push my luck, going for my most likely victim. I had Travis with me alone after he helped me get settled into bed for an afternoon nap.

And I tried to work my magic, a kiss that lingered too long, with more tongue and teeth than was necessary. Sliding my hand up under his shirt, he groaned, crawling up onto the bed with me, hovering over me as I internally smiled, getting further than I had managed all week to getting them to break their own self-inflicted celibacy.

And then Eli barged in like he knew what I was up to.

Kill joy.

The worst part about the whole thing was I had Travis right where I wanted him. Hard. Horny. Desperate, just like I was.

"You can't," Eli glared at me with his hands on his hips, and Travis actually groaned in a pout back at him.

"Don't listen to him." I kissed Travis again, pulling him

back to me as he chuckled, kissing me deeper as Eli grunted from the doorway. "He's a cock block."

The door shut behind him, and then Travis was yanked off the bed to stand at the side with a smug-looking Eli, and I huffed in frustration.

"Not fair." I pouted.

"Yeah," Travis stuck out his bottom lip in a very dramatic way that was so not him, maybe he was closer to breaking than I thought. "I'm horny."

"Then I'll take care of you." Eli said, shocking me speechless as I sputtered.

I watched Travis's pout morph into something sinister as Eli pulled him in, kissing him deeply.

"Holy fucking balls." I groaned, mouth hanging open, body on fire.

There was no hesitation on either of their parts, no tentative exploring or indecision.

It was raw, and powerful, and needy.

So fucking needy.

I moaned when Travis put his hands on Eli's hips, pulling their bodies flush before Eli dropped his hand to the front of Trav's jeans, palming his hard cock that I put there with my kiss a moment ago.

"What the hell have I missed this last week?"

Travis groaned and smiled up at the ceiling as Eli pulled back to stare up at him as he stroked his dick. "We've kissed a lot." Trav replied. "But not like this. Fuck yes, Sunshine."

Trav's hips flexed, pushing against Eli's hand, and I sat up higher on the pillows to watch my favorite porno.

I didn't even care that they weren't giving me any attention, even though I was on the brink of a full-on tantrum moments ago. I needed to see what they were doing more than I needed to come.

I *had* to see it.

"Sunshine!" Emmie called out from the kitchen, "Saw!" and the guys parted like they were burned by each other's touch, chests heaving and both of their jeans were tight in the crotch. "I'm hungry!"

"I'll be right there!" Trav called back, rubbing his hands over his face as he took a few calming deep breaths before glancing over at me where I sat on the bed, hanging on by a thread over the whole thing. "Duty calls."

"I hate you." I hissed, glaring at both of them. "Before, it was just him!" I pointed at Eli defiantly, "But now, I hate you both."

My men both grinned, dismissing my claims before walking back out to take care of my kids.

I huffed, falling back onto the pillows, but even as much as I tried, I couldn't keep the stupid grin off my face as I replayed their sexy kiss in my mind.

Damn, I was a lucky woman.

And not once in my life had I ever thought that about myself.

50 - TRAVIS
No Going Back

THE LIGHT over the sink was the only one on as I leaned against the counter, taking a deep breath. Eli moved around the kitchen, fingers tapping the countertop as he shuffled things around endlessly.

"You're wound tight." I said, voice low.

He gave me that easy smile, but it didn't quite reach his eyes. "It feels so damn good to have her home. Even better knowing she's finally safe. But—" He trailed off, scrubbing a hand through his hair.

I didn't need him to finish. I felt it too—the tension in the air.

"You're the one who made the no-touching rule." I raised

an eyebrow at him, "Say the word and I'll support breaking that rule."

He groaned, fisting his hair and falling back against the island across from me. "We can't fuck her, man. She's still too sore."

"But," I deadpanned.

"But it feels wrong finding release with you if we can't give her that." He groaned, "She practically climbed me like a tree in the shower earlier at the hospital. I was supposed to be washing her hair for her, and then she was wet and naked in my arms, rubbing herself against my abs, and I—fuck—I almost gave in. One inch, and I would have been inside of her."

"Don't you think we should listen to her and what she needs?" I questioned. "There are a lot of ways to get her off without rutting into her."

He made an animalistic noise and rubbed his hand down his abs, but stopped right above his belt like he was just barely stopping himself from grabbing his dick at just the mention of fucking our girl. "Not for me. Not right now." He shook his head, haunted. "I'm wound too tight. Too crazed with need. I'll be too rough."

"You need rough?" I leaned up off the counter, and his chest fell with a needy exhale as I stood toe to toe with him. "I can give you rough. You won't break me."

We had kissed a lot during Frankie's absence. It was odd and weirdly fucking normal at the same time. But we hadn't taken it further.

Even though I knew we both wanted to. We just wanted Frankie to be a part of it.

"Fucking hell, Trav." He glared at me, "Careful what you say, I'm a hair trigger away from bending you over the bed and fucking you." I raised an eyebrow, surprised at the intensity of his words, and the heat behind them. But I was more surprised by the way my body hardened at the thought of what he was threatening. "I just need—" He sighed, "relief."

"Then let's go get you some relief." I nodded toward our bedroom down the hall and held his stare until he felt how serious I was about it. And then he was off, walking ahead of me to our room, quietly opening the door in case Frankie was asleep.

"Fuck," He groaned, pushing the door open wide after peeking in, and I looked over his shoulder to where Frankie lay in our bed. "My God."

"Oh, Shade." I whistled, walking around Eli's frozen body and shutting the door behind him with a quick flick of the lock. "You naughty, naughty girl."

She moaned, throwing her head back in ecstasy as she pushed her vibrator in her pussy, bottoming out and coming all over it. She was a man's biggest fantasy, legs spread, nightgown pulled down to reveal her big, lush tits, and pretty pink pussy on display, dripping wet and needy as she played with it.

"I gave you the opportunity to be the one to make me come." She moaned, lifting her head back up off the pillow, pulling the vibrator from her body to strum it across her clit in lazy strokes. "But you just wouldn't give me what I needed, so I took matters into my own hands."

"How did you—" Eli paused, glancing at the tall chest of drawers in our closet that held all of her toys in the top drawer.

"I'm not proud of the bum shuffle I did to get across the room." She panted, rolling one of her perfect nipples between her fingertips as she dipped the toy back into her needy body. "But desperate times call for desperate measures."

"Minx." I walked over to the bed, and leaned over her

face, with my hand on the pillow next to her head. "The whole room smells like your sweet pussy, how many times have you come so far?"

"Mmh," She smiled up at me with a sex high dreamy look in her eyes. "Too many to count. But it barely feels like I've scratched the surface. I'm a very horny woman, with two sexy men here to help me."

"Wrong." I said dominantly, and she instantly scowled at me. "No sex for you."

"Goddamnit, Travis!" She hissed, pointing her finger up at me angrily. "I'm so over this overprotective bullshit that you like to use against me! I'm a fully grown woman, who is fully capable of making my own decisions about my body, and my body wants cock. Right now!"

Eli groaned from the end of the bed, leaning forward with two fists in the blanket to stare at her wet pussy lips like a deranged man.

"You're not getting fucked tonight, Shade." I repeated, and she sputtered, but I put my hand on her mouth, silencing her. "Because tonight, we're going to take care of Eli." Her jaw snapped shut under my hand, and her scowl turned curious as I looked at our partner until she followed my gaze to the man between her legs. "Look at him, baby. Look at how deranged he looks right now." She shook my hand off her mouth, and I let my fingers glide down over her neck and collarbones, to the swell of her juicy tits that I wanted nothing more than to stick my face in between right now. And I wasn't even a tits man, I was just a Frankie man. But I was going to take care of both of my partners tonight, long before I worried about my needs. "He needs relief. But he's so worked up, he knows he can't be gentle with you. Which you need. So, it's up to me to take the edge off for him."

Her big green eyes snapped to me and widened. "You."

"Mmh," I nodded once. "And you're going to watch us, while you play with this pretty, tight little pussy for us to watch." I dipped one finger down between her spread thighs and pushed it into her tight pussy. She was soaked, and the sound of it filled the air as I pushed and pulled my hand, fucking her with just one single finger until all of my knuckles were wet with her. "Got it?"

"But—" She whimpered when I pulled my finger out.

"No." I commanded, tracing the finger that was wet with her arousal over her pink nipples until a moan left her lips. "If you don't play by my rules, then I'm going to take our guy into the bathroom and lock you out while I suck him off in the shower for the first time."

"Fuck!" She hissed, hips rising on their own as my dirty words teased her.

The problem was, they also teased a feral Eli, and his bright eyes flashed to mine from the foot of the bed. "Isn't that right, Sunshine?"

"I don't care how you get me off," he stood up to his full height and my eyes fell to the erection fighting against his jeans, licking my lips for his benefit, "But you better do it soon, before I lose any ability to think straight."

I kissed Frankie's shocked lips, pushing my tongue into her mouth until she sucked on it greedily, moaning into my mouth before pulling back. I led her idle hand, vibrator still buzzing, to her pussy and slowly pushed it in for her. "Keep playing with this pussy so he can watch. Got it?"

She nodded her head frantically, "Yes, Sir."

"Good girl." I growled, and both of them moaned in response, bringing a smile to my lips. I loved playing with my toys.

I stalked Eli around to the end of the bed, as he stood solid and unmoving, but his eyes were wild like he expected me to pull a punch line any second, changing things up. There was zero chance of that happening though, so I fisted the front of his shirt and pulled him in until our mouths crashed together.

He pushed his tongue into my mouth instantly, and I wrapped my hand around the back of his neck, dominating him, angling him how I wanted and setting the pace. He fell into line perfectly, rocking his hips forward for friction he desperately needed. I'd never seen Eli so frantic for anyone like he was right now.

He needed us.

And he was going to get us.

"I'm coming." Frankie's small whimper filled the air as I turned Eli's head so he could watch her as I kissed his neck, biting the smooth flesh he kept shaved before sucking his ear lobe into my mouth. He moaned loudly, and Frankie's whimpers intensified under his stare. "Tell me what our girl is doing to come."

"Fucking herself," He gulped, grabbing my biceps for stability as I started pulling his shirt up. "So hard. So deep."

"Mmh," I groaned, pulling back long enough to pull his shirt off over his head as I kept biting him. He loved it, moaning and groaning with each mark I left on him as I moved to his chest. His chest was soft and smooth, so similar to Frankie's, where mine was rough with coarse hair and weathered skin. I liked it. "She wants your cock, doesn't she?" I asked, pulling back far enough to glance over at our girl, and she nodded eagerly.

"Yes."

"Too bad." I chided with a wink her way as I pulled his belt open and then the button and lowered the zipper against his hard dick. "It's mine tonight."

I wasn't embarrassed or shy about taking our relationship

to the next level; I didn't let uncertainty or fear into my mind. I simply fed off his need, my desire, and her approval.

That was all that mattered.

I turned back to Eli, pushing his jeans and briefs down as he stared up at me with such deep desire in his bright eyes. "I've got you." I said confidently as he swallowed, giving me a small nod before I took him in my palm. My strokes were slow and gentle, but his eyes still rolled, as his head fell back with a curse falling from his lips as I looked down between our bodies.

His skin was flushed everywhere. His muscles were tight like he was coiled around a fragile band of restraint, and then his hands fisted in my shirt, pulling me closer, kissing me while I pleasured him.

I growled at the dominance he gave through the kiss, thriving on the barest of emotions, the purest reaction to my touch as Frankie moaned next to us again.

"Is it always like this?" She panted, "This desperate and fueled with lust?"

"Always," Eli gasped, pulling back as I started kissing his neck again. "He's too—" He faded off when I started biting and sucking a trail down his chest, crouching and then lowering myself to my knees in front of him. "Travis." He moaned, nostrils flaring and hips flexing as I stroked him right in front of my face, staring up at him as he teetered on the edge of control. "He's too much, too perfect for us."

Frankie sat up on the bed, scooting to the end and glaring at me when I raised an eyebrow at her, tempting her to follow my rules. "Shut up." She hissed at me. "I have to see this up close and personal." Her chest rose and fell nearly as fast as Eli's did as we watched her. "Because he's right, you're too perfect for us."

I grinned with a wicked smirk aimed at her, "I think I like this praise from the both of you."

Eli grunted, flexing his hips when I lowered my free hand to his balls, rubbing them the way Frankie taught me to drive him crazy. "You would have a praise kink, you big bastard."

"I think I have a voyeur kink," Frankie panted, "Because I've never been more turned on in my life."

"I have a kink for blowjobs." Eli gasped, desperation dripping from his lips. "And pussy licking. In that order."

I stared up at him, playing into the role completely for their fantasies as they both stopped talking, stopped breathing, living on the edge of their seats as I slowly stuck my tongue out and rubbed the head of my best friend's cock across it.

My lover.

My boyfriend.

My girlfriend's boyfriend.

Fuck.

I was getting harder the more I thought about the dynamics and felt the lust radiating off both of their bodies.

Eli's jaw hung open, eyebrows pinched together as I closed my lips around him, rocking my neck to take him into my mouth.

And then I gagged.

And Frankie giggled.

And Eli cursed, throwing his head back and pushing himself back into my mouth, deeper, making me do it again.

"Oh, my fucking god." Eli gasped, tightening his hands into fists at his side. "I'm going to come."

"God," Frankie moaned, reaching over to stroke the base of his cock as I worked to take him deeper into my mouth.

I didn't even hesitate as he started roaring, biting his fist to keep the noise down as he orgasmed into my mouth.

I wasn't quitting.

I was fulfilling the whole fantasy. For both of them.

"Good boy." Frankie purred, rubbing the back of my neck as I kept rocking forward, sucking him down. "You're doing such a good job."

Yep, I definitely had a praise kink.

Who knew?

Eli stilled, chest panting like he'd just run a mile, and I slowly, gently pulled off him, watching him closely for his normal crash out after an orgasm between us. But he didn't retreat into himself. He didn't hide. He didn't glow with shame.

No, the only thing radiating from Eli was—wonder.

Amazement.

Love.

Acceptance.

Thank God, he finally accepted himself. And me. And Frankie.

"Let me taste." Frankie turned my jaw with her gentle fingers before leaning over to kiss me.

I pushed my tongue into her mouth as I rose up, leaning her back on the bed to grind against her eager pussy, keeping her legs spread wide around me so I didn't bump or irritate the burns on her ankles and feet.

"His come tastes so good on your tongue, big guy." She purred, rocking up against me. "But now it's his turn to give."

Eli chuckled, pushing me out of the way as I laid down next to our girl, pulling her lips back to mine as he lowered his to her pussy.

The guttural moan falling from her lips made my cock weep as he pushed his fingers into her while he sucked her clit into his mouth.

"I needed this." She panted, opening her eyes to look at me, and then sobered up a bit. "Are you okay?"

I nodded, pressing my forehead against hers, "Why wouldn't I be?"

She giggled and shrugged before moaning as Eli did something she liked extra. "Because you just swallowed down your first load of come like it was your entire purpose in life."

Eli grunted, pulling up, lips wet and a cocky grin on his flushed face. "Damn good blowjob, by the way."

"I'd say," I leaned over and sucked Frankie's nipple into my mouth. "You came in two seconds flat. Chump."

"It was all a little overwhelming for me." He pinched my thigh, next to Frankies and then popped his head back up and grimaced. "Why are you still fully clothed?"

I shrugged, laying back on the bed and propping one arm behind my head to watch the two of them. "I'm in no hurry. I want to watch our girl shatter a few more times for us."She moaned, grabbing the back of her thighs and spreading them wide when Eli started really putting in the work between her legs. "I'm not sure my poor heart can handle more orgasms." She said and then instantly grabbed Eli's head, pushing him back down when he pulled away to give her a break. "After this one."

I snorted and rolled back over to her, kissing her soundlessly as Eli worked all his charm on her. And within a few minutes, she was shaking, gasping, and coming all over his face with a satisfied sigh before melting into the bed.

"Okay, I'm done now." She murmured, looking over at me. "Your turn."

"I don't need—" I started and then scoffed when Eli moved over to where I lay on the bed and started undoing my belt. "Eli."

He paused, hands hovering over my fly. "You don't want—?"

As soon as his name left my lips, I regretted it, because the fear was evident in his eyes as he froze, automatically doubting that I could want him to touch me. Like it was wrong.

We'd come so far tonight, I hated watching him recede into that doubt.

I sat up, legs spread wide around him on his knees, and grabbed the front of his throat, pulling him in for a kiss. "Don't finish that sentence. Or I swear to God, I'll bend you over and redden that ass so fucking bad you'll be on bedrest with Frankie for the next week."

He gulped against my hand, eyes widening under the intensity of my threat, and Frankie even popped up on one elbow, legs dangling safely away from us as I put him in place.

"Do I want these sexy lips wrapped around my cock, sucking me off like I just did for you? Do I want to lose myself in you like I've been fantasizing about since the first time we kissed, for Frankie? Do I want to crash through euphoria with the two people I love?" I asked, and his pupils widened as I leaned in against his lips. "The answer to all of those things is yes. Without fail, every time, yes." I bit his bottom lip, and then finally released the tight grip I had on his neck and relaxed now that his eyes were full of lust again instead of doubt. "More than that though, I want to simply take care of you both." I turned to look at Frankie, hearts practically radiating out of her dark soulful eyes back at me. "Tonight was about seeing to your needs." I looked back at Eli and took a deep breath, "Healing something that was eating you from the inside out."

"And you did." He replied firmly, steady and strong, like he found his strength from mine. Which made my pride soar.

"And now I have another need I need you to fulfill." He dragged my zipper down, making me groan as the pressure intensified in my aching cock. I resolved to go without tonight, and I would get pleasure from seeing to their needs. But now that they were both satisfied, it was harder to ignore my desire. "I want to tear you apart, break through every tough part of you, until you're putty in my hands."

"You want to suck my cock?" I growled, and he licked his lips, making my balls tighten.

"Can't say as I've ever wanted to suck a cock before in my life." He raised one eyebrow at me defiantly, "But I want to wreck you, Trav. Until you're mine. The same way you belong to Frankie. I want that too."

I watched his face, looking for any hesitation, but there was none.

Slowly, I reached up and pulled my shirt off over the back of my neck, tossing it onto the floor and then leaned back on my elbows so I could see him. Frankie curled up on her side, teasing her fingers up and down my abs.

"Do it." I demanded.

51 - ELI

Eternal

SLIDING my fingers under the waistband of Trav's boxers, I stared straight into his eyes as he lifted his hips and let me strip him. My spent cock twitched at the mere thought of it.

I pulled his clothes off, finally matching him to me and Frankie in our nakedness, and then let my eyes travel to his lap.

Fucking hell, he was so big.

Of course he was.

Tree trunk thighs.

Deep barrel chest.

Shoulders as wide as the houses he built.

He was the very definition of a dominant, testosterone-filled man. Yet, twenty minutes ago, he had fallen to his knees at my feet and sucked me dry, taking me deep past every boundary he had.

And now, I was going to break him down, with my own need to top him from my knees until he was a wreck for me.

I wanted everything.

"Color?" I asked, giving him a tentative smile as I laid my palms flat on his thighs, dragging them down to his knees and back up.

"I'm seeing sounds right now." He bit back, jaw clenched tight as his cock hardened, all on its own until it lay heavily against his stomach, so thick it couldn't stay upright under the weight of itself.

I grinned and finally slid my hands toward the center of his body, slowly, but surely gripping his cock in my palm. His hips flexed involuntarily, and a rumble sounded in his chest. Turning to our girl, who silently watched, letting us test every bit of new freedom she was giving to us, I leaned over and kissed her.

She threaded her fingers in my hair, kissing me back soundly as I slowly stroked our lover. "Do you remember the first time I felt Trav through your body?" I hummed, "You were on my lap, my come deep in your pussy as he lined up from behind and slammed into you. He fucked you so hard, you slid up and down against me until I came again."

"Yes," She nodded her head, lips against mine. "It was the start of all of this."

"It was the day I knew I loved you." I corrected her. "You accepted me. Accepted us. Gave us space and safety to explore things we didn't know we needed until you gave us the place to do it. The love to do it." I hummed, looking over at Trav with his pitch-black eyes and tight, corded muscles in his neck as he reacted to my words just as viscerally as she did. "Now look at us."

"All of us." He added. "Happy."

"In love." Frankie hummed, kissing my cheek before turning to him and kissing him. "So desperately in love with each other."

"Thank you, baby," He growled, kissing her deeper as I watched them hungrily, hardening again. "For letting us share you."

She giggled, turning to me and flicking her glance down at Trav's thick cock in my hands, where I still lazily stroked him, warming him up to my touch and teasing him until his body kept flexing, silently seeking more. "I'm the luckiest woman in the world. Everything I've survived—" She closed her eyes, "Was for this. For this deep, satisfying, eternal happiness."

"Eternal." I tried the word out on my lips before slowly lowering them to the crown of Trav's cock. His eyes were wild as he watched me, Frankie's nails dug into his chest as she watched the teasing second hand. "I like the sound of that."

Slowly, I brought my tongue out and swiped it up the length of him, from root to tip, feeling the ridges and grooves, tasting him.

His growl was inhuman.

Perfectly, Travis.

"Take it." He demanded, clenching his teeth, "Take it into your mouth, Eli."

And then I did just that.

Holding his stare, I started sucking him, widening my jaw to fit his monster thickness into my mouth, working every inch of him I could. I was hard again from simply pleasuring him, making him curse with ecstasy as his head fell back, hanging between his shoulders.

"Good boy." I hummed, joking about his newly discovered praise kink. "You like that, don't you?"

"Fuck yes, I do." He dropped his chin to his chest and

then ran his fingers through my hair, gripping the back of my head in his big hand and setting the pace.

I hated it.

But only because it made my dick harder.

Also, because he was lasting far longer than me, just to be rude.

"Like this," Frankie purred, scooting down to sit on the edge of the bed again as she spit on her palm and ran it over his big tight balls. "He has a magic button."

"Frank—" He growled and then hissed when her finger disappeared behind them. "Fuck!"

She grinned devilishly, leading my hand to his taint, pushing my fingers against it before gently leading my head back down to the crown of his dick. "Suck him while you roll your fingers over it."

"I'm—" Trav growled, gripping the sheets in his tight fists. "Fuck,"

He spread his thighs wide, and I pressed my dick into the end of the bed, thrusting against it as I watched him fall apart in my hands.

"That's it." Frankie murmured, with awe on her face as she watched us. "Look at him breaking apart for you, Eli."

What a fucking sight it was too, seeing the big dominant man between us crumble because of me. For me. My erection tingled with pleasure, and I knew I was going to come the second he broke completely.

"Harder." Trav growled, "Press harder."

And I did, loosening my jaw to take him all the way to the back of my throat as he bellowed, grabbing a pillow and biting it hard as he came, filling my mouth with his come as I eagerly kept stroking, sucking and watching him, taking it all.

Every fucking last drop.

"God, he's coming too," Frankie moaned, reaching down

to slide her hand over the head of my cock and stroke as I filled her palm with come. "From making you come."

Frankie looked so damn proud of herself as she laid soft, gentle kisses across his chest, as he came down and I pulled off him, slowing down and then laying my hand on his thighs as we both gasped for air.

"Holy hell." He finally sputtered, and I got off my knees, stretching out in triumph.

"It may not have been two seconds flat like my chump ass," I grinned, "But I think I'm still pretty impressed."

He snorted, burying his head in Frankie's neck when she laid back against him. "I'd say."

I collapsed on the other side of her, all of us panting with sweat beaded on our skin, wrapped in heat and something deeper.

It wasn't about getting off. Or finding pleasure in ourselves.

It was about trust. About giving each other permission to feel, to explore, to need.

As I looked down at her flushed face, Travis's lips still brushing her skin, I knew this was only the beginning for us.

Eternal.

EPILOGUE
Frankie

THE GLASS RATTLED under my palms as I pounded on it, screaming until my voice cracked and went hoarse. "Eyes up, Emmie! You've got this! Track it!" I screamed as the puck soared through the air, shot hard and fast from the outside, narrowly missing the big defenders that stood in her way, blocking her view. It didn't matter though; my girl never let a puck past her. "Yes, girl!" I screamed, jumping up and down as she blocked yet another goal.

I didn't care how feral I looked; I didn't care that everyone around me was laughing. My daughter was less than a minute away from finishing her very first championship game, as the starting goalie, without a single goal on her net.

That was something worth screaming about.

On the bench, Travis bellowed plays out like a drill sergeant, his body tense and oozing dominance as he controlled the menaces on the ice like a well-executed dance.

Eli was right beside him, golden retriever smile flashing as he slapped helmets and shouted encouragement. *My men*, coaching my daughter, all while looking like they were born for it.

Behind me, Toby wasn't even watching. He was moving up and down the bleachers like a miniature bookie, hand out, palm full of crumpled bills. "Last chance, folks! Final buzzer coming in hot—Coach Saw drops the F-bomb, and I'll double your payout!"

Half of the parents groaned, half laughed while they dug in their pockets for their chance at the obvious win. Coach Rick sat next to me with a bag of popcorn, muttered, "Kid's got my retirement plan figured out."

I pinched my nose as I shook my head, giving it up to God to keep my youngest out of the slammer because there wasn't a chance that I was missing a second of Emmie's game to scold him.

The worst part of the whole thing was that he wasn't wrong. Thirty seconds later, Travis barked, slapping his hand against the boards like he was an ornery player instead of a respected coach. "Goddamnit, cover your wing!"

It was loud enough the ref glared, and Eli shoved Travis to the other end of the bench with a grimace and a friendly wave at the man officiating. The buzzer hadn't even finished echoing before Toby was raking in his winnings, with a grin that was all trouble.

The team erupted, benches clearing as they celebrated their hard-fought, well-deserved championship win. They were the underdogs, a team of misfits with a tiny girl in goal that everyone underestimated.

And they freaking won it. Won it all.

When the team congregated at the snack bar for their celebratory snow cones, wearing their new medals with bright, sticky smiles, I sat back and soaked it all up. I freaking lived for the high of motherhood, because days like this one made it all seem worth it.

"Alright!" One of the parents called, grabbing everyone's attention, "Kids, gather your bags and line up! The cars are parked at the curb, and we're off for the lock-in sleepover at the arcade!"

Heaven help the parents who volunteered to host that event, I wasn't going near it with a ten-foot pole.

Especially because they invited the siblings of the players too.

"Don't burn the place to the ground, okay?" I called, hugging Emmie tight as she adjusted her backpack, no doubt filled to the brim with snacks instead of clean clothes or a sleeping bag.

"Got it, Mama." She winked, pulling one of Eli's signature moves before she grabbed Toby's arm, dragging him after her.

"Don't worry, Mama!" Toby said with a smirk. "Eli took my matches, but Trav taught me how to make sparks with sticks and rocks!"

"Lord help me." I groaned as my men in question flanked me, waving everyone off for the night as we faced cleanup duties. I wasn't sure where they had been for the last twenty minutes while I wrangled the team at the snack counter, but they also deserved a break now that the season was over. So, I wasn't going to ride them too hard.

The silence circled us in the chilly air of the rink. No kids. No parents. Just me, my men, and the ice that started everything.

A year ago, I'd been bartending here, scraping by on two hours of sleep and pure stubborn determination.

And now I had a business degree and the corner office at Hayes Family Construction, with a shiny plaque outside my door telling everyone how freaking badass I was.

My plans had given Trav the courage he needed, and the stubborn kick in the ass, to take the plunge and expand his operation. He had triple the employees, double the projects running, and HFC was building things he had always dreamed of.

God, it felt good to see him succeed.

And Eli was now a part-time firefighter, working two days a week at the station, and a full-time fire investigator. It eased some of the worry in my chest knowing that most of the time, he wasn't going into the buildings until the fire was out.

"Black Cat." Eli said, sliding his fingers over my back, teasing the slice of skin at the hem of my jersey before sliding under it. "We have a surprise for you."

My eyes widened as I looked from him to Trav, on my other side, looking deliciously up at something. "Does it involve a filthy trip to the locker room?" I teased and Trav laced his fingers with mine, as they both led me to the stairs leading down to the main rink below.

"Something like that." Eli smiled.

The air rushed out of my lungs, my feet freezing in place as I took in the scene.

Candles. Literally everywhere.

Rose petals, black and red, sprinkled across the ice to a red carpet that led to the center.

"Guys." I whispered in awe.

"Let's go, Shade." Trav said, pulling me down the steps, and opening the gate in the boards so I could walk out onto the red carpet. When the three of us got to the center, there was a bucket with champagne in it and a million other candles surrounding the space in a circle.

"Frankie," Eli whispered, taking my other hand in his, until my men stood shoulder to shoulder in front of me. His eyes were red, despite the magical smile on his lips as he lifted my hand to them, kissing my knuckles. "You told us once that no one had ever done anything nice and thoughtful for you before, so we knew when we did this," He took a shuddering breath, and my own breath escaped with a shake, "That we had to do it big."

"This?" I whispered, turning to look at Travis as he gave me a gentle one-sided grin.

"Proposing." He replied firmly, always steady and sure. "We want to make this official, we want to make it real. Actually, I wanted to do it a year ago when we brought you home from the hospital, but—"

"Jesus Christ," Eli elbowed him in the gut with a roll of his eyes, and I giggled. "What he means is, we know you've done this before. We know you've been married, hoping to get the magical fairy tale ending you so desperately deserve, baby."

Travis squeezed my hand as tears fell over my eyelashes, "And we know you didn't get it that time, and we're glad. Because it means you came back to Cedar Bluff. To us. For this."

Eli pulled a box from his pocket, holding it between them as they both fell to one knee, making my tears turn into sobs, as my vision danced and swayed as I tried to see them lift the lid of the box open.

"Black Cat,"

"Shade,"

"Will you marry us?" Eli smiled.

"Will you give us the world?" Travis added.

"Will you let us be the men in your life forever?"

"Will you let us be the fathers your kids deserve?"

"Oh my God," I cried, melting to my knees in front of them as I nodded my head, forcing the lump in my throat away. "Yes!"

They engulfed me, swallowing me up with their big strong arms, and warm love, and I welcomed it.

I embraced it.

There was nothing else in the world that I needed, outside of them and my kids.

Our kids.

Our family.

We were whole.

EPILOGUE
Eli

THE CEREMONY LOCATION WAS BEAUTIFUL. The flowers were perfect. The weather was spectacular for July in Wisconsin.

And everything else was absolute chaos.

"Where's Toby?" Travis barked, tugging at his tie like it was choking him. The tie was non-negotiable on Frankie's part, but Trav bartered it for the black cowboy hat he was wearing.

Something I planned to make him wear later with nothing else.

I had spent all day imagining Frankie in her sexy little white lace lingerie that I happened to sneak a glimpse of when she packed her bag last night. And Trav wearing nothing but a cowboy hat while he fucked her senseless was right there next to it in my mind.

Shit, I was going to have to go jack off again if I didn't get my mind out of the gutter.

"Selling bets out front," I muttered, already bracing myself. "He's got a jar going on how many times Coach Rick cries before the reception."

"Damn kid," Travis grumbled, but the twitch at the corner of his mouth gave him away. Toby was turning out to be quite the mix of us, mastering Trav's steady confidence with my ornery shenanigans to keep things interesting.

Meanwhile, Emmie was a full-blown mini-Frankie, through and through.

Bossy.

Moody.

And right, one hundred percent of the time.

Like currently, as she marched up and down the aisle, like a pint-sized general, making sure every flower petal was perfect in the bouquets, scolding bridesmaids three times her size.

"It's late." Travis groaned, pulling at his tie again. "We were supposed to start ten minutes ago."

I chuckled, pulling him behind the building we were supposed to wait in until we got the cue. "Come here."

He begrudgingly followed me until we were hidden away from everyone, and then he pushed me against the wall. "I'm manic."

"I can tell." As he pinned me, I chuckled and pulled him in for a kiss, deepening it. "Today will be perfect, even if she's late." I said when I finally pulled back, and his nostrils flared as his dark eyes stared back at me.

"You don't think—" He stopped himself, like cutting open his vulnerability was still too hard for him to do, even though we were about to get married. This marriage was as much for him and me as it was for us and Frankie.

"That Frankie is running off into the sunset and away from this marriage while we are left in the dust?" I deadpanned when he didn't immediately acknowledge the absurdity of that. Fears didn't always make logical sense. "No, Trav. I don't think she's running. I think she's probably in her bridal suite, having a panic attack, thinking we're the ones running."

His jaw fell open like he hadn't even considered that, "Then we should be there! Reassuring her!"

He tore away from me like he was going to march across the venue to the bridal suite and do just that. "Get back here with your big dumb head." I snapped, pulling him back and pinning him to the wall as a look of outrage burned in his dominant eyes. It wasn't very often that I would put him in his place, it was usually Frankie and I being overdramatic, but right now, he was taking the cake. "She will murder you if you ruin this first look for her. She's literally crafted this whole wedding over watching you cry like a little bitch in front of all of our loved ones." He shoved me, but I expected it, and countered it, pushing him back with a grin. "She's fine. You're fine. We're all fine. And soon, we're all going to be married."

He sighed as if it was physically painful to take a deep breath under the weight of all his worry.

"Would it help you relax if I told you a secret?" I asked, leaning in and teasing him just the slightest with my hips pinned to his and my lips hovering.

"Maybe." He growled, grabbing my waist and pulling me in harder.

"I'm taking your last name." I whispered, feeling his body tense against mine. "Just like you wanted me to."

His hand came up, gripping the back of my neck as his lips crashed against mine, drawing every ounce of need and passion from my body in no time flat. Jesus, he was the absolute worst when I was trying to keep my head on straight and my dick soft. "You told me no. You told me you were okay if Frankie took Hayes and not Torres, but that you couldn't change."

"I know." I replied, drawing on his strength. "But I changed my mind. Because you were right. We should be unified. We should be one. A family. So, by the end of the night, we'll be The Hayes Family, party of five."

"God, Eli." He whispered, kissing me again. This time softer and more passionately, and I could feel how moved he was by it. "I love you, Sunshine."

"I love you too." I smiled against his lips. "And your big dumb head." I flicked the brim of his cowboy hat and ducked when he went to bite me for it. "Oh, and by the way," I said, stepping back to adjust my annoyingly hard dick for him to watch, "Tonight, when I'm fucking you from behind, while you're balls deep in our *wife*," I said, lowering my voice until he could feel the promise in it, "You're wearing that fucking hat, and nothing else."

"Sunshine—" He took a menacing step forward, like he was going to test that theory right then and there before Emmie's bossy voice called out from the side of the building.

"Dad!" She huffed annoyed as she found us standing there, thankfully not humping each other against the wall anymore. We were open about our relationship with the kids at home, but they never saw us do anything more than kiss and hug. The same way any other kid should see their parents love openly.

And my heart still did a stupid little backflip every time she or Toby called us dad or daddy. It was their idea, and I was a freaking mess the day they asked if they could, like we'd ever be able to deny them giving such an honor to us.

We were so unworthy of their love. But we were trying every day to earn it, nonetheless.

"Yeah, pipsqueak?" Trav replied, walking out and blocking me while my hard-on crashed out to normal size in no time at all. To be honest, Frankie's mini-me scared me a little when she got bossy like she was right now.

"Mom's ready." She put her hands on her hips, "You guys ready?" She eyed me suspiciously as I joined Trav, standing side by side and united.

"So, freaking ready." I smiled at her, and her shoulders deflated as she dropped her fists happily.

"Good," She nodded as she turned and took both of our hands. "Because I'd hate to have to be the one to break the news to Papa Hal that he lost the bet."

Trav snorted, rubbing his face, "What is Papa Hal betting on now? Let me guess, Toby is collecting the money."

"Duh," She rolled her eyes, "Papa Hal bet it would be Mom or Daddy to be the one to run out on the whole wedding thing. Not you. He said you were too boring to make life that interesting."

I tipped my head back and laughed loudly, earning myself a wink from Emmie, who peeked up at Trav next.

"Did he?" Travis deadpanned with a shake of his head. "Well, he's right, I'm in it for the long haul, kid." He said and then scooped her up, tossing her over his shoulder with her sweet little baby pink dress billowing in the wind as she squealed and laughed. "You're not getting out of line drills that easily."

"Let's go get married, kiddo." I booped her nose as she hung upside down over his shoulder, and the smile she gave me back was worth everything in the whole world.

These damn kids, and their tragically, breathtakingly beautiful mother, were the only reasons my heart beat in my chest.

My family.

My life.

EPILOGUE

Travis

"FUCK," A voice echoed through the bedroom door as I silently walked down the hallway. "You're a bitch when you want to be."

Eli.

Sounding, very un-Eli like.

"You love it, and you know it." Frankie's smart tone snapped back as I silently pushed the door to our bedroom open, revealing what was happening inside.

And holy fucking damn.

"Shut up, and fuck me." He groaned, throwing his head back as Frankie slammed into him harder for good measure.

He was hanging from a sex swing in the middle of our bedroom, something I hadn't seen before, or hung. I was a little more upset that they put holes in my cedar plank ceiling than I was about the fact that they were using fun new sex toys behind my back while I was supposed to be at work.

Eli moaned, pulling my attention away from the hardware in the ceiling as I leaned against the doorframe to watch them fuck.

Or really, to watch Frankie fuck him.

Something I'd been begging to do to him for *years*.

Okay, fine, I was most upset about that part.

He laid back on the black swing, naked, legs spread and supported in stirrups as his shoulders hovered in a hammock, swinging on and off our wife's brand-new strap-on she bought last week.

A toy we were going to break in together at some point but hadn't even opened yet.

And Frankie? Fuck.

She wore black leather lingerie that I was pretty sure was crotchless, like it had been plucked straight out of my dirtiest fantasy.

"Fuck, you feel so good," He groaned, fisting his cock and stroking it as she fucked him.

"You're supposed to be getting punished." She slapped his hand away, gripping his hips and slamming into him harder. "Not enjoying it."

He grinned, face flushed as he gripped the handle above his head, bracing for her savage thrusts as his hard cock bobbed against his abs. "Then you're doing it wrong, because I am most *definitely* enjoying this."

"Bastard." She hissed and then pulled out, standing a foot away as he sputtered in shock.

"Evil." He grunted, lifting himself up in the swing to glare at her. "Diabolically evil."

"What the fuck are you two doing?" I asked loudly from

the doorway, making them both jump, and I wish I had been thinking to snap their picture. Mouths agape, eyes wide, and both of them looking guilty as fuck.

"Shit," Eli groaned, fighting with the straps as he tried to get his feet free. "It's not what it looks like."

"Like I'm being left out of something I've wanted for years?" I crossed the room, glaring at both of them, before looking up at the ugly-ass eyebolt hanging from the ceiling. "Did you even check to make sure that was in a ceiling joist?"

Frankie grinned, "To be honest, no."

"You said it was secure!" Eli yelled, swinging harder trying to get out of the swing, but I grabbed his foot, tipping it up and planting his ass back into the swing as I glared at him.

"Explain yourselves."

He huffed, but crossed his arms across his chest like he wasn't spread eagle, with his lubed-up asshole on display as I glanced down at the strap she was using on him with interest.

Damn, it was almost as big as me.

"You ruined it now," he said with a pout. "So, it doesn't matter."

"I ruined it?" I asked, raising my eyebrows at him dominantly as I turned him, so I stood between his spread legs and leaned over him, wrapping my hand around his throat. "Come again?"

Frankie snorted, tipping her head back as she fell into giggles, earning a scathing glare from me before she started taking off her strap.

"He was trying to surprise you for our anniversary." She droned on, unimpressed. "I told him whiskey was probably safer, but he insisted on giving you his ass." She shrugged. "I'm innocent in all of this."

"Bullshit." I snapped and pulled her over, so she was pinned between him and me, folded over his chest as I spanked her ass. She moaned and arched into it as Eli shifted to hold her to his chest with a weary look at me over her shoulder.

"Are you mad?" He asked. "I wanted to surprise you."

"You let her take your ass virginity with a toy instead of letting me have it?" I cocked my head to the side, spanking her again, drawing another moan from her lips as I slid my hand down between her cheeks to prove myself right that her outfit was crotchless and pushed two fingers into her soaked pussy. "And you got off on it." I barked.

She giggled, spreading her legs as best she could, always willing to take it rough when I was worked up. "To be fair, I was punishing him because I found him in here, playing with my new toy without permission, trying to prep himself for your big cock."

My dick hardened in my jeans as I got to the bottom of it all. "How very Domme of you." I pinched her clit, and she shrieked, trying to crawl up Eli's body to get away from it. "But not your job. That was my prize. And you took it."

She panted, glancing over her shoulder at me. "Are you going to punish me for it?"

My wife.

The minx.

Always ready to play with us as if we were her two personal toys.

Because we were.

"Fuck yes, I am." I said, picking her up by her waist until she straddled Eli's waist in the swing, his still-hard cock pinned between them. "And you're not going to like it."

I stepped back from them, and stripped out of my work clothes, stroking my hard cock as I walked back over to them.

"Are you sure about that?" Eli asked, adjusting her so she was sitting back, hovering over the ground between his thighs, just how I wanted her. "Because I think we're both about to like this."

I lined up and sank into our wife's wet pussy without another word, making her hiss and dig her nails into our husband's chest as she took it.

"Yep," she moaned, "I like that a lot."

Fisting a hand in her long dark hair, I pulled her up, so she was sitting up and then I reached around her body and pulled her lingerie to the side, revealing both of her massive tits to our guy, who was always down to play with his favorite toys. "Who bought the swing?"

"Me." Frankie panted. "It was my gift to you both for our anniversary. I hung it up this morning before I ran to the store to get some steaks for dinner. I was going to fill you both with delicious dinner and then bring you in here and let you do dirty, depraved things to me."

"Interesting." I glanced up at the ugly hook in my ceiling and slammed into her again, making them both moan with pleasure. I held her still as Eli leaned forward and started playing with her tits, while I fucked her pussy until she was moaning, and begging to come.

She knew better than to do it without permission on a fuck like this.

She knew I'd demand her submission before I gave it to her.

Which was why I didn't give it to her.

Instead, I picked up the toy she had laid on the bench at the end of the bed, and chuckled when I saw what was on it.

A condom.

She glanced over her shoulder at me and grinned. "It was supposed to make his ass burn with the tingling shit," She shrugged, "but the bastard liked it."

"Hmm." I said, pulling the condom off and taking the dildo out of the harness before pouring lube over the head.

Frankie's eyes squinted as she watched me prep it, and almost as if she knew what was coming, she started to scurry off Eli's lap.

But he was two steps ahead of her and held her tight around the waist as I lined it up with her ass, pushing her toy in. "Fucking hell, Trav." She hissed, but leaned back on it, taking it in one slow, steady thrust.

My wife thrived with a toy in her ass, and we all knew it.

She moaned, pushing on and off it, fucking herself with it as I held it firmly before I let go of it and pushed her up Eli's chest. Sputtering, she looked back at me. "What the fuck?"

"You stole my prize." I shrugged, stroking my cock, still wet with her arousal, as I grabbed the bottle of lube again and poured it over it. "So now you get to sit there, stuffed, but unfulfilled."

"Dick." She hissed, but her eyes were alight with fire, from what I was about to do.

Our husband was a little more reserved. "Trav, wait."

"No." I walked back to where he sat, so on display and at my mercy, and pushed my cock against his asshole. Something I had wanted for years. Something he held off on, out of fear of my size, but he was always eager to fuck my ass though. Which I wasn't complaining about, there was nothing better than taking it from him while I gave it to Frankie at the same time.

"Jesus, I'm not prepped to take you there yet." He groaned, tensing. "I haven't taken anything that big yet."

"Which is a shame. Something I would be willing to help you with if you had just come to me with it." I pushed, breaching that tight ring of muscles at the entrance, cursing at how tight he was. "But now you're going to take me, ready or not, because you hid it from me."

"I was trying to surprise you." He hissed, holding onto the swing, gripping it tight in his fists. "Because you're the absolute worst to buy a present for."

"He's got you there, big guy." Frankie smirked. "You're impossible to buy for."

"Am not." I groaned, notching my hands around his hips where his legs met his sides and bracing him as I pushed in and pulled out, taking him slowly but keeping the motion continuous. If I kept moving, the burn wouldn't come as forcefully. I knew that. "This." I moaned, "This is what I wanted."

"Fuck," He dropped his head back and widened his legs, pushing onto me as best as he could in the swing, as I went deeper. "Jesus, that cock is so thick."

"You can do it." Frankie murmured, laying kisses all over his chest and neck, tempting him and distracting him like a good little wife. She was perfect for us. "You're doing so good, baby." Reaching behind her, she grazed my chest with her fingertips, grounding me, "How does he feel, Saw?"

"So tight," I licked my lips, pushing all the way into him, and his cock jumped between them. "So hot."

"Mmh," She moaned when his cock tapped against her clit, and then she looked at me. "Can I grind on him?" Her green eyes were burning with passion as she swallowed. "Like that first night all three of us were together. Just like this."

"Good girl." I praised her, and her hips instantly lowered so his cock was pinned between her and him, rocking to rub against it.

Eli let a slew of curses fly that would have impressed a sailor as his hands gripped her hips, controlling the pace and pressure of her on his cock. I knew firsthand that he was battling an overwhelming amount of stimulation, and let him have that control.

Like a good, compassionate lover would.

Even if I weren't blind with need.

Which I was.

I gripped the flared end of the dildo, holding it as her rocking hips forced it out and then back into her own ass, making her frantic with the need to come.

"Beg him." Eli demanded, knowing how close she must be from the dual stimuli. "Beg big daddy Travis to come all over his toy and my cock."

She grunted, groaning as I twisted the toy, changing the angle toward the front wall of her pussy, just how she liked.

Finally—finally with fire in her eyes—she looked over her shoulder and pouted like the pretty little sex fiend we all knew she was. "Please, can I come? You both feel so good, baby. I want to come all over your toy."

"No." I replied, picking up my pace in our husband's ass, making him curse and groan as she kept rocking against his cock, trying to keep him in the right headspace as I fucked him for the first time.

"Bastard." She hissed, her skin on fire, beads of perspiration rolling down that delicious line of her spine to the dimples over her ass. "Please!" She cried, desperate for it. "Please, Trav."

"No." I repeated, and slid my hand between their bodies, grabbing his cock and pulling it up. "But you may take him deep into your pussy. I want to see you stuffed tight with cock."

"Fuck yes," He begged perfectly, "Please baby, fuck my cock. Ride it. Just put it in, I don't even care. I need it."

"Damnit." She cursed, and then took him, every long inch of him until she was so fucking pretty and stuffed. "God."

"I'm close." Eli cried, "Fuck her ass with it. Please!" He frantically gripped her hips so tight I knew she'd wear his fingertip prints for days. "Fuck me, harder. For the love of God, just let me come!"

I slammed in deep and then pulled out and did it again, rocking him in the swing as he tipped his head back in ecstasy before I gave in and gave them both what they needed.

I pulled her toy out and started fucking her with it, in perfect sync to my own thrusts, and both of them fell apart, incoherent cries and pleas falling from their lips as they lost their minds.

"Come for me." I demanded, biting my lip to hold my own release off as I finally gave them what they wanted. "Both of you. Fill her up. Fill our wife up with your come while I give you mine."

"Yes!" He roared as she shot off like a firecracker, squeezing down on his cock and her toy. "I'm coming, fuck yes, Trav. You're making me come, baby. Black Cat, you feel so fucking good."

"Good boy," She purred, coming down off her high, but kept her hips moving to milk him as I roared, filling him up. Her green eyes found mine, pride and love beaming through them as I got what I wanted from them both until my knees nearly gave out in pleasure. "You too, Big Guy. You're so fucking good to us."

I wanted to collapse onto our bed and catch my breath, but I couldn't do that, not when they needed me.

I took care of them as I cleaned them up, rubbing their limbs back to life, regaining circulation as they stared at me with such wonder and trust in their eyes before I crawled into bed beside them.

Frankie curled into my chest, pulling Eli up against her

back as he put his arm over my side, holding us all together with a content little smile on his pretty boy face.

Even years later, he was still such a fucking, shiny bright spot in our lives. I didn't know how Frankie and I didn't darken him with our broody dimness. But he was still just right. Perfection, really.

And Frankie, the literal glue that held our family together, bonded Eli and me together in ways we never longed for until we met her.

"Does this mean I have to return your gift?" she asked with a sly smile on her face as she hid it in my chest. "Since you're obviously mad at us."

Eli bit her shoulder with a wink, "No way, Black Cat. That was way too much fun to get rid of."

She chuckled, looking up at me. "Are you still mad?"

"I was never mad." I kissed her forehead, looking over at Eli. "Not for one second."

"Just once I wish you'd get jealous," Eli smarted with a smirk. "For even just a second."

I snorted and waved him off, "I was more worried about my poor ceiling."

Both of them scoffed at me with mild outrage before I soothed it, giving them the news I came home to share with them.

"But we're not going to be able to enjoy your dirty little swing for a while." I sighed as if it were a big disappointment.

"Why?" Frankie raised her head to look at me with a scowl. "What did you do?"

I shrugged as if it were no big deal. "Booked us a vacation in Italy for two weeks."

They both jumped up to their knees in utter shock and excitement. "I'm sorry, excuse you, what?" Eli barked. "How the—"

"Well, that's a lie." I sat up, "It's a week in Italy. And then a week on the French Island of Corsica."

"Oh, my God!" Frankie screamed, shaking her head back and forth. "Wait! The office! And the kids! And—"

"All taken care of." I said, cutting her off before kissing her deeply. "The office will go on without us because you run such a great team. And the kids are going to have a blast exploring a foreign country or two with us. And Grandma Blake is going to be the best babysitter to entertain the kids at night while I do all the dirty and depraved I have planned for you both while we're there."

"Jesus," Eli sighed with a smile on his face as he threw himself back down on the pillow next to me. "You really do always take care of everything."

"I take care of you." I corrected, kissing him. "Happy anniversary, Husband." Turning to Frankie, she kissed me eagerly, with an excited smile on her face. "Happy anniversary, Wife."

"And to think," She murmured sweetly against my lips. "Years ago, I almost let a sexy, smile-happy firefighter take me home after I had a meltdown in the middle of the hockey rink thanks to my crazy kids." She turned to Eli, and he beamed at her warmly, "But he kissed me senseless and then pushed me at his best friend and said something powerful that started it all."

"What did he say?" I asked, trying to remember every detail from the night we both first kissed Frankie.

"Think of me when you kiss him goodnight." Eli replied with a smirk. "And what a wild ride it's been since then."

The End.

More spice, obviously!

Come back to Cedar Bluff in book 2 of the series with **<u>Sugar on Ice.</u>** This delicious why choose romance brings the heat with a FFM dynamic. Here's the blurb!

Stay tuned for more details coming soon!

Marigold "Goldie" James is the heart and soul of Cedar Bluff. Her bakery, Honey & Hearth, is the beating center of town, where warmth, laughter, and the smell of fresh bread make the long winters feel a little less cold. But when disaster strikes and her bakery floods overnight, Goldie's world is turned upside down. And so are her feelings for two very different people who rush to help her rebuild.
Rhea Dalton, the dominant, no-nonsense firefighter with smoke in her smile and confidence that crackles like flame, makes Goldie feel alive in ways she's never dared to imagine. And Tanner Brooks, Cedar Bluff's golden-boy officer, has a

steadiness and charm that makes her feel like she's already home.

When the three of them are brought together for the town's biggest event of the year—the Cuffs and Hoses Charity Hockey Tournament—things start to heat up on and off the ice. The fire department and the police department may be competing for the championship, but it's starting to look like the real game is for Goldie's heart.

Goldie doesn't want to choose.

She loves Rhea's fire. She craves Tanner's loyalty.

And somewhere between the tension, the laughter, and the spicy late-night confessions, she starts to realize maybe she doesn't have to.

But as their passions grow, something darker brews beneath Cedar Bluff's picture-perfect surface. One by one, local shops begin to suffer mysterious "accidents," and whispers spread of a powerful developer trying to buy out the heart of downtown.

To protect the town they love, Goldie, Rhea, and Tanner will have to put their rivalry aside and work together—on the ice, in the streets, and in the warmth of Honey & Hearth—before Cedar Bluff loses everything that makes it home.

When fire, steel, and sugar collide—someone's bound to get burned.

ALSO BY A.M. MCCOY

The Line Walkers Series

Stalker

Psycho

Bully

Beauty in the Ink Duet

Twisted Ink

Twisted Lace

Bailey Dunn & Co Duet

Bailey Dunn

Christmas With The Camdens (Novella)

Shadeport Crew Series

Elora Dax

Carly James

Laila Manning

Kings of Hawthorn Series

Claiming What's His

Indulging His Desires

Earning His Eden

Standalones

Sinister Vows
Guilty For You:
Secrets Within Us:

ABOUT A.M. MCCOY

Born and raised in New York, Ally had to find a way to keep warm through those long winter months. So she mastered writing those one-handed reads to stay busy. When she's not dealing smut, she's chasing chaos around her home and imagining all the dark and twisted turns she will create for her characters.

Stalk me...
Figuratively, of course.